Mad

About

Murder

Also by Cindy Vincent

It's a Mad, Mad Murder
A Maddie Montgomery Mystery

Bad Day for a Bombshell:
A Tracy Truworth, Apprentice P.I.
1940s Homefront Mystery

Swell Time for a Swing Dance:
A Tracy Truworth, Apprentice P.I.
1940s Homefront Mystery

Yes, Carol . . . It's Christmas!

The Case of the Cat Show Princess:
A Buckley and Bogey Cat Detective Caper

The Case of the Crafty Christmas Crooks:
A Buckley and Bogey Cat Detective Caper

The Case of the Jewel Covered Cat Statues:
A Buckley and Bogey Cat Detective Caper

The Case of the Clever Secret Code:
A Buckley and Bogey Cat Detective Caper

The Case of Too Many Clues:
A Buckley and Bogey Cat Detective Caper

The Case of The Perfect Pretty Picture:
A Buckley and Bogey Cat Detective Caper

The Mystery of the Missing Ming:
A Daisy Diamond Detective Novel

The Case of the Rising Star Ruby:
A Daisy Diamond Detective Novel

The Light
A Destiny Moments Novel

Cats Are Part of His Kingdom, Too:
33 Daily Devotions to Show God's Love

Mad About Murder

A Maddie Montgomery Mystery

Cindy Vincent

Whodunit Press
Houston

Mad About Murder

A Maddie Montgomery Mystery

Published by Whodunit Press

A Division of Mysteries by Vincent, LLC

For information, please contact:

WhodunitPress@gmail.com

ISBN: 978-1-932169-93-5

Printed in the United States of America

Dedication

To Sara,
Friend, world-class encourager and
outstanding math teacher—
you asked for another Maddie Montgomery
book, so here it is!

Chapter One

The smell of bacon sizzling around shrimp filled my oversized, designer kitchen. When the timer went off with a loud *beep-beep-beep,* I pulled the pan from one of my double ovens and placed it on a cooling rack that I'd set on the dark granite countertop. Just like clockwork, my seventeen-year-old son, Parker, materialized from somewhere and plopped onto a barstool in front of my huge kitchen island. And since he'd gotten home from school a half an hour ago and already eaten the "healthy" snacks I'd left for him, he really shouldn't have been hungry.

In theory anyway.

But theory never, ever applied to Parker's stomach. To be honest, I secretly thought of the kid as a "human hoover," given the way he could practically inhale every ounce of food in the kitchen and never put on a pound. Amazingly, he considered afternoon snacks to be a mere warm-up meal, getting him prepared for the big event of the day—dinner. Whereby I usually tripled—if not quadrupled—whatever recipe I happened to be making that night.

So sure enough, there he sat, ready to do his best in his quest to eat us out of house and home. He was followed by our two cats—patent-leather-shiny, black Agatha, and orange, longhaired Ellery—who were also willing participants in Parker's perpetual eating plan. Naturally, the kitties had learned long ago to stick close to my son whenever he entered the kitchen. Because Parker was also extremely generous when it came to tossing them bites of whatever he happened to be eating.

Which happened to be a lot.

And Parker, like the rest of the neighborhood, had a real preference for my bacon-wrapped shrimp with honey-garlic sauce. It was but one of the scrumptious recipes that I, Maddie Montgomery, had included in my culinary mystery novel series that featured my regular heroine, Blaze McClane. A young woman whose hair color matched the high-dollar and highly polished copper cookware in her kitchen that was absolutely "loaded with lethal weapons." Much like most kitchens are full of things like knives, meat forks, rolling pins, and cast-iron cookware—implements that can be used for self-defense.

And that was all before a person got creative.

Parker raised dark brows above dark eyes, features he'd inherited from his father and my late husband. "Ummm . . . Mom, would you mind if I had a couple of those shrimps?"

"Way ahead of you, kiddo," I told him as I put a dozen on a plate for him. "But the rest of these are for the new people who just moved in across the street. I'm taking them over to welcome them to the neighborhood."

He managed to down a shrimp a mere millisecond after I set the plate before him. "Don't people usually take cookies? You know, you *could* stand to bake a few more cookies around here."

I couldn't help but laugh. Never mind that I was nearly a gourmet cook, and I fed my son like he was a pampered passenger on a cruise ship. He still preferred cookies. And for that matter, this wasn't the first time we'd had this conversation as I tried to steer him toward healthier foods.

"Everybody takes cookies to people when they move in," I explained as I glanced around my kitchen, with its white cabinets and backsplash tiles of seafoam-green glass, a color that was repeated in a slightly darker hue on the walls. "So the new neighbors will probably end up with tons of cookies and brownies and other desserts."

Parker chomped on another shrimp and tossed a few tidbits to the kitties. "Is that a bad thing? Maybe we should think about moving," he added with his usual goofy grin. "We could probably make quite a haul when it comes to cookies. We might even score some snickerdoodles."

I rolled my eyes and tried not to laugh again. "We're not moving, Parker. And the new neighbors might find my shrimp to be a welcome change. Something savory. And a little salty."

"Since they're probably loaded down with *all* those cookies," he said, his eyes glazing over. "Do you think the new people will need help eating the stuff they get? I could probably down a bunch for them."

Truer words were never spoken.

For I've seen him devour a dozen cookies in world-record time, and Lord only knows what he could do with two dozen. As always, I wondered where all those calories went, though as I looked at his thin frame now, I thought he might have grown another inch. He was already taller than most of his classmates, and I wondered if he was going to fit into his car much longer. Lately, he'd been complaining that it was a little uncomfortable.

What kind of car did really tall people drive?

Though I knew the car that Parker *wanted* to drive—the one my late husband had left me, a 1956 Continental Mark II. Black. It had been Charlie's pride and joy. And now I only drove it when Parker and I went to church on Sunday, and then to lunch at the restaurant of his choice. Which usually meant pulling up to the drive-through at Abbott's Big Burgers. The burger joint was a favorite here in Abbott Cove, Texas, a bedroom community of the greater Houston area.

I pulled a pretty platter from my cupboard and started to plate the rest of the shrimp. Once I was done, I covered it with tinfoil and spooned the honey-garlic sauce into a separate container.

"I don't think they'll need your help eating whatever food they might get, but you're welcome to come with me and say hello," I told him. "They might have some kids your age."

"Not interested, Mom. Since I'm leaving for college in the fall."

I put the lid on the container holding the sauce. "Even if they have a cute, teenage daughter? You never know . . ."

Parker paused mid-shrimp. "Well, okay . . . maybe. Do I have to be polite and everything?"

"Yes, you have to use your manners."

"All right. I can do that. I'll carry the food."

"Just let me change and I'll be right back. Don't touch that plate while I'm gone."

He flashed me a look of pure, angelic innocence, much like the kitties who stared up at me with a similar expression. I rolled my eyes again and raced off to my bedroom. Then I slipped into a cornflower-blue sundress, since the April temperatures here in the Houston area already rivaled that of the surface of the sun. I ran a brush through my not-so-naturally blonde hair and rimmed my blue eyes with a little eyeliner and mascara. With a swipe of peach-colored lip gloss, I considered myself to be presentable.

I returned to the kitchen to find my son staring at his laptop which was now open and sitting on the kitchen island. Judging from the way his jaw had practically dropped to the top of the counter, I immediately wondered what he'd been watching. Especially after he let out a long "*whoooaaa . . .*"

"Are you okay, Parker?"

"Mom, you've gotta see this girl's video," he insisted as he slowly shook his head, his eyes wide in amazement.

I glanced at the clock on my oven. "Can it wait, kiddo? How about if I look at it after we get back?"

Parker gulped. "Nope, Mom. I think you'd better see it right now. This is major."

Which was the most recent "Parker-speak" for anything that involved high drama. Something I fear he'd become addicted to ever since I'd solved my first murder mystery and almost become the killer's next victim along the way.

Unfortunately, Parker had played a much bigger role in unraveling that case than I ever would have liked. I'd barely gotten him past being so overprotective of me when he'd come home to find that I'd just tied up all the loose ends—a term that proved to be much more literal than usual—and caught the neighborhood killer. Afterward, Parker reverted back to his old ways, watching out for me much like he had right after Charlie's death. Not that I should have been surprised, given that we'd been a military family, and my son had grown up knowing that he might become "the man of the house" at any time.

"Okay, I'll look at it for a minute," I acquiesced. "And we can finish watching it after we get back."

Parker shook his head. "I think you're gonna want to see the whole thing, Mom." He returned the video to the beginning and clicked the arrow to start it again.

Rap music thumped from the computer, and I saw a screenshot that read "Maddie and Mindie."

"Maddie . . . does she mean me?" I asked.

"Yup, Mom. She's talking about you."

A few seconds later, a twentysomething woman appeared before the camera. She pulled her waist-length, dark-brown hair into a messy bun and waved enthusiastically to her unseen audience.

"Hi, everyone! I'm Mindie! Today I'm starting my own personal challenge of cooking every single one of Maddie Montgomery's recipes that she has in her mystery novels. My mom has every one of her books, and I want to see if Maddie Montgomery's recipes really work or not. So I plan to try them all out by the end of July. A tough challenge, I know, but I'm up for the task!"

I thunked a hand to my chest. "Oh, Parker, this is wonderful! This girl is adorable, and I love that my books and recipes have inspired young people to cook!"

To top it off, Mindie even reminded me a little of my own daughter, Lyndi, who had graduated from culinary school and actually surpassed me when it came to cooking skills. These days, Lyndi worked as a Navy cook on an aircraft carrier, somewhere in the middle of the Atlantic. Or at least, I think that's where she was. I never really knew for sure, to tell you the truth. Regardless, I was so incredibly proud of her. Not only for her cooking skills, but because she'd followed in her father's footsteps and decided to serve our country.

Parker frowned and paused the video. "Hang on a second, Mom. Maybe you'd better watch the rest of this first."

I glanced at him, confused. After all, I was really happy with the recipes I'd included in my books. I'd personally tested each recipe myself—repeatedly—to make sure they worked. And I made them as simple as possible, so that even the most "cooking challenged" readers could complete each dish successfully and put something tasty on the table. I also rated my recipes according to difficulty.

Meaning, someone new to cooking could start with the easier ones first and then move on to the more challenging ones as they gained experience.

And now, cooking videos created by a young woman like Mindie would be fantastic for introducing my recipes and my novels to the next generation. Or, as they say in today's world, it could help promote my brand.

Something that made me very excited, considering I'd recently become an "Indie" author and no longer relied on the marketing of a large publishing house.

So the concern on my son's face didn't exactly add up to me. Especially since Parker had helped with the marketing of my books, and he knew full well how videos like this could boost my sales.

So why didn't he seem happy about it?

I felt a twinge at my temple. "Okay . . . let's see the rest of this then."

He nodded and hit the forward arrow for the video again. "You got it, Mom."

Right away, a very animated Mindie continued. "When I was little, I used to help my mom bake brownies all the time. She would crack the eggs while I emptied the mix from the box. So I know everything I need to know about cooking! You might even say I'm an expert in the kitchen."

"Everything?" I repeated dumbly. "An expert?"

Somehow, I wasn't sure that helping someone bake brownies from a box qualified her as much of an expert. Even so, I did appreciate this young woman's energy.

"This is going to be a whole lotta fun," she went on. "So I hope you'll join me as I live stream my new cooking show!"

I crinkled my forehead. "This is live streamed?"

"It was, Mom. Now it's on playback."

"Okay," I said as I continued to stare at the screen.

"Today," Mindie announced, "I'm going to start with something simple. I'm going to bake Maddie Montgomery's chocolate chip cookie recipe, the one found in the back of her book, *Soufflés and Assassinations.*"

"Well, that sounds good," I told Parker. "It's a very easy recipe. It'll be wonderful advertising for my book."

But he shook his head. "Give it a minute, Mom."

So I continued to watch.

"First, I'm going to start with the butter," Mindie said to the camera. "Personally, I like lots and lots of butter. So I'm going to double up on it in my cookies," she explained, before she proceeded to take a double-sized stick of butter and plop it into a small, glass measuring cup.

"That'll never work," Parker and I both muttered at the same time.

"Next," said an extra cheerful Mindie, "I'm going to melt the butter in the microwave, so it'll be easy to work with."

Then she flung open the door of the microwave, and with a great flourish, she stuck the measuring cup inside and slammed the door shut. She flashed a huge smile at the camera and then proceeded to set the control panel and timer, which made a loud *beep-beep-beep-beep* sound.

"Wait a minute . . ." I gasped. "That was too many beeps. How long did she set that for?"

"That's why I wanted you to see the whole thing, Mom," Parker said with a groan. "She set her microwave for fifteen minutes. On full power."

"*Fifteen minutes*?" I repeated, feeling a cold chill pass over my body.

"Oh, yeah."

Suddenly, I found it hard to breathe. "That's way, *way* too long. That butter is going to . . . to . . ."

"Yup, Mom, you got it. It's going to blow like a firecracker on the Fourth of July."

"Maybe she'll stop it early," I suggested hopefully.

But Parker just sighed, while I stared at Mindie as she preened for the camera and went on talking about her wonderful memories of baking with her mom.

None of which probably included what happened next.

And while Parker and I watched in horror, the microwave timer simply counted down the minutes, and the glass turntable went around and around and around. As I've heard people say, it was probably like watching a train wreck. Because no matter what, we couldn't look away.

And a few seconds later, there it was—a bright, brilliant, yellow explosion inside of Mindie's microwave. Accompanied by a loud *ppppuuumfph*!

Mindie reacted by running to the microwave and whipping the door open wide, only to have a small river of hot, molten butter come splashing out and all over the front of her apron-less shirt. She screamed and ran to her kitchen sink, while butter continued to drip in huge globs from the roof of the microwave, before it flowed out past the open door, oozing along in a glowing yellow stream.

That's when I dropped my head into my hands. "I don't believe this . . ."

"I told you, Mom," Parker said as he closed his laptop. "You needed to see this."

Though right at that moment, I wasn't so sure.

Chapter Two

For a minute or two, I just sat there, frozen to the spot, with my head in my hands. I was breathing like I'd just run a marathon. Not that I'd ever run a marathon, mind you, and for that matter, had any *intentions* of running one. But after watching Mindie make mincemeat out of her microwave while using one of my recipes, I was in complete and utter shock. And since she'd managed to connect my name to that whole disaster of a baking incident, I was well aware that her video might actually *damage* my brand. Not to mention, hurt my book sales. It certainly wasn't going to do much for my reputation.

"Easy, Mom," Parker told me. "Don't have an aneurysm or something."

"An aneurysm?" I managed to sputter.

Mostly because I was pretty sure Parker had no idea what that word meant, though he'd certainly been using it a lot lately. Usually in reference to me.

"Well, Mom, you *are* pretty old, you know," he explained carefully, like someone talking to a patient in a nursing home. "You might want to start taking it easy these days."

I wasn't sure whether to laugh or be annoyed. I was about to tell him that my being forty-eight didn't exactly qualify me to join a senior citizen center, but I didn't get the chance. Not when my phone rang and interrupted us, loudly playing my ringtone, the theme song from Peter Gunn.

Judging from the lack of a discernable number on my caller ID, I knew exactly who was calling. It was my mysterious and somewhat eccentric neighbor, Spencer Poe. An almost-elderly man who would admit to having once worked for the government, though he continued to be very vague and elusive as to what he actually did for Uncle Sam. My late husband had once mentioned that Spencer had a military background, though the details were sketchy, if not perfectly fuzzy, on which branch or what role he'd been in. And of course, Spencer was an absolute expert when it came to avoiding any kind of explanation about his past. Though from what I'd seen, I was pretty sure he was a former spy for the CIA. Something I could never prove.

Especially not the "former" part.

"Good afternoon, Mrs. Montgomery," came his gravelly voice through the phone. "I hope I haven't caught you at a bad time. Your breathing patterns convey signs of severe stress."

I fought the instantaneous reaction to tell him that he could call me Maddie. But I knew his reply would be exactly as it had always been, that it would be disrespectful to my late husband "the Colonel" to address me so informally.

"No, it's not a bad time," I assured him. "I've just had a bit of a shock, that's all."

"Nothing serious, I hope," he said in response.

"I hope not, too," I told him, still trying to wrap my brain around the video I'd just seen.

"Are you in need of assistance?" he asked with the same concern in his voice that my father always had for me when he was still alive.

"Oh, no, but thank you anyway. Parker and I were about to take some food over to welcome the new neighbors to the neighborhood. And you're *welcome* to come with us, if you like."

"Only if you feel that you and young Parker might require protection. Though taking into account the manner in which you dealt with your recent murder investigation, I do believe you are quite capable of handling many such situations by yourself. Regardless, the offer still stands."

I crinkled my brow. "Wait a minute . . . Why would we need protection?"

A question that was met with another question. "Have you met the new neighbors, Mrs. Montgomery?"

"No, not yet. Have *you* met them?"

"Not precisely," he informed me. "Not in person anyway."

What other way was there to meet them? That's when I had to remind myself that I was talking to Spencer Poe. And considering what I believed he'd done for a living, who knew what he meant.

I blinked and shook my head. "So . . . is there anything I need to know about these neighbors?"

"I'm sure you'll deduce any idiosyncrasies once you're in their presence."

"Idiosyncrasies . . .?" I repeated. "What do you mean?"

But as always, he breezed right past the question.

Speaking of idiosyncrasies.

"That's neither here nor there, Mrs. Montgomery," he finally said. "And I don't want to hold you up. I was merely calling to let you know that we are supposed to have a sudden and severe thunderstorm this afternoon. A rogue cell, it would appear."

"I didn't see anything in the forecast," I murmured as I glanced out my kitchen window.

But sure enough, I spotted a dark cloud far off on the horizon, above the tall treetops of my cul-de-sac.

"I'm afraid this one simply popped up," he told me.

"Thanks for the warning," I told him, with my brain in a whirl. "We'll head over to the neighbors now and be home before it hits."

"Very wise, Mrs. Montgomery. I shall keep an eye out. And remember, I'm just a few doors down should you need me. Though I won't have my drone in the air for your assistance today. Given the impending storm."

"Probably for the best," I told him before we said our goodbyes.

Then Parker and I left through the front door of my burgundy-brick, two-story home and headed across the street. As I carefully carried my bacon-wrapped shrimp, I kept wondering why Spencer Poe thought we might need his brand of chivalry today. To be honest, it only made me more discombobulated than I already was. I barely even noticed that the wind had picked up by the time we reached the neighbors' walkway, and the birds all seemed to be chattering away and battening down the hatches, so to speak.

It had been a while since we'd walked this direction in our cul-de-sac, and a lot had happened since then. I had solved the murders of a couple of neighbors and restored peace and safety to our tree-lined neighborhood. But I'd also found a few gold coins and what looked like a treasure map that had been in my husband's possession before he had died. Items I'd known absolutely nothing about until I found a lockbox in a storage unit. Though I'm sure Charlie hadn't planned on leaving this life and going on to the next one without locating who knew what. Now, Parker and I had inadvertently been left with what was a complete riddle, one that we'd decided to keep just between us.

But more about that later.

We headed up the new neighbors' walkway, lined with Vincas and Pentas that bloomed with abandon in shades of pink, red, purple, and white, bringing to life the phrase "an explosion of color." Probably thanks to the team of gardeners who had been hard at work in the front yard weeks before the moving van had rolled in, something that now made the house a standout even in our normally beautiful neighborhood.

And something that also made the sparkling white van in the driveway look dull in comparison, though the words "Bugsy's Bye-Bye Bugs, We Put the 'Extra' in Exterminators" in big, bloodred letters definitely popped out. Especially since they were situated right next to a huge, cartoon bug, one that was lying on its back with all six legs sticking up in the air and a giant knife sticking out of its chest. The *X*s where the eyes should have been truly symbolized that this insect was, without a doubt, a goner.

I shuddered at the thought, just as Parker and I reached the front door and rang the bell. Seconds later, I heard what sounded like high heels clicking on the hardwood floor of the front entry. Then the door was answered by a thirtysomething woman, one who was tall and thin and could have given any runway model a run for her money. She was wearing a beautifully cut emerald-green dress that most likely sported a designer's label.

I gave her my friendliest smile. "Hello, I'm Maddie Montgomery, your neighbor from across the cul-de-sac. And this is my son, Parker. We wanted to welcome you to the neighborhood and bring you this," I told her as I handed her my plate of bacon-wrapped shrimp.

"Well, aren't you sweet," she said with a bright smile of her own as she lifted the plate to her nose and took a good sniff. "Wow, this smells delicious. Lots of neighbors have brought us food. We obviously picked a great place to live."

"I hope you'll be very happy here," I told her. "And I hope we haven't caught you at a bad time. It looks like you're all dressed up and ready to go out."

She glanced down at her dress that matched her emerald-green eyes. "Oh heavens, no," she said, shaking her full head of dark-auburn hair. "I'm just unpacking and getting things put away. I'm Olivia Degill, by the way. And you said you're Maddie. And you're Parker."

"That's us," I confirmed.

Then her extra-long lashes suddenly flew up. "Maddie Montgomery . . . the famous mystery author?"

"Not really *that* famous," I sort of murmured, brushing off her comment with a laugh. "And yes, I write mysteries."

Of course, I didn't tell her that fame had never been something I'd aspired to, and to be honest, it wasn't something I especially enjoyed. Sure, I wanted the titles of my novels to become household names, and I definitely wanted to sell tons and tons of those very books. But having my own name front and center didn't matter that much to me. I loved writing mysteries almost as much as I loved life itself. Besides that, writing books was how I managed to keep food on the table and a roof over our heads. And given Parker's ability to eat enough for five people, my grocery bill wasn't exactly cheap.

But all that was probably much, *much* more than this new neighbor wanted to know.

She beamed at me and let out a loud, "*Oooooh*! I love having famous people over to my house!"

Which I figured was my cue to change the subject. "Well, your house is beautiful. I absolutely love all the flowers and the gardens you've put in. It looks like you did a lot of work around the place before you moved in."

She blinked a couple of times. "Well, *I* didn't do any of the work. I simply hire people with really good reviews to do the work for me. The only reason I'm unpacking my own stuff today is because the workers I hired this morning walked out on me. It's all so annoying. To tell you the truth, I'd rather be a famous author just like you. Back in high school, one of my teachers told me I should write a book. You'll have to teach me how."

I would?

Okay, I have to admit, this wasn't my first rodeo when it came to someone saying something like that to me. Never mind that I'd spent years learning my craft and putting in the hard work to rewrite and improve every one of my manuscripts. Plus there was the money I'd spent for classes and conventions and more, to build on the skills that I'd already acquired. After that, I went to all the work of finding an agent and publisher and getting my first book in print. Along with the next twenty-nine books before I went Indie and essentially became my own publisher.

So needless to say, I was never crazy about someone else thinking it was my job to teach them what I knew.

For free, no doubt.

But over the years, I'd found a great way to handle situations like this one, without being overtly insulting. Especially since I did enjoy encouraging new authors to learn the craft and hone their skills.

"I'm afraid I don't teach writing classes," I said sweetly. "But I can send you some links to some great online courses. And they're not too terribly expensive."

Olivia's green eyes turned dark, much like the thunderclouds that were suddenly careening across the sky above us. "Oh . . . I guess. I've got a fantastic idea for a murder mystery. It's about a wife who bumps off her husband. I've got the whole murder mapped out, down to the way the killer hides her tracks. But that's the tough part, since the police always suspect the wife first. So maybe I could run it past you sometime and you could give me some ideas."

Words that caused the little hairs on the back of my neck to stand at attention. And something inside told me it would be a good idea to dodge this request, too.

"I've got some wonderful online sources that can help you there as well," I said with a wave of my hand. "Because I've got way too much on my plate these days. I'm in the middle of writing my new book, and I've got a pretty tight deadline to get it to my editor. Which means I'll be spending most of my days and nights glued to my desk chair."

Parker reacted with a very exaggerated nod. "It's true. My mom needs to get a life."

This from the child who mere minutes ago told me I needed to take it easy. Because of my age, no less.

Though you'd never know he was capable of saying such things, given the way he now poured on the charm. "It's really nice to meet you and your house is so . . . umm . . . nice," he said with all the politeness of a British butler, albeit one with a definite Texas drawl, as he held out his hand to shake our new neighbor's. Right before he broke out with, "Do you have any kids?"

Olivia shook her head again, causing her long tresses to swing back and forth in a hypnotic motion. "My husband and I don't have any children. We've only been married for a few months. And he doesn't have children with any of his ex-wives, either."

Naturally, I was dying to know *exactly* how many exes, and to be honest, my curiosity almost got the better of me. But I managed to hold my tongue. I'd already told Parker that he had to use his best manners, so it wouldn't set a good example if *I* didn't. Instead, I simply smiled and followed as Olivia motioned for us to step inside. Then she casually led us on an obstacle course around moving boxes that were piled everywhere, in various stages of unpacking.

"This is a familiar sight," I told her with a smile. "My late husband was in the military, and we went through plenty of moves. How about you? Where did you move from?"

"From downtown Houston. I wanted us to live in my husband's old condo, but that didn't work out, and we needed to get away from that place. Too many memories . . . and too many complications," she finished as we entered the spacious, mostly white kitchen.

Then Olivia promptly pulled the tinfoil from the bacon-wrapped shrimp and slid it onto the only open spot left on the large island. Between the kitchen things she'd been unpacking, and plates and plates of cookies that had probably been brought over by other neighbors.

Much to the delight of Parker's growling stomach. Not to mention, his bulging eyeballs.

She seemed to notice his reaction. "Go ahead and have some cookies, Parker. We've got tons of them."

I looked at my son, and I could practically see the muscles in his jaw clenching as he worked hard to summon every ounce of self-control he could find and rein in the urge to devour every cookie there. I really had to give him credit for showing such restraint, since I was pretty sure his willpower was barely hanging on by a thread.

"Well, maybe just one," he replied, practically panting.

"One?" came Olivia's surprised voice. "C'mon, Parker, take a handful. We can't eat all these by ourselves."

"Well, if you insist," he said with a grin and a quick glance at me.

I smiled and nodded that it was okay. Then I watched as he went from plate to plate and grabbed a whole variety of cookies. Just as a tall man strolled in, his eyes glued to his cell phone.

The man could've easily been Cary Grant's twin. In his fifties, that is, with a good sprinkling of silver in his dark hair. A characteristic that only added to the man's classically handsome features.

"This is my husband," Olivia informed us as she pointed to him.

Yet her words and tone sounded oddly reminiscent of someone pointing out their refrigerator. Or maybe their vacuum cleaner. Or, at best, a favorite reading chair. Either way, it didn't exactly sound like the kind of gooey, starry-eyed language someone would expect from a newlywed.

Not that her husband noticed. In fact, he didn't so much as glance up at us, clearly mesmerized by his cell phone.

"Honey," she said, waving at him to get his attention. "This is our new neighbor. Maddie Montgomery. And her son, Parker."

At long last, the man finally raised his head and stared at us as though he were looking at some distant object. Then after a few uncomfortable seconds, the light seemed to dawn in his eyes, and he focused in on me.

"Maddie Montgomery . . ." he repeated, apparently letting my name roll around in his brain before he finally exclaimed, "The mystery writer!"

"Uh-huh, that's right," I managed to utter.

He slammed his phone down on the white granite of the island countertop and strode right up to me. "I can't believe it! Maddie Montgomery. In the flesh," he said over and over again. "You write the Blaze McClane mystery novels."

"Yes, Blaze is the main character in my series," I told him. "It sounds like you've read them."

"No, but I know plenty of women who absolutely love your work. It's amazing to meet you," he went on. "I can't believe the famous Maddie Montgomery is right here, in my very own kitchen. I will always remember this day and the moment I met you." He reached out a large hand and took mine.

And held it.

And held it some more.

"You're so wonderful," he said smoothly. "And special. And your books are fantastic. Being a famous author sounds so glamorous."

I let out a little laugh and tried to pull my hand away.

With no success.

"I'm afraid you may have been misled," I said. "Writing books is mostly just a lot of hard work. It's hardly ever glamorous."

Now the man showed me a toothy, perfectly whitened smile. "Women like you fascinate me. Such beauty, and a mind that can create characters and a world around them. Tell me, how do you do it?"

If I thought Parker had been laying on the charm a bit thick, well, it was nothing compared to this man who practically had it oozing from his pores.

In the meantime, I was simply trying to get my hand away from his, since he seemed to believe our palms were lined with superglue and stuck together. For life. Even so, I tugged harder, trying not to create a scene. But this handholding had gone from uncomfortable to downright creepy.

Especially with the way he was staring deep into my eyes. Without blinking.

I furrowed my brows. "Umm, excuse me . . . but would you mind . . ."

"My name is Dexter," he interrupted. "But you can call me Dex."

Mostly I just wanted to call myself "free."

I glanced past the kitchen island to his wife, who was now shooting daggers at me with her eyes.

But she wasn't the only one.

I turned my head to see the man who must have been their exterminator, coming down the stairs. He was tall and muscular, and he looked like he could probably wrestle anything that came his way. Including alligators. His sandy blonde hair had been cut extra short, military style, and went well with his perfect, military posture. The embroidered name badge on his dirt-smudged, white jumpsuit proclaimed that he was "Bugsy" of Bugsy's Bye-Bye Bugs, who put the "Extra in Exterminator."

And judging from the scowl on his face, Bugsy was no happier about the handholding scene than I was. In fact, he looked out-and-out irate.

Right about then, I really and truly wished I'd taken up Spencer Poe's offer to escort us over to the new neighbor's house.

Because, if there were ever a time when I could have used a fatherly, possible former CIA agent who probably knew all kinds of kung fu, it was now.

Chapter Three

With my new neighbor continuing his python-like grasp of my hand, I quickly passed the point of being creeped out and was now completely peeved. I only hoped that Bugsy—a man who was probably an expert when it came to rescuing terrified residents from *actual* snakes—might come to *my* rescue. Unfortunately, he didn't show any signs of playing knight in shining armor, and I was pretty sure his scowling stare wasn't going to do the trick. And since Parker was too busy trying to figure out exactly how many cookies he could stuff into his mouth at one time to notice my predicament, I figured I was on my own to break free from this man who was holding my hand hostage.

Which meant I had no choice but to resort to some kind of self-defense tactic. Something I'd had quite a bit of training in, and, for that matter, even had a little experience with, when it came to real life situations. Of course, my main character in my mystery series, Blaze, often employed a wide range of self-defense techniques, ones that usually involved kitchen utensils and cookware that did double duty as lethal weapons. But now, much to my annoyance, I was too far from the kitchen to grab a thing.

Thankfully, I wasn't forced to make any fancy moves since I was saved by the bell. Or rather, by "the blue." More specifically, a huge, blue gem that adorned Olivia's hand as she held it up and wriggled her fingers, thus flashing the most stunning sapphire ring I have ever seen.

Outside of the British royal family, that is.

"Well, Maddie, you're just in time to see what my husband bought me," she said through a smile that didn't even reach her cheekbones, let alone her eyes. "My new ring arrived today. It's a seven-carat sapphire. And it cost a fortune." She moved her hand under a pendant light that hung above the kitchen island, making the blue stone glow like it was radioactive.

And that's when Dex finally dropped my hand.

If only I'd known such a maneuver would work, because I would have flashed my own ring at him long ago. Though the one I had on wasn't nearly as substantial as the one his wife was wearing. In any case, I took a step back and wiggled my own fingers to get the circulation going again.

Parker stared at the ring and his dark eyes went wide. "Wow, that's a really nice stone, Mrs. Degill. Sapphires, or corundum, are a nine on the Mohs' scale for hardness. Right below a diamond. Is that a Ceylon sapphire?"

And as part of a National Science Fair winning team, my high-Q and handsome son knew his gems and minerals. Someday, he was going to make some very lucky young woman a fantastic husband. And her engagement ring would be stunning.

"Yes, it is," Olivia told Parker, emphasizing every single word.

"That's so cool," Parker raved, moving in for a closer look. "The clarity looks perfect. I can't see a single inclusion. Not without a loupe anyway."

"Because it's flawless," Olivia said smugly. "Like I said, it cost a fortune."

I moved in her direction to get a better look myself, (and to get away from Dex), being careful not to get *too* close to her or her ring. Just in case this couple was from some culture where constant handholding was de rigueur.

"Your new ring is gorgeous," I couldn't help but gush.

"It certainly is," she agreed in an icy tone. "By the way, Maddie, please meet my exterminator, Bugsy," she said with a nod toward the man in the white jumpsuit. "I found a few pests around the place, and I decided to have them eliminated. Immediately." She stared directly into my eyes as she spoke, sending a cold chill running right through me.

Then without even blinking, she turned from me to Dex, who now looked oddly nauseated. He gulped while she continued to stare.

I took a step back and glanced toward the exterminator. "Nice to meet you, Bugsy," I said with all the manners I could muster at that moment. "I'm a neighbor from across the street."

Bugsy gave me a salute. "Ma'am. Glad to meet you," he said in a deep-from-the-heart-of-Texas drawl. "You might want me to take a look at your place, too. If there are bugs over here, they're probably over there as well. They can be sneaky, little varmints, ma'am. Sometimes you don't even know you've got 'em till one slithers out from under the baseboard."

Words that made my skin crawl.

Bugsy whipped out a business card from the top pocket of his jumpsuit and handed it to me. "Here's my card, ma'am. My mama had them made up."

"They're very . . . expressive," I said as I read his name listed as Bugsy Barkowski, along with his company name and his slogan, "We put the 'Extra' in Exterminators." Not only did I wonder what that "extra" might be, but I also wondered if his mama had actually named him "Bugsy."

"Call me if you need me, ma'am," he went on. "I'd be happy to come over to your place and *kee-eell* any pests you've got running around."

Then without waiting for a reply, he turned and headed upstairs again, leaving me and Parker and the Degills alone. And from that moment on, the conversation was as chilly as the tone between the newlyweds.

So I said a few more niceties about their house and then excused Parker and me, saying I needed to get back to work on the next chapter of my book.

"Oh, yes, that's right, you work from home," Olivia said as the realization suddenly seemed to hit her. "So you're in the neighborhood every single day."

Which she made sound like a bad thing.

"And I have been for years," I replied, not sure what to make of her comment.

One minute she wanted me to teach her how to write, and the next minute she didn't seem too pleased that I was so close by.

Regardless, I had the overwhelming urge to wash my hand, so we said our goodbyes and let ourselves out the front door.

We were practically blown away the second we stepped out onto the covered front entryway. Parker had to help me pull the door shut since the wind seemed to have grown into a full-fledged life-form of its own, causing the trees in our cul-de-sac to sway wildly. Thunder rumbled in the background and lightning flashed through the clouds. Apparently, the storm that Spencer Poe had warned me about had officially arrived, along with several of its friends and a few relatives who had decided to join the party.

That left us with two choices: Either we stayed huddled on the Degills' front stoop, or we carefully made our way across the street. Neither choice looked all that terrific to me. Especially as a mom who'd constantly preached to her kids to stay inside during a thunderstorm.

I glanced at the dark clouds above us. "What do you think, Parker? Should we brave the storm and get home?"

"Sure, Mom," he told me, grinning despite the oversized raindrops that now hurled themselves straight at us, Kamikaze style. "Our odds of making it are pretty good. Statistically anyway. As long as we stay away from the trees. Lightning usually hits the tallest stuff first. So if it's gonna hit, it'll hit those big pines, travel down to the ground and create a ground current."

"Good to know," I managed to say, trying not to think about it.

"But we'd better not run," Parker informed me. "We've gotta move slow."

"Okay, lead on McDuff," I replied as I glanced toward our house.

Which now felt like it was a million miles away.

And that's when I noticed the car parked against the curb just to the left of our front walkway. A car I didn't recognize. It was a silver Crown Victoria, the kind of vehicle that had been popular with police departments for years. I had no sooner spotted the car when a flash of lightning lit up the area around us. It also illuminated the driver, who appeared to be a woman with golden-blonde hair up in a topknot.

Right away, I racked my brain, wondering if I'd forgotten an appointment. Or if someone was supposed to be coming over. But for the life of me, I couldn't think of anyone we were expecting.

I pointed to the Crown Victoria, which appeared to have dirt caked and probably baked on top of even older dirt. "Parker, did you have someone stopping by this afternoon?" Though in reality, I doubted the woman, who looked to be a little younger than me, was there for my son.

He shook his head and nodded toward the car. "Nope, not me."

"Hmmm . . . I wonder who that could be."

"I dunno, Mom, but maybe we could find out when we get over there. Because we should get moving."

And so we did. We took a few measured steps down the walkway just as the huge droplets of rain pelted us even harder. Water ran in rivulets down our faces as we moved forward, ducking our heads and taking the long way around the huge, tree-filled island at the end of our cul-de-sac. Thus avoiding the danger of standing under any tall trees, like my sciency son had warned against.

All the while, I fought the urge to simply take off running for my front door. But since I had agreed to Parker's idea of moving at a snail's pace, I just kept on inching onward. I did manage to get in a few quick glances at the car next to the curb, but with the wind and the rain in a whirl, it was hard to see much of anything.

Though I was pretty sure the woman in the car wasn't having the same problem. Especially after another flash of lightning lit up the area again, and I got an even better look at her.

And the huge pair of binoculars she was holding up to her eyes.

Apparently, she was watching us. Up close and personal. But why? Whatever her reason, I decided her actions needed an explanation.

Immediately.

"Parker, I'm breaking formation," I hollered above the storm. "I want to find out what this woman is doing here."

But I had barely started my march toward her when I promptly slipped on the slick street and fell forward. Thankfully, I managed to land on my outstretched hands, without injury. Not only that, but I was now essentially in the starting position of a sprinter.

That's when I heard the engine of the Crown Victoria turn over, and brake lights suddenly lit up. That meant this woman was about to take off, without giving me a chance to find out what was going on.

So I jumped to my feet, just in time to see her roll down her window and snap off a few pictures of me with her cell phone. The window went back up as I raced forward, forgetting all about the trees and the lightning.

Of course, thanks to my years and years of writing mystery novels, I knew enough to get a license plate number. So I glanced toward the rear of the vehicle and tried to blink away all the water running down my face and into my eyes. Yet despite my best efforts, I couldn't make out the number. Mostly because of all the dirt on the car, which was now running off like a scaled-down version of the mighty and very muddy Mississippi. If nothing else, at least I could make out the telltale peach of a Georgia license plate.

But I wasn't done yet. I sped up, splashing in the high water as I went slipping and sliding toward the driver's side of the car. I noticed lots of minor dents in the vehicle just as I started to get closer. And that's when the woman put the car in gear and peeled out, turning the wheel hard to the left. Her maneuver sent a huge spray of water right at me, along with a sampling of mud, gravel and road debris.

I screamed and jumped back, while she hit the gas and careened around the cul-de-sac. From there, she had a straight shot out of our neighborhood. And she took it, practically hydroplaning as she went.

Leaving me in the middle of the street, hands on my hips. What in the world was going on? And why did that woman seem so interested in me? And my son?

"Mom, are you okay?" Parker asked as he came up beside me.

"Yeah, kiddo, I'm okay. Let's go home and get out of this mess."

"Way ahead of you, Mom!"

A statement that proved to be quite literal as my son quickly bounded in front of me and raced up our walkway to the front door of our house. He pushed it open and held it, waiting for me to join him. We both jumped inside only seconds before a bright flash of lightning blazed across the sky.

"Wow, Mom, what was that all about?" Parker asked as he shook the rainwater from his hair, much like a puppy shaking after a bath.

"I wish I knew," I told him. "But I have no idea what that woman was up to."

"You know, Mom, some people make a really big deal about you being famous and everything. Maybe it was one of your fans. You know, wanting to get a picture of you."

"Hmmm . . . I don't know, Parker," I said as we walked through the dining room on our way to the kitchen. "My readers usually show up at scheduled events, and well, they're very nice people. They usually want their picture taken *with* me. They don't just want a picture *of* me. Especially not one where I'm being drenched in the rain."

Parker shrugged. "I dunno, Mom. It's hard to say."

I ducked into the laundry room and grabbed a couple of warm, fluffy towels from the dryer, which I'd thankfully left drying before we'd left the house. I tossed a towel to Parker and kept one for myself. But before I could finish drying off my arms and face, my phone rang.

It was my neighbor, Spencer Poe. "Are you all right, Mrs. Montgomery?" he asked with great concern in his raspy voice. "I witnessed the events in the street as you tried to return to your residence. Were it not for the storm, I would have sent my drone out to assist you. Were you harmed in any way?"

"Well . . . no, not exactly," I started. "I'm just a little shook up. But it was pretty strange when that woman rolled down her window and snapped off a few pictures of me. Right before she vamoosed and aimed for me as she went. I tried to get a license plate, but I couldn't see it well enough to read it. Though I could make out that it was a Georgia plate."

"I attempted to get a read on her plate as well," he told me. "But with the deluge, I'm afraid I was unsuccessful. That woman was clearly up to something, and the storm proved to be the perfect cover for her illicit activities. It was rather aggressive of her to drive straight into that huge puddle and spray you like she did."

Parker pointed toward the back staircase. "Gonna go change clothes, Mom," he whispered.

I nodded, before he took off up the stairs.

"Yes, she was very aggressive," I told Spencer. "I only wish I knew who she was. And what she wanted."

"I will keep an eye out for her. Since we do not know her motivation or what her intentions were, it is quite possible she may return."

"I hope not," I replied, while my imagination took off racing in a serpentine pattern across my brain, dodging reality altogether, as I tried to figure out what she was doing out there in the first place.

"I suggest you keep your doors locked and your alarm on," came my neighbor's advice. "And if I may ask, Mrs. Montgomery, how was your visit to the Degills' home?"

"Uncomfortable," I said, not sure if I should go into detail about the whole hand-hostage incident. "I don't think I'll be a regular visitor to their place." I shuddered at the mere memory of Dex's touch.

"Just as I feared, considering the two ex-wives who live nearby and the number of females he's been affiliated with. I hope he did not make inappropriate advances toward you."

Inappropriate was one word for it, though I could certainly think of a few more.

But I saw no need to upset my almost-elderly neighbor with the details. "I think Olivia has figured out how to keep her husband in line," I assured him. "Judging by the size of the sapphire ring she was wearing. She claimed it was a gift, but her husband didn't seem so happy about it."

"I would suspect not. In any case, if he should cause any problems for you, and if you should need my assistance, please do not hesitate to ask."

"Well, thank you, Spencer. That's very sweet of you."

"In the meantime, I hope you will relay the events that took place in front of your house to your new beau, Detective Reagan. I would think he would be concerned, if not helpful, in case of any future incidents."

"I'll be sure to let him know," I agreed before we both said our goodbyes.

Which left me with a bit of a predicament. Should I call Remy now, and tell him about the woman in front of my house? Or should I wait until he picked me up for dinner tomorrow night?

Because my new beau wasn't exactly "a beau," per se. Not yet anyway. No, Detective Remington "Remy" Reagan was a man that I'd gone out to dinner with twice. With a third date set for tomorrow night. And since things had been going so well, I hoped there might be more dates to come. And maybe, just maybe, the spark between us might grow into something more.

But I also wanted to take things slow and allow the relationship to evolve naturally on its own. Which was why I felt a little funny calling Remy at this exact moment. Because we hadn't reached the stage where we were in touch throughout the day, either by text or phone call. And I knew I wouldn't like it if he tried to take this relationship a lot faster than I was ready for, and I certainly wanted to respect his wishes to take things slow, too.

So would it look like I was pushing him if I called him right now? Or God forbid, would I come across as clingy and smothering? To be honest, I didn't know the parameters of dating these days. I'd been used to being married for so many years that starting over was foreign territory to me. And probably for him, too.

As I considered my own budding romance, I couldn't help but think of the so-called "romance" across the street. Though the Degills were newlyweds, they hardly acted like they were madly in love. And then there was the information that Spencer Poe had just passed along, saying that Dex was on wife number three, and apparently had racked up a number of other romantic "affiliations" as well. Meaning, it sounded like Dex got around.

And judging by the way he went after me with his unabashed handholding this afternoon, I got the feeling he was *still* getting around. Something I imagined wouldn't sit very well with his current wife. And from my knowledge as a culinary mystery writer, I had to say, that sounded like the perfect recipe for murder.

Chapter Four

After a few minutes of debating whether to call Remy or not, in the end, my curiosity got the better of me. Meaning, I was dying to hear what he might say about the woman who had been sitting in her car outside my house. So I dialed his number.

He answered after a couple of rings. "Maddie, this is a surprise. How's my favorite writer?"

His words made me laugh. "Do you know any other writers besides me?"

"Do I need to?"

Touché. The man definitely had a way with words himself.

"I hope we're still on for tomorrow night," he said, sounding concerned. "I hope you're not calling to cancel."

"I wouldn't miss it for the world," I told him, remembering that I had a hair salon appointment in the morning, so my hair would look gorgeous for the night. "But I'm calling to ask you about something that happened in front of my house this afternoon."

"Uh-oh. That sounds ominous, given some of the things that have happened in front of your house in the past. Give me the scoop."

And so I did just that.

"Did this woman threaten you in any way?" he wanted to know.

"Well, sort of. When she sped off, she turned hard to the left, not far from me. And she sprayed me with water from a huge puddle. This was after she took my picture."

"Have you ever seen her before?" he asked carefully.

"Not that I can recall. She didn't look the least bit familiar. And to be honest, I didn't really get a good look at her, since water was running down my face."

"Hmmm . . . Did she show up on your doorbell camera?"

I quickly called up the app. "You can see the car, but it's kind of blurry because of the storm. And the license plate isn't visible."

"That's what I was afraid of. Unfortunately, Maddie, there's not much we can do about the situation. Unless she shows up again and harasses you. It would be pretty hard to find the car, and I doubt the department would really want to spend the resources to locate her. Not unless she's committed some other crime. So do me a favor and call me if she shows up again."

"I can do that."

"And whatever you do, don't approach her on your own," he added.

"Why, Detective, how thoughtful of you to care."

"I'm serious, Maddie. Leave the investigating to the professionals. Remember, you're not trained to deal with criminals, even though I know you played a role in capturing a killer not long ago."

Words that suddenly got my hackles up, had I possessed actual hackles. *Played a role*? That was the understatement of the century.

"Ummm . . . excuse me, but as you will recall, I actually *caught* the killer. *Then* I called the police. That's where you came in."

He chuckled on the other end of the line. "Yes, I remember it well. And yes, I concede, you caught a dangerous criminal. But from now on, please stick to *writing* mysteries. Not solving them. I don't want anything to happen to you. Now I've gotta run. See you tomorrow night?"

"See you tomorrow night," I said with all the sugar I could manage to pour on at that moment.

But I couldn't exactly squelch the irritation I was feeling by the time we got off the phone. After all, I'd only investigated the murders in our neighborhood because the police had ruled the first death an accident. And they refused to look beyond that. So that's when I stepped in. Thanks to some serious urging from Spencer Poe, that is.

Then I ultimately cracked the case. Which meant I clearly had some skills when it came to crime solving, probably a by-product of my years of researching and writing mysteries.

So now, I had to wonder, what was the big deal if I wanted to investigate a strange incident that happened in front of my very own house? For all I knew, the woman in the Crown Victoria was up to something that could affect Parker or me. Not to mention, the rest of the neighborhood.

On the other hand, I could also understand where Remy was coming from. And he did have a point—I wasn't a law enforcement professional. But what if I were in a similar situation as I had been before, with a murder taking place in my neighborhood? One that the police ignored. Was I just supposed to sit back and do nothing? I could no more do that than I could burn my best Yorkshire pudding and pot roast recipe.

I stared out the window at the sun shining brightly through the clouds, signaling that our sudden storm had officially blown over. Maybe the real problem was that I'd felt a great sense of satisfaction from putting the pieces of the puzzle together and figuring out who had committed the double homicide in our neighborhood. And the truth was, if another mystery presented itself, I would probably jump in with both feet and try to solve it, too. Something Remy would probably be opposed to, no doubt.

I heard the padding of little paws on the back staircase, only seconds before Ellery and Agatha trotted into the kitchen, tails held high. An occurrence that usually foreshadowed Parker's arrival into the kitchen, too.

And just as all signs had indicated, my son came bounding down. "Mom, I've gotta show you something. I think I just figured out a clue from that treasure map of Dad's. I'm pretty sure our first stop is the Glenwood Cemetery."

Despite myself, I couldn't help but smile. Remy may have given me a subtle command—or rather, a *very* strong suggestion—when it came to solving mysteries. Regardless of that, and my great attraction to Detective Remington Reagan, he couldn't stop me from secretly following this treasure map with my son.

Wherever it might lead us.

I nodded to Parker. "Okay, tell me what you found while I get dinner going."

He slid onto a barstool at the kitchen island. "Sounds good, Mom. I'm starving. What's for dinner anyway?" It was the very question he asked me every day around this time, in what had pretty much become a ritual.

I stared at him for a moment in disbelief. How could this child possibly be hungry? It had been less than twenty minutes since he'd practically inhaled at least a dozen cookies, not to mention a dozen bacon-wrapped shrimp, as well as his after-school snacks. Yet here he was, hungry again.

"Your favorite gourmet pizza," I told him, much to his great joy. "Or rather, I should say 'pizzas.' With Italian sausage, artichoke hearts and spinach. And lots of cheese."

"That's Lyndi's favorite, too."

"Yes, it is," I said, smiling as I thought of my daughter out there in the world, possibly making pizza herself tonight. For an entire ship full of sailors, that is. In fact, it had been her idea to start adding Italian herbs to the pizza dough we made at home. It was a nice touch, and a recipe that I was using for tonight's dinner. Having made it earlier, I grabbed it from the refrigerator now, along with the other ingredients that I planned to use for toppings.

"So what did you figure out?" I asked Parker while I halved the dough and rolled it out.

Though he'd been gung ho to tell me something important when he'd first flown into the room, he now appeared completely mesmerized by the pizza dough that I was stretching onto pans. In fact, he looked like he was close to drooling.

I turned on both of my ovens and set the temperature to 450 degrees. "Umm . . . Parker? There was something you wanted to show me?"

He blinked a few times before turning his attention to the folded, yellowed paper that he'd brought with him, something we'd found among my late husband's things not long ago. And something we believed to be a treasure map. The brittle paper was clearly very, very old, and from what I could tell, contained some poorly drawn landmarks. Along with some highly cryptic directions.

I wondered if those landmarks would still be there today.

Apparently, Parker seemed to think so as he carefully unfolded the paper. "Look at this," he said, pointing to a note that had been written on the front, in the top, right-hand corner.

I glanced at the letters *GWt* over the letters *ROT*. And while I knew Parker was extremely adept at problem solving, I couldn't say I was on board with the direction he thought those letters were taking us. Frankly, I thought they looked more like initials for some couple. Or maybe even siblings.

I brushed olive oil across my newly formed pizza crusts and popped each one into an oven to prebake. "Hmmm . . . I'm not sure I can make heads or tails of that," I said carefully to my son, not wanting to squelch his enthusiasm. "The ink looks like it's from a modern pen. Not some gold-nib, dip pen from days of old. So what makes you think it leads to the Glenwood Cemetery? I believe that cemetery was established in the eighteen-seventies. And somehow, I think this map looks older than that."

"I hear ya, Mom. So I looked it up. The cemetery goes back to eighteen seventy-one. But I'm pretty sure Dad wrote this stuff here on the top. It looks like his writing."

"Well, yes, I guess it *does* look like his handwriting. He always wrote in block letters and in all caps. But I'm not sure about that lowercase *t*," I said before I checked on the pizza crusts.

Parker was already nodding. "I wasn't sure either, Mom. So I looked at it with a magnifying glass. That's when I figured out that it wasn't a *t* at all. I think it's a cross."

I leaned in to take a closer look. "You know, I think you might be right . . ."

"At first, I thought it could be for a church or something."

I pulled the nicely crisped crusts from the ovens. "That makes sense."

"Then I looked up churches. But I couldn't find any that fit with the initials *GW*. Not any old ones anyway. So I tried to figure out what else a cross might mean. And I thought of those crosses that people put by the road to show where someone had died. From there, I wondered if the cross in Dad's notes was for a gravesite."

"Could be."

"And the *GW* part could stand for 'Glenwood.' The cross next to it would make it the 'Glenwood Cemetery.' Everyone in town has heard of that place."

"Very true. It's pretty famous."

"But I can't figure out what Dad could've meant by the *ROT* part. I don't think he meant a body rotting in a grave."

I started to add toppings to the pizza crusts. "No, that sounds a little crude for your father. I wonder if it's someone's initials."

"That's what I thought, too, Mom. Maybe Dad was looking for the grave of someone whose initials were *ROT*."

"Isn't there a way to look that up online?"

"I tried. But nothing fit. It didn't help that I only had initials. And not a name," he added as he stared at the paper, looking at it from different directions.

With the pizzas fully loaded, I slid them back into the ovens. It wasn't long before the spicy aroma filled the kitchen.

"Would you like to set the table?" I asked Parker. "Let's eat in the dining room. So we have extra space for the pizzas."

Without a word, he jumped up and grabbed plates from a cupboard, followed by napkins, knives and forks. And parmesan cheese. Holding everything against his stomach, he raced to the dining room with his stash. All the while, the kitties just watched him, wide-eyed.

Five minutes later, (though according to Parker, it was more like a full year of his life, and he almost didn't survive), I had the pizzas on the table, and we quickly filled our plates. The treasure map was mostly on Parker's mind while we ate dinner, though honestly, he was so busy devouring his food that he barely had time to talk. In the meantime, I savored the three slices I'd managed to keep for myself.

"Can we go to the Glenwood Cemetery and check it out?" he asked.

"Sounds just dandy," I told him, a word that never failed to elicit his regular goofy grin. "It'll have to be on a weekend."

"Maybe we can go out to lunch, too. For some serious burgers."

I couldn't help but laugh. Only Parker would be planning to eat one meal while he was already eating another. And of course, the "uniqueness" of my teenage son wanting us to visit a historic cemetery did not escape me. Because I was pretty sure that most parents took their kids to ball games or museums or the zoo or something like that on the weekends. Yet here I was, about to take Parker to a cemetery.

Somehow . . . something just didn't seem quite right with that picture. In fact, his request for burgers afterward was probably the most "normal" thing about the whole situation.

Which reminded me that he still needed to eat the following evening while I was out. "Do you think you can come up with some dinner on your own tomorrow night?" I asked. "Since I have a date?"

"No prob, Mom. I'll make grilled cheese sandwiches. And soup. Where is this guy taking you anyway?"

"Detective Reagan is taking me to that new French restaurant at the top of the Abbott Building."

He raised his brows. "Fancy. Are you going to marry him? Is it time for me to have a man-to-man chat with the guy?"

A question that made me choke on my pizza.

"I don't have any plans anytime soon," I said after I regained my composure. "We've only gone on a few dates. Marriage isn't even on the table."

"Maybe he'll buy you a big sapphire ring like Mrs. Degill has."

I rolled my eyes. Truthfully, I didn't think it was likely. Especially since he lived on a detective's salary.

Which instantly made me wonder how Dex Degill could afford such a high-dollar ring for his wife. In the time that we'd been at their house, no one had mentioned his occupation. And while I'd been busy fighting for custody of my hand, I didn't have the presence of mind to ask, "By the way, what do you do for a living?"

Whatever he did, apparently, he was also able to afford the little, red sportscar that I now saw backing out of their driveway. The floor-to-ceiling windows of my dining room gave me a good view of Olivia at the wheel, with her auburn hair floating all around her like a halo.

And that's when it occurred to me, maybe Olivia was the one with the money.

Though somehow, I doubted it. She didn't seem to be employed, and if she'd been independently wealthy, I didn't think she would have been able to flash her giant, blue ring and get her husband to "heel," so to speak. No, from the way he'd reacted, it seemed that ring had caused him some financial pain, and it was much more reminiscent of a punishment rather than a present. Yes, she'd used the word "gift" when she waved it for all to see, but his nauseated response said otherwise.

And now I wondered if the pretty, red car might be another "gift." From what I could tell, it appeared to be brand-new and fresh off the lot. In fact, I was pretty sure I'd seen it in several car ads. Which meant the car must have been a very recent purchase. And if the car and the ring were both 'guilt gifts,' I wondered what Dex might have done that had forced him to pay so dearly. Literally. Not only that, but I also wondered if it was something that had happened recently, or if Olivia had found out about something he'd done long ago. Maybe even something that could ruin him if it ever leaked out. Though if all those suppositions were true, it meant Olivia was essentially blackmailing her own husband.

Probably not a good arrangement for a happy marriage.

Regardless, like it or not, the very idea of it was now on my radar. Coupled with the way she'd more or less informed and expected me to teach her how to write mystery novels, I wondered if she was pretty good when it came to manipulating people. And the more I thought about it, the more I began to picture Olivia as an expert at getting what she wanted.

Which brought up yet another question—if that was the case, exactly how far would Olivia go to get her way?

Chapter Five

Olivia finished backing her red car into the street before she revved the engine and took off like a jet fighter pilot leaving an aircraft carrier. Except she didn't go vertical.

"Wow, she's in a hurry," I commented to Parker.

"If I had a car like that, I'd put the pedal down, too," came his instant reply.

I stared at him.

He grinned back at me. "Kidding, Mom. Just kidding."

"This from the young man who's been angling to drive the Continental to prom for a while now," I said, shaking my head.

The "Continental," of course, being the 1956 Continental Mark II that I had inherited from my late husband.

Parker's eyes lit up. "It would be so cool to take Dad's old car. Maybe I could find a nineteen-fifties tux to wear."

"Do you have a date for this prom?"

He shrugged. "Maybe. I haven't asked her yet."

Words that made my heart skip a beat. "Are you going to?"

"If it means I get to drive the car," he added, his eyebrows raised. "Maybe she could dress up nineteen-fifties style, too."

I couldn't help but smile. "That sounds like a lot of fun."

"So is that a 'yes'? Can I take the Continental to prom?"

"We'll see. I think we'd better take you for a test-drive first. That car doesn't handle quite like your own car does."

"Cool, Mom! Can we go tomorrow?"

"How about this weekend?" I suggested with a laugh. "We could take the Continental when we go to the Glenwood Cemetery. It would be the perfect place for you to practice driving it."

Especially since the parklike cemetery had *very* low speed limits posted across its various lanes. Besides that, since most of the people there were already dead, I didn't need to worry about him hitting someone, should he have trouble steering at first. A factoid that I didn't say out loud, for my son's sake.

"Consider it booked," came Parker's reply as he polished off the rest of his dinner. "I'll get used to driving Dad's old car. And we can look around and see if we can figure out Dad's clues."

"In the meantime, you've got kitchen cleanup."

He gasped and went limp in his chair. "You know, most of my friends don't have to do so many chores."

"You'll thank me when you're an independent and very capable adult."

"In that case, I want to invent a better way to clean the kitchen," he responded with another grin. "I could probably pull the garden hose in through the window. Then I could hose down the dishes. And use a blow dryer to finish them off."

By now, I couldn't help but smile. "You know, we do have a dishwasher."

"Yeah, but you have to rinse and then load. It's an extra step."

"It's what we've got, kiddo."

"Hmmm . . ."

I laughed, grabbed my plate and headed for the kitchen, with him following and doing some kind of Frankenstein walk. Then I left my plate in the sink and left him to do his worst, knowing full well that my kitchen would be sparkling clean and in good working order the next time I stepped into it. Mostly because his dad had taught him military organization and neatness when he was young. Charlie had even found ways to make picking up toys a fun game for Parker.

And to this day, it had paid off.

And speaking of paying for things, I needed to get back to work on Blaze's latest book: *Diamonds à La Carte*. That's because I was the bread winner these days. The sole bread winner. And that meant I had to produce book after book.

But first I headed to my closet to figure out what I was going to wear on my date the next night. I decided on a sleeveless, black dress, one with a slight A-line flair to the skirt that hit just below the knee. Then I picked out my red, block-heel sandals and a bold, gold bracelet and nearly matching earrings. The entire outfit looked simple but elegant. Dressy but not too dressy.

And perfect for my date with Remy.

Just thinking about it made me feel warm all over. Aside from his insistence that I avoid investigating or solving mysteries, things had been going so well between us. Not to mention, the mere sight of the man made my heart go pitter-pat. Dating as a widow had been challenging, without a doubt. But now I had to wonder, was it possible to fall in love a second time around?

Regardless, I could hardly wait to see him again.

I was smiling when I headed upstairs via my curved front staircase and turned left at the second-floor landing. Then I strolled down the hardwood floor of the hallway to my home office. My happy place. While my kitchen was the place where I created culinary delights, my office was the place where I created characters and stories that were near and dear to my heart. And now as I stepped into the room and flipped on the light switch, I made a quick visual survey of my collection of mementoes, trophies, award plaques, and photographs that were sitting on every available surface or hanging on the walls. Though not on the wall behind my desk, which only displayed framed covers of every one of my novels.

I sat at my desk and let out a relaxing sigh, all ready to see where Blaze was going next. Agatha and Ellery came trotting in and trilled up to me, before taking their usual spots on the seat cushion of my bay window. I cooed to them and started my regular writing warm-up—a couple of minutes of pure stream of consciousness writing. Then I deleted those words and got right into the zone and back into Blaze's world.

Her latest culinary mystery involved international jewel thieves who moved their stolen goods via a series of cooking contests that traveled from state to state. In the current chapter I was working on, Blaze was explaining it all to her boyfriend, Detective Angus Steele, as I wrote:

"'So how did you find out about the diamonds?' Angus asked, clearly fascinated by Blaze's ability to uncover hidden clues.

Blaze let out a little laugh and tossed her long, copper-colored hair over her shoulder. 'Naturally, I first became suspicious when I noticed how possessive Chloe was of her cooking implements. She practically traveled with a full kitchen, considering all the tools and utensils and small appliances that she took everywhere. Packing and unpacking was quite an ordeal, and she always had unknown visitors appear and help for a short time at each stop. Before they took off. Never to be seen again.'

'All of which could appear to be perfectly legit,' Angus commented, crossing his arms and putting an index finger to his perfectly square chin. 'And simply make her look eccentric. Or obsessive and controlling.'

Blaze nodded and gazed out the window of her designer kitchen. 'Mostly it just made her look annoying, so people wanted to avoid her. That's why her cover worked so well.'

Now Angus flashed a bright smile. 'But you, Blaze, brilliant girl, saw right through her ruse.'

Blaze returned his smile, her eyes sparkling and her heart pounding, just like it always did whenever he was near. 'Because I noticed Chloe didn't like anyone touching her things. That is highly unusual in the cooking community, since most of us are happy to share if someone needs something. But when Chloe wasn't looking, I borrowed her salt mill, and I quickly understood what was going on.'

'And that's when you found the diamonds,' he murmured, running his hands through his golden hair. 'But how did you know they were inside the salt mill?'

'That, my dear detective, is where my many decades of being a gourmet cook came into play. Because I have seen all kinds of salt in my life. Sea salt, Himalayan salt, kosher salt, and just good old table salt. And if there is one thing I've learned about salt crystals, it's that they don't sparkle when the light hits them. But diamonds certainly do.'

'You have such amazing instincts when it comes to crime solving, Blaze, my love. Where would I be without you? And speaking of diamonds . . .' Without fanfare, he slid his arm around her tiny waist and pulled her close."

Right at that moment, I couldn't help but let out a sardonic chuckle. "Isn't that interesting . . .?" I muttered aloud. "Detective

Angus Steele *never* tries to hold Blaze back when it comes to solving crimes. Unlike a detective that I happen to know . . ."

Never mind that one detective was fictional, and the other was, well . . . not. Nonetheless, I wrote on, and before I knew it, I had whipped out four pages. I was halfway through the next when I heard a loud *vroom-vroom-vroom* coming from outside my window.

Something that wasn't a normal sound at the end of our usually quiet neighborhood. I immediately wondered if the woman in the Crown Victoria had returned. So I jumped up to look out my bay window, and thankfully, I didn't see a silver car.

But unfortunately, I did see Olivia's little, red car out in the street, and instead of taking a left into her own driveway, she took a right, heading in the direction of my house. Then she drove slowly around the cul-de-sac, hitting the gas a few times and making more loud engine sounds. Of course, I wondered if she was simply testing out her engine. Meaning, I wondered if she might be having a problem with her car.

Naturally, I assumed she would simply pull into her driveway when she reached her side of the street. But I was dead wrong. Instead, she embarked on another go-around of the tree-filled island. And just as she approached my house, she hit the gas a few more times, making an even louder *vroom-vroom-vroom*!

From what I could tell, she was also making sure that I heard it.

Parker came marching into my office. "Umm . . . Mom . . . Why is Mrs. Degill out there revving her engine? Right in front of our house?"

I shook my head. "That's a good question, kiddo. To tell you the truth, I have no idea why she's doing that."

"It seems kind of weird, Mom."

"Yup, it does."

"We've sure had a lot of people doing strange things in front of our house lately."

He could say that again. First the woman in the Crown Victoria, and now Olivia out there gunning her engine. Both scenarios gave me a very uneasy feeling. Like they were just the icy, protruding tips of something much bigger that was happening just below the surface. I watched as Olivia made one more round and then pulled into her own driveway and straight into her garage. Seconds later, I saw the garage door come down.

Oddly enough, I breathed a sigh of relief.

"Well, it looks like she went home," I told my son. "Let's hope she stays there."

Parker raised his brows and nodded. "I think I'll go hit the hay, Mom."

"Sounds good. Sleep tight."

Of course, I didn't add that I was about to go and make sure the house was locked up and the alarm was on.

Yet as I stared out my window, I couldn't help but wonder what Olivia had been up to. It seemed like she had wanted me to notice her driving around our cul-de-sac. But why? And what did she hope to accomplish from it?

The obvious answer was that she was sending me a message, and that maybe she was blaming me for the way her husband had latched onto my hand earlier. Of course, there might be a hundred other reasons for her behavior, none of which were terribly rational.

But one answer stood out front and center in my mystery-writer brain.

"She's trying to establish an alibi," I murmured. "That, or she's simply trying one out, to see if anyone notices her," I explained to the kitties, who were now sitting at attention.

But if she was going to need an alibi, that only meant one thing—Olivia was planning to commit a crime. And a very premeditated one at that.

I shivered at the thought and immediately closed the blinds against the coming night.

And whatever else might be out there.

Chapter Six

The next morning after Parker left for school, I was still thinking about Olivia in her red car and the woman in the Crown Victoria. I was about to head to the salon to have my hair done, but I didn't go anywhere without glancing out my dining room windows first, just to make sure the silver car wasn't parked out front again. And then when I finally did back out of my driveway, I took a quick peek at the Degills' house before I drove down the street.

Evidently, I was becoming paranoid. But what I was paranoid about exactly, well, I couldn't say for sure. Yes, there'd been a strange woman parked in front of my house yesterday, one who took my picture. And then there'd been Olivia's behavior the night before which had been . . . well, odd. To say the least. But that was hardly a reason to start looking over my shoulder at every turn. After all, I lived in a safe neighborhood with mostly nice people.

Though it was true, there had been that one murder—okay, two, actually—but I'd already uncovered that killer. So what were the odds of another one happening?

Yet something inside me said there was much more to the situation than met the eye.

And speaking of "meeting the eye," I glanced at my hair in the rearview mirror, blatantly aware that I needed a trim and a touchup, and who knew what else. Of course, I was also well aware that getting my hair done on the morning before my big date with Remy was probably pushing my luck. Big-time. But I'd been so busy writing my new book that I'd done a first-rate job of procrastinating when it came to making a salon appointment.

Even so, I'd been going to the same hairdresser for years, and I knew I could count on Lucy to resurrect my limp locks. So I figured the risk was minimal as I drove through the streets of Abbott Cove, with the sun shining happily through my windshield.

I arrived at Sleek and Chic Shears a few minutes early and smiled as I approached the new, redheaded receptionist. "Hi, I'm Maddie Montgomery, and I'm here for a nine-thirty appointment with Lucy."

The young woman reacted like I was speaking in a foreign tongue. Without saying a word, she simply stared at me, stone-faced. Perhaps the custom of whatever land she'd come from. In any case, she did not show any signs of comprehending what I'd said.

I was just about to resort to some kind of gesticulation when she finally mumbled, "I'll go get the manager."

Which was definitely not the response I was expecting. Or hoping for.

While she stalked away, I glanced down the length of the mirrored salon to Lucy's spot, surprised not to see her there. Or anywhere else, for that matter. But just because I couldn't see her, and just because the young receptionist was acting oddly, there was no reason for me to panic.

Or so I told myself.

As I waited and waited. And waited some more.

Thankfully, the receptionist finally reappeared with a very tall and very icy, platinum blonde woman in tow. A woman whom I guessed must be the manager.

"I'm sorry," the woman said, "but Lucy quit. And we hired a new hairdresser to take her place. She'll be doing your hair this morning."

Again I told myself not to panic, even though my heart had started to pound out a rumba beat with a loud *thunk-thunk-thunk-a-thunk.*

"Wait a minute . . . Lucy quit?" I managed to utter. "When did that happen? I just made my appointment a couple of days ago."

"Oh, it was all very sudden," the manager explained. "And we are certainly keeping our end of the deal by providing someone to do your hair."

"But why did Lucy quit?" I asked, immediately worried about her. "Is she okay? She seemed fine the last time I saw her."

Sparks flew from the manager's gray eyes. "I'm afraid I'm not at liberty to say. But don't worry. We've got you covered. Deirdre will be doing your hair this morning."

"Deirdre?" I repeated, trying to buy time to think.

The manager plastered a smile on her face. "You'll love her. I promise. Now please follow me."

Which left me in an awkward position. Did I follow? Or did I cancel and walk away? I hadn't booked an appointment with this Deirdre, and I didn't know a thing about her. Namely, whether she was a good hairdresser or not. And since she'd just been hired, I wondered if the salon knew much about her, either. Not only that, but I would have appreciated a few minutes to mull things over.

"I think I'll come back another time," I said.

The manager frowned. "Are you sure? Deirdre will be taking over Lucy's clientele. She's really good."

"Well . . ." I hesitated.

"Oh, come on. Deirdre is so much fun and so bubbly. You'll love her. And your hair looks like it could use a little work."

Well, she had me there.

"Now please follow me," the manager insisted.

Then before I could give it another thought, my feet completely betrayed me and overrode all the red flags that my brain was busy sending up. And I numbly trailed along behind her and walked to Deirdre's chair.

Which used to be Lucy's chair.

Deirdre gave me a hearty welcome. "Good morning, Maddie. Don't you worry about a thing. I'll do a great job. Trust me."

Words that always unnerved me. No matter who said them.

But if nothing else, Deirdre herself had beautifully styled chestnut hair, which was stunning in combination with her vivid blue eyes. And if she looked that nice, then she had to be a good hairdresser herself, right?

Except that she probably hadn't done her own hair.

"So what'll it be this morning, Maddie?" she asked as I took a seat. "A trim? A whole new style? Or something more daring, like fuchsia or maybe a nice blue-black color?"

"Ummm . . . just a trim and a blowout would be great," I told her. "Nothing drastic, thanks."

She nodded, and her mouth put on quite a show of smiling while her eyes suddenly teared up. Though hopefully it was merely a reaction to all the hair-product fumes that were floating around the shop and not from my obvious hesitation about having her work on my hair. But the mere thought that my actions might cause her to cry made me decide to give her the benefit of the doubt and be a little more friendly. After all, I'd been the "new" person plenty of times in my life, and I remembered what it was like.

"Let's get you shampooed," Deirdre said with a sniffle.

"That would be great," I replied, offering her an encouraging smile.

She quickly wrapped a black cape around my neck while my eyes zeroed in on the ornate scissors that were lying on her small counter. Scissors that were adorned with inlaid crystals. Sort of like the handles of old-time swords that were adorned with precious gems. In fact, the scissors themselves even had a "swordlike" appearance.

"Those are stunning," I said with complete sincerity. "I've never seen scissors with inlaid crystals before."

"Oh, those aren't crystals," she informed me as she motioned for me to go with her to the shampoo station.

I followed behind and took the chair that she indicated. "They're not? You mean they're . . ." I started to ask as she leaned me back and turned on the water.

"Uh-huh," I could barely hear her say over the sound of water running past my ears. "They're real gems," she explained as she lathered my head with shampoo. "I had them done at Flause Jewelers. After I graduated from stylist school and got my license. A couple of weeks ago."

That's when my breath caught in my throat. Did she just say, "A couple of weeks ago?" Had I heard her right?

But before I could say a word, she went on with, "Those are sapphires and emeralds and rubies. And citrines. Oh, and a few diamonds," she informed me as she rinsed my hair.

And then skipped the conditioning part of the routine.

Right before she demonstrated that she was a fan of the drip-dry method when it came time to toweling me off.

"Okay, let's go back to my station now," she instructed.

"Umm . . . could I have a towel, please?" I asked.

"Oh, sure. Of course, Maddie. Sorry, but I've been a little distracted lately. What with all that's been going on in my life."

She pulled a towel about the size of a facecloth from a cupboard and dropped it onto my shoulder. Whereby I did my best to blot the water from my forehead and eyes before I followed her back to her chair, leaving a virtual river of water in my wake.

I managed to slide onto the chair before I glanced into the mirror, noticing that I now resembled a drowned rat. But apparently, I wasn't the only one who was dripping, since Deirdre now had a couple of big tears rolling down her cheeks.

"Are you all right?" I asked gently.

She waved me off. "Oh, I'm fine. Just fine. So how much should I cut off your ends, Maddie? Have you ever thought of a nice, short haircut?"

Despite myself, I gasped. "Short . . .? Oh, no. No, no. I absolutely do not want short hair. In fact, just a blowout would be great."

"Nonsense! You definitely need a trim. I saw your frizzy ends the second you entered the shop." By this time, tears had begun to flow freely from her eyes, making me wonder if my "frizzy ends" had upset her so much. I also wondered how much her eyesight was impaired by her tears.

But mostly I just wondered how I could get out of there without causing a major scene. Because I truly did not believe that Deirdre was in any condition to perform a task where eye-hand coordination might be required. Especially one that involved sharp scissors.

"No, really, I like frizzy ends," I told her. "My mother had frizzy ends. Just like my grandmother did. We're a frizzy ends kind of family. So all I need today is a style, and we'll call it good."

But again, my words fell on deaf ears.

"You need at least an inch off," she insisted as she started to section my hair, combing the front half over my face.

"Okay . . . just an inch. But no more," I conceded from beneath my dripping wet mane that now covered my face like a curtain.

And while I could no longer see her, I could hear her crying and sniffling from behind me. Along with the steady *snip-snip-snip* sound of her cutting my wet hair.

At long last, she finished one section and combed down another. "This will be such a boost for my career, Maddie. I heard you're a famous author, and now I can tell everyone that I'm your hairdresser. Plus, I get a chance to use my new scissors. They're really amazing. They're called sword-blade scissors."

"I thought they kind of looked like a sword," I said, my voice muffled by the blanket of wet hair hanging over my eyes, nose, and mouth.

Not that she heard me.

"But right after I got them," she went on, "I realized I probably shouldn't have had all those gems put on the handle. They do kind of hurt my hand after a while, and it makes me drop them a lot."

Which was when I froze, not daring so much as to breathe. I tucked my feet under the chair, hoping to get my sandaled toes out of the line of fire. I was already doubtful about getting my hair cut; I didn't need anything else cut off as well. And given the sharp pointiness of her shears, I could easily envision punctured or severed toes.

"These scissors are worth a fortune," she went on, finally getting to the front of my hair. "I really didn't have the money to get them decorated right now, but I wanted them done so badly. Because I really needed a symbol of my new life without my ex-husband. Rotten, cheating scumbag that he was. So thank goodness, the jeweler did it all for pretty cheap, along with the exchange of my old engagement ring that had a big diamond in it. After all, Gage, the owner, sold us that ring."

"That was nice . . ." I managed to get out, while she combed my hair.

"I'm sure Gage knew all about how Dex, my ex, cheated on me. And the only reason I became a hairdresser is because Dex left me destitute."

Dex? As in Dex Degill? The man who had moved in across the street and wanted us to be permanently attached by our palms? Or was it possible that Deirdre was talking about another "Dex?" It wasn't exactly a common name these days.

"It's the only reason I went to beauty school," Deirdre went on, still sniffling. "I mean, what else could I do? I had to make a living. And Gage helped me out by doing such a great job decorating my scissors."

"Customer service is so important," I agreed, holding as still as I could and praying that she didn't accidentally stab me.

"It's the truth, isn't it?" she went on before she dropped her scissors.

Which made a loud clattering sound when they hit the floor.

And made me jump a mile.

Deirdre sighed and picked up her scissors. "See what I mean, Maddie? These things are kind of hard to hold on to . . ."

For the life of me, I couldn't think of the correct response to such a statement. Instead, I just went with, "Deirdre, you never told me your last name."

"Oh, I kept Dex's last name. It's Degill," she practically sobbed. "You know, Maddie, your hair really does need a deep conditioning treatment. I've got just the thing for you."

Never mind that she hadn't even bothered with conditioner at all. But right about then, I didn't really care. I was mostly just thankful that she had finished the trim, and I didn't appear to be bleeding anywhere.

"I'm sorry, Deirdre, but I need to be going," I told her gently as I leaned up in the chair, ready to leave.

But she grabbed me by the shoulders and leaned me back. "Oh, no, Maddie. Your hair is just too dry. We've got to fix that."

Though I seriously questioned how she could determine that my hair was dry at all, given the way that I was still dripping. And apparently, so was she, as I noticed more tears welling up in her eyes and spilling onto her cheeks.

How could I possibly say no to a woman who was so upset? In any case, I decided it wouldn't hurt for me to go through with the conditioning treatment. After all, it sounded simple enough, and certainly nothing that could damage my hair. For all I knew, it might even make my hair look good.

Or so I told myself while I watched her squirt some murky liquid into a little bowl. Then, using a paint brush, she started to brush the goop onto sections of my hair.

"I never, ever should've married Dex in the first place," she bemoaned while her tears flowed faster, and she slathered on more and more of the gooey conditioner. "I was in love with another man. I'd been dating him for a couple of years, and we'd just gotten engaged."

"So why didn't you marry him?" I asked.

Deirdre sniffled and kept on slathering bigger and bigger gobs of goop onto my head. "Oh, I don't know. Dex was a really competitive guy, and he more or less competed with my fiancé for my hand in marriage. And I do mean 'my hand.' Because the minute I met him, he took my hand and wouldn't let go. It was so romantic."

I shuddered at the memory of Dex hanging onto my own hand. "Well, I guess some women might call that romantic," I managed to get in before she flipped on her hair dryer and hit me full blast.

This lasted for a few minutes before she turned it off and turned her curling iron on.

"Oh, Maddie, it really *was* the most romantic thing ever," she went on, not missing a beat in her story. "Especially since Dex was already married, and he even left his wife for me. Nothing says 'I love you' like a man who wants you *so* badly that they'd turn their whole life upside down for you."

Somehow, I didn't think Dex's other ex-wife would see it that way.

Deirdre paused and smiled bravely through her tears. "Of course, it didn't hurt that Dex was super rich. And I do mean rich! He was always surprising me with jewels and things. He was very generous. A lot more than my fiancé. That's why I dumped him and married Dex."

At that point, I was stumped as to what to say. That, and I was too busy watching her fuse this so-called "conditioner" to my hair with a white-hot curling iron.

"When Dex left me," she went on, "I had no choice but to get a job. But the truth is, Maddie, I hate it so much! And I hate that I even have to work at all." At that point, she began to sob loudly. "I could absolutely kill Dex for doing this to me!"

Words and actions that left me speechless. Along with my image in the mirror, and the awareness that my hair now looked like I'd accidentally walked through a car wash during the "Wax" cycle.

As I stared at myself, I tried hard not to hyperventilate.

"There, now don't you look lovely?" Deirdre said, blowing her nose. "You're all ready for a night on the town."

A night on the town? As in my date with Remy tonight?

Clearly, I would have to cancel, and for that matter, I would probably need to move out of state for a while. At least until my hair returned to normal again. Because there was absolutely no way that I could ever, ever, *ever* let someone see me like this.

Deirdre put the curling iron back in its stand and glanced at me in the mirror. "Oh, it looks like I cut the right side of your hair shorter than the left. I don't know why I always do that. I guess we'll have to start over."

"No . . . *Noooo*!" I managed to get out before I started to choke. "It's fine. It's great. I'll just keep my head tilted in that direction."

Then I stood up and pulled the black cape from my neck.

"Okay, good," she said, mustering up another smile. "I gave you an extra bunch of this treatment, since your hair was so dry. So it should last about three months. You can pay up front. And you can choose how big a tip you'd like to leave. You'll get a prompt of anywhere from twenty to thirty percent. Don't forget that I really need the money," she added with another onslaught of tears.

Which left me completely flabbergasted. Did she really expect me to pay for this? Though by then, I was so shell-shocked that I simply wanted to do whatever it took to get out of there.

Mostly since I was absolutely dying to get home and wash out whatever she'd put in my hair.

I ambled to the front reception area, realizing that my head was now dripping with the greasy, synthetic concoction. Possibly the same stuff my mechanic used when he changed the oil in my car.

The young receptionist's eyes went wide when she saw me. She eyeballed my hair from root to tip and gave me a sneer. As though this train wreck of a hairdo was *my* idea. Not to mention, my fault.

Then after I'd paid and overridden the section asking for a tip, I raced to my car, well aware that the shirt I'd worn today was now completely ruined. Somehow, I doubted the stuff that was oozing from my hair shafts was going to be easy to wash out.

I also wondered if I needed to avoid open flames.

I held my breath the whole way back to my neighborhood, praying that no one I knew would see me. I thought I was home free when I turned into my cul-de-sac and saw my driveway, dead ahead.

There was just one problem.

A silver Crown Victoria was parked on the street in front of my house. And the blonde woman behind the wheel was hanging out the window.

Filming me with a camera.

Chapter Seven

Right at that moment, I forgot all about my horrible hair, and I became a woman on a mission. No matter what, I was going to learn the identity of this woman who was sitting in front of my house. And more importantly, I was going to find out *why* she was there.

Or die trying.

Which, I hoped, wasn't even a remote possibility.

So I quickly parked my car at the end of my driveway, flung my door open and bounced out. But I was not about to go in empty-handed. Taking a page from Blaze's books, I reached behind my seat and grabbed the fifteen-inch cocktail stirring rod that I kept there "just in case." Not so I could stir cocktails on the go, of course, but rather because the thin-glass rod made for one heck of a weapon.

A baton, if you will.

Then I made a beeline for the Crown Victoria, a car that now sported a Texas license plate. Yet I would have bet my favorite sauté pan that the plate wasn't hers, considering I'd spotted a Georgia plate on her car yesterday after she'd splashed me and sped away.

Remy's words rang through my brain as I raced to the driver's side door. "Whatever you do, don't approach her on your own," he'd insisted. Along with, "Leave the investigating to the professionals."

"Fat chance," I muttered as I saw the woman reach over to the passenger side and set her camera down.

Was she about to drive off again?

But much to my amazement, the blonde woman just turned and stared at me, her eyes wide and her mouth open. It was the first I'd gotten a good look at her, and she was probably the kind of woman who could be described as "voluptuous." In part thanks to the pink tank top she was wearing, which was at least two sizes too small for her.

In any case, it was clear she wasn't insecure about what the good Lord (or possibly her plastic surgeon) had given her, since a great portion of it was barely under wraps. If not on display.

Along with the huge diamond solitaire on the silver chain that hung just above her décolletage.

As the gem sparkled in the sunlight, I guessed it was probably about a four-carat stone. Yet something so expensive seemed a little incongruous with her unwashed, dented car and her attire in general. Had the necklace been a gift?

"Oh, my God, what happened to you?" she gasped. "Were you cleaning a grill with your hair? Or a deep fat fryer? Dex is not gonna like that look." She pulled out her phone and snapped off a few pictures.

"Dex? My neighbor? Why would he care about my hair?" I asked in my most stern tone.

She smirked. "Well, he definitely won't think you look too pretty like that."

"Who cares what Dex thinks?" I said, putting my hands on my hips. "Let's talk about you instead. Who are you and what are you doing out here? And where did you get that Texas license plate?"

She sighed and stared at my front door, giving me a chance to glance inside her car. She had an open laptop sitting on the passenger seat beside her. And that seat, along with the whole back seat, was filled with files and papers and a few books and all kinds of things. To be honest, the items inside her vehicle looked more like they belonged in an office, or on a desk, rather than riding around in a car.

"I traded plates with someone in my apartment complex," she admitted.

"Does that person know about it?"

"Well, not exactly. But I'll have the plates traded back before she even realizes it. I mean, seriously, what else could I do? I couldn't risk anyone getting my real license plate number."

"Why in the world not?" I asked, while my mind conjured up a million possibilities as to why someone would want to conceal their plate number.

None of which were good.

"It's complicated," she informed me.

"You still haven't told me who you are," I said, doing my best to remain formidable and firm.

"I'm Belinda. And you're Maddie. I researched you online, so I know all about you."

Words that made the little hairs on the back of my neck stand on end.

And made me glad I'd brought my stirring rod with me.

"How nice," I said, chomping on the words. "Now tell me why you're parked right in front of my house and taking pictures of me."

She shrugged. "Because you were with Dex."

I stared at her in disbelief. "I haven't 'been with' Dex. And that's the second time you brought up my neighbor. Why?"

"I saw you walking out of his house yesterday," she informed me, flipping her long hair over her shoulder.

For a moment, I was stunned. "I took food over to him and his wife to welcome them to the neighborhood. Big deal. Why are you so interested in Dex? And Olivia?"

Her hazel eyes were suddenly filled with stars. "Because Dex and I dated. And I know that, deep down, he still loves me."

"Does *he* know that? And would he really be married to someone else if he loved *you*?"

Without responding to my question, she flashed me a dreamy smile, much like a teenager in love. It was as though she hadn't even heard me at all.

"I met Dex a while ago at a speed dating event, right after I moved here," she finally murmured, practically purring. "You know, they have them all the time at the Lytely Char and Grill Restaurant and Lounge. They're a great way to meet people. Trevor Lytely runs them. Of course, the men he invites are all rich, and it makes such a difference. So those speed dating nights are a lot of fun. Though for me, it was more than just fun. It was love at first sight when I met Dex, and he took my hand. And he held it. And he wouldn't let go. Unfortunately, he came with a minor complication—he was about to marry Olivia."

I glanced at the house across the street. "I would think that might put a damper on his dating life."

She tilted her head and sighed. "No worries. He'll be leaving her soon."

I wiped away some of the oily stuff that had dripped from my hair and onto my cheek. "But if you're after Dex, why are you parked in front of *my* house?"

She sighed. "Well . . . there is a little matter of that restraining order. I'm supposed to stay two-hundred feet away. So I figure I'm safe over here."

A restraining order?

"So you're a stalker," I clarified.

"I find that word highly offensive," she chastised me. "It has such a nasty ring to it. I prefer the term 'Tracker-American.'"

I crossed my arms. "Whatever you want to call it, not only are your plates illegal, but stalking is against the law, too."

She huffed. "When it comes to true love, there are no limits to what a person would do. Besides, I'm an upstanding citizen. I work full-time, as you can see. I'm a medical transcriptionist."

"You work from your car," I intoned, shaking my head.

"Well, I would much rather work from my apartment, but then how would I keep track of Dex? People have no idea how hard it is to keep track of someone. And how much time it takes."

"That alone might be a good reason to give it up."

She tilted her head at me. "Oh? What would you do for true love? For Dex?"

"Not this," I said with a flourish. "As for Dex, he's a married man. And even if he were single, I would have absolutely no interest in him. It sounds like the man is a complete philanderer." Memories of his handholding stunt came flooding back into my mind, making me shudder.

"You say that now," Belinda went on. "But sooner or later, all women are taken in by his charm. He's like a magnet and women are the metal. And no matter how strong you are, and how much you try to resist, you'll find yourself attracted to him and drawn in eventually."

To which I responded with a loud "*Eeeewwww*!"

And that was about the time when I decided to call Remy and have him arrest this woman and take her away. But then I realized there was one very big problem with that whole scenario. Namely, my hair. Meaning, I hadn't had a chance to wash all the gunk out and try to save it from itself, so to speak.

Then again, I wasn't sure if my hair actually *could* be saved. Not before tonight anyway. Which meant there was still the possibility that I might have to cancel my date with Remy.

So I decided to take a different tack when it came to Belinda.

I looked her directly in the eyes. "You've got two options right now. You can get out of here and not come back, or I will call the police and have you arrested. The choice is yours."

To which she hissed at me like a cat, which, sadly enough, wasn't even the oddest thing about our exchange.

"Your hair looks terrible, by the way," she tossed over her shoulder as she drove off, speeding around the island of the cul-de-sac and onto the straightaway leading out of our neighborhood.

All the while, I couldn't help but wonder—was Dex's dalliance with Belinda the reason Olivia had gotten a new, big sapphire? And a cute, little sportscar? Either as punishment or guilt gifts?

Belinda was barely out of sight when I noticed a drone heading my way. One that looked like a big, metallic firefly. And when it hovered and blinked its little lights, I actually thought it was kind of cute.

I even had a name for the little craft.

Evinrude.

I headed for my car and grabbed my phone out of my purse, since I knew what would be coming next—a call from Evinrude's owner. Spencer Poe. And sure enough, my phone played my Peter Gunn ringtone.

"Mrs. Montgomery, have you been harmed?" my neighbor asked frantically, the second I answered. "Did that woman spray you with some kind of toxic chemical? It appears to be all over your head. I can have a Hazmat team there in a matter of seconds."

For a moment, I wondered if it might take a Hazmat team to wash this stuff out. Especially since it continued to ooze oily blobs onto my shirt. But I decided to start with shampoo first, and move onto something more industrial strength later, if I needed to.

"I'm fine, Spencer," I said into the phone. "It was just a bad experience at the beauty salon."

"You can never be too careful, Mrs. Montgomery. Spies frequently work as hair stylists. They lull unsuspecting victims into a state of relaxation, thus making them susceptible to revealing classified information."

"Well, thankfully, I don't know any classified information. And I'm afraid this hairdresser was much more interested in her own problems than in me."

"Thank goodness for small favors," he said in all seriousness. "Then I shall bring my drone back home. But if you have any issues later, please don't hesitate to request my assistance."

"Thank you, Spencer."

Then I waved goodbye to Evinrude and drove my car into the garage.

After that, I washed my hair.

And washed my hair.

And washed it again.

Four washings later, and the oily stuff appeared to be going nowhere. If anything, I thought it might actually be expanding.

That was when I sat down and started to cry like a lovesick sixteen-year-old who couldn't go on her big date to the prom. But I quickly reminded myself that I was a grown-up and not a kid, and that I had been through so much worse than a bad haircut and conditioning treatment that wouldn't go away.

So I took a deep breath and splashed cold water all over my face. I was a little more composed by the time Parker rolled in.

He froze in his tracks the instant he saw me. "Mom, what happened to you? Did some extraterrestrials try to beam you aboard their mother ship, but they didn't succeed and they just gooed you up instead? Or were you attacked by a band of brain-eating zombies, and you've got brain fluid leaking out? Though I've never heard of brain fluid being so greasy . . ."

If I hadn't been so upset about my hair, I would've rolled my eyes. "No, nothing like that."

He moved in for a closer inspection. "Wow, Mom, I don't know what you've got on your hair . . . but is it supposed to be dripping like that?"

"No, Parker, it's not. Can you help me get this stuff out? I've washed it four times, and I can't get rid of it."

He rubbed a couple of strands between his fingers. "Let's see, it looks like some kind of synthetic polymer and formaldehyde compound."

"You mean . . . embalming fluid?"

He shook his head. "Not exactly, Mom. Did they do this at your salon place? Because this stuff doesn't belong on somebody's hair. It belongs on the International Space Station. It's really amazing. I've never seen anything like it."

"Okay, that's nice. But can you get it out?"

He stood back and stared at my hair some more. "Yeah, Mom, I'm pretty sure I can. I'll go see what I've got in my old chemistry set."

Visions of my hair going up in smoke flashed through my brain, and I wondered how fast I could get a wig delivered.

"You know, Mom, maybe you should go put your feet up in the living room. You shouldn't get all stressed out at your age."

Finally, I did roll my eyes at him, seconds before I decided to take his advice. Like it or not, it had been a trying day, and a little down time might be a good idea. And to think, I'd been looking forward to my date with Remy for a full week. And now, unless Parker came up with some miracle concoction that could save my hair, preferably without removing it completely, I was about to call and feign an illness and reschedule.

But between Remy's schedule and mine, who knew when we might be able to go out again?

I sat on one of the oversized, gold-toned couches in my living room, being careful not to let my hair touch the back. The twin to this couch faced me, with a glass coffee table between the two, and a white shag rug on the floor below. A white-mantled fireplace stood regally on the adjacent wall, with a Vincent Van Gogh giclée print—*Café Terrace at Night*—centered on the wall above it.

Seconds later, the kitties joined me, Ellery on one side and Agatha on the other, both leaning in close. Clearly lending their moral support.

I sighed, feeling good and sorry for myself, only seconds before Parker appeared before me.

He held out a big test tube full of blue, gooey stuff. "Okay, Mom, I think this is what you need. It should work on your hair."

I only prayed he was right.

Chapter Eight

I emerged from the shower with squeaky, clean hair. Thank God. Whatever oily compound had been fused into my long locks was now gone, and yes, I breathed a huge sigh of relief. More than one, truth be told. Right before I grabbed an old pair of haircutting scissors and trimmed about a half an inch from the left side of my hair, the side that Deirdre had left longer. So now, both sides officially matched.

And after I dried and styled it, I had to say, my hair looked wonderful. Stunning, even. Lots of body, fantastic shine, and a perfect length. Honestly, it had been a while since my tresses had looked so lustrous. And it was night and day from the results of my disastrous appointment with Deirdre.

As far as I was concerned, the transformation bordered on miraculous. Meaning, my son was a genius. Because whatever potion he had come up with had absolutely saved me from my "hairy" situation. Now I wondered if he should patent his formula and sell it. Surely there were others out there who might need a product like this. Who knew what kind of greasy situations such a concoction might clean up?

I stepped from my bathroom and into my bedroom, feeling as calm and happy and relaxed as the colors that decorated the room. Dark blue, white, and seafoam, with just a hint of pink. All the colors of a Bermuda bay.

Smiling, I donned my black dress, added the jewelry I had picked out the night before, and slipped into my red sandals. I spritzed on just a bit of perfume and glanced at myself in the mirror.

I hardly even recognized the woman staring back at me. In a matter of an hour, I'd been completely transformed. And now I was looking forward to my date with Detective Remington Reagan with every fiber of my being. Visions of Cinderella dancing with the prince played through my head. Along with thoughts of a moonlight stroll through a magical garden. Who knew what wonders tonight might bring?

Still smiling, I practically waltzed out of my bedroom, high heels clicking on the hardwood floor. I found Parker in the kitchen, gathering up the ingredients he needed to make his dinner.

He raised an eyebrow when he saw me. "Hey, Mom, you cleaned up pretty good."

"Thanks to the stuff you gave me," I told him, absolutely beaming at my brainy boy. "What was in that vial anyway? I mean, what kind of chemicals did you put in? Was it a complicated formula?"

"No, not really."

And to think, the child was modest, on top of it all.

"I can't believe how well it worked," I gushed.

He shrugged. "Well, it *should've* worked. It's the same stuff they use to clean ducks after an oil spill."

That's when my mouth dropped open wide. "Wait a minute . . . Do you mean . . .?"

"Yup, Mom. It was dishwashing soap," he told me with his usual goofy grin.

"Oh."

So much for that patent I was thinking about.

"Do you have everything you need to make your dinner tonight?" I asked, taking stock of what he had on the counter.

"Got it all right here. I think I can handle this."

"I'm sure you can," I encouraged him. "After all, you'll be cooking for yourself when you go to college."

Whereby he let out a loud sigh. "Yup, Mom, I will. But since I'm going to A&M, I'll still be close enough to come home on weekends. When I get tired of all that cooking."

Something I wouldn't get tired of at all.

Parker pulled a saucepan and a large frying pan from the cupboard. "So what time can I expect you home? You do know this is a school night," he added with another grin.

I would have ruffled his hair if he hadn't been so much taller than me.

"Well, since we're going to that French restaurant at the top of Abbott Building, we won't be far away. Not like driving into downtown Houston. So I should be home around ten or ten-thirty. What do you plan to do tonight?"

"Oh, you know, nothing much. I thought I'd take the Continental out for a test drive."

And that's when I was pretty sure my heart stopped. For a moment anyway.

Until Parker laughed. "Kidding, Mom. Kidding. I'm just going to study for finals. And me and the felines are going to spend some quality time."

Which most likely meant my pantry would be completely bare by the time I got home. But it was a chance I was willing to take and something that completely slipped my mind when I heard the doorbell ring. I strolled to the front entry and opened the door to find a tall, dark-haired man with navy-blue eyes looking directly into mine. Then there were those broad shoulders that were about chin level to me, and that dark, wavy hair.

Remy.

Right away my pulse started to pound, and I remembered exactly why I was so smitten with the man.

He reached an arm around my waist and gave me a quick kiss on the cheek. Something that sent shivers across every inch of my body.

"Are you ready?" he murmured. "Traffic is terrible. We'd better get going if we want to make our reservation."

"I'm ready. Let me just say goodbye to Parker."

"Oh, right," Remy said with a nod. "I'd better say hello to the man of the house myself."

I led him directly into the kitchen, where Parker had now opened up a can of tomato soup and was carefully spooning it into the saucepan. I noticed he had pulled out eight slices of bread, presumably for the grilled cheese sandwiches he planned to make.

"How's it going, Parker?" Remy asked.

Right before he did something that completely impressed me—he held out his hand to shake my son's. Treating him with great respect and like the almost grown-up man that he was.

And even better, Parker gave him a firm handshake in return.

"Going good, Mr. Reagan," Parker replied. "Sure you don't want to stay here and have grilled cheese sandwiches? Instead of some fancy French food?"

Remy smiled. "Sounds tempting. Can I take a rain check?"

Parker saluted him with his spatula. "You know where we live."

Which made Remy laugh. "Yes, I do. But now I'm going to take your mom out for a nice dinner. I promise I'll take good care of her."

"You better. She's the only mom I've got," Parker told him before he made a *V* with his fingers, pointed to his eyes, then to Remy's, and then back to his own. In a perfect "I'll be watching you gesture." To top it off, he couldn't help but laugh at his own joke.

That was about the time when I shook my head and rolled my eyes.

"Message received," came Remy's smiling reply. "And don't forget, buddy, we're only a phone call away if you need anything."

"Got it," Parker said, making a shooing motion with his hands. "Now get out of here. I've got food to cook. Go have fun and bring me back a steak or two."

I shook my head and laughed. "Good night, kiddo. I'll see you later."

"Back at'cha, Mom."

With that, Remy and I headed for the hallway and out the front door. I was careful to lock it behind me, just to make sure the place was secure while Parker was home alone. Especially now that I'd met Belinda, the "Tracker-American," who seemed to think a restraining order was a mere inconvenience when it came to pursuing the man she loved.

"He's a terrific kid, Maddie," Remy told me as we walked to his dark sedan. One that looked like it had just gone through the car wash. Such a welcome change compared to Belinda's unkempt car.

"He really is," I agreed. "I am so fortunate to have two fantastic kids."

"Well, I suspect you had a lot to do with that."

I smiled at the dear detective as he held the car door for me. "I've done my best. Just like I'm sure you did with your two daughters."

"I'm afraid I can't take as much credit for them turning out so well," he explained after he got in behind the wheel. "That was mostly my late wife's doing. My job has always been very demanding, so I wasn't around as much as I would've liked. But thankfully my wife survived until our kids got into college, even though she was going through chemo while they were in high school. Still, it gave my girls a better start in life."

I nodded. "It's hard on kids to lose a parent at such a young age. I know it was tough for both my kids, but I think it hit Parker the most, since his father was his role model."

"But it looks like he's doing great. Just like my daughters who are grown and on their own. One lives in Houston and the other moved to Lubbock with her husband. Though we don't see each other as much, I'd like to think we're still very close. I guess we really learned to lean on each other after my wife passed away."

"It's so nice to have them, isn't it? Of course, I say this right now . . . But I may change my mind if we come home to see flashing red lights blazing in the cul-de-sac, with Parker standing out in front of the house," I added with a laugh.

He smiled and shook his head. "Let's not even think it."

"Deal," I agreed.

Remy started the car and just stared at me for a moment or two. "Your hair . . . You look like an angel," he added as he reached over and touched my cheek.

Gently and tenderly.

Taking my breath away.

Right at that moment, I didn't have the heart to tell him what my hair had looked like mere hours ago, thanks to my horrendous salon appointment. And how I almost had to cancel our date because of it. Not to mention, my complete avoidance of calling him after I'd tangled with Belinda today. No, as far as I was concerned, there was no need to tell him all that now. What he didn't know wouldn't hurt him. So I just smiled and looked deep into his eyes.

"I suppose we'd better get to the restaurant," he finally said, breaking the spell.

From there, the conversation flowed freely, and I found myself leaning slightly toward him. He drove with his left hand on the wheel and leaned in toward me, too. Then after we arrived and parked in the Abbott Building lot, he strolled around the car and opened my door. With a warm smile, he took my hand and helped me out of the vehicle. He offered me his arm as we entered the ground floor of the building and took the elevator to the restaurant at the top. The place was nicely darkened when we walked in, and we were led to a table for two in front of a huge picture window, with Abbott Cove itself—the bay for which the community of Abbott Cove was named—visible in the distance. Candles were lit on every table, giving the place a relaxed and romantic atmosphere.

The hostess left us with a wine list and menus.

Right away, Remy turned to me and laid his hand on top of mine. "Okay, Maddie, I know you're an expert when it comes to wine and gourmet food. But I've got to confess—I'm actually a little clueless about this stuff. I'm more of a beer and burger kind of guy. Which you probably noticed since I took you to my favorite haunts on our first two dates."

"There's nothing wrong with beer and burgers," I encouraged him. "Good food is good food. And I loved going to those off the beaten path places. The burgers were delicious."

He nodded. "They absolutely were. But tonight, I wanted to take you some place a little bit fancier . . . okay, make that a *lot* fancier . . . But I'm not really an expert when it comes to ordering wine. Would you mind taking the lead on this?"

I smiled at him, my eyes meeting his again. "Not at all. For starters, it depends on what you want to eat tonight."

"Hmmm . . . I don't even recognize the names of half this stuff. What do you like on the menu?"

"Oh, I'm definitely looking at the flounder with the capers and Beurre Blanc sauce," I answered without hesitation.

He raised his brows. "Okay, good. Fish. I like fish. All kinds of fish. Especially when I catch them myself."

I nodded. "Freshly caught fish is fantastic. And just for the record, I enjoy cooking freshly caught fish. Of any kind. Though if you ever wanted me to cook some for you, you'd have to catch enough for Parker, too. In any case, we'll probably want a white wine to go with the flounder. It looks like they have a nice Sancerre from the Loire Valley of France. Which would pair beautifully with the fish," I told him, pointing to a reasonably priced wine on the list.

"I'm game. Let's try it," he said as he accidentally knocked the case that held his sunglasses off the table.

"Would you like me to put that in my purse?" I offered. "I'm forever leaving sunglasses all over town."

"That would be great. I'm the same way," he said, picking up the case and handing it to me.

I slipped it into my purse, just as a tall, very polite waiter appeared before us, and Remy expertly ordered a bottle of the Sancerre. Like he'd been doing it all his life.

Minutes later, the waiter reappeared with our wine and a chiller on a stand. He smoothly uncorked the bottle and poured a little in Remy's glass and then in mine.

"Is this the part where I'm supposed to do some kind of ritual?" Remy murmured to me.

"Just follow my lead," I whispered in his ear.

Then I picked up my glass, swirled the wine a little, took a sniff of it, and finally sipped the golden liquid. "Mmmm . . . This is very nice," I said with a smile.

In the meantime, Remy was following along and repeating my actions. Until it came to the tasting part, and he downed his wine sample in one full gulp. "Oh, that is good. I'm impressed."

The waiter smiled and nodded to us both. "So will this be satisfactory?"

"Yes, I think so," Remy replied, catching my eye.

After which, the waiter poured a small glass for each of us, before setting the rest of the bottle in the wine chiller.

Once the man was gone, Remy held up his glass, ready for a toast. "To a wonderful night," he said softly. "And to the most beautiful woman in the restaurant."

At that moment, I was glad the place was dark so he couldn't see me blush. "That's very sweet," I said, clinking my glass with his.

Then just as I took another sip of the Sancerre, Remy added, "And to your beautiful, glowing hair."

Which nearly made me choke on my wine.

"And just for the record," he went on. "I'd be happy to bring some fresh fish over to see what magic you can perform in the kitchen. But I would solve the Parker situation by taking him fishing with me first."

"Oh, he would love that," I gushed, right before the waiter reappeared to take our orders.

After that, the night was magical. Soon it seemed like the waiter and everyone else around us practically disappeared. It was just Remy and me, his eyes bright even in the candlelight. Conversation was easy, and we talked about all kinds of subjects, from the places we had lived, and where we'd grown up, and what we liked to do for fun. Not to mention, our work. On top of it all, the wine was delicious and an excellent pairing with the flounder. Which, by the way, was done to perfection.

And as we ate and talked, we shared a casual touch here and there—his fingers brushing mine, or a rub on the shoulder, or his hand sliding across my back. Every time he touched me, I felt tingles, and I was completely mesmerized. If not completely smitten.

On the way home, he even took my hand and kissed it, leaving me breathless. I pictured us cuddled up together on the couch later. Me, resting my head on his shoulder, with his arm around me, and my arms around his waist with his heartbeat so close to mine. I even wondered if we would share a real kiss before he had to say good night.

That, or we'd be making out like a couple of teenagers.

Suddenly, I felt so alive, like I was young again. Especially when he reached over and stroked my hair. Did all this mean I had a boyfriend? It seemed so funny to use a term like that at my age. Regardless of what I called him, I was truly happy being around Remy. And I couldn't help but wonder where this relationship might lead, and if we would one day have a happily ever after of our own.

But that would be a long way down the road. For now, I took his hand, and he gave me an enticing smile in return. More than anything, I didn't want the night to end. I wanted to stop time, or at least, slow it down for a while. So that nothing could break the happy trance that we seemed to be in. It had been so long since I'd felt this way.

And I suspected he felt the same, since he seemed to be taking his time as he drove us back to my house. We were almost there, and he had just turned his car onto my street, when his mood suddenly changed. Probably thanks to the flashing red lights that lit up the sky at the end of my cul-de-sac.

Police cars.

I put a hand to my chest. "Parker!"

Then I frantically searched the area with my eyes, looking for my house. And looking for him. Where was he? Was he okay?

Thankfully, I finally saw him standing on our front walkway as we drove closer. And from what I could tell, he seemed to be fine. Along with the house. In fact, the house with some kind of emergency appeared to be one across the street.

Dex and Olivia's house, to be specific.

I jumped when Remy got a hands-free phone call. From my research, I knew the police codes well enough to know what the police dispatcher was saying to him. Along with the address she was talking about.

"Homicide . . ." I murmured as Remy quickly parked the car in front of the island of my cul-de-sac. "Someone was murdered. A male, in his fifties."

It had to be Dex.

Remy turned to me, the romance erased from his face and his voice, and his features now made of stone.

His work face, I guessed.

"Maddie, I want you to go home and stay there. Lock your doors," he commanded. "I'll talk to you later."

"But . . . but . . ." I protested. "I want to go, too. Those are my neighbors. This is my neighborhood."

"No, Maddie, you can't," he said firmly. "I have to go to work. And you need to stay away. Somewhere safe."

Naturally, I wanted to say more, but I figured there was no use arguing with him at this point. Especially when he jumped out of the car without so much as a "Good night."

In a daze, I climbed out from my side of the car, with my curiosity running at full throttle. In fact, you might even say my curiosity was killing me.

Though I suspected that wasn't the cause of death for the man across the street.

And now I couldn't help but wonder, what was the cause of death?

And more importantly, who had murdered the man?

Chapter Nine

I shut Remy's car door behind me, still in shock. Even though it was a warm spring night, I suddenly felt chilled, and I wrapped my arms around myself. It was amazing how quickly a night could go from being so warm and romantic to being so utterly cold and harsh.

But a murder in the neighborhood will do that.

I glanced toward the Degills' house and noticed that Remy had already been swallowed up by all the cars and flashing lights and police tape. Oh, how I wish he'd asked me to go with him, because I was absolutely dying to know what had happened. If Dex had been killed, was Olivia okay? Or had she been hurt, too?

I closed my eyes for a moment and shook my head. Sure, my brief visit to their house had been strange enough, and yes, I'd seen some "idiosyncrasies" with the pair, as Spencer Poe had put it. Even so, it was still upsetting and hard to believe that my new neighbor had been murdered. And before the couple had even finished unpacking.

So what was the scoop?

I remembered Olivia telling me that they'd moved to the suburbs to get away from something. And I tried to remember exactly what she had said. Something about there being too many memories . . . and too many complications.

Had those complications followed them out of the city and into our suburban neighborhood? Or had it been a domestic situation, as they say? Then again, his murder could have been some random act of violence, maybe from an attempted home invasion.

With so many questions racing through my brain, my head was starting to spin. Yet despite all the possibilities, something inside said his death had been nothing more than an old-fashioned, premeditated murder.

Which also meant there was a murderer on the loose.

A thought that made my pulse start to pound. I glanced at Parker, who was now standing in the middle of our driveway. And as I headed in his direction, I noticed a crowd had begun to form on our side of the street, not far from our property. I paused for a moment and searched the group for familiar faces. While I saw many of our neighbors there—some in bathrobes and others in something they must have just thrown on—I didn't see the one face I was looking for.

Belinda.

Or more specifically, Dex's stalker.

I thought of the conversation I'd had with her earlier today, and that's when I realized I had information that Remy needed to know. Because I'd avoided telling him about the woman who'd been sitting in front of my house in the Crown Victoria, and that she had been stalking Dex. Though when I did tell him, I realized it would probably be a good idea to skirt my reason for not saying something sooner.

Oh, the power of a bad hair appointment.

Of course, there was also the complication of his having "ordered" me not to approach the woman. Something that didn't exactly sit well with me. Because I'd been running my own life quite well for a long time, thank you very much. And I didn't need him telling me what to do.

But that was an issue we would have to deal with later. Right now, it was important to get the killer behind bars, so he or she couldn't kill again.

I finally reached my son, who had moved to the end of our driveway. He was wearing sweatpants and a t-shirt, and judging from the condition of his hair, I guessed he must have been in bed before the police cars probably came screaming down the street.

"Are you okay?" I asked, putting an arm around his shoulder.

"Yup, Mom. So far anyway. Do you know our street has a ten percent murder rate per capita? We're gonna get a reputation. Maybe we should move."

Like it or not, Parker did have a point.

I looked back at the Degills' house. "So what happened?"

"I don't know for sure. I was studying in my room and I fell asleep. Then the sirens woke me up. There were lots of them. And they kept on getting louder. Until they stopped over there, across the street."

"Oh, Parker, you should have called me."

"No time, Mom. It all happened right before you got home. The word online is that Mr. Degill was murdered. Geez, it's really weird. We were just at their house yesterday."

"'Weird' is the word," I agreed.

"Did Mr. Reagan go over there?" he asked, nodding toward the other side of the cul-de-sac.

"He did."

But before I could say more, my phone rang.

Not surprisingly, it was Spencer Poe. "Mrs. Montgomery, are you and young Parker all right?"

"Yes, we're fine," I told him. "Shook up, but fine. How about you? Are you okay?"

"I am unharmed, and my property has not been compromised," he confirmed. "Though I regret that I had my cameras down tonight for charging and repairs, and I should not have let my guard down like that. So I'm afraid I did not capture any footage of an assassin driving in and out of the neighborhood. That is, *if* the person who committed the crime approached the Degills' house by motor vehicle. The killer could have come on foot, of course, and jumped the fence from the property behind theirs. Or they might have repelled in by helicopter, though I didn't pick up on any aircraft in the area at the time."

Purely by reflex, I glanced up at the sky, even though I knew his suggestion was probably a little far-fetched. Not only that, but the murderer might have already been in the house. Meaning, Dex could have been killed by his wife, Olivia.

"I'll check my front door camera later," I told Spencer. "Though I doubt it would have picked up anything, since it doesn't usually pick up images from across the street very well."

"Unless a vehicle drove around the cul-de-sac as it was leaving. In any case, it will be valuable information for the police. Is your Detective Reagan at the crime scene now?"

"Remy is over there," I told him.

"I assume you will be joining him shortly. Now that you know young Parker is all right."

"I'm afraid Remy gave me strict instructions to stay away," I said with a sigh.

"Hardly a valid order, Mrs. Montgomery," Spencer went on. "You are not in his chain of command. And frankly, having met Mr. and Mrs. Degill, you most likely possess vital information that could assist the police in their investigation."

"Well . . . umm, yes, I suppose that's true . . ." I said, fully aware that my curiosity was growing and expanding like one of Parker's science experiments, bringing it dangerously close to bursting at the seams.

"Don't forget, Mrs. Montgomery, that you recently solved a murder that had initially been ruled an accident by the police. So not only have you gained experience and expertise that could be quite valuable when it comes to unmasking yet another murderer, but coupled with your experience and research as a mystery writer, you are the perfect person for solving a case like this."

"Thank you for saying that, Spencer, but I'm still not sure if . . ." I started to respond.

But he interrupted me before I could finish, something he rarely did. "If not for yourself, then do it for young Parker. Solve this case for the safety and security of your neighbors and all of us who live on this street."

Okay, I had to admit, when he put it that way, it was hard to say no. Because the last thing any of us wanted was another murderer wandering our cul-de-sac. Besides, what was the worst thing that could happen if I went over and took a peek at the scene of the crime?

"All right, Spencer. You talked me into it."

"Excellent, Mrs. Montgomery. Let me know if I might be of assistance," he said before we got off the phone.

With that, all I needed now was a good excuse to go over to the Degills' house. And that's when I remembered I still had Remy's sunglasses.

"I'll be right back," I told Parker. "I've got to take something to Remy. And I have some information that I need to pass along to him."

"I'll stay here and hold down the fort," he said with a salute.

"If anyone can do it, it's you," I told him. "I won't be gone long."

Then I made a beeline to the other side of the cul-de-sac.

Which put me smack dab into the middle of a tricky situation. From all my research when it came to writing murder mysteries, I also knew I wasn't *really* supposed to walk into an active crime scene. But if I looked like I knew what I was doing, well, maybe I could talk my way in. And that was an entirely different matter.

So I strode purposely to the other side of the street, head held high and arms swinging. Like I was supposed to be there. I made direct eye contact with the first uniformed police officer I saw—a petite, dark-haired woman who looked as fierce as a bulldog.

I stayed in the shadows as best I could and held up Remy's black, sunglass case for but a second. And gee, it was hardly my fault if the officer might have mistaken it for a badge holder in the darkness.

"I've got something for Detective Reagan," I told her as officially as I could, using my deepest, most serious, cop-like voice. You might even say I tried to mimic Spencer Poe.

But before the officer had a chance to respond, she got a message over her shoulder mic. She took it while she motioned me inside.

Which meant I was *actually* going in. To the scene of the crime.

A place I wasn't really supposed to be.

That's when my heart started to race like I'd just downed four cups of coffee in under a minute. I almost felt like I was a spy in the late 1970s who'd just sneaked behind the Iron Curtain. Which meant it was possible that I was imitating Spencer Poe much more than I realized. Especially when I knew full well that my little trick to get in never should've worked in the first place.

Even so, this was not the time to drop my act, and I did my absolute best to look as serious and professional as a woman could look in a little, black dress and red heels. I even frowned when I passed a uniformed officer or two, trying to play the role of a law enforcement person whose night had been interrupted because of a major crime.

Though I did take a few detours around some of the moving boxes that were still unpacked and stacked three high—something that also provided perfect cover, in a sense—while I slowly made my way toward the kitchen. As near as I could tell, nothing looked out of place or out of the ordinary along my route.

Yet as I edged closer to the kitchen, I could tell it was the area where most of the action was taking place. Quietly, I stepped into the large room and hesitated for a second or two. Near the kitchen island, I saw Remy kneeling as he leaned over a body.

More specifically, Dex's body, which was lying face down on the floor.

Using every ounce of subterfuge I could muster, I quickly snapped off a photo or two with my phone, before I slipped it back into my purse.

Strangely enough, the place didn't look all that different from the way it had the day before. Well, except for the pool of blood on the floor, and the police who were running around. From where I stood, I could even hear Olivia being interviewed in the family room nearby.

A very cool, collected, and indifferent Olivia.

A new widow who didn't sound like she was too terribly overcome with grief.

All the while, as I inched closer, I wasn't sure what my game plan should be. I was halfway to the island when Remy looked up, and his blue eyes went wide in shock.

That's when I thought my heart might pound right out of my chest.

So I did my best to stay casual, and I just waved and held up his sunglass case. "These were in my purse. I wanted to make sure you had them for tomorrow."

He immediately stood up, annoyance creasing his otherwise handsome features. "Maddie, you shouldn't be here."

"But I have to talk to you. I have information that you need to know about."

"Seriously, Maddie, you have to go. Thank you for bringing my glasses. I'll call you later," Remy told me as he motioned to a uniformed officer. "Get her out of here," he commanded the tall man.

"You got it," the officer said firmly.

That's when I knew I was licked. I handed the sunglass case to the younger man and said, "Please be sure Detective Reagan gets these."

"Yes, ma'am, I will." Then he took my upper arm and started to rather forcibly escort me in the direction of the door.

But just as I turned, my eye caught a glimpse of something sparkly. Something that flashed in the overhead lights.

Scissors encrusted with gems.

Scissors that I immediately recognized, because I had seen those very scissors earlier today.

Deirdre's scissors.

And they were now sticking straight out of Dex's back.

Chapter Ten

I didn't resist as the police officer led me from the Degills' house, mostly because I was too dumbfounded to even attempt to argue my way back inside. And if I thought I had questions racing through my brain before, well, it was nothing compared to what was going through my head right at that moment. After seeing the scene of the crime.

First and foremost, I was trying to figure out how Deirdre's jewel-covered scissors had ended up so firmly planted in my neighbor's back.

Had Deirdre put them there?

Yes, I had a pretty good idea that Deirdre was off her rocker, and while she certainly did a good job of murdering my hair, I never would have suspected her of *actual* murder.

Not unless she was thoroughly provoked. And even then, she would've needed a lot of anger and adrenaline to have the strength to thrust those scissors so deeply into Dex's back. A feat that a weaker woman couldn't have pulled off.

Though from what I knew, the one person who seemed to provoke Deirdre the most was her ex-husband. Not only that, but she'd come right out and told me she could kill him for what he'd done to her.

So did Deirdre murder Dex?

Possibly.

And for that matter, *probably*. The obvious evidence pointed to her.

But if there was something I'd learned from writing mysteries and from life in general: Things were never as simple as they seemed.

And I couldn't help but think about the very tangled web that Dex had woven, only to get caught up in his own handiwork. He was married to Olivia, who appeared to be keeping him under wraps via an odd form of blackmail. But Dex was also being stalked by Belinda, who claimed she had dated him while he was about to become a married man. On top of that, he also happened to be Deirdre's "rotten, cheating scumbag" of an ex-husband, whom she'd ranted on and on about. Not to mention, he had another ex-wife wandering around out there somewhere.

So despite Deirdre's scissors being used as a murder weapon, I wasn't fully convinced that she had committed the crime. Because I suspected there was more than one person in the world who might have wanted to see Dex dead.

I left my police escort halfway down the Degills' front walkway and then crossed the street, nodding to my neighbors but not stopping to chat tonight. After all, I was already walking on thin ice, so to speak, where the Abbott Cove police were concerned. Or rather, one detective in particular. So I figured it probably wasn't a good idea to give any indication that I was sharing what I'd seen with the people who lived near me, thereby "tainting" any future police interviews of the neighbors.

That, and for all I knew, Dex's killer might just be standing there in that crowd, watching everything.

The thought of it chilled me to the bone, making me feel like I'd just walked into a blast chiller.

I shivered, but I managed to keep my focus on Parker as I joined him on our driveway. "I'm afraid it's true," I told him. "Mr. Degill has been . . ."

"Bumped off? Exterminated? Sent with a one-way ticket into the afterlife?"

I'd forgotten that Parker had picked up vintage P.I. language after reading some of the classic mysteries I had in my personal library. "Yes, Parker, something like that."

"Was it really . . . umm, gruesome, Mom? Over at their house?"

"Yes, and no. But maybe we should go inside and talk about this if you like. I think you've had a pretty big night. And you do have school in the morning," I added, though I certainly wasn't going to push the issue if he didn't feel like going the next day.

Parker yawned and stretched. "Sounds okay, Mom. I am kind of hungry. Did you bring me a steak?"

In any other situation, I would have rolled my eyes. But not tonight.

"How about a milkshake?" I suggested as we walked into the house. "That should hold you till morning."

With any kind of luck.

"Make it a double," he said.

And so I did. One chocolate and one vanilla. I could tell Parker was close to dropping off as he consumed both shakes at the same time, with one straw sticking out of each glass.

In the meantime, I folded my arms and leaned back against the kitchen counter. Though my eyes wandered momentarily to the dying hubbub out in the street beyond my window.

Minutes later, I closed my blinds and returned my attention to my son. "Did you want to talk about what happened to Mr. Degill?"

He shrugged and petted Ellery and Agatha who had jumped up on a stool beside him. "I dunno, Mom. Not much to talk about. We had another murder in the neighborhood, and it's just bizarro. And kind of creepy, if you ask me. How do I know you'll be okay while I'm at school tomorrow?"

"Well, I think it might be a good idea for us to practice some extra security for a while. Until the person who killed Mr. Degill is behind bars. So I'll keep the doors locked and the alarm on during the day."

"And don't answer the door to any strangers," he added, staring at me.

"Got it," I agreed.

Though I knew full well that the person who murdered Dex Degill might not be a stranger at all.

It was a thought that stayed with me long after Parker headed off for bed. And because I knew sleep would elude me, I went to my home office and tried to focus on my latest work in progress. Needless to say, I had a hard time concentrating, and I found myself jumping up to look out the window every time I heard a noise. Of course, the irony of the situation did not escape me, that an *actual* murder in the neighborhood was inhibiting my ability to write about a *fictitious* one.

To pass the time, I looked up Deirdre's bio from the Sleek and Chic Shears Salon's website. But when I found her picture with her name printed below, I had to wonder why she hadn't gone back to her maiden name after she and Dex had divorced. Was there a part of her that believed she and Dex would still get back together? Maybe she thought he would come to his senses when it came to his relationship with Olivia.

But maybe she'd just officially found out otherwise. Something that could certainly evoke enough ire to make her a clear-cut candidate when it came to playing the role of killer.

"But she's hardly the only one," I murmured aloud, thinking of the stone-cold sound of Olivia's voice when I was over at the Degills' house this evening.

I glanced out the window one more time and noticed that Remy's car was still there. I hoped he would see my office light was still on and show up on my doorstep when he had finished across the street. Then we'd have a chance to sort out what had happened between us after we'd come home from our date. Sure, maybe I wasn't too pleased that he hadn't even bothered to say good night. And okay, he might be upset with me for showing up at his crime scene, meaning I possibly deserved his, well . . . *irritation*. But surely if we talked about it, we could put it behind us and go on like we had before. Maybe write in another date on the calendar. I could even invite him over for a home-cooked meal the next time.

But none of that happened.

I didn't hear from him at all, and somewhere along the line, I forgot to keep checking out the window. Probably since I'd finally gotten into the zone with my writing, and it was pushing two A.M. when I came up for air. That's when I stretched and glanced outside again. The crowd in the street had dispersed, and all but one police cruiser had left for the night. Unfortunately, Remy's car was also gone, and I hadn't even seen him leave.

So much for the way I'd imagined tonight would end.

I sighed and headed for bed. But not before checking all the doors and setting the alarm. Ellery and Agatha were both waiting for me in their usual spots on my bed, though they were clearly too keyed up to sleep. Pretty much like I was, with my heart racing and my skin feeling prickly. It didn't help that the kitties spent a good half an hour just peering into the darkened hallway with wide eyes.

Yet even after they dozed off, I stayed vigilant and watchful. A murder taking place just across the cul-de-sac was way too close for comfort as far as I was concerned. And until the person who committed the crime was apprehended, who knew if they might just strike again?

That was, *if* that person was apprehended. More than ever, I wished I'd been able to tell Remy about Belinda, since it could save him a lot of time and trouble. Otherwise, he'd have a lot of catching up to do, just to discover what I already knew. And all that wasted time meant more hours for a murderer to be out on the street.

Quite likely the very street that Parker and I lived on.

A thought that kept rattling around in my overtired brain, especially when I replayed the scene of Belinda sitting in her car in front of my house the morning before. One way or another, I needed to let Remy know what I knew about Dex's stalker. Though before I did, it would be helpful to have a last name to go with her first.

Of course, I knew just how to find it.

Because Belinda had mentioned that she'd met Dex at a speed dating event at the Lytely Char and Grill Restaurant, and she'd even told me the name of the man who ran those events. Trevor Lytely. Somehow, I had a hunch that Mr. Lytely was well acquainted with Belinda, since I doubted the speed dating event where she'd met Dex had been her first rodeo, so to speak. And since Belinda wasn't exactly the closed mouth type, I guessed Trevor probably knew a lot more about Belinda than just her name.

And a visit to Mr. Lytely in the morning could mean I'd hit the mother lode when it came to mining information about Dex's stalker. Then later, after I passed what I'd learned onto Remy, he might actually appreciate my contribution to crime solving.

Funny, how having a plan in hand made me feel so much better. I finally fell asleep and even woke up before my alarm, just raring to go. I quickly fed an overtired Parker a huge breakfast, and since he'd been up so late the night before, I allowed him a cup of full-strength, caffeinated coffee. Something I didn't usually do. In the meantime, I downed a little breakfast myself, before I saw Parker out the door and on his way to school. With my promise that I would set the alarm after he left.

Which was exactly what I did. Then, fueled by two cups of coffee with real cream and a nice helping of sweetener, I quickly showered and donned a casual, teal-green dress. I followed this with a couple of swipes of mascara and matching pink lip gloss. After some morning chores, I was out the door before ten o'clock. I drove to the outskirts of Abbott Cove, where I found the Lytely Char and Grill Restaurant and Lounge, a place I'd never been before.

Though I had to say, while the outside could have used a good power washing and a touch-up on the paint, the interior of the place surprised me the minute I walked in. For some reason, I'd expected a restaurant and lounge that rivaled a dark, sleazy 1970s-style bar. But this place was exactly the opposite.

The walls were a nice calm ecru, with a gold, black, and plum art deco wallpaper on an accent wall. The same color scheme was repeated in the plum chenille chairs, and the tables covered in white tablecloths were nicely highlighted with gold silverware and brass salt and pepper mills. Along with black, art deco vases with a single red rose that adorned each table. To top it off, the art on the walls appeared to be real, and framed in a variety of gold and black frames.

In other words, someone had put a lot of thought and money into decorating the place. And I had to admit, it worked. It had kind of a modernized Great Gatsby feel to it, and it was both calming and energizing at the same time.

But best of all, mere seconds after I asked the receptionist if I could speak to Trevor Lytely, he appeared from a back room and headed my way.

The first thing I noticed about the man were his eyes. Soft brown and sweet. Puppy dog eyes. Something that seemed at odds with his chiseled jawline, and brown hair with blonde streaks. I guessed he was in his early fifties, and he was dressed in a rumpled, gray suit that looked like it had once been expensive, but probably not given a lot of care over the years.

"Hi, doll, I'm Trevor," he oozed as he took my outstretched hand and held it as though he were about to kiss it.

Yet thankfully, he never did.

"And I'm Maddie," I told him, pulling my hand away and not meeting any resistance. Then I started in with a big, giant fib, something I was eminently unqualified to do. "I was wondering if you could help me. I'm trying to get in touch with a woman who told me she attended your speed dating events. I think her name was Berniece . . . no, that's not right. It might have been Beatrix . . . or maybe Belle . . . or . . ."

"Belinda?" he supplied.

I rewarded him with my brightest smile. "Yes! That sounds right. I think. But what is her last name?"

He let out a little chuckle. "I'm sorry, but we never give out information about our customers."

I let my mouth dip into a frown. "Oh . . . that's too bad. Because I really need to get ahold of her. Could you make an exception just this once?" With some extra effort, I even managed to produce a little pout.

"Sure, I'd be happy to, doll," he said with a smug grin. "As long as you grease my palm."

My eyebrows shot up. "Excuse me?"

"Honey, information isn't free around here. If you want to know something that I shouldn't be telling you, then you'll have to pay me for it."

"You mean, you would charge me money just to tell me Belinda's last name?" I asked with all the innocence I could muster.

And that was about the time when his eyes went from puppy dog to pit bull. "Don't play dumb with me, lady. You came in here batting your lashes and using your girly charms to get me to open up. Well, if you want information, you'll have to pay for it."

Okay, I had to admit—he was right about me trying to use my feminine wiles. Trying and failing, that was. Some big crime solver I was proving to be. I couldn't even manage to find out something as simple as the last name of a suspect.

With no other ideas in mind, I finally asked him, "Okay, how much?" All the while, I tried to do a mental inventory of what cash I had in my purse.

For some reason, he found my question to be funny. Uproariously so. Because he laughed till he had tears in his eyes.

"If you have to ask, doll," he said between guffaws, "you can't afford it."

I folded my arms in front of me. "How do you know whether I can afford it or not? Unless you give me a number, how am I supposed to know how much your great information costs?"

He put his hand on my shoulder. "You are one crazy dame, you know that? I don't know why you want Belinda's last name, and frankly, I don't care. But I'll tell you what, beautiful—you can ask her yourself at our next speed dating party on Saturday night. She'll be there. This event is for a more mature crowd, people forty and above. And a knockout like you would be a big hit around here. I'll even waive your fee this first time."

"Ummm . . . no, thanks. I think I'll pass."

Now the puppy dog eyes returned. "Are you sure? I don't see a wedding ring. I'm guessing you're single. You never know, you might have some fun and meet some great guys. All the men who attend these events have money. Gobs of it. I make sure of that. They're the kind of men who would happily spend their dough on a doll like you."

I shook my head. "Sorry, but I'm not interested."

"Just give it some thought," he said as he handed me his card. "Call me if you change your mind, and I'll get you set up for Saturday night. We only have a couple of spots left."

With that, he gave my arm a squeeze and then turned and raced off to what I could only guess was the kitchen. Clearly, I had been dismissed. Not unless I was willing to attend his next speed dating event.

Something I had absolutely no desire to do.

I headed for my car and drove straight home, feeling completely deflated. Here I'd been so sure that I could gather info about Belinda, something that might lead to finding Dex's murderer. But instead, I'd come up with a big, fat bupkes. Though if nothing else, I could still tell Remy about Belinda being in front of my house the day before. It wasn't as much as I'd hoped to tell him, but it was still something.

I barely walked in the door and turned off the alarm when my phone rang inside my purse.

It was Remy.

"Hi, I'm so glad you called," I started. "Our date ended so abruptly last night. We didn't get a chance to say good night."

Naturally, I expected one of his usual witty and warm remarks, like the kind I'd gotten used to from him. With an allowance for his being up late last night, of course.

Only, that wasn't what I got at all.

Instead his voice had a hard, robotic quality to it. "Listen, Maddie, I don't have much time to talk. But I wanted to let you know that I'm going to have my hands full for a while with this case. And I'm not going to have time to date. So we're going to need to cool it."

"Cool it?" I repeated dumbly, not sure I'd heard him right.

"Yeah, Maddie. I'm really sorry, but this is a very big case. And I've got to give it all my attention. Do you understand?"

So far, I wasn't understanding this at all.

"Is this because I showed up at your crime scene last night?" I asked carefully. "Okay, maybe I should have waited for you to finish and come over here. But I've got some important information for you. Something that will help you solve this crime. Would you like to come over for coffee? Then I'll give you the scoop."

"No, Maddie, I don't think so. It's obvious that you want in on this case, and like I told you before, you've got to leave the investigating to the professionals. I mean it. Stay out of this. Don't interfere with an official police investigation. I'll probably call you sometime. But now I've gotta run."

And that was that. Again, no goodbye and no listening to what I had to say.

I put my phone on my kitchen counter and just stared at it for a minute or two. What had just happened? How was it possible that the two of us had been so lovey-dovey last night, and now, all of a sudden, it sounded completely uncertain whether we'd even see each other again?

For the life of me, I couldn't wrap my head around it all. Was he really that upset that I'd gone over to the Degills' last night? Or was there something else I'd said or done that had really turned him off?

Though you never would've known it, judging by the way he'd been acting on the way home the night before.

So what in the world was going on? And since Remy had given me absolutely no explanation whatsoever, how could I even begin to make sense of what had just happened?

But then another realization hit me like a lightning bolt: Had I just been dumped?

I shook my head a few times, trying to put the pieces into place. To be honest, since Charlie and I had met when we were young, I really didn't have much experience when it came to dating. Or being dumped, for that matter. Sure, there was a guy I'd dated off and on in high school, and the relationship had ended when he went away to college. And yes, I remember going through some highly hormonal, adolescent upset, but that was about it.

Now, despite myself, I felt like that teenager once more, with a rollercoaster of emotions overriding my brain. Not to mention, my better judgement.

How was that possible at this age?

Unfortunately, my inner adolescent—who suddenly seemed to be taking over—also had the overwhelming urge to get even. Or rather, to teach this nasty man a lesson. Of course, I could easily do that by simply going out on a date with another man, thus proving that Remy had made a huge mistake. But if I really wanted to "show him," the number one way I could do that would be to solve the Degill murder before he did.

I shook my head, wondering how such thoughts and emotions could be taking over my grown-up, mature mind. It was childish to have such a reaction to his saying goodbye. And it would be the dumbest reason on the planet for me to really enter the fray and crack this case, as they say.

Then again, there was one very good reason for me to solve it, and that was for the safety of Parker and me. Along with the rest of my neighbors.

Or at least, that's what I told myself as I pulled out Trevor's card and tapped his number into my phone.

He answered on the third ring.

"Hello, Trevor? This is Maddie again. I met you this morning?"

"Oh, yeah. I would never forget a woman as gorgeous as you. Have you changed your mind about Saturday night?"

"Yes, I have," I told him. "Count me in."

"Glad to hear it, doll. But I need your firm commitment. You'll be taking the last spot I have for a woman. So I can't have you changing your mind and backing out at the last minute. Do you promise to be here?"

I cringed and closed my eyes. "Yes. I promise I'll be there."

"Great! Be here at seven, sharp. You'll have a terrific time, believe me. And you won't regret this."

Funny, but as I got off the phone, a very big part of me already did.

Chapter Eleven

Shortly after I ended my call to Trevor, I just stood there and stared at my phone. I couldn't believe what I'd just done, signing up for something called speed dating. To tell you the truth, I wasn't even sure what speed dating was. Or how it worked. Though worst of all, I couldn't believe what had spurred me on to do such a thing.

I shook my head and poured myself a cup of coffee. Then I doctored it nicely with plenty of cream and sweetener, all the while thinking back over the events of the last few days. A very odd and very active few days that didn't even seem real right now. But what stood out the most was my dream date with Remy, followed by a neighborhood murder, which was followed by Remy snipping our budding relationship in the, well . . . in the bud. Of course, it didn't help that I'd reacted to it all by completely "overreacting," whereby I'd turned into the emotional equivalent of a sixteen-year-old girl.

What in the world had come over me?

I took a sip of my coffee and closed my eyes for a moment. Sure, I realized the events of the last few days were beyond upsetting. And yes, it was true, that I'd had very high hopes for my relationship with Remy. Spencer Poe had even taken to calling him "your Detective Reagan," so apparently, I wasn't the only person who had seen the spark between us.

Still, it wasn't like we were engaged or anything. We weren't even a long-term couple. And to be honest, I didn't really know Remy all that well. We'd only gone out on three dates. So for all I knew, he might be famous for subjecting women to intense romantic extremes and sending them on emotional roller coaster rides. Maybe he'd put his late wife through such "hot and cold" moments on a regular basis. But the fact was, I would probably never know.

Regardless, my turning into a teenage trainwreck over a relationship that didn't get off the ground was hardly a great way for me to react. If I wasn't careful, I might become the kind of woman who made a living by writing revenge songs about every guy she went out with. Though in my case, it was more likely that I would simply bump off those men, (or rather, man) in my latest novel. A thought that made me chuckle.

That was right before I reevaluated my overwhelming desire to defy the orders of an esteemed member of the Abbott Cove Police Department. Especially since I was mostly doing it out of spite. Though I had to admit, I was hardly doing anything wrong by attending a speed dating event and finding out more about Belinda. Maybe she was the one who had murdered Dex Degill, and I might end up gathering enough evidence to send her up the river. With or without Remy. Because he wasn't the only police officer around, and another member of Abbott Cove's finest might be happy to receive the information I had to pass along.

Either way, I needed to forget about Remy and get back to my own life. After all, I'd lived almost five decades without the man, and after a few days, I figured he'd be nothing more than a blip on my radar.

So I took a deep breath, grabbed my cup of coffee and called to the kitties, who happily followed me upstairs to my home office. Then I settled in at my desk and quickly got into the zone with my writing. I started on the next chapter in Blaze's new book and forgot all about the world around me. I had just finished writing my first two pages of the day when the doorbell rang. I sighed and glanced to Ellery and Agatha, who were enjoying the sun on the window seat of my bay window. An idyllic scene if ever there were one.

But the sound of the doorbell presented me with an immediate dilemma. Did I get up and answer it? Or did I just hope that whoever was out there would simply go away? Because I preferred to stay in Blaze's world and continue writing uninterrupted for hours. If not all day. In fact, most writers absolutely hate being interrupted while they're working. And ever since I'd started my life's adventure as a novelist, I had learned to guard my work time zealously.

Including now. Until the doorbell rang again, and this time, I decided that whoever was at my door was not going to go away. And since I'd left my phone downstairs, I couldn't just take a glance at the camera app to see who was out there.

I sighed, saved my work, and headed down my curved staircase.

"Coming!" I hollered.

My right foot had just touched down on the hardwood floor of my front entryway when I suddenly remembered my promise to Parker to keep the doors locked and the alarm activated. A promise I'd already broken, since I'd forgotten to reset the alarm when I got back home this morning.

Right about then, I also recalled saying something about not opening the door to strangers. But when I looked through the peephole, much to my surprise, I saw Olivia Degill on my doorstep. But she wasn't a stranger, was she? She was my neighbor.

A neighbor I actually knew very little about. Though one prominent fact about her did stand out loud and clear—her husband had been murdered.

And no doubt, Olivia was a prime suspect.

So, did I open the door to her or not?

Most likely she just needed a shoulder to cry on and some words of comfort. And what kind of a person would I be if I snubbed a teary-eyed widow, one whose eyes were probably rimmed with red from crying all night?

"A person who won't become the next murder victim in our cul-de-sac," I answered my own question under my breath.

Then without giving it another thought, I unlocked the door and tugged it open, all ready to give poor Olivia a big hug and just let her cry if she needed to.

But the dry-eyed woman on my doorstep was nothing like the widow in the grips of uncontrollable grief that I'd envisioned. Not even close. Not even in the same universe, for that matter. Because other than wearing a different designer dress, Olivia looked almost exactly like she had a few days ago, clear down to her big sapphire ring.

Still, I knew full well that people expressed grief in different ways, and the way one person might react could be completely different from the way another person might react. Meaning, it wasn't time for me to be judgmental.

"Olivia, I'm so sorry for your loss," I said with complete sympathy. "And for all that you're going through."

But her only response was to simply knit her eyebrows into a deep *V* and stare at me, as though she had no idea what I was talking about.

"About your husband?" I prompted.

Recognition must have dawned, because she finally nodded. "Oh, right. Thank you."

"I'm surprised to see you here," I said gently, in what was possibly the understatement of the year. "I'm a widow myself, and I know how rough it can be."

"I wanted to bring your plate back," she intoned as she handed me the platter that I'd taken to her house a few days ago, loaded with bacon-wrapped shrimp. "It was empty. The food was all gone."

"Well, I'm glad you liked it," I told her.

She shook her head. "Oh, no, I only ate one. And my husband didn't eat more than a couple. I can't eat stuff like that and look like this."

Fair enough. Though clearly, *someone* had eaten all that shrimp. Given how much everyone always raved over the dish, I doubted she'd just tossed them out.

"Well, you didn't have to worry about bringing back my plate. My goodness, I'm sure you've got more important things to deal with right now."

She returned to staring at me. "Aren't you going to invite me in, Maddie?"

For some reason, her question completely unnerved me. Not to mention, sent my senses into full alert mode.

"Ummm . . . sure," I said on autopilot, since I couldn't think up a quick excuse. "Would you like a cup of coffee?" I added, managing to come up with my best concerned-neighbor expression.

"Uh-huh," she said, her gaze now going up my staircase and settling on the Juliet balcony of the second-floor landing.

I stepped aside to let her enter, then I shut the door and led her to the kitchen. “Have a seat,” I told her, indicating the kitchen table. “How do you like your coffee? I have real cream and sweetener.”

“I’ll just have the sweetener,” she told me as she took a chair and glanced around the room. “I love your kitchen. I’d like to do my kitchen just like this.” And before I even had a chance to respond, she took out her phone and started taking pictures.

Something that only added to my anxiety. Didn’t people usually ask before they started photographing the inside of your house?

But before she could take more photos, I distracted her by setting a coffee cup in front of her and handing her the sweetener and a spoon. Just like I’d hoped, she put down her phone to doctor her coffee.

“So . . . how are you holding up?” I asked as I refreshed my own coffee and added more cream. “You’ve been through such an ordeal.”

“Oh, I’m fine,” she said without emotion. “The police interviewed me this morning. They asked me to come down to the station and make a statement. After they questioned me for hours last night. Of course, I had to spend the night in a hotel. Since my kitchen was a crime scene and they had it taped off.”

“Oh, my goodness. How did that go? Being grilled by the police can be a pretty big ordeal.”

But she just smiled and polished her sapphire ring, before staring at it with great adoration. “Not with that detective, Remington Reagan. Wow, he is so hot. Seriously, his eyes are the same color as my new ring . . . I could have stayed there and led him on all day. Telling him all kinds of things. He just looked into my eyes and hung on my every word. It was so romantic.”

“Did you say Detective Reagan?”

Her smile turned smug. “That’s him. And I could tell the attraction was mutual. He was hitting on me the whole time I was there. At the end of the conversation, he even took my hand and held it and told me he’d be in touch. So I know I’ll be hearing from him again soon. And I fully expect him to ask me out to dinner. After all, I’m a free woman now.”

And to think, all this when the body was barely even cold.

Speaking of cold, Remy must have ended our relationship mere minutes after he finished interviewing Olivia. Something that gave credence to Olivia's take on the way Remy had been acting toward her. But was that all it was—an act? Nothing but a means to gain information from her? His version of good cop, or rather, charming and flirtatious cop?

Or had he been after much more than mere information? Had he actually been interested in . . . well, a very wealthy, attractive widow?

Talk about things that make you go, "*Hmmm . . .*"

Especially considering that I was a widow myself. And while I certainly wasn't *wealthy*, by all outward appearances, I probably looked pretty well-to-do to other people.

So had Remy dumped me because he'd found a younger, more financially endowed widow? Sure, I felt like he'd been way out of line when he talked to me this morning. There was no question about it. But somehow, I doubted Remy was a widow chaser, mostly because I was only hearing Olivia's side of the story. It was very likely that Remy had a whole different version of things.

Not that I would ever hear it.

On the other hand, if Olivia was right, and Remy really was interested in her, that meant he had a clear-cut conflict of interest when it came to investigating this crime. Something that was completely unprofessional. And if he had a "thing" for the woman who was undoubtedly a top suspect, he certainly wasn't going to implicate her for killing her husband. Which also meant this neighborhood murder might go unsolved.

And we could have a killer living across the street.

That was, unless someone else stepped in, considered *all* the suspects and cracked the case. A concept that, in my own mind, pretty much answered the question of my involvement in this situation once and for all. In fact, as far as I was concerned, it practically gave me carte blanche to uncover the killer myself. And with one of the lead suspects sitting smack-dab in the middle of my kitchen, I had the perfect opportunity to gather more information.

So I took the chair across from her. "Did the police keep you very long at the station?"

Her eyes lit up. "Not long enough, because I could have stayed with that man forever. But at least they let me back into my house. I've scheduled professional cleaners to come over. They said no one will ever be able to tell that someone was murdered there by the time they're done."

Nothing like blotting out a bloody crime.

"Wow, that was fast!" I responded, unable to hide the surprise in my voice. "I didn't think the police ever allowed people to return home so quickly."

She gave me a sly smile. "That's because I sweet-talked the detective into letting me go home. Believe me, he wasn't about to tell me no. I don't think I'll have any problem getting my way with him."

I stared into my coffee cup. "But I'll bet the detective wanted to know if you had an alibi."

She shrugged and took a sip of her coffee. "And I do. I was out last night to dinner with some friends. When I got home, I found Dex lying on the kitchen floor. He'd been gone for a while and there was no use calling an ambulance. So I just called the police. And I gave the detective the names and numbers of the friends I was out with."

"What other kinds of questions did he ask you?"

"Oh, just the usual."

The usual?

I fought to keep my eyebrows from shooting up my forehead. "So . . . does that mean you have experience with this kind of questioning?" I asked as casually as I could.

She tilted her head from side-to-side. "Umm . . . sure. Once or twice. Dex was always involved with something or another. Though I think the people who questioned him . . . and me . . . were federal agents. Not the regular police."

This time, my eyebrows got the better of me, and I couldn't even begin to hide my surprise. "Oh! What was he involved in?"

She shrugged. "I don't know. Something to do with his business. I didn't keep track of those things. And nothing ever came of the investigation anyway."

"So, he wasn't arrested or anything?"

"Nope, not Dex. He was really good at covering his tracks. Believe me, I would know."

"Oh?" I responded, trying to encourage her to say more.

"Yeah, he was a rich guy. And women everywhere went for him in a big way. But I figured out how to keep him in line." Once again, she stared at her new sapphire.

"Did you tell Detective Reagan about all of this? About his being questioned by the feds?"

She waved a perfectly manicured hand in front of her face. "Of course not. It was none of his business. Besides, if he wants to know more, he can ask Hayes."

"Hayes?" I repeated.

"Hayes Hawthorne. Dex's business partner."

"Was he questioned by federal agents, too?"

Olivia let out a little chuckle. "Oh, yeah, and he was pretty steamed about it. He told Dex that if he had stayed on the up-and-up, then they wouldn't be having trouble."

"Wow. What did Dex say to that?"

Olivia smiled again. "Dex set him straight. He told him that sometimes you've got to take chances and cut some corners if you want to make money. Real money. Besides, Hayes knew what Dex was like before he got into business with him. They'd known each other forever. They even went to college together in Austin."

"What kind of business was it?"

Olivia shook her head. "It's complicated. But they had their hands in real estate development, and import/export, and all kinds of things. I never really kept track of it all, and I pretty much tuned him out whenever he talked about work. I just knew that he made a lot of money."

"But who gets the business now? Now that Dex is . . ."

"Dead?" she supplied without batting an eye. "Hayes gets most of it. But it doesn't all go to him. And that's what I wanted to talk to you about. Because I know who killed Dex."

I nearly fell out of my chair. "You do?"

"Oh, yeah," she told me, her unblinking gaze directed right at me. "It was his first wife, Cissy."

"How do you know . . .?"

Sparks flew from her green eyes. "She gets a chunk of the business, so she'll probably sell it out to Hayes. And make a lot of money. And that money should be mine. Plus, I know she wanted

Dex dead. She was still furious that he'd cheated on her and left her years ago. She never got over it."

"But the scissors . . ." I blurted out before I caught myself.

Olivia raised her brows. "How did you know about the scissors? Yes, they belonged to Dex's second wife, Deidre. His first wife used them to frame his second. Cissy hates us both."

I sat back in my chair. "Olivia, are you sure about this?"

She nodded. "Absolutely. Go check her out. You'll see what I mean. She wanted to get back at Dex. By killing him. And it was going to make her even richer."

Then before I could say another word, Olivia handed me a piece of paper that was a little bigger than a business card. I glanced at it and read the name "Cissy Degill," along with an address underneath.

"Go meet her and see what I mean. She's always home on Friday afternoons, because she gets ready to go out and party that night," Olivia informed me. "Ask her a few questions and you'll know that she's the killer."

"Did you tell the detective about Cissy?"

She shook her head. "No, we mostly just talked about me. Because Detective Reagan wanted to know everything about me. Like I said, it was very romantic. He asked me a few boring questions about Dex, but then he always came back to me," she added with a dreamy smile.

Okay, yes, I know it was pretty odd that Olivia was pushing me to check out Dex's first wife as a possible murderer. But the question was, why? And for that matter, why hadn't she told Remy about her so-called suspicions? Sure, it was true that I was keen to investigate this case. But Olivia couldn't possibly have known that.

Unless, of course, some of the neighbors had spilled the beans, so to speak. And she might have gotten an earful about my recent crime solving caper. While Remy might not have appreciated my ability to uncover a killer, the people who lived around me certainly did. Well, most of them anyway. With the exception of those who went to jail, of course.

Olivia took a good gulp of her coffee. "I've got to go now," she said as she stood up from the table, leaving a half-full cup of coffee behind. "Check out Cissy. And you'll see what I'm talking about."

Yet as I walked her to the door, I still couldn't believe that Olivia was trying to get me to investigate her husband's murder. Yes, she seemed upfront about it all, but deep down, I didn't exactly buy it. And I had a pretty good idea that she truly thought she had just played me.

And I had just let her.

Since, like it or not, my curiosity was already getting the better of me. And while I was dying to go check out Dex's first wife, I was also well aware that Olivia's actions only made her look more guilty. Like she was trying to divert attention away from herself. Which meant there was one fact that stood out loud and clear to me—I needed to find out more about Olivia.

And I knew how to do just that.

I locked my front door and raced to my kitchen. Then I went through the little pile on my counter where I kept my bills and cards and various things. I kept searching until I found what I was looking for—the business card of Bugsy Barkowski.

Right away, I wondered why he hadn't listed his real first name along with what I guessed must be his nickname, Bugsy. Maybe he didn't like his real name, or maybe it was one of those names that got him teased throughout his childhood.

"Or maybe he has something to hide," I murmured to myself before I picked up my phone and tapped in the number.

He answered on the third ring.

"Hello, Bugsy?" I replied. "This is Maddie Montgomery calling. I met you a couple of days ago at the Degills' house."

"*Y-e-s-s-s* . . ." he answered with a surprising amount of hesitation.

"Bugsy, I think I've got a problem with palmetto bugs. Could you come over and take care of them for me?"

Words that apparently made him perk right up. "I live to *kee-eell* bugs, Ms. Montgomery. I can be there tomorrow. Bugs get started early and so do I. I'll be there at daybreak."

Daybreak? As in sunrise? I couldn't even think of the exact time the sun came up in the morning. But either way, I had to get Parker off to school first before I had time to talk to Bugsy.

"Make it nine o'clock," I told him.

"Ma'am, yes, ma'am. I will be there at oh-nine-hundred. On the dot."

From his tone of voice, I almost got the feeling he was saluting me from the other side of the phone.

"Thank you, Bugsy. I'll see you then," I told him.

I put my phone back on the counter and instantly started to think of questions I wanted to ask him. Questions designed to get him to dish the dirt about the Degills. Olivia, in particular.

In the meantime, I needed to scrounge through my garden and hope I could find a few palmetto bugs. Then I had to capture them and keep them in a container until Bugsy arrived at 0900 hours the following morning.

Just to give the perception that I really and truly had a problem with bugs.

All so I could quietly investigate the murder that had taken place across the street. Because I knew full well that I needed to come in under the radar. So the man who had just dumped me and ordered me to stay away would have absolutely no idea what I was up to . . .

Chapter Twelve

I had just gotten off the phone with Bugsy when I remembered the photos I'd taken the night before from the scene of the crime at the Degills' house. Pictures I probably shouldn't even possess. Yet the very idea that I *did* possess them gave me an odd sense of satisfaction.

Especially when I opened them up and found nice, clear images that captured the scene perfectly. Still, it was hard to see the details on the small screen of my phone. So I raced up to my desk and transferred the photos to my laptop that was connected to a big monitor. Then I opened them up again.

And much to my amazement, I could see everything clearly. Perfectly. There was Dex, lying face down on the floor, with Deirdre's jewel-covered scissors embedded firmly into his back. The rest of the house looked pretty much like it had before, and I didn't see any chairs or boxes turned over. Or plates scattered around, or anything. In fact, the plates of cookies and things were in the same places that I'd remembered them, though clearly some cookies had been eaten, and my shrimp plate was empty. But nothing was on the floor, and from what I could tell, there were no signs of a struggle. And no blood on the floor aside from what had probably gushed out when Dex was stabbed.

Stabbed in the back, mind you.

Meaning it wasn't a direct confrontation, and Dex hadn't been facing his killer when that person plunged those dagger-like scissors right into him, sending him into the afterlife ahead of schedule. So either the murderer had surprised Dex, and Dex had no idea that the person was there, or Dex had turned his back on his killer, right before he was stabbed. Which brought up a very big question—did Dex know his murderer? It certainly could've accounted for his turning around, thus setting himself up for a surprise attack from behind. Maybe he thought the killer was someone he could trust, or at the very least, a person he wasn't afraid of.

There were just so many possible scenarios.

But any way I looked at it, I had to say, the crime reeked of rage.

And when it came to uncontrolled rage, Deirdre certainly fit the picture. My bad hairdo the day before only attested to her tendency to be overtaken by her emotions. And for that matter, they were *her* scissors that had been shoved into Dex's back. But Belinda, the starry-eyed, stressed-out stalker, probably had the potential to become irrationally irate herself, given her complete disregard for personal boundaries. I also added Dex's first wife's name to my list, thanks to Olivia's insistence that Cissy had been mad at the man herself.

Oddly enough, the only one who hadn't appeared to be overtly angry at Dex was wife number three, Olivia. She had told me, (and the police), that she'd been out for the evening and returned home to find her husband dead. Was it the truth? Or was it pure fiction?

That's when I realized I might have a way to check out her alibi. I logged into my doorbell camera account and played back the recorded events from the evening before. The camera didn't pick up things from across the street very clearly, in part because of the trees growing in the cul-de-sac. Even so, I could make out Olivia's red car backing out of her driveway and zooming around the cul-de-sac a couple of times before taking off down the street. No doubt, she had gunned her engine like she had the night before, but this time I hadn't heard her, probably since I'd been in the shower and too busy getting ready for my date with Remy to notice what was going on outside. Her departure was about an hour before Remy arrived and parked in front of my house. Then shortly after we'd driven off, a car drove into the Degills' driveway.

So it appeared that Dex did have a visitor while Olivia was out.

That, or Olivia had simply returned in another vehicle.

This second vehicle appeared to be a very nondescript, four-door, dark sedan. In my camera playback feature, it looked like a million other cars, and from my front-door view, I couldn't even begin to identify the make or model of the vehicle. It didn't help that the image was also distorted somewhat by the camera's wide-angle lens, and for that matter, it also looked a lot like Remy's car did on playback. The car appeared to stay at the Degills' house for about ten minutes before it drove away.

After that, I kept going through the rest of the events that had been recorded from my doorbell camera, and I noticed that shortly before Remy and I had arrived back in the neighborhood, Olivia's red car had pulled into her driveway. A few minutes later, police cars came roaring in with red flashing lights. I stopped watching when I noticed Remy's car bringing us into the cul-de-sac, and I saw him race from the driver's side and barely take time to slam the door. And definitely not take time to say good night.

But there was no need for me to relive *that* moment.

I saved the recorded images seconds before a very tired Parker dragged himself in after school. I greeted him in the kitchen and watched as he half-slid and half-flopped onto one of the barstools of the kitchen island.

"Coffee, please, Mom. Make it a double. An expresso or something." He dropped his head onto his arm.

As always, I fought the urge to laugh at his antics. "Sorry, kiddo. Have an apple. The natural sugar will give you a boost."

"Nothing could give me a boost right now, Mom. I'm way too tired."

I grabbed some carrots from the refrigerator and set them on a little plate, along with a nice slice of Havarti cheese. Then I washed and polished a Red Delicious apple, grabbed the peanut butter from the pantry and set it all in front of him. He managed to lift his head and down one of the carrots in three bites. I poured him a glass of milk and set it next to the plate.

The kitties immediately joined him on adjacent stools, though they knew his afterschool snacks rarely involved something they might like. Even so, they did sniff at the little bites of apple that Parker set before them.

He glanced up at me. "Any news about the murder, Mom?"

None that I would share with him, of course.

"Nope, not a thing," I told him. "All quiet all day."

Parker shook his head. "Weird. Some days nothing happens and then other days—it's sayonara!"

By now, I couldn't help but laugh, especially with Parker's word choice. "Sayonara?"

"You got it, Mom. So are you and the man going out on another date? I need to know so I can get it on my schedule."

Speaking of sayonara. "Well, umm . . . no. I don't think that's going to happen."

Parker froze just as he was about to take another bite of his apple. "What? What gives?"

Which left me in an odd position. I really didn't want to drag Parker into the ups and downs of my love life. Limited though it may be. On the other hand, he kind of needed to know. But how did I explain something that I couldn't even explain myself?

So I settled for saying, "Detective Reagan is busy with this case and won't have time to date. I guess you could say that we've tabled our relationship for the moment."

He raised a dark eyebrow. "Tabled it? What does that even mean?"

"It means we won't be going out right now."

His jaw dropped. "Oh, no, Mom! You got dumped?"

"No, I did not get dumped, Parker."

Now he shook his head. "I'm pretty sure you did, Mom. And he's probably going to ghost you. I can't believe it. My own mother—dumped! I'm going to let him have it the next time I see him."

I laughed. "No, there will be no letting anyone 'have it.' It didn't work out and that's that."

"That's lousy, Mom. Even I've got a date."

Joy leapt in my heart, and I thunked a hand to my chest. "Parker, that's wonderful! Who is she? And where are you going?"

"To prom, Mom. I'm taking her to prom. After all, you told me if I wanted to take Dad's car to prom that I had to get a date." He gave me his usual goofy grin.

Funny, but I didn't quite remember the agreement that way, that if he got a date, he could drive Charlie's car. In fact, I was pretty sure I hadn't completely agreed to letting him take the car under any circumstances. "What is this girl's name?"

His face lit up. "Cassidy. Cassidy Carmichael."

"Beautiful name. What's she like?"

"Pretty. And smart. Supersmart. Straight A's. And she has a good sense of humor."

"Do you have a picture of . . ." I started to ask.

"Way ahead of you, Mom. I told her I had to take her picture because I knew you'd be giving me the third degree." He munched on a few more carrots while he scrolled through the photos on his phone.

I laughed again. "Do you even know what the third degree is?"

"Umm . . . something I read in one of those mystery novels you have in our library," he said before he held out his phone and showed me her picture.

"Oh, Parker, she is so pretty!" I exclaimed as I looked at the heart-faced teen with strawberry blonde hair and big, blue eyes. "What a nice smile, too. I can hardly wait to meet her."

"Ease up, Mom. It's just a prom date. But she is good with the whole dressing up fifties style. You know, to match the car. Now I've just gotta find an old suit."

"Well, there's an old tux in the attic. It was your grandfather's tux. Your dad inherited it when your grandfather passed away. I'll bet it would fit you. We might have to make a few adjustments, but I think we could get it to work."

Parker's dark eyes went wide. "Cool, Mom!"

"Plus, you've got your dad's old, stingy-brimmed fedora. And I think there might be some skinny ties in a trunk somewhere, if you wanted to wear one of those instead of a bowtie. It might look more 'Rat Pack.'"

Parker's grin never dipped. "Nice . . ."

"But let's go up there and look for it another night. When we're not so tired."

"Good plan, Mom."

"Though there is one thing I was hoping you would do for me tonight."

"Name it, oh, mom of mine."

"I need you to capture a few palmetto bugs tonight after dinner. Out in the garden."

He looked at me sideways. "Palmetto bugs? Really? Now you've got me worried. You're not jumping on that whole, bug-eating craze, are you? Maybe you're in worse shape than I thought. After being dumped and all."

"No, Parker, I'm fine with what happened between Detective Reagan and me," I sort of lied as I turned away, presumably under the guise of grabbing an old refrigerator storage container from a drawer. "In any case, I'm not going to start eating bugs."

"You sure?" he asked with a gulp while he stared at the container that I slid in front of him.

"Yes, I'm sure."

He raised his brows. "How many of those bugs do you want me to find?"

"A couple. Maybe a few more."

"You're not going to start putting bugs in my breakfast, are you?"

I rolled my eyes. "I don't have any plans to. Not yet anyway. But it might save on my grocery bills."

"That's a good sign, Mom. You're joking again. And as long as you're okay, there's something I need to show you."

"This sounds serious."

He downed the last of his snacks and grabbed his computer from his backpack. "It is, Mom. But there's no getting around it. You've gotta see this." In a flash, he had his computer open and booted, and he pulled up a video. "You're not going to believe this, Mom, but she did it again."

I was about to ask, "Who did what?" when I saw a shoddily designed logo that read "Maddie and Mindie." Something new since the last video I'd seen with that moniker. But before I could say a word, Parker hit the play arrow on the video, and some rap music sounded on his computer.

Seconds later, there was Mindie, smiling before the camera as she pulled her long hair before her, resting half of it on either side of her front. "Hello, all my wonderful fans! It's me again, Mindie," she said as she stroked her hair like she was petting a couple of ferrets.

"You've all been so nice to me after I had such a rough time with that last Maddie Montgomery recipe. And I want to thank everyone for all the nice comments and all the support you gave me. So you'll be happy to know that I don't give up easy, and I've decided to continue my quest to make every one of the Maddie Montgomery recipes from her mystery novels. Maddie puts a skill level rating on each one, so I thought I'd go for a hard recipe this time. You know, since I'm an expert in the kitchen and so I can get it over with. Then I'll work my way down to the easy ones."

"What?" I gasped. "Bad idea," I murmured to the young woman in the screen. "Very bad idea . . . start simple and work your way up. Practice your skills before you move on . . ."

"I hear ya, Mom," Parker murmured with a sigh.

If only the overconfident young woman on the screen could have heard me, too.

"So today," she continued, "I'm going to follow a recipe that Maddie has in her novel called *Cherry Picked For Murder*."

That's when I felt my stomach drop to my knees. Mostly because I had a pretty good idea which recipe she was talking about. And if I was right, it was a recipe that was, no doubt, way beyond her skill set.

"Not the Cherries Jubilee . . . please, no . . ." I intoned.

"This time," Mindie went on, "I'm going to make something extra special. I'll be making Maddie's recipe for Cherries Jubilee."

"*Nooooo* . . . no, no, no," I said to the computer screen as I slid onto one of the island stools. "This is not going to end well!"

"Easy, Mom," Parker coached me. "Take really deep breaths."

So I tried to do just that for the next few minutes, while I watched her mix sugar and orange zest and cherries in her pan. At long last, she added the brandy. "Now it's time for me to flambé my dessert," she explained to her audience. "Which is just another way of saying 'light it on fire.' I guess it burns off the alcohol."

Then she pulled out a long lighter and tried to flick it on. But no matter what she did, no flame appeared.

"There seems to be something wrong with this," she explained. "So I'm going to use a match instead," she added as she produced an old matchbook with a few matches left in the pack.

"Matches?" Parker repeated. "Nobody uses those kind of matches anymore."

"She needs to use a long, wooden kitchen match," I told him. "They hold the flame longer. It's in the recipe."

But clearly, Mindie hadn't bothered with such a pesky, little detail and went barreling forward with the small, cardboard matches. After a few tries, she managed to light one and tossed it into the cherries mixture.

Only to have it immediately burn out.

"That didn't work at all," she complained to her viewing audience while she used a fork to scoop it out. "But since I'm a person who never gives up, I'm going to try it again. But first I'm going to add a little more brandy to the mixture to make sure it lights up good."

"*Nooooo* . . . please, no . . ." I said again, as though my words might possibly stop this trainwreck.

She poured in a few good slugs of the brandy and then tossed in another match. But the match went out before it even hit the dessert.

"Geesh, this is really hard," she said into the camera. "Maddie Montgomery recipes are *really* hard. And this one doesn't call for enough brandy to light it on fire. So I'm going to pour in a little more."

And she did just that. I could even hear the *glug-glug-glug* of the liquid gushing from the large bottle of brandy.

Then she tilted her head. "You know, I think I'll put in one more swig. Just to be sure."

By now, the bottle was almost empty.

I put my hand to my chest, hoping to ease the pounding of my heart.

Mindie glanced at her lighter again. "Oh, wait a minute, I was supposed to open my lighter by clicking this little button. So now that I've got that figured out, I'm going to try lighting my Cherries Jubilee with the lighter again . . ."

All the while, I watched in horror as she did, in fact, click her lighter and produce a nice, big, blue flame. She even managed to turn it up a little, so the flame looked huge before the camera.

Then she grinned broadly and said, "Okay, here we go."

I cringed as she slowly moved the lighter closer and closer and closer to her cherries mixture. I barely saw the flame touch the liquid.

Followed by an enormous *Pmmmffftt!*

The bright blue and yellow flash of the explosion even shook the camera. After which, big, red and purple blobs of cherries went sliding down the lens. Eventually, Mindie wiped the lens off with a towel, giving us a good view of the aftermath. Her hair was now covered in cherries and red goo, along with the ceiling and every square inch of her entire kitchen. Huge red drops of gunk oozed across the counter and flowed onto the floor. Blobs of cherries dripped from the ceiling, falling onto Mindie. And everywhere else.

"Well, that didn't go very well," a teary-eyed Mindie whined into the camera. "Maddie Montgomery recipes are really hard. That's for sure. They don't work at all. Anyway, until next time, this is me, Mindie, signing off."

I groaned and dropped my head into my hands. "I don't believe this. This can't be happening."

Parker shut the lid to his computer. "I feel your pain, Mom. But the bad news is, she said 'until next time.'"

"Next time . . .?" I gasped. "You mean . . . you mean . . ."

"Yup, Mom. I think she plans to keep it up."

That's when I closed my eyes and tried not to hyperventilate.

Chapter Thirteen

Even after Parker packed up his laptop and headed up to his room to do homework, I was still in a daze. Which meant I had a hard time concentrating when I went back to my office and tried to work until it was time for me to cook dinner. Of course, I didn't get very far, considering I got three phone calls from three of my author friends from around the country. All of whom had seen the latest Maddie and Mindie video.

"Maddie, I'm mortified," said my romance writer friend, Tillie, from her huge, log home in Montana. "That so-called cooking demonstration was a complete catastrophe."

I closed my eyes and cringed. "'Catastrophe' is the word. Especially when it comes to the condition of her kitchen. I've never seen such a mess."

"Me, either," Tillie agreed. "In fact, I didn't think it was a real cooking video at first. I thought it was a comedy sketch. But then I realized this girl was dead serious. I'm guessing you didn't authorize that video. Or the other one she put out."

I glanced out the window at the perfect spring weather. "No, I absolutely did not authorize that girl's project. I'd never even heard of her until she started filming herself while she was annihilating my recipes."

"So you saw it online for the first time, just like the rest of us?"

I felt my heart skip a beat. "The rest of us?"

"Oh, yeah," Tillie told me. "I was in an authors' group online, and it was all they could talk about. People kept playing it over and over, just to see those cherries blow up again."

"She'll be cleaning cherries off her ceiling for a long, long time," I said with a wry chuckle. "Hopefully that'll keep her busy for a while."

And so the conversation went. By the time Tillie and I got off the phone, my head was spinning. I took a few deep breaths and tried to get my bearings, right before my Peter Gunn ringtone started to play again.

This time it was my friend, Callie, a fellow culinary author from Louisiana, who was calling. "Wow, that Mindie is a complete dumpster fire," she exclaimed, her voice ringing with shock. "On top of it all, she's trying to piggyback off your fame by using your name in her project. So while she's becoming famous, she's making you look like, well . . . like a fraud. When it comes to your recipes anyway."

I ran my fingers through my hair. "I know, when it's really the other way around. You would think she might actually have a few cooking skills before she attempted to do something like this."

"I couldn't agree more, Maddie. But I don't think completing your recipes is her real goal. I think she's just looking for a way to become famous. Pure and simple. Probably since her mom is one of your fans. So now this girl wants to use your fame to create her own. Have you seen the number of hits she's gotten? I'm pretty sure she's gone viral with this."

I sighed. "I'd like to think the old adage is true, that there's no such thing as bad publicity."

"I would, too. But I think there are exceptions to every rule. And I wonder if this might be one of those exceptions," Callie warned. "Because, amazingly, while this Mindie is gaining her moment in the sun, she's dimming your star."

A point that hit home shortly after Callie and I said our goodbyes.

Because I had barely put my phone back on my desk when another author friend, Erin, called from South Carolina. "Maddie, is there anything you can do about this person? Maybe call your lawyer?"

"I suppose I could. But what would I have him do? Send this girl a 'cease and desist' letter? She'd probably just post it online and make me look even worse."

"It's very likely. Still, it's not right for her to bumble her way into ruining your reputation as a culinary author. I wonder if you could turn the tables somehow."

Words that sent possibilities whirling through my brain. "Hmmm . . . I've been making cooking videos of my favorite recipes for a long time now. So maybe I could make some specific videos to counter hers," I said, thinking aloud. "Since she's busy claiming my recipes are too hard, I could redo some of them and show the world just how easy they are. Then I could emphasize the importance of following the instructions and using the right amount of ingredients. I could show some very basic techniques when it comes to cooking and point out where Mindie went wrong. Without actually using her name, of course."

"Of course," Erin agreed with a laugh. "It sounds like a great idea to me. It might even boost your book sales. Then you could capitalize on her stuff instead of the other way around."

"I'll give it some thought. If she keeps it up. After her last two fiascos, she'll probably just give up and fade into the background," I added, noticing how hollow my words sounded the second they left my mouth. "In the meantime, I've got to finish my new book."

Not to mention, solve the latest murder in my neighborhood.

So shooting and editing videos right now was the last thing in the world I had time for.

Nonetheless, I did feel much better after my phone conversations. Though I wasn't sure if I'd solved my problem, it was still nice to know I had friends. I was even smiling when I started to cook dinner. And I kept on smiling while I served up chicken pieces that had been roasted to perfection in my air fryer, along with mashed potatoes mixed with sour cream and olive bits.

Parker, on the other hand, was so tired that I thought he might fall asleep before he finished his dinner. Yet even with his eyes half-closed, he managed to polish off a huge mound of potatoes and seven pieces of chicken.

I stared at him in astonishment. While plenty of parents worried about their kids sleepwalking, I wondered if my son might be in more danger from "sleep eating." Was it possible that I would wake up one night and find him in the kitchen, unconsciously downing every item in the pantry?

For that matter, I wasn't completely convinced he was awake now as he downed the last crumb on his plate. And because he was so tired, I decided to let him off the hook for dishes duty tonight. That was, right after he went outside and captured the palmetto bugs I'd requested.

He returned to the kitchen just as I finished the cleanup.

"Here you go, Mom." He presented me with the container, much like when he was ten and presented me with the annual grade school gift that the teacher had instructed the kids to make for Mother's Day. "The best samples I could find. I had to dip into the neighbors' yard to get one of them. And one flew right at me. Just like palmetto bugs always do. You never did tell me why you wanted these."

I chuckled. "No special reason. I've got an exterminator coming over tomorrow, and I wanted to show him some bugs."

"Exterminator? As in 'pest control'?" he asked as Ellery and Agatha jumped onto the barstool beside him, eyeballing those buzzing insects.

I checked to make sure the lid was on nice and tight. "Yup, pest control. He'll be here in the morning."

Parker crinkled his brows. "I know I'm tired, Mom . . . But I'm pretty sure we don't have a problem with bugs. Not on the inside anyway. The felines always hunt down anything that gets in."

"Yes, and Ellery and Agatha do a great job," I assured him.

"So why do you have a bug guy coming over?" he asked, mere seconds before his eyes lit up and he grinned. "Wait a minute . . . did you call that guy we met across the street? You invited him over so you can grill him about the Degills, didn't you, Mom?"

Much like Parker seemed to be grilling *me* at the moment.

"Well, umm . . ." I managed to murmur, trying my best to stall.

Trying and failing, that is.

All the while, Parker kept on grinning at me like he'd just won the lottery. "So that's why you wanted me to find those bugs. You're using them as an excuse to talk to that bug guy. And while he's looking around for more bugs, you'll be asking him all kinds of questions."

For once, words completely failed me.

Parker, on the other hand, didn't seem to be suffering from a shortage of words at all. "That's so sneaky, Mom. But you're not normally sneaky. There's only one reason you'd do something like that. You're investigating Mr. Degill's murder, aren't you?"

His deduction left me even more tongue-tied, and once again, scrambling, as I tried to figure out how to deal with my supersmart son. "All right, yes," I finally admitted. "I didn't think it would hurt to look into this a little."

Except for the fact that an Abbott Cove homicide cop had specifically ordered me not to do so. But I saw no need to mention that to Parker.

His grin went even wider. "Cool, Mom. I can help."

"No, kiddo. I don't want you mixed up in this. Besides, you'll be in school."

"Yeah, school . . . hey, I've got an idea," he said, his dark eyes dancing with excitement. "I can ask Mrs. Degill if I can look at her sapphire. Under a microscope and stuff. I can say I'm doing a report for school on gems and minerals. Then I'll have to go over there. To her house. And you'll have to come with me. And since you're so sneaky now, you can sneak around their house and look for clues. While I'm checking out her ring. She won't even know what you're up to. Because she'll have to stay with me and her ring. So I'll take my time and do a whole, big analysis on that stone," he went on, the words flying from him like a runaway train.

And that was the moment when I put a stop to things by kicking into full-blown "Mom mode."

"Oh, no. No, no, no," I said in no uncertain terms. "That's a very bad idea. You will not be going over there."

Yet judging from the way his grin never dipped, I could tell my words had gone in one ear and out the other. Regardless, I decided there was no use talking about it more tonight, and I sent him up to bed instead. With the hopes that he'd have forgotten all about it by morning.

But no such luck.

When he appeared for breakfast the next day, it was apparent that he'd given it even more thought during the night. And he continued to chat about "his role" in my investigation during the fifteen seconds that it took him to down the breakfast I'd just spent twenty minutes cooking.

"I mean it, Parker. I don't want you getting involved in this," were my final words to him as he left the house.

Of course, it did not escape me that I'd pretty much said to him what Remy had said to me, when he'd strictly forbidden me to look into the murder of Dex Degill.

But that was completely different. Parker was a child—my child—and it was my job to protect him. I, on the other hand, wasn't a child who needed protecting. Not only that, but like Spencer Poe had told me, I wasn't in Remy's chain of command.

And just like I'd more or less ignored Remy's commands, I was afraid Parker was ignoring my commands, too, as he walked out the door. Though he did pop his head back in long enough to remind me to keep the doors locked and the alarm on.

Then he was gone.

I let out a deep sigh as I poured my second cup of coffee. Who was the parent here and who was the child? Sure, I wanted Parker to become an independent young man, and frankly, I felt like I'd done an excellent job of guiding him there. Especially after losing Charlie and becoming a single parent.

Yet Parker seemed to think that his becoming a grown-up qualified us for some kind of role reversal. Funny, but most new adults complained that their parents didn't treat them like grown-ups. But in our case, it seemed I needed to remind my son that I was still an adult and quite nicely in charge, thank you very much.

Or at least, I hoped I was. I had my doubts for a moment or two as I raced through my morning routine so I could be ready for my appointment with Bugsy at "oh-nine-hundred." Because here I was, pretending to have an insect infestation, just to "grill" a man about a murder that I wasn't supposed to be investigating.

Maybe I wasn't as "in charge" as I thought.

But now was hardly the time to hash it over in my mind. Not when Bugsy arrived on my doorstep precisely at nine o'clock. Not a minute before and not a minute later.

He stood there with perfect military posture, like he was in line for inspection by a drill sergeant. "Good morning, ma'am. I'm here, reporting for duty. How are you this fine day?"

"I'm very good, Bugsy. Should I call you Bugsy? Or do you prefer to be called by your real first name?"

He stared at me for a moment or two, as though weighing his options. "No, ma'am, everyone just calls me 'Bugsy.' That will be fine."

"Please come in, Bugsy," I told him as I held the door wide to let him enter.

And as I shut the door behind him, I suddenly realized that this was the second day in a row when I'd allowed someone to step into my home. Another virtual stranger, and this time, a very big guy who was sizing up my house, no less.

Just as Agatha seemed to be sizing him up, judging by the way she made a beeline for him, strutting and slinking along like Bugsy was the greatest gift to feline-kind the world had ever seen. She practically threw herself at Bugsy's feet, rolling and lolling around on the floor and putting her tummy on full display. In all the years that I'd had Agatha, a cat who had been spayed long ago, I'd ever seen her act like such a "hussy."

Sure, I know she was only a cat, but I still found the whole scene to be a little awkward. Especially when she continued to writhe and trill up at him with wanton abandon.

I picked her up and held her next to me, trying to control her impulses. "I'm so sorry, Bugsy. I don't know what's gotten into my cat."

He raised an eyebrow and nodded. "No worries, ma'am. Nothing I'm not used to. Happens all the time. She's smelling the residue from my bug spray. It's plant-based, and it seems to drive the female cats crazy."

"Well, I hope it does more than that to the bugs," I told him as I passed him the container with the palmetto bugs.

He held it up to the light and gave it a thorough inspection. "No worries, ma'am. It'll *kee-eell* them. It'll *kee-eell* them dead. All of 'em."

"Sounds good, Bugsy. But . . . plant-based?" I repeated, not quite able to keep the surprise out of my voice.

"Yes, ma'am. Lots of plants are poisonous. Half the stuff out there in your garden is poisonous. Deadly, even. When it's distilled down and concentrated," he told me with a glint in his eyes.

A fact I realized I wasn't completely unfamiliar with, thanks to my years of research for writing murder mysteries. Though somehow, I hadn't thought about it in terms of a concentration that could be used to kill insects. Not to mention, something that could be put in a canister and sprayed.

Now I glanced at the canister that Bugsy had brought with him and set on my hardwood floor. Or, more specifically, I looked at the skull and crossbones symbol on the silver container.

A symbol for poison.

And that's when it hit me: Had an autopsy been done on Dex Degill? From what I'd seen of the crime scene, it looked like Dex had died from stab wounds.

But was it possible he'd been poisoned first? Or even simply drugged? Something that had rendered him more pliable and easier to stab? Before the murderer finished him off with Deirdre's scissors?

More than one classic mystery novelist had used such a scheme in a book. And I'd even written this method of murder into my fifth Blaze McClane book, *The Saucy Assassin*, which featured a Southern Belle serial killer.

But if that's what had happened to Dex, it meant it wouldn't have taken someone with super strength to stab him. Or someone who was fueled by adrenaline while in the grips of uncontrollable rage.

No, it meant that any old Joe or Josephine could have plunged those scissors into the guy. And the person who had murdered my neighbor could just as easily have been a woman as a man. That also meant the suspect pool just got a little wider and a little deeper. And who knew what kind of monster lurked below in those deep, dark depths?

Speaking of lurking, I glanced up at Bugsy again and suddenly remembered a few other interesting tidbits that I'd learned from my research. Sure, poisoning was usually a woman's choice when it came to murder, and men tended to use more physical means. But that didn't mean that men didn't break the mold every now and then.

Especially if that man was already in a profession where they used a deadly substance on a daily basis. Not to mention, a job where they already "*kee-eelled*" for a living. Albeit insects, but a form of extermination all the same.

Despite the warmth of the day, a cold chill passed across my bare arms. I managed to give Bugsy a feeble smile, yet all the while, I couldn't help but wonder if I'd made a huge mistake by inviting the Degills' exterminator into my own home.

A mistake that I might regret for the rest of my life.

Which, considering the spray cannister of poison that this man had brought with him, might not be all that much longer.

Chapter Fourteen

To say I felt on guard around Bugsy all of a sudden was probably the understatement of the century. Okay, that might be a little melodramatic, but I think you get the picture. After all, not only had he been at the Degills' house the day before Dex was murdered, but he'd probably been *all over* that place. Purportedly looking for bugs. Which meant he would have known every single nook and cranny of the home. And he could have secretly left a door or window unlocked, making it easy for him to sneak back in later. Then he could have hidden anywhere inside that big house and waited for the right moment to do the dirty deed, so to speak.

But why would a big, linebacker of a guy like Bugsy resort to poisoning Dex and then stabbing him with some very specific scissors? It didn't make sense, considering Bugsy probably could have killed Dex with his bare hands if he'd wanted to.

Unless the crime had been well-thought-out, emphasizing the word "premeditated" in the term "premeditated murder." Because the truth was, it would take a pretty strong man to kill another big man with sheer strength, a fact that could whittle down a suspect list in a hurry. Whereas incapacitating someone with a plant-based insecticide before stabbing them was something that would likely throw the police off the trail.

Not to mention, make for the actions of a very clever killer.

Yet somehow, as I looked up at Bugsy, "clever" was not the first word that sprang to mind. Bless his heart. Yet for all I knew, his big, dumb guy persona was nothing but an act, designed to hide his true self. That, or he could have had an accomplice. Someone who had the brains to map the whole thing out and simply convinced Bugsy to go along with it.

But any way I looked at it, as long as he was casting a very large shadow across my front entryway, it was time for me to focus in on the real reason I'd invited him over. Meaning, it was time for me to "grill" Bugsy, as Parker had so delicately put it.

So I forced my smile to go from feeble to full-blown Southern Belle. "Say, Bugsy, did the Degills have the same problem with palmetto bugs that we have over here? You mentioned that, if their house had bugs, then our house probably did, too."

He nodded and glanced around the room. "Yes, ma'am, they did. At least, according to Olivia, they did. She said she saw all kinds of bugs, and she showed me some Black Widows in a jar. Just like you showed me your palmetto bugs."

"Black Widows?" I gulped and glanced around the room myself, fighting the urge to jump on top of my dining room table.

And stay there.

"That's right, ma'am. But they were already dead. And they'd been dead for a long time."

"Funny, but I don't remember any neighbors mentioning Black Widows before."

His pale-blue eyes lit up. "I've never seen 'em in this area, either, ma'am. But I don't think the spiders came from here. I think they came in with the moving boxes. From the Degills' old place."

"Good to know," I told him.

"But it seems like she would have noticed them before," he went on. "She was pretty jumpy when it came to bugs."

I remembered that Olivia had said something about needing to move from their old place because of "too many memories" and "too many complications." So had those complications included a problem with spiders and other bugs? Though moving to get away from insects seemed like an awfully extreme solution to the problem. Especially when it appeared the insects had traveled with them to their new home.

"How about Dex?" I asked with all the innocence I could muster. "Was he worried about insects, too?"

That's when a cloud practically passed over Bugsy's face. "Bugs were the last thing on that guy's mind."

"Oh? How's that?"

Bugsy shook his head. "Well, ma'am, he was married to a beautiful woman, but he never paid any attention to her. He didn't appreciate her one bit. He was too busy looking at other women."

I felt my eyes go wide. "Wow. And to think, they were newlyweds."

Bugsy scowled. "You couldn't tell by the way he acted. He was drawn to pretty women like June Bugs to a porch light. But you saw what he was like. When you were over there."

"Oh, yeah," I agreed with a nod. "He latched onto my hand and wouldn't let go. Not even when I tugged and tried everything I could think of to get free. Without making a big scene."

"Yes, ma'am, I know. You weren't the first one he went after with his handholding trick. While he said all those nice things. Sometimes in front of his wife and sometimes not. And some of those ladies even seemed to like it."

"Are we talking about a lot of women?" I asked carefully, trying to conceal my shock.

Bugsy pulled a small flashlight from his pocket. "Yes, ma'am, from what I could see. There was a decorator who showed up once and never came back. Then there was a mail lady and a few other delivery women. And some women from his office. Plus his two ex-wives showed up out of the blue."

Naturally, I wondered how much time Bugsy had spent at the Degills' place and exactly how many bugs he'd had to kill. Then I wondered why Dex's two former wives had shown up at his new house that he owned with his new wife.

"His ex-wives were there together?" I tried to confirm without choking.

He shook his head as he moved from my front door down the hallway, shining the flashlight on the baseboards as he went. "Nope. They were there different times. Lookin' for money."

"Do you know if he gave them any?"

"I think it took a bit, but he finally did. But I don't think they got as much as they wanted. And this was after a whole bunch of cuddling and handholding. He sure didn't act like he was divorced from either one of 'em."

A fact that surprised me, considering the venom that Deirdre had been spewing the whole time she'd been taking it out on my hair.

I watched the beam of Bugsy's flashlight as I followed behind him and kept my eyes peeled for anything with eight legs. "Wow, where was Olivia while this was going on?"

"She was out. Both times. Or I think she would've been pretty upset."

"I can imagine."

Bugsy stared into the room off the hallway that I had turned into a library. "He did not deserve her. Not one bit."

"I'm glad my husband didn't do things like that."

His pale eyebrows shot up his forehead. "You're married, ma'am?"

I smiled and nodded to a picture I had sitting on an end table in my library, one of Charlie and me at a formal dance. "I *was* married, Bugsy. I lost my husband a few years ago."

He stepped over for a closer look at the photo, shining his flashlight beam onto it before his eyes went wide. "Your husband was a . . . he was a Colonel?" He gasped, stood ramrod straight, and then gave me a snappy salute.

Not sure what to do, I just smiled in return. "Yes, he was. But you don't have to salute me, since I wasn't the one who actually signed up. Even so, we were certainly a military family."

His posture never dipped. "Oh, ma'am! Thank you for your service, ma'am."

"Thank you for thanking me," I said in return. "Are you a veteran, Bugsy?"

His face fell, along with his shoulders. "I wish, ma'am, but no, I'm not. I tried to get in, but they wouldn't take me. My four brothers all got in, and they've been moving up through the ranks. One of 'em is special forces. Sure wish I could'a joined 'em. But I'm making the most of it, ma'am. I just do battle with the bugs instead. The way I see it, they're the enemy, and we're at war. So it's my job to take 'em out."

"That sounds very noble," I said, hoping to console him. "Especially since you're helping people who are terribly scared of bugs. Like Olivia. Not only that, but insects can do a lot of damage, and that damage can cost homeowners a lot of money."

He was already nodding. "Yes, ma'am. It sure can."

"Plus . . . when you think about it, since some insects are venomous or carry diseases, you might even be saving lives," I went on, well aware that I was probably laying it on a bit thick.

Yet for some reason, I couldn't seem to stop myself, and I couldn't understand my sudden urge to bolster this man who had been turned down by whatever branch of the military he'd tried to join. And to think, only minutes ago I'd been a nervous wreck around the guy, wondering if he might actually be capable of murder. Something I hadn't completely ruled out at this point. Yet here I was, treating this man like he was one of my kids. First Agatha had turned into a virtual tramp of a cat around Bugsy, and now I'd turned into the man's mommy. Was it possible that I was under the influence of his pesticide residue, too?

Regardless, he seemed to take my reassurance to heart.

"Ma'am, yes, ma'am," he said, blinking hard. "Now don't you worry, ma'am. I'll make sure this home is safe and sound for you and your family. Right away, ma'am. I'll get those bugs for you. I'll *kee-eell* them all."

"Sounds good, Bugsy. Let me show you around so you'll know where you're going," I told him as I led him toward the kitchen.

But we'd barely walked to the end of the hallway when the doorbell rang. Bugsy frowned before he followed me back into the foyer like a trusty guard dog. I opened the front door to find my neighbor, Spencer Poe, standing on the doorstep, holding a glass measuring cup.

Okay, I had to say, that wasn't exactly a sight I saw every day. Or *any day*, for that matter. Not only was I shocked that he actually owned such a kitchen implement, but I was also amazed to see *him* there in person. Clearly, he'd broken his own protocol of leaving his house unattended, for fear some government spy might sneak in while he was gone and bug the place.

A concept that, after I'd gotten to know the man, might not be as far-fetched as it sounded.

"Well, hello, Spencer. Nice to see you," I said, using my best Texas manners. "What brings you by?"

I was always fascinated by how truly "nondescript" the man really was. Beige pants, beige jacket, nearly bald head, sunglasses over gray eyes. Average height. The kind of person that would be hard to pick out in a crowd. In fact, when I thought about it, there was next to nothing about him that would distinguish him from any other man his age.

In other words, the perfect spy. He could slip in and out of places and nobody would ever give him a second glance. He was also an expert when it came to avoiding any kind of questions that might "confirm" the possibility of his ever having worked for the CIA.

Right away, his gaze zeroed in on Bugsy, and while his expression was completely neutral, I had a feeling he was sizing up the other man. "Good morning, Mrs. Montgomery. I wondered if I might borrow a cup of sugar."

Huh?

For a moment, I wasn't sure I'd heard him correctly. "You want to do what . . .? When have you ever . . .?" I started to ask but held my tongue, having been raised with good manners. "Spencer, have you taken up baking?"

"Oh, you never know," he replied with his usual "answer without really answering" tactic. "My, it's a nice day, isn't it, Mrs. Montgomery?" he went on as he casually passed me the measuring cup.

One that had a small, folded note lying flat on the bottom.

I fought the urge to roll my eyes as I took the cup and picked up the note. I unfolded it to read "Mrs. Montgomery, if you are under duress or in danger from this man in your home, blink twice, then pause, and blink three more times. If not, then blink seven times in succession."

"Do what . . .?" I crinkled my eyebrows, before I did my best to blink. One, two, three, four . . . Or was that five?

"Wait a minute," I finally said. "No, Spencer, I'm fine. I hired Bugsy here to take care of any bugs that might be in my home." I opened the door wide and motioned for my neighbor to come inside.

He stepped across the threshold, keeping his eyes on my new exterminator. "Bugs? Are you referring to short-range or long-range?"

"Range?" I asked dumbly, getting the sense we were speaking different languages.

"Listening devices, of course, Mrs. Montgomery," Spencer said matter-of-factly, as though it were obvious.

I shook my head. "No, Spencer, I'm talking about *actual* bugs. Insects."

Now Bugsy squared his shoulders and stared directly at my neighbor, who, in turn, stared right back, in what appeared to be our neighborhood's version of the showdown at the O.K. Corral. Thank goodness neither of them was armed.

Or at least, I didn't think they were. Though Bugsy was now wielding the wand of his cannister like a light saber, albeit one that could spray out poison, and who knew what kind of device Spencer might be carrying. Knowing him, it was quite likely that he was. Carrying something, that is.

Thankfully, I knew exactly how to diffuse the situation.

"Bugsy was at the Degills' house a few days ago," I explained to Spencer. "He was there killing insects."

That's when Spencer Poe seemed to relax a little. "Oh, I see, Mrs. Montgomery. So he's met both Olivia and Dex. And he probably saw or overheard a great many things when he was over there," he finished, giving me the quintessential conspiratorial wink.

With Spencer officially appeased, I turned to Bugsy and presented him with his personal kryptonite. "Mr. Poe is my neighbor, and he was also in the military."

Bugsy's face lit up like an LED light, and he gave Spencer an even snappier salute than the one he'd given me. "Sir, yes, sir! Thank you for your service, sir."

Spencer saluted him back. "At ease, soldier. Which branch did *you* serve in, son?"

Bugsy's face fell. "They wouldn't take me, sir. Old football injury."

"I'm sorry to hear that, son," Spencer Poe replied in his gravelly voice, sounding very much like a senior officer. "No doubt, you would have made a fine soldier."

Bugsy's eyes went wide. "Yes, sir, thank you, sir! How about you, sir? Which branch did you serve in?"

It was the very question that I'd asked Spencer myself a few times. But since Spencer was practically an Olympic medalist when it came to the exercise of dodging questions, I'd never gotten an actual answer. In fact, the only reason I even knew that Spencer was former military and had also worked for the government was because Charlie had told me. Yet the truth was, Spencer himself had divulged very little about his background to me.

And now I wondered how he would get out of answering the question this time.

"Wish I could give you details, son," Spencer said firmly. "But I'm afraid it's all classified."

A concept that seemed to enthrall Bugsy to no end. "*Cooool . . .*" he breathed, before he added another salute.

"Why don't you head to the kitchen and get started, Bugsy," I told him, pointing him in the right direction. "I'll be with you in a few minutes."

"Yes, ma'am. Thank you, ma'am!" Then he closed his eyes and took a few deep breaths, clearly bolstering himself for something big. "I'm going in!" he finally announced, like a paratrooper about to make a major jump.

"Vaya con dios, soldier," came the response from Spencer Poe.

"Thank you, sir," Bugsy beamed. "Nice to meet you, sir." And then he was off, taking long strides down the hallway. A man on a mission as he quickly came to the end of the hall, executed a perfect parade pivot, and headed toward my kitchen.

As he did, Spencer pulled an envelope from his jacket pocket. "From what I can tell, Mrs. Montgomery, it appears you are not under any imminent threat from that young man."

"I don't think so, either, Spencer. But I can't help but remember that I'd seen him at the Degills' house the day before Dex was murdered."

Spencer's gray brows furrowed across his forehead. "If you have any concerns about him whatsoever, Mrs. Montgomery, simply say the word. I am here to assist or protect you, should you require it. Out of respect for your late husband, the Colonel."

"Thank you, Spencer. That is very thoughtful of you. But as long as Bugsy doesn't see me as 'the enemy,' I think he's pretty harmless. Still, I wonder if a guy like him could easily be manipulated. Especially when it comes to a damsel in distress. And I haven't fully ruled him out as a suspect."

Spencer gave me a paternal smile. "I'm pleased to see you're still on the case, Mrs. Montgomery. Have you made good progress?"

I smiled in return. "You know I'm actually not supposed to be investigating this murder . . . At least not according to Remy."

"But who better than you to investigate, Mrs. Montgomery? With your research into the criminal mind and your superb investigative skills, I can't imagine anyone better than you to 'crack the case,' as they say. And do not forget your previous work of solving our first two neighborhood murders, committed by the same killer."

"Thanks for the vote of confidence, Spencer," I said as I handed his measuring cup back to him. "I'm assuming this cup was only a ruse to come over here and make sure I was okay. And you don't really need any sugar?"

"I wouldn't touch the stuff, Mrs. Montgomery. The government has been putting dangerous additives into sugar for quite some time now. But your statement also makes the case for your being the perfect person to solve this crime. Because you do not miss the subtleties of human behavior."

"That's very thoughtful of you to say."

Though I wasn't sure how true it was, given the way I'd completely missed the subtleties of human behavior when it came to my short-term relationship with Remy.

"One other thing, Mrs. Montgomery," he said as he pulled an envelope from his pocket and handed it to me. "Another piece of your mail was mistakenly placed in my box. This one appears to have taken the slow boat from China. Possibly quite literally, since the postmark is no longer legible."

I took the envelope from him and tried to wipe off the smudges. "Wow, this looks like it was run over by a truck."

Not to mention, it appeared the letter had taken several wrong turns and been on quite a journey before it landed in the wrong mailbox. If nothing else, it had gotten close, and thankfully, ended up in the box of a neighbor who was very good about bringing me my misdelivered mail. A common occurrence in our neighborhood, given our mailman seemed to treat mail delivery as though it were a game of chance, whereby he randomly tossed mail into the boxes of our cluster mailbox at the end of our cul-de-sac.

Spencer Poe's expression turned serious. "If you like, Mrs. Montgomery, I could have it checked for specific tire treads. As usual, I have already x-rayed and scanned it, to make sure there were no microdots or toxins inside. For your protection, as well as mine. You'll be pleased to know that it came out clean."

As was so often the case, I wasn't sure whether to be annoyed or to thank him.

"Nonetheless, the wording of the letter was interesting," he went on.

"The wording? Spencer, you did not read my mail . . ." I half-stated and half-asked, remembering that we'd had this conversation before.

"Not intentionally, of course. But I'm afraid the x-ray process did inadvertently reveal some contents of the letter. It appears the sender thinks you need to become more familiar with Texas history. Perhaps someone wants you to join the DRT. If you are not already a member, that is."

"The DRT?" I repeated.

"Yes, the Daughter's of the Republic of Texas. The oldest women's patriotic organization in the state, and one of the oldest in the country. You would need to check your lineage to be eligible to join."

"I guess I hadn't even thought about it. But it's strange, because Parker and I were planning to go to the Glenwood Cemetery on Saturday morning. Maybe I can look around and see if I have any ancestors buried there. Any of the original Republic of Texas members."

Spencer's face froze. "Surely, Mrs. Montgomery, you are not going to the cemetery because you or young Parker are ill."

I smiled. "No, Spencer. I'm giving Parker a driving lesson. So he can practice driving the Continental."

Words that made Spencer Poe beam. "The Colonel would be so proud."

"Yes, he would," I agreed.

"But . . . why . . . if you don't mind my asking, are you going to a historic cemetery for a . . . driving lesson?"

"It's complicated," I told him as I pulled the wrinkled but clean letter from the envelope.

I immediately read, "The Battle of San Jacinto. The Texas Declaration of Independence. The beginning of the Republic of Texas."

And that was all the letter said. On three separate lines.

"Who could have sent this to me?" I wondered aloud. "And why?"

I glanced at what was left of the postmark on the outer envelope, and if I squinted a little and tilted my head a certain way, I could barely make out the name "Houston," though the date was too smudged for me to read. There was no return address.

Frankly, it amazed me that a letter that had been mailed locally could arrive in such bad shape. And for that matter, I wondered exactly how long ago the letter had been mailed. Because, when I looked at who the letter had been addressed to, I couldn't tell if it said "Mr." or "Mrs." Montgomery.

But that was hardly my takeaway, since the name "Republic of Texas" was now echoing through my brain.

Over and over.

Republic of Texas. *R-O-T*.

Weren't those the initials on Charlie's treasure map?

Tingles raced across my skin as I quickly put the pieces together. Because, if somebody had sent me information regarding Charlie's map, that meant . . .

Somebody else knew about it.

And it was possible they either *knew* or had *guessed* that I might be looking for the treasure, too.

Chapter Fifteen

It was just past noon when Bugsy finished giving my property a thorough going over. From what I could tell, he had inspected every square foot of my attic, along with every drain and baseboard inside the house. That was before he headed outside for a nearly inch-by-inch, microscopic examination of my yard.

In the end, he pronounced that Parker and I were safe from anything that creeped or crawled and might be venomous. But he also warned me that, though he didn't actually see many bugs—and certainly nothing alarming—he could still sense their presence. According to him, he had the ability to detect the most minute, nano-vibrations caused by any insect, and thus using this great superpower, he was sure the bugs had simply "gone underground." For the moment anyway. Then he left strict instructions to call him the minute I spotted a flying roach or a cobweb. All of which, he insisted, were telltale signs that "I was not alone."

A creepy thought, to say the least.

Literally.

In the meantime, I stuck the letter that Spencer had brought over to me in my office safe, where I also kept the old, gold coins that I'd found among Charlie's things. Of course, before I hid the letter away, I gave it the once-over, still trying to figure out why someone had sent it to me in the first place. And what those three, cryptic lines were supposed to mean.

On top of it all, there was the question of who the letter was actually addressed to, since I couldn't tell if the writing on the envelope said Mr. or Mrs. Montgomery. But was it really possible that someone had mailed it to Charlie, and it had been rumbling around in the system all this time and just showed up, a few years after his death?

Somehow, I found that hard to believe.

And as I jumped in my car and headed to downtown Houston—my arms tense as I navigated traffic that rivaled an Indy 500 race—another thought popped into my head. Maybe the sender wasn't aware that Charlie had died. Which meant the sender would not have been someone who'd been in close communication with my husband.

And while that was certainly possible, in reality, it was most likely the envelope had simply been addressed to me. That meant someone out there knew I had the map. Or at least, they suspected I had it.

Did that also mean that Parker and I were in danger? Maybe from some treasure hunter, bent on finding a hidden stash of really old coins? And who knew what else?

Yet judging from the tone of the cryptic letter, it sounded more like someone was trying to lead us *toward* the treasure. By giving us clues. Rather than someone trying to threaten us. That, or maybe they were leading us to find the treasure so they could swoop in and nab it from us.

So many questions. All without answers.

But I let it go for the moment as I pulled into a parking garage that was near the luxury condo building where Dex Degill's first wife, Cissy, was supposed to live.

According to Olivia anyway.

I only hoped she'd told me the truth as I walked to the street. I waited for a car to pass before I strolled across the crosswalk and then to the sidewalk in front of the building. Thankfully, I managed to jump inside the front entrance by catching the door behind a tenant. And as I stepped into the ornate lobby, I tried to act like I belonged there. Even so, I couldn't help but pause for a minute, taking in the stunning architectural features that were clearly from another era. The highly polished, black-and-white tiled floor was a perfect complement to the buttercream of the walls and contrasting white woodwork. As well as the black wall sconces. For a moment, I almost felt like I'd stepped onto a movie set from the Golden Age of Hollywood.

But any way I looked at it, one thing was clear—the whole building practically screamed "expensive."

And even though I was in awe of the place, I still wrestled with the reason why I was there in the first place as I rode the elevator up to Cissy's floor. Yes, I knew full well that I was taking the bait that Olivia had so blatantly dangled right in front of my nose after she'd practically shoved her way into my house. But why had I so willingly complied? Had my curiosity simply gotten the better of me? Or did I think Olivia was actually steering me to find out who had killed Dex?

Regardless, I couldn't ignore the likely prospect that Olivia had sent me on a very nice wild-goose chase, one that would distract me from looking at her as the chief suspect. For all I knew, she could have killed her husband. In fact, the first time I met her she was talking about a plot for a mystery novel, one where the wife murdered her husband and then managed to cover her tracks. So had Olivia just been talking about a book? Or had she actually been plotting a crime?

My mind was in a whirl by the time I stepped from the elevator and followed the hallway around to Cissy's door. It was one of but a few on this floor, which meant that—if I did the math correctly—her condo must be utterly enormous.

Not to mention, cost a small fortune.

Yet now, as I got closer to her door, a part of me hoped she wouldn't be home, since I really hadn't thought of any angle or excuse for my impromptu visit. After all, I was a total stranger and essentially a nosy neighbor playing amateur sleuth.

But a very *big* part of me also hoped that Cissy would be there like Olivia had said. Mostly because I didn't want to believe that I'd just driven all the way downtown and dodged all that traffic for nothing.

Though when I thought about it, I wondered how Olivia seemed to know that Cissy would be home at all. Did Olivia really keep tabs on Dex's first wife? And if so, why? Out of pure jealousy, or for some other reason?

In any case, since I was here at Cissy's place, and I'd come to investigate Dex's murder, I decided I might as well do it right. So I stood up tall, put my shoulders back, and knocked on the door. I barely had a chance to take a deep breath when she flung the door open wide. She was dressed in a fuzzy, pink bathrobe and cradled a half-full glass of white wine in one hand.

Or maybe I should say, half-empty.

"Oh, my goodness, you're early!" she squealed with delight.

Her eyes were as green as Olivia's, and her hair was a deep, chestnut brown, barely a few shades darker than Olivia's. Though Cissy's hair color most likely came from a very high-end salon and probably not the kind of place that might employ the likes of Deidre. If I didn't know better, I would have said that Olivia and Cissy were related, with Cissy being a decade or so older.

"Good afternoon, Cissy . . ." I managed to get in before she took over.

"I'm so happy to see you! I wasn't expecting you for a few hours yet!" She immediately wrapped an arm around my neck and gave me a one-armed hug. "I'm so glad you're here already. You're an *absolute* lifesaver!"

I was?

"It's nice to meet you . . ." I tried again.

"Oh, you, too. Come in! Come in!" She took my arm and ushered me into her gigantic front room.

I stepped in, my brain still spinning as I tried to make sense of things. This was hardly the reaction I'd imagined from someone who could possibly be a murder suspect.

"Umm . . . Cissy . . . you were expecting me?" I managed to say, now wondering if Olivia had warned her that I might stop by.

But that hardly seemed like the action of a woman trying to frame the death of her husband on an ex-wife.

"Yes, honey! Absolutely!" Cissy insisted. "It's a total emergency."

"An emergency?" I sort of gasped.

"Oh yes," she gushed, putting a hand to her forehead, much like a Victorian woman who was about to faint. "It was awful. It happened at work today."

"Oh . . . what kind of work do you do?" I tried and failed to keep the surprise out of my voice while I wondered what kind of emergency we were talking about. "You must have a very hazardous job."

Of course, my mind was already teaming with possibilities of dangerous professions. Air ambulance helicopter nurse, police officer, skyscraper window washer. To name a few.

She shut the door behind us and motioned for me to sit on her off-white couch with a gilded, wooden frame. A piece of furniture that would have been right at home in Trump Tower.

"Oh, honey, my job is super hazardous!" she soldiered on, her voice going up an octave. "I'm an administrative assistant. At one of the smaller oil companies here in downtown Houston, and I broke a nail trying to put a new toner in my printer. I made a real mess of it."

"The printer?"

"No, no, honey, my nail!" She held up her pinkie finger so I could see a practically nonexistent ridge on the edge of her acrylic nail. "Like I said, this is an emergency. A nail emergency! Seriously, I don't know how I could possibly go out tonight looking like this!"

I sat on the couch, suddenly speechless. First of all, I could barely even see this great breakage that Cissy seemed to think was so life changing. It was nothing an emery board couldn't take care of in under a minute. And second, if she thought a broken nail was an emergency, I wondered how she would react to the death of a husband. Albeit an ex-husband, but someone she'd once been married to, all the same.

"It sounds . . . trying," I said with all the sympathy I could muster. "You have been very brave." Then I reached into my purse and grabbed my diamond-bit nail file, all ready to smooth her jagged nail as well as her jangled nerves.

"You can't *even* imagine how upsetting this has been! I've worked at my job for years now, and something awful happens every single day. Oh, the trials I've been through! Day in and day out! But thankfully, I may not have to work much longer." She smiled brightly and took a sip of her wine.

Then she fluttered a hand to her chest. "Oh, but where are my manners? Let me get you a glass of wine, too. This is gonna be fun. I love getting my nails done. My hairdresser will be here in an hour, too. It's going to be an afternoon full of pampering. Just what I need after all the trauma I've had to endure!"

Without waiting for me to respond, she grabbed her glass and raced for her kitchen, presumably to get me a glass of wine that I had no intention of drinking. Not in the middle of the afternoon anyway.

While she was gone, I glanced out the windows that were nearly two stories tall, giving me a fantastic view of the sparkling skyscrapers of the city. The adjacent wall showed exposed brick with framed artwork that was illuminated by perfectly aimed ceiling lights. Yet despite all that beauty, it was the vintage woodwork—the arched doorways and coffered ceilings, and crown and baseboard molding above even more molding—that stood out the most to me. To reproduce something so intricate today would have cost a small fortune. Much like I guessed the high-end, off-white furniture with gold-and-black accents had cost a fortune. In fact, I was pretty sure I'd seen some of it a few years ago in an ad for the city's most exclusive and expensive furniture store. In any case, all put together, the room was stunning.

To say the least.

Curious what the rest of the place looked like, I leaned over the edge of the couch and caught a glimpse of a bedroom down a very wide hallway. The walls had been sectioned with quarter-round carpentry, and those sections had been paneled with gold damask fabric. The tray ceiling was stenciled with gold leaf in a fleur-de-lis pattern. And the huge, four-poster bed was covered with a cream-colored comforter that appeared to be pure silk satin. It was utterly exquisite, but I think the expression "no expense spared" probably summed it up the best.

Yet somehow, I didn't think her condo and furnishings were something a person could afford on an administrative assistant's salary. So I guessed she'd either inherited a lot of money somewhere in her past, or she'd had a good divorce lawyer and come out smelling like one of the long-stemmed red roses that she had in a crystal vase. But if that were true, had she gotten enough money to afford her high-on-the-hog lifestyle for *life*?

After a few minutes, Cissy returned with the wine and plopped a glass down on the gilded coffee table in front of me. Then she slid into an overstuffed armchair adjacent to the couch and took a good gulp from her own refilled glass. Oddly enough, she hadn't even asked my name yet, and for that matter, I hadn't volunteered it.

"Where's your kit?" she wondered aloud, as she glanced at the nail file I was holding.

"My kit?" I repeated. "What kind of kit did you expect me to bring?"

Her extended lashes fluttered in panic. "Your nail kit. You are the new manicurist I sent for, right?"

"Cissy, I think there may have been some confusion," I said gently. "Because I'm not a manicurist, though I'd certainly be happy to fix your nail for you. Instead, I'm here for, well . . . for another reason. I came to bring you some news, and I'm afraid it's not exactly good news."

Her eyes went wide. "Are you with the police?"

I gave her a slight smile. "No, nothing like that. I'm just a concerned citizen. A neighbor, actually."

"A neighbor? But I know all my neighbors." Now she squinted at me, her dark brows suddenly dropping into a deep line across her forehead. "Wait a minute . . . whose neighbor? What is this? Who are you and what are you doing here?"

Naturally, her words reminded me that the next time I wanted to question someone, it would be a good idea to have a game plan before I went off half-cocked, as they say. Even so, I hadn't gotten where I was in life without learning a thing or two when it came to interviewing people and getting their stories. In fact, I'd interviewed experts in a whole variety of fields, to gather information for my mystery novels.

So I silently bolstered myself and said, "I'm sorry, Cissy, but I'm still in shock over what happened. I'm not exactly thinking straight."

She folded her arms and stared at me. "What do you mean, 'what happened'?"

"Well, I live in the neighborhood where Dex Degill lives. Or rather, where he *used* to live."

"What about him?"

"I'm afraid the man is no longer with us. The sad truth is, he's deceased. And the neighbors and I wanted to make sure that everyone was notified. We learned that you were an ex-wife and thought you should be notified, too. Because you know how it is, nobody ever tells the ex-wives anything. Yet they probably want to know. And for legal reasons, they might even *need* to know."

Anger flared in her eyes. "Let me guess . . . that scheming, little wench Olivia put you up to this, didn't she? What crazy plan has she got cooked up now? I want you to tell me everything. Don't leave out a single detail."

"Umm . . ." I started to say, not quite sure where to take this conversation. To buy some time, I picked up my glass of wine and took a sip.

And was instantly surprised.

"Wow, this is fantastic," I gushed. "I love a good Sauvignon Blanc, but this is the best I've tasted in a while. It's very soft. Is it French?"

"Yes, Pouilly-Fumé."

"Oh, my goodness. Did you buy this locally?"

"Yes, I order it in. Now quit stalling and spill it. And I don't mean the wine."

"Okay," I said before I took another sip. "Dex didn't exactly die from natural causes, and just so you know, he was, well . . . he was murdered."

Without batting an eye, Cissy leaned forward in her chair. "Yes, I'd caught wind of it. Did Olivia kill him? I'm sure she's in the will, and she'll probably inherit a boatload, if not an actual boat. Though who knows for sure. I know Dex forced her to sign a prenup, which is only effective in the case of a divorce. But the will is a different matter."

Not to mention, a motive for Olivia to kill her husband. Funny that Cissy should bring that up. Was it because she wanted to redirect the conversation and steer me off course? So she wouldn't look like a suspect herself?

Either way, I decided to keep the focus on Cissy. "I realize this must all be very upsetting for you . . ."

"Oh, please," she replied with a wave of her hand. "Life with Dex was always upsetting. To put it mildly. He considered beautiful women to be nothing more than another 'merger and acquisition.' As you can imagine, it made our marriage pretty horrible," she added before she took a good-sized gulp of her wine. "But then he'd apologize, and I'd forgive him, hoping he would change his ways.

Only, he didn't, and then he up and divorced me for some ditz named Deidre. Though God knows why. That woman is a total drama queen. All drama, all the time."

This from a woman who considered a chipped nail to be a major emergency.

"I believe I've met Deirdre," I said before I took another sip of the amazingly delicious wine.

Cissy scoffed and gave my hair the once-over. "Deirdre and her scissors. Covered in jewels. Like some kind of dagger from the Middle Ages. Give me a break."

My jaw dropped. "You know about the scissors?"

She let out a mirthless laugh. "Oh, yes, I heard. Ironic, isn't it, that they should end up in Dex's back? Serves him right for cheating on me with Deirdre and ending our marriage. But maybe I should ask, how do *you* know about the scissors? Since you live in the neighborhood, what did *you* see that night?" Her tone suddenly sounded as chilly as the air conditioning in her condo.

I shivered and took a good gulp of my wine. "Not much. I didn't know anything was going on until the police showed up with their flashing lights. Then I just stood outside with the rest of the neighbors."

"Hmmm . . ." She looked me up and down, as though analyzing me to see if I was telling the truth. "Olivia probably wasn't with you and the rest of the crowd. She was probably being detained by the police."

I shrugged, doing my best to be nonchalant. "Well, as far as I know."

"But she must have blabbed about it later, to somebody on your street. I'll bet she landed on someone's doorstep and started in with one of her big, ole sob stories. The woes of Olivia. Otherwise, you wouldn't be here now. And you would have no idea who I was."

That's when a whole array of red flags hoisted themselves inside my brain. "Did you and Olivia communicate much?"

She glanced toward her kitchen. "Unfortunately, yes. But not by my choice. That girl was a thorn in my side, and she had some weird obsession with me. She always found a way to contact me, no matter what I did to stop her. Or she'd have Dex contact me with weird requests."

I felt my eyes go wide. "Really? Like what?"

"One time she wanted some of my silver serving dishes. Things that Dex and I got as wedding gifts. And she wanted a necklace that Dex gave me a long time ago. Because she thought it should be hers. I gotta say, I'm surprised *I* wasn't the one who was murdered. I think she wanted to get rid of any woman who had any kind of connection to him. Or that he was attracted to."

A statement that caught my attention, considering the way Dex had gone after me. And if Olivia was our new neighborhood murderer, was it possible that I was on her radar, too?

Cissy gave me a sly smile and stared at me, as though she could read my thoughts. "You know, you're exactly the kind of woman Dex would have gone for. I'll bet Olivia thought so, too. I'd watch my back, if I were you."

"But I had no interest in Dex," I clarified.

Not to mention, the concept itself didn't exactly make sense, since *Dex* was the one who was murdered. If Olivia had wanted to eliminate any competition so she could have Dex to herself, then why murder *him*? It didn't add up. Then again, from my years of research as a mystery writer, I had learned long ago that "logic" rarely applied when it came to a killer.

Cissy laughed. "I don't think Olivia cared whether a woman was interested in Dex or not. Because Dex had a way of winning women over. It was like a game to him, a challenge. And he wanted to win at all costs."

And from what I could tell, it had cost him a lot. Including his very life.

"So he was like a big game hunter," I added with a shudder.

She nodded. "That was him to a tee. And Olivia knew it. Though I'm not sure if she ever really loved him, or if she just wanted to own him. Though I do know she loved his money, and she definitely did not want to share it. Which is why I think she's trying to pin his murder on me, and she's not exactly keeping her mouth shut about it, either. Maybe she thinks she can blackmail me into giving her some of my inheritance. So either I give her money, or she'll convince the police that I killed Dex. That's the way she operates."

"Blackmail? Do you think Olivia is capable of blackmail?" I asked ever so innocently, despite the image of her big, sapphire ring sitting front and center in my mind's eye. Meaning, I'd seen Olivia in action, and from what I could piece together, she seemed pretty talented when it came to manipulation.

On the other hand, I wondered if Cissy was half as innocent as she made herself out to be. Especially after I remembered what Bugsy had said about Cissy dropping by to see Dex, asking for money. Not to mention, it was pretty hard to blackmail someone without some kind of evidence that they'd done something wrong.

"Olivia is capable of all kinds of things," Cissy assured me without batting an eye. "Including murder."

"So you think Olivia is after whatever you'll inherit. It sounds like Dex must have remembered you in his will, too. It must be a lot if Olivia wants to get her hands on it."

She nodded. "It is. As stated in our divorce agreement, upon his death, I get a third of the business. Since I helped him start it. His partner, Hayes, has already agreed to buy me out. So I'll be rolling in cash. Though Hayes will be buying it for a lot less than it's worth. And naturally, Olivia wants a piece of that pie. Which is especially annoying since, again, I'm sure she's in the will somewhere. No doubt she'll get the house and all the immediate assets, since they were probably in her name, too. Plus, I'm sure she'll get money on top of that."

I glanced around the room. "What about this stunning condo? Is she after it, too?"

"Dex and I once owned it jointly, but I fought hard to get it in the divorce. Then Olivia did her best to try to take it from me. She really thought it should be hers. She even tried to take it over when I was out of town for a couple of weeks."

I shook my head. "Wow. And what about Deirdre? His second wife?"

Cissy laughed sarcastically. "Oh, she'll get everything she deserves. Which is absolutely nothing. She'll be left out in the cold. It couldn't happen to a better person. All thanks to that prenup she signed before she married Dex."

"Did Olivia sign a prenup, too?"

"Yes, she did," Cissy snickered. "And I'm sure she found out early on that Dex didn't let a little thing like a marriage certificate interfere with his dating life. And if she had divorced him for it, she would have been out on her ear, too. Just like Deirdre."

Then before I could ask more, we were interrupted by a knock on the door.

"That'll either be my hairdresser or my *real* manicurist," Cissy said with a cold, hard stare. "So it's time for you to leave."

"Thank you for the wine," I told her, not wanting to stick around a second longer.

In fact, I was more than a little thankful for that knock on the door. Because this was one conversation that was making my skin crawl. And every fiber of my being was screaming for me to get out of there. I even beat Cissy to the door and opened it to find a young woman with bright red hair and leggings that matched. She walked in with a huge case just as I walked out.

Cissy greeted her as I made a beeline for the elevator.

Then she yelled after me, "You never did tell me your name."

Without responding, I turned and hit the push bar for the stairs instead. Then I raced down to the street and stepped outside, suddenly grateful for the fresh air.

Though my head wasn't feeling all that fresh. In fact, it felt a little fuzzy from the wine. So I headed to the coffee shop right next door to Cissy's building. I sat on a stool facing a counter in front of a big, plate glass window and ordered a cup of coffee and a piece of homemade cherry pie.

It wasn't until the waitress brought my order that I realized the pie was probably a bad idea. Mostly because all those cherries reminded me of Mindie's ill-fated attempt to recreate my Cherries Jubilee recipe.

Something I'd just as soon forget.

But I rolled my eyes and dug in anyway, feeling my head start to clear little by little. Needless to say, I'd gotten an earful at Cissy's place, and now I had to put those pieces into place. Yes, Olivia had sent me down to meet Dex's first wife, but did she know that Cissy would actually give me more reasons to suspect Olivia as being the one who had offed her husband?

Somehow, I didn't think so.

And yet there was still the question of why Olivia had even enticed me to go downtown in the first place. Either she thought I could—or would—help her, or she thought I was nothing but a pawn in whatever game she was playing.

Yet as I ate my pie (which turned out to be delicious, by the way), I couldn't help but wonder—was Olivia better off with Dex dead or alive? While he was alive, she didn't seem to have any problem spending his money. Big-time. But with him dead, did she stand to inherit more than she could have spent every day? Whether she really loved him or not was questionable, but regardless, she probably still hated the fact that he cheated on her. And apparently, on a regular basis. It was hard on a woman's ego to have a philanderer for a husband. And even if money were her main motivation for marrying the man, with her prenup, she must have been pretty insecure that the money would dry up if he left her for someone else. A fact that was highly likely, given his history, and something that could have happened at any time.

Which basically meant, she might have been better off being his widow rather than just another one of Dex's exes.

I took the last bite of my pie and sat sipping my coffee while I stared out the window. Much to my amazement, I noticed a woman with loads of chestnut hair step into the crosswalk nearby and take long strides toward the parking garage across the street. When she turned for a minute, I caught a glimpse of her face, and I could hardly believe my eyes.

Cissy.

I froze for a second, with my coffee cup to my lips. What was she doing out there? If she'd had a hair appointment at her condo, the stylist had certainly been quick. And what about her big "nail emergency," along with that appointment she'd had with a manicurist? Why was she now racing across the street, wearing black yoga pants and a gray sweatshirt, clothes that were probably pretty sloppy for her? It was like she'd just grabbed the first thing she could find and pulled it on. Which gave me the impression she'd left her place in a hurry.

Minutes later, her actions confirmed it when she practically peeled out of the parking garage and flew down the street.

But why? What had happened after I'd left that sent her scurrying away like she was evacuating from a hurricane? And while a million questions zoomed around in my mind, it was the vehicle that she was driving that really captured my attention—a dark, four-door sedan.

A car that was a dead ringer for the car I'd caught on my doorbell camera.

I started to choke, and I quickly downed the last few sips of my coffee. Then I signaled for the check.

Where in the world was Cissy going? And was there any chance I might follow her?

Though apparently, I wasn't the only one who had that idea. Because I spotted another vehicle pulling out of that same parking garage, barely a half a block behind Cissy.

A silver Crown Victoria.

"Belinda?" I whispered with a gasp.

Was Dex's stalker now stalking his ex-wife?

The waitress showed up with my bill, and I immediately paid her with cash. I was about to get up from my stool and leave when I spotted another dark, four-door sedan pull into the same parking garage. The car looked a lot like the one that Cissy had been driving, though I was sure it wasn't the same vehicle.

Mostly because I thought that car looked familiar. And I confirmed it just as soon as I saw a tall, dark-haired man emerge from the parking garage and enter the same crosswalk that Cissy had just taken. He was moving in a huge hurry, like a man on a mission. To top it off, I could spot the frown on his face from clear across the street.

My heart skipped a beat, and my breath caught in my throat when I recognized the very attractive man who seemed to be racing my way.

A man whom I was very familiar with and hadn't seen for a few days. And for that matter, didn't exactly want to see now, given where I'd just been.

And the reason why I'd been there.

Because the man who appeared to be making a beeline right for me might not be too pleased if he knew.

Remy.

Chapter Sixteen

For a second or two, I just sat there and stared out the window, dumbfounded, as Remy trotted across the street and appeared to be heading straight for me.

The dark-haired waitress, who was about my age, leaned closer to the window for a better look. "*Whew*! That guy is *soooo* hot, isn't he? You don't see many men out there like him."

"Handsome is as handsome does," I told her, wondering why I suddenly sounded like Forest Gump.

As I'm sure she did, too, judging by the strange look she gave me.

"It's what's on the inside that matters," I clarified, thankfully sounding more like myself again. "Yes, the man is incredibly good-looking, but it doesn't matter if he only ends up making a girl feel miserable."

Her blue eyes went wide in surprise. "Honey, do you know that guy? Did he do something rotten to you?"

Much to my amazement, her questions stabbed me right through the heart. In fact, I couldn't believe how much they hit home. Though I probably shouldn't have been so surprised, since I thought Remy and I had been hitting it off pretty well. Okay, *really well*. But evidently, I had misjudged the situation, given the way he'd completely cut me off like he had. Or "dumped me," as my teenage son had so delicately put it. And because I considered myself to be a very good judge of character, it was hard for me to reconcile *my* perception of things with the reality of it.

But all that was probably much, much more than this waitress wanted to know.

So I just responded with, "Yes, I've gone out with him."

"It's always the good-looking ones," she said with a *tsk-tsk*. "They think they can get away with treating a woman badly, and the sad truth is, they probably can." She patted my shoulder before she headed back to the counter.

Oddly enough, her attempt to console me stung even more. Because that was the weird thing—up until the moment when he started to investigate Dex Degill's murder, Remy hadn't been treating me badly at all.

Yet as I sat here now, I couldn't help but wonder if the look of pure irritation etched across his features was meant for me. Especially when his words of warning echoed through my brain, his insistence that I not get involved in this murder investigation. So I had a hunch that if he caught me in this coffee shop, right next door to the building where Dex's first ex-wife lived, Remy might be pretty peeved about it all. And if he figured out that I'd just been "chatting" with Cissy, well, who knew how the man might respond.

So I slid off my stool and instinctively took a few steps back, deeper into the coffee shop. I had the restroom door in my sights, and I figured I could get there in about ten steps. Five, if I ran. Four, if I dove for home, so to speak, where I would be safe from the ire of the man headed my way.

"Honey, are you okay?" the waitress asked me as she came closer again. "Do you need me to call the police?"

Naturally, I didn't have the heart to tell her that it was "the police"—or at least, *a* policeman—that I was trying to get away from.

And that's when it hit me—was I really going to hide from Remy? Someone I would still be dating if it had been up to me? As for his looking annoyed, when I thought about it, if anyone should be looking annoyed right about now, it should've been me. Given the way Remy had so coldly put the kibosh to our romance.

Besides all that, what was really *so* terrible about my stopping in to chat with Cissy? I was simply there to make sure she knew about the death of her ex-husband, and I had gone at the behest of Dex's third wife. It was something any good and decent neighbor would do. And the fact that I'd managed to ask a few questions and gather some information while I was there—information that might be pertinent to solving Dex's murder—well, that was all just purely coincidence.

Or so I tried to tell myself.

Right before I let out a loud sigh and closed my eyes. Seriously, who was I kidding? I knew full well that I'd come racing downtown to check out Cissy's story simply because I'd allowed my curiosity to put a chokehold on my better judgment. Not to mention, I wasn't fully confident that Remy would actually solve the case, especially not if he was now interested in Olivia, like she had claimed. I, on the other hand, had a vested interest in this crime, given that I lived right across the street from the house where the dastardly deed had taken place. And I wanted to make sure my neighborhood was safe once more.

So I stood my ground, you might say, and planted my feet right where I was standing. I was not about to run away like a child who thought she was "in trouble." Come what may, if Remy was looking for me and thought I was interfering with his case, well, we could duke it out right here and now. I was ready to face the music and the man I had mistakenly thought I might have a future with.

"Thanks," I told the waitress. "But I will be fine."

"Okay, honey," she said. "But holler if you need anything."

"That's very sweet of you," I replied with a smile.

Funny how life could turn on a dime. Just days ago I'd been cuddled up to the great-looking guy headed my way, blissfully happy in a romantic haze, and now here I was, dreading an interaction with him. Because, if there actually was an interaction, I fully expected it to be contentious.

I took a deep breath and watched him move ever closer to the curb. And that's when it dawned on me—how could Remy possibly know where I was and what I'd been doing the last few hours? I knew he couldn't have planted a tracker in my purse because I'd changed purses since I'd last seen him. Plus, I was pretty sure he wasn't having me followed. I doubted he had the desire or the departmental resources to keep track of me.

Which, all in all, meant he had no way of knowing what I was up to. And for that matter, probably didn't care.

A point that was completely proven to be true when I watched him make a slight turn and head for the door to Cissy's building. Right next to the coffee shop.

I rolled my eyes and almost laughed. No doubt, Remy was here to see Cissy. Not me. And for that matter, I was pretty sure he hadn't even spotted me in here. So I gave him a few minutes to get inside the condo building next door, and then I took off, practically running across the street to the parking garage. After all, I figured Remy wouldn't be on Cissy's floor for long.

Given that she wasn't home.

Once I was inside the cement parking structure, I took the elevator to the floor where I'd left my car. Within a matter of minutes, I was behind the wheel and headed for the exit, passing Remy's car on the first floor as I went. But before I turned onto the street, I glanced at the crosswalk to make sure he wasn't there already. Thankfully, the coast was clear, so I hit the gas and headed for home.

I didn't breathe easy until I was on the interstate that took me straight to Abbott Cove. Much as I hated to admit it, a very big part of me was glad that Cissy had left before Remy arrived. So she wouldn't have a chance to mention the "blonde neighbor" who had just been there to see her. Though I did find it interesting that I'd gotten to Cissy before Remy had. Not only that, but I also wondered if Remy even knew about Dex's stalker, Belinda, since he'd cut me off before I could even tell him about her.

It was a question that brought up yet another question—why did Belinda appear to be stalking Cissy now? As a "Tracker-American," as she'd put it, had Dex's passing left such a hole in her life that she needed to find a new person to keep track of? It hardly seemed likely, considering stalkers usually had some kind of romantic interest in their victims.

I also wondered if Cissy knew about Belinda, because Cissy certainly didn't seem nervous about people coming over to her condo. She hadn't even bothered to get my name before she ushered me right on into her place. Hardly the actions of someone who was being stalked.

But why had Cissy left her place so abruptly? Especially when she'd told me she had several in-house appointments that afternoon?

Was it possible that someone had tipped her off and told her the police were on their way to talk to her?

Yet if she was innocent when it came to killing Dex, she had no need to suddenly take off. In fact, she would have been wise to get a police interview over with, so she could put it behind her.

Unless Olivia had been right, and Cissy really had murdered her ex-husband. After all, Cissy had admitted that Dex's death had been a rather lucrative turn of events for her. And given her lifestyle and her complete disdain for that whole, pesky "having to work thing," the idea of sending her ex into the afterlife ahead of schedule might have seemed pretty tempting.

But was it tempting enough to spur her on to actually murder the man?

I shook my head, trying to make sense of it all. Then I hit the gas, changed lanes and took the exit ramp for Abbott Cove, easing my navy-blue SUV between two big pickup trucks. I had to admit, this crime was just as complicated and convoluted as something I might write into one of my mystery novels. Yet like clarifying butter, the stuff to be discarded had yet to descend to the bottom of the pan and a clear-cut suspect had yet to rise to the top. And it seemed there were more than a few people who might not exactly be bawling their eyes out over Dex Degill's untimely demise. Mostly women, from what I could tell.

It was interesting how a man who seemed to love women so much had managed to make so many hate him.

I slowed my car as I came to a stop light and then took a right onto the main road that ran through Abbott Cove, just as my phone rang. Thinking it was Parker, I took the call hands free.

"Mrs. Montgomery," came Spencer Poe's raspy voice through my car's speakers. "It appears you are not at home, and I believe there is a situation brewing here that you need to be made aware of."

At once my heart started to race, and the first thing I thought of was my son, who was due home from school about now.

"Oh, no, is it Parker?" I gasped. With another red light up ahead, I eased to a stop behind a huge line of cars.

"I'm afraid it is, Mrs. Montgomery," Spencer Poe informed me in his most solemn tone.

A million images flashed through my mind. Was Parker sick or hurt? Had he been in a car accident? Kidnapped? Taken hostage by a roving band of hyper-hormonal, teenage girls?

Or had he been murdered by the same assassin who had killed my neighbor from across the street?

"What happened? Is Parker okay?" I barely managed to squeak out. "Please tell me he's all right."

"I would hope so, Mrs. Montgomery, but I can't say for certain. Thus I am calling and offering to intervene if you wish. So that young Parker would have a supervisory adult on the scene if you think it best."

Words that didn't exactly make sense or fit into any emergency scenario that I had already conjured up.

"Intervene? What's going on?" I fought to keep my eyes on the road and the herd of cars in front of me.

"I'm afraid young Parker has made his way across the street and to Mrs. Degill's front door. Immediately after his arrival home from school today at fifteen-hundred hours. My drone camera picked up his actions."

"He's done what?" I blurted out, all the while wondering why Spencer had his drone out this afternoon.

But that was a question for another day. Right now, I needed to figure out what Parker was up to. Thankfully, it didn't take long before the light finally dawned, (both in my brain and the green traffic light up ahead), and I knew exactly what scheme he had going. Though I wasn't sure what bothered me the most—the fact that he had blatantly disobeyed me or the fact that he seemed to be a chip off the old block.

And that I was the "old block" in this situation.

I rolled my eyes and groaned. "Thank you for the report," I told my neighbor. "I'm afraid Parker wants in on this investigation, and he's figured out how to get his foot in the door. In this case, literally. He wants us to snoop around Olivia's house and look for clues, as he put it. But he's doing it under the guise of examining and measuring the sapphire in her new ring. Using all his scientific methods."

"Ah, of course . . ." Spencer responded. "I should have recognized his strategy. And in order for him to implement his operation, you, no doubt, will be required to go with him, in the role of parental supervisor. Then while he acts as a distraction and takes his time examining the stone, you can quietly disengage and sneak off to case the place," he added with a chuckle. "I must say, your son has developed a rather outstanding op."

"I suppose so," I responded through clenched teeth, holding my tongue when it came to telling Spencer that Parker wasn't supposed to be *implementing* any operation. Or his "op," as my neighbor had called it. "Though I'm not sure why he went over there by himself, since he needed my involvement for his plan to work."

"No doubt, he's laying the groundwork and completing the preliminary setup, so everything will be in place when you arrive home."

Something that Parker and I were going to have a long, long talk about later.

"Just remember, Mrs. Montgomery," Spencer went on. "Be prepared to hide if necessary and have an alibi ready in case you get caught."

"Got it," I told him, recalling that he'd given me the same advice the last time I'd been investigating a murder. "And thanks for letting me know about Parker. I'll be home in a few minutes."

"I have my drone ready, and I'll keep an eye out for him until you arrive, Mrs. Montgomery. I shall be at your service if you need my assistance."

I thanked him again and continued to maneuver my way through Abbott Cove, dodging traffic and watching for brake lights and bad drivers. Clearly, I had headed home about the same time that plenty of the people who worked downtown had embarked on their evening commute. Finally, after a few more turns, I made it onto my street and made a beeline for my house. A quick glance at the Degills' house showed that Parker wasn't on the front stoop, talking to Olivia.

I drove into my driveway and spotted the open garage door with Parker's car inside. I pulled my SUV in next to his car, glancing around and looking for my son. But he was nowhere to be seen. Right away, I wondered if he was still at the Degills' house, and maybe in the very kitchen where Dex had been murdered.

The mere thought of it made my pulse start to pound.

But thankfully, I spotted my kitchen door opening slowly, before Parker staggered out, carrying his microscope in one hand and an open box atop his laptop in the other. His arms were so full that I wasn't sure how he'd managed to get the door open at all.

"Oh, good, Mom, you're home," he said impatiently. "I was just about to call you. I already went over and talked to Mrs. Degill. I got everything set up. She's waiting for us right now."

I folded my arms and leaned against my car door. "Not so fast, kiddo. I told you I didn't want you getting involved in this."

He beamed at me with a huge grin. "Too late, Mom. I already asked her, and she already agreed. She even has a bunch of other jewelry that she's going to let me look at, too. So it would be pretty weird if we didn't show up now."

I put my hands on my hips and leveled my gaze at him. "Parker, we need to talk about this. Because I specifically told you . . ."

His grin never dipped. "Please, Mom, can we talk when we get back?"

Which left me with a major dilemma. Did I blatantly tell him no when he was already standing there ready to go? Or could I let this behavior slide for a moment and have a frank—and very firm—conversation with him after we got back?

Parker was a good kid. A great kid, actually. And truth be told, he'd given me very little trouble over the years. Still, I couldn't say I'd ever read a single parenting book with a chapter titled: Allowing Your Child to Help You Solve a Murder. A murder that I wasn't even supposed to be trying to solve myself.

"All right, Parker," I conceded, though I kept a little indignation in my voice. Just to let him know that I was not entirely okay with the whole thing.

He let out a "Woo-hoo!" and pushed the box he was carrying into my arms. "Can you take this for me, Mom?"

I stared into the open box. "What's in here?"

"My refractometer and my reflectometer. And the spectroscope I borrowed from the lab at school. Plus it's got my caliper and charts and a whole bunch of stuff. But don't worry, Mom, I'll carry my microscope and my laptop myself."

"Wow, Parker, you're putting on quite a show. You sure you're not really doing a paper for school?"

"Oh, I'm doing that, too, Mom. But mostly I'm just buying some time so you can go snoop around her house."

"Sorry, but I left my magnifying glass at home," I informed him, my voice dripping with sarcasm.

"Oh, no worries, Mom. I brought it, too. It's in the box. So you can search for clues."

It took everything I had not to roll my eyes. Funny, but after my close call with Remy—which turned out not to be a close call at all—I wasn't exactly in the mood for anything that required any derring-do on my part. But unfortunately, not only did Parker have the whole thing arranged, but it was hard to squelch his enthusiasm.

So onward we went. Down the driveway, across the cul-de-sac and up Olivia's front walkway. A white van with the words "Crime Scene Cleanup, Inc." emblazoned on one side was just pulling out as we arrived.

Something that only served to remind me that we were about to step into a house where a murder had recently taken place.

"Hold on there a minute, Parker," I said to my son. "Maybe this isn't such a good plan." Despite myself, I almost used the word "op."

"No worries, Mom," he said, moving forward full steam ahead. "We've got this. I'll distract and you investigate. Piece of cake."

I was about to say more when Olivia swung her front door open wide, clearly expecting us. That's when I realized that backing out now might do more harm than good. I had no doubt that Parker would balk, and making a scene in front of Olivia would look more than a little suspicious. Not to mention, put us firmly on her bad side.

Something I didn't exactly want to do, not when she appeared to be so happy that we were there. If only I could have said the same. Because right at that moment, I couldn't help but wonder if we were walking straight into the lions' den.

One that was run by a very clever lioness, a woman who had possibly—no, make that *probably*—killed her husband.

That's when chills set a land-speed record running up and down my spine.

Chapter Seventeen

While I followed my son into Olivia's house, I couldn't help but notice the smile on her face and the gleam in her green eyes as she held her front door open for us. Yet somehow, her smile struck me as less "welcome to my home" and more "gotcha in my clutches."

"You can set up in here," she said as she directed us to the dining room.

So we trudged on in, carrying all of Parker's equipment, to find that she'd made plenty of room for him to work on her dining room table. A trio of black vases had been scooted to one end of the gold table runner that adorned a cream-colored tablecloth. A black jewel box with a gold lock sat prominently in the center of the table.

"The crime scene cleaners just finished in the kitchen," she informed us in a tone that was reminiscent of someone simply talking about the weather. "You know, cleaning up any stains that might be leftover."

Leftover from Dex's murder, I thought, completing the sentence in my mind while I fought the urge not to say it out loud. Regardless, those very words seemed to dangle in the air. And to be honest, I wasn't sure what the proper response to her statement should be. Something like, "Oh, good, I hope they got that big blood stain out," or maybe, "it's important to know a good service who can clean up after a brutal murder."

But I managed to hold my tongue while I helped my son unpack and get his equipment in place. "I *really* hope Parker isn't imposing on you this afternoon. I didn't realize he was going to stop by and get this set up. I got home a little later than usual this afternoon."

Olivia gave me a smug smile. "Oh, right, because you were downtown. Interrogating Cissy."

All of a sudden, my breath caught in my throat. How did Olivia know I was downtown this afternoon? After all, I hadn't openly agreed to go chat with Cissy, and I certainly hadn't told Olivia "when" I might go. So was Olivia keeping track of my movements?

I forced a chuckle. "I didn't exactly 'interrogate' her," I clarified, while Parker got his microscope into position. "I simply told her about Dex's . . . passing. But how did you know I was there?"

"She called me right after you left, and she was furious," Olivia said nonchalantly. "Though the funny thing was, she didn't seem to know your name. And of course, I didn't tell her. But I could, you know. Next time I talk to her."

Words that sounded an awful lot like Olivia had just threatened me. And as far as I was concerned, her days of manipulating me were done. Sure, I'd allowed my curiosity to take over, and I'd gone downtown at her request. And yes, I'd gathered valuable information when it came to figuring out who had killed Dex Degill. But I drew the line when someone started to threaten me. Or even blackmail me.

Much like I believed she'd blackmailed her late husband, and like Cissy had feared Olivia would blackmail her, too.

"You tell her whatever you like," I replied, hoping to take the wind out of her sails and put the kibosh on any blackmail plans.

Olivia stared at me. "I also told her that Detective Reagan was on his way over."

Something that accounted for Cissy taking off in such a hurry, and something that probably made her look pretty guilty. And, for that matter, might have been Olivia's goal all along. Still, how did she happen to know that Remy was on his way downtown?

And if she knew that he was headed to Cissy's place, had she sort of set it up for Remy and me to run into each other? Because we almost did. And sure, without a doubt, he would've been upset. But more importantly, it probably would've put an end to any plans I had to investigate the murder, once and for all.

Which made me wonder if Olivia *really* did want me to investigate. Or was she actually trying to prevent me from doing so?

But it was something I'd have to ponder later. Because, right now, I wanted to get Parker's project done and over with, so we didn't have to spend another minute longer in this house than we needed to.

With that said, I also wanted complete and total evidence about what he was doing when it came to handling her jewelry. So there couldn't be any backlash should any of her pieces mysteriously go "missing." So I attached his phone to the camera tripod he'd brought and placed it directly in front of him. To record his every move. Then after he took a seat, I put the phone's camera on the video setting and hit the record button.

"Are you ready, Parker?" Olivia asked.

"Ready, Mrs. Degill," he told her with a nod.

Just as the doorbell rang.

Olivia let out a loud "*Huuffff!*" Then she glanced angrily out the front window. "Who can *that* be? I'd better go check this out," she muttered before she stomped off.

For the life of me, I hoped it wasn't Remy, and that Olivia wasn't playing some kind of game by inviting him over. I'd barely managed to evade him once today, and I wasn't in the mood to go through that again. Plus, I was pretty sure he wasn't going to buy the whole "I'm here for my son's science project" routine.

But when two raised voices reached our ears—Olivia's and some man's—I knew it wasn't Remy at the door.

"Not now, Hayes!" Olivia shrieked. "Not unless you're here to give me money!"

Hayes? Wasn't that the name of Dex's business partner?

The man, whom I now knew to be Hayes, yelled back at Olivia. "You won't be getting a dime out of me, you little gold digger! And you would've found that out if you'd bothered to take my phone calls! So now I'm here to inform you once and for all. In person. You won't be getting one red cent from the business!"

"Then I'll just have my lawyer sue it out of you!"

"Fat chance. You know as well as I do that Dex didn't leave any of his part of the business to you, and you don't have a right to one iota of it! So you can threaten to sue all you want. But he made it very clear in the will. It's as plain as that nose job on your face that Dex managed to turn into a tax write-off!"

"Well, if Cissy gets part of the business, then so do I!" Olivia shouted back, her voice coming nearer. "Now go away, Hayes! Leave! I'm busy," she continued to yell as she came marching back into the dining room.

She was followed by a man who, quite frankly, took my breath away the second I laid eyes on him. He was so strikingly handsome that he could have easily graced the cover of any men's magazine, as long as they were featuring a chiseled, middle-aged man who clearly knew his way around a gym. He had pale-blue eyes, dark brows and salt-and-pepper hair. Though the style was a bit confusing to me, given the way some of his hair lay down flat, and other sections were shorter and spikier. Clearly, the man had been blessed, (or more likely cursed), with the kind of course, stiff hair that no amount of conditioner could ever tame. Probably not even the kind of otherworldly, oily treatment that Deidre had put on my hair.

"Maddie, meet Hayes!" Olivia now directed her yelling to me. "The greedy, hard-hearted, tightwad who is trying to cheat me out of my inheritance!"

"None of which is true," the man said in his own defense, his eyes locking with mine. "If anyone was cheating, it was Dex. The man was a gourmet chef when it came to cooking the books. Sorry you have to be in the middle of this, Maddie," he said before he held out a hand to shake mine. "I'm Hayes Hawthorne. Very nice to meet you."

"You, too," I said in response, while butterflies danced in my stomach and my heart beat like a smitten seventeen-year-old at the mere sight of this man.

And speaking of seventeen-year-olds, I nodded to my own. "And this is Parker, my son. He's here to do a science paper on Olivia's gems."

Parker barely had a chance to smile at the man, before Hayes took off with, "Oh, yeah, Olivia's got plenty of those! Makes you wonder where Dex got the money to buy all that stuff, doesn't it? Sure, our business is good, but not that good. But that didn't stop Dex from being a big spender when it came to women. Why a man would waste all that money on jewelry, I'll never know."

"That's because you're a complete cheapskate," Olivia shot back. "And you won't give me the money I'm owed from Dex's business."

"You're not owed a thing, Olivia. Again, Dex didn't leave you a single cent from the business."

Right about then, I wondered if *now* might be a good time for Parker and me to duck out and escape. I glanced at my son who merely raised a dark eyebrow and gave me a barely perceptible shake of his head. Meaning, he wasn't about to go anywhere, now that he was on his "op," such as it was.

Olivia finally pointed in the direction of the front door. "Get out, Hayes! Now! Or I'm calling the police. And for your information, I'm on very intimate terms with Detective Remington Reagan, and I will have him over here in a flash!"

"Intimate?" Hayes scoffed. "Why doesn't that surprise me? Dex barely dies and you've already got another chump on the line. But fine, I'll go! Just know that a police officer won't make the kind of money that you're used to," he added with a loud laugh.

He flashed me a million-kilowatt smile before he strode away, while Parker raised his eyebrows. No doubt, questioning how Remy might already be involved with Olivia. This time, I was the one to give a barely perceptible shake of the head. Because I wasn't going to talk about my relationship with Remy right at this moment.

Or probably any other time, for that matter.

Olivia let out another huff. "Okay, Parker, let's get back to your school assignment."

Then she unlocked her jewelry case and opened the lid. And it was like someone had turned on a switch and lit up a Christmas tree. In the light of the overhead chandelier, gems glittered up to us in every color of the rainbow. Red, purple, green, yellow, white, and blue.

For a few seconds, I just stood there mesmerized.

Parker's jaw practically dropped to the top of the table. "Wow, Mrs. Degill. Those are some really nice gems. This is going to make a great report. I don't get to see gems like this up close and personal very often. The gems my mom has are a whole lot smaller."

I fought the urge to roll my eyes.

"My husband bought most of them for me," Olivia said proudly. "Even before we were married. As you can see, he also bought me a super big engagement ring." With that, she pulled out a gold ring that sported a diamond that was so large it could have doubled for a small ice cube.

That's when I realized she was no longer wearing her wedding and engagement ring. For some reason, this struck me as a little odd. Sure, I know every widow acts differently, but "when" to stop wearing your wedding ring was typically a big issue for most women, a true symbol of the finality of death. And yes, I realized she and Dex hadn't been married all that long, but still, it seemed awfully quick for her to stop wearing her rings. It had taken me six months before I stopped wearing mine after Charlie had died. Even now, my ring finger felt naked.

"Here, Parker, take a look at this," she said, handing her diamond engagement ring to my son.

He grasped it between his thumb and forefinger, before placing it carefully under his microscope. "This is a really nice diamond, Mrs. Degill. Just a couple of tiny pinpoint inclusions. But you can only see them under a scope. And the color is brilliant."

Olivia crinkled her brows and nodded, as though not quite understanding the significance of what he'd just said. In the meantime, Parker put the diamond ring through the paces, giving it a thorough examination and using all the instruments he'd brought with him. And of course, he recorded every measurement on his computer, along with a few notes on the gem. Then he also held it up to his laptop camera and clicked off a few nice photos.

When he was done, he handed the ring back to her with a smile. "Really cool diamond, Mrs. Degill."

Olivia slipped it onto her right-hand ring finger and smiled at it, adoringly. "Thank you, Parker. I thought you might like it. Now take a look at my ruby ring," she said as she pulled a brilliant red ring from her case.

Parker's mouth dropped open. "Is this a pigeon's blood ruby?"

Olivia smiled again. "Yes, it is, Parker. Very expensive, of course."

Once again, he carefully placed the ring on the plate of his microscope. "Wow, Mrs. Degill. This is . . . this is . . . well, I've never seen anything like it."

And for that matter, I'd never seen anything like the look on his face. First his eyes went wide, but then he looked sort of grim. Eventually, he smiled, though it looked largely forced.

His reaction made my antennae go up as he removed the ring from his microscope tray and proceeded to photograph it. He pulled out another instrument, took a few quick measurements, and then recorded a few notes on his laptop. Having finished, he handed the ring back to Olivia.

Though I noticed he hadn't used even half the equipment he'd brought over when it came to examining the ruby. Much like he didn't use all his equipment when he examined the emerald she passed him next.

"This is . . . umm . . . amazing," he said in a surprisingly subdued voice. "Do you know where these gems came from, Mrs. Degill?"

"Absolutely! Everything came from Flause Jewelers," she said proudly. "Gage Flause is the owner, and he really knows his stuff. And that gives me an idea," she murmured as she pulled her cell phone from her pocket. "Let me text him right now. And see if he can meet with you and show you some of his best stuff. For your paper. You'll love it," she added as her thumbs flew across her phone.

"Oh, no, Olivia, you don't have to go to the trouble," I demurred.

"No trouble," she insisted. "And here, he's already answered. He can meet with you tomorrow at one-thirty. Does that work for you?"

"Sure," Parker replied, without an ounce of hesitation. "Mom and I can go then," he agreed, barely even glancing up at me.

And certainly not bothering with pesky little things like asking my permission.

The little hairs on the back of my neck suddenly stood at attention, since I was acutely aware that Olivia had just managed to set me up with another appointment. Via my own son. So what did she have in mind this time? A wild goose chase? Or possibly a setup and confrontation with Remy, now that she claimed to be on such "intimate terms" with him and seemed to think he was at her beck and call?

Needless to say, I would be sure to cancel our "meeting" with this Mr. Flause the minute we got back home.

"Gage found some incredible deals for Dex," Olivia trilled on. "So Dex got me some really great gems. But eventually, I started buying jewelry from Gage myself. In fact, I picked out this sapphire ring from him, and believe me, this one cost a small fortune. I made sure of it. But after what Dex did, he deserved to pay, and I deserved this ring."

Before I could form any kind of response, Parker jumped in with, "Mrs. Degill, could I please look at that sapphire next?"

"Sure, Parker. I love to show it off," she said with another smile.

Then Parker went through his pared-down routine with the blue ring and handed it back to her.

"What did you think, Parker?" she asked, beaming.

He gave her a feeble smile. "I can honestly say I've never seen a more perfect sapphire."

"Here, check out this diamond necklace next," she insisted, handing it to him.

So Parker slid the large, pear-shaped center stone of the necklace under his microscope lens. "Amazing," he uttered, only seconds before he handed it right back to her.

Much to my surprise.

And while I couldn't tell what was going on with Parker, I knew it was something I'd have to ask him about after we left. I also realized that if I planned to do any snooping, it was now or never.

I smiled at Olivia. "Would you mind if I use your restroom? I haven't had a chance to go since I got home."

"Sure," she told me. "Use the one at the top of the stairs. The one down here is still drying from all the cleaning chemicals. It takes a lot to fully get rid of blood, you know."

Something I actually *did* know, thanks to my research as a mystery writer.

But I chose not to respond to her gory comment, and I simply said, "Thank you. I drank way too much coffee when I was downtown."

Olivia tilted her head. "Coffee? But Cissy doesn't serve coffee. I don't think she even drinks it."

"I wouldn't know," I responded, before making a point of checking to see that the phone camera was still rolling, so to speak. "Be right back," I told Parker.

"Sounds good, Mom. And you might want to hurry. I've got to get home and write this all up. So it'll be ready to go for Monday."

A statement that caught me off guard. Meaning, it was clear he didn't want to stay there much longer. Which also meant I wasn't going to have much time to snoop. And because of this surprising development, I probably wouldn't have gone at all, except that I really did have to use the bathroom.

That meant whatever investigating I was going to do had to be quick. So I power walked out of the dining room and into the kitchen and family room, where the cleaning crew had done a miraculous job. Needless to say, I knew I wouldn't find anything interesting in this area, given the whole place was now cleaned from within an inch of its life.

So I ran up the staircase from the kitchen and found the guest bathroom right away. I did what I came to do, and then I tiptoed from the large room. And I continued to tiptoe throughout the upper hallway, glancing into bedrooms as I went. Again, nothing stood out as being suspicious or out of the ordinary.

That was, until I reached the master bedroom. And that's when my jaw practically hit the off-white shag rug that partially covered the beautiful hardwood floor. Because it seemed like I'd seen this room before. And I quickly realized where I had seen it, and not that many hours ago. Because the room was almost an exact replica of the master bedroom at Cissy's condo. Down to the throw pillows on the silk-satin bedspread.

Okay, to say I was shocked—and a little creeped out—was probably a gigantic understatement. Who on earth decorates their own bedroom to be a carbon copy of their husband's ex-wife's bedroom? And whose idea was it to duplicate Cissy's bedroom? Was it Dex's idea? Or Olivia's?

My mind was in a whirl by the time I made my way back down the stairs. But I fought hard to put my game face back on and not reveal what was really going through my brain. I even plastered a smile on my face as I returned to the dining room.

Parker, on the other hand, was looking deadly serious. "Oh, good, here's my mom," he said quickly to Olivia. "I think I've got all I need, Mrs. Degill. Thank you so much for letting me look at all your gems. That was really nice of you."

Then he gave me a strange look, one that I couldn't completely read. Not that I had a chance to anyway. Because he proceeded to pack up all his stuff at warp speed. Apparently, he was done, and in a major hurry to get out of there.

I thanked Olivia and carried my share of Parker's stuff as he practically made a beeline for the door.

But I waited to quiz him until we had reached the middle of the cul-de-sac. "What's going on, Parker?"

"Mom, I'm kinda in shock."

"Me, too. That fight between Olivia and Hayes *was* pretty shocking, wasn't it?"

"Yeah, it was weird. But that's not what really got me."

"What happened?" I asked with great concern as we moved toward our side of the street."

"It was her gems, Mom."

"They were beautiful."

"Yeah, on the outside they looked good. Really good. Like they're super nice stones. Perfect, even. And the diamond from her engagement ring *really* was a great specimen."

"Okay. I sense a 'but' in there somewhere."

"Oh, yeah, Mom," he said, sounding off-kilter. "And I wonder if Mrs. Degill knows . . . but I don't think she would have shown me all her jewelry if she did."

I looked at my son as we neared our driveway. "What is it you think she doesn't know?"

Parker stopped dead in his tracks. "They're not real, Mom."

I paused momentarily beside him. "Huh?"

"Yup, Mom. They're fakes. Every one of them. Except for the big diamond in her engagement ring."

For a moment or two, all I could do was sputter. While a thousand questions flew through my brain, my mouth couldn't seem to form words.

"I know how you feel, Mom," Parker told me. "They're really good fakes, that's for sure. But they're fakes, all the same."

That's when I nearly tripped on the curb.

Chapter Eighteen

I've always heard about people who were shocked to the point of being speechless, and, truth be told, I'm sure I'd even assigned such a state to a few characters in my books once or twice. Though, of course, never for my main character, Blaze, who had no problem when it came to thinking on her feet and never, *ever*, would have experienced a speechless second herself. Yet here I was, returning to our house through the garage with my son, and we were both shocked to the point of being completely speechless.

Parker was the first to finally break the trance. "I don't get it, Mom," he said as we set his stuff on the kitchen island. "Did Mrs. Degill know those gems were fakes? And if she did, then why did she let me look at them?"

Why indeed?

Which was just one of many questions that was ping-ponging around inside my brain.

I shook my head. "That's a very good question, kiddo. And I honestly don't have an answer. Because it all seems pretty strange to me. But I'm not sure she does know the truth about her gems. Since she always acts like she's so proud of her jewelry. And she's been showing off her new sapphire ring like it was a newborn baby."

Not to mention, from what I could gather, she had used that sapphire ring to get her husband to release my hand and be a "good boy," simply by wiggling her fingers and flashing that big, blue stone at him. But how could that be possible, if she knew the stone was nothing but a fake? Albeit a good fake, according to my son.

"Tell me, Parker," I said carefully, "are you sure those gems weren't real?"

"No doubt about it, Mom. I've looked at lots of them in Earth Science class. And even more when our class took a field trip to the Natural History Museum. So I know what to look for. And I can tell the difference between real and fake." Ellery and Agatha appeared and began to rub around Parker's legs, obviously there for moral support.

I picked up Ellery and cuddled him. "So just out of curiosity, how could you tell?"

"Lots of ways, Mom. But mostly, because her gems were too perfect. *Way* too perfect. No variation in the color, and not a single inclusion. Anywhere. Real stones that big are never that perfect. Or at least, it's really, *really* rare."

"So you believe that every single one of those gems you looked at was a fake," I repeated, still trying to let it all sink in. "Except for the diamond in her engagement ring."

"Yup, Mom. I could see if just one of those stones was totally flawless. But all of them?"

Right about then, the questions inside my brain seemed to reach critical mass, and I could barely even think straight. Let alone, think at all. More than anything, I needed to get all the chaos inside my mind sorted out. And there was only one way I knew of to do just that.

To quote my main character, Blaze, "When the going gets tough, the tough get cooking." Spending time in my kitchen always made me feel grounded, no matter what was going on in my world.

"Why don't you take your stuff upstairs while I get dinner ready," I suggested to my son. "We can talk about it more then."

"Sounds good, Mom. I'm starving," he said before he trudged up the back staircase, followed by our two felines.

Still in a daze from the day, I dug into the pantry and the refrigerator until I had all the ingredients I needed. Tonight's menu? My famous chicken cacciatore.

Just the thought of it had my mouth watering as I set the oven for 350 degrees and pulled a ceramic baking dish from a drawer.

While the oven preheated, I grabbed a container of my homemade marinara sauce from the freezer and put it in the microwave to defrost. Then I filled a pasta pot with water and set it to boil on the stove. I dusted chicken pieces with flour and browned them before putting them into the ceramic dish.

As I got into my usual rhythm of cooking dinner and moving around the kitchen—grabbing a spatula here and some seasoning there, and a mixing spoon here and a salt mill there—I went into sort of a dance, you might say. A dance that was familiar, comfortable, and oddly relaxing. By the time I dropped linguini noodles into the boiling water of the pasta pot, I was cooking on autopilot, and my mind immediately started to contemplate the truth about Olivia's jewels.

First of all, I found it hard to believe that nobody knew the gems were fake. It seemed that someone along the food chain must have known. If not Olivia, then maybe Dex. And if not Dex, then the jeweler, Gage. So who, if any of them, did know those gorgeous gems weren't real? One of them? Or two? Or maybe all three?

I also wondered if Olivia had been suspicious about them herself. It could account for why she'd so openly welcomed Parker to come over and take a look. So he might confirm what she believed to be the truth. Then again, maybe the stones had started out as the real deal, and Olivia had replaced them with look-alikes. And maybe she wanted to see if the fakes were good enough to fool my son, a kid who knew his gems and minerals.

Because, if they could fool him, they could probably fool anyone.

I drained water from the pasta, all the while wondering who knew what and when they knew it. Not to mention, what the motivation was behind the phony jewels. Clearly, someone was trying to deceive someone. But why? For money? Or for appearances?

Something inside me said there was much, much more to the story.

That's when I remembered that Olivia had set us up with a visit to her jeweler, Gage, the next afternoon. Once again, I had to wonder why. Were her motives pure, and she just wanted to help out a kid with a science paper? Or was she actually looking for some answers herself?

Or was she simply playing another one of her games?

I had to admit, since Olivia seemed to be so good at manipulating people, it was quite likely she'd figured out a major weakness of mine, that my curiosity tended to get the better of me. So maybe she was simply sending me off in another direction, so I wouldn't focus in on the real killer. Namely, Olivia herself.

And yes, I know I'd vowed that I was done with Olivia's manipulations. But after finding out about the fake jewels, I could hardly wait to meet with Mr. Gage Flause. Not to mention, I was dying to have my son examine some of the gems in his store and see what Parker found. All under the guise of doing research for a science paper, of course. Maybe then I could uncover some answers to this case that seemed to be getting stranger by the second. So for better or worse, I decided to go through with the jewelry store appointment the next day.

I pulled plates from the cupboard just as Parker magically appeared from the back staircase. Followed by his two sidekicks, Ellery and Agatha.

He helped me set the table and once I gave him the okay, he loaded up his plate until it resembled Mt. Vesuvius more than a dinner plate. Then he was on his usual "race against time" to down his dinner in world-record speed.

"Slow down, Parker," I said with a laugh. "Someday, when you're out on a date, eating that fast would be considered bad manners."

His eyes went wide, and he nearly dropped a drumstick. "What do you mean, bad manners? How'm I supposed to eat? If say, for instance, I was out on a date?"

"Well, for one thing, you don't want to devour all the food before anyone else gets a chance to eat any."

He glanced at his plate and then at mine. "Umm . . . okay. Duly noted. What else?"

The question made my antennae pop up, and I wondered why Parker wanted to know this now. He'd never cared about his eating etiquette before. Despite my many, many, *many* attempts to get him to eat in a more, well . . . civilized fashion. But since his friends at school all ate exactly like he did, he really didn't see the need to change. And so far, my efforts had gone unheeded.

"When you go out to dinner with someone," I explained, "you're supposed to be there for the company and the conversation. You're supposed to enjoy the food and each other. And you're supposed to take your time."

He tilted his head from side to side. "Oh. Interesting. Who knew?"

"Parker, is there any special reason you want to know about this?"

"Ummm . . . maybe."

I felt my eyes go wide. "Maybe?"

"Okay, Mom. Don't go gonzo on me . . ."

Despite myself, I couldn't help but laugh. "Gonzo? When have I ever gone 'gonzo'?"

Parker rolled his eyes. "I just don't want you to make a thing out of this. But I sort of have a date. On Tuesday."

That's when I fully understood Parker's "gonzo" reference, because, right then and there, I really and truly did want to go gonzo. Or at the very least, let out a little squeal.

But I fought with everything I had to control myself. "Is it with the girl you were telling me about? Cassidy?"

Parker sighed. "Yes, Mom. It is. Her family is going out for pizza on Tuesday night. And she asked me to come with them. I guess they want to meet me. Since I'm going to be taking her to prom."

By now I couldn't stop smiling. And smiling and smiling and smiling.

"How nice, Parker! I'm so happy! I hope to meet her myself someday soon."

His eyebrows went up. "Okay. How about Saturday night?"

I was but a split second away from saying yes, when I suddenly remembered that I'd signed up for speed dating that night, where I hoped to find Belinda. And get the scoop on her tracking/stalking activities.

I shook my head. "Sorry, Parker, but I'm afraid I can't. I've got plans. Let's pick another night."

His jaw dropped open, showing a mouthful of food. "Huh? What do you mean, you've got plans? Are you going somewhere?"

"Don't talk with your mouth full," I chided him with a laugh. "And yes, I'm going out."

He quirked an eyebrow and finished chewing. "Another date? With the guy who dumped you and ghosted you? Let me guess. I'll bet he came crawling back. Kind of like those palmetto bugs I had to go out and catch so you could tell a big fib to that bug guy."

I rolled my eyes. "No, nothing like that, kiddo. Okay, maybe kind of like that. I've got to go out to . . ." And that's when I hesitated, because more than anything, I didn't want to tell my son the truth.

And while I quickly tried to come up with an acceptable excuse—a lie, essentially—I immediately decided against it. Aside from Santa Claus or the Easter Bunny or the Tooth Fairy, I didn't like lying to my kids. Mostly because I figured it was a bad example and made it perfectly acceptable for them to do the same in return.

Still, I needed to come up with some kind of explanation.

"I'm going out to investigate this case," I confessed.

More or less anyway.

"Investigate? Then I'm coming with you."

I laughed and shook my head. "Not this time. You can't go where I'm going."

His brows dropped into a deep *V* across his forehead. "What? What do you mean I can't go with you? I don't want you running around out there where it's dangerous. On a Saturday night. No way are you going alone. You know what happened last time."

Yes, I *certainly* did. I remembered exactly what had happened the last time I gave in and let Parker come with me on a murder investigation.

Just one more reason why he wouldn't be coming with me on Saturday night.

I finished the last bite of my chicken. "No, Parker, I'm going to an adults' only . . . event."

He stared at me. "Adults only? Mom . . . that doesn't sound good."

I laughed again. "No, it's nothing like that. It's for grown-ups. 'Mature' I think is the word they used. I'm going to a speed dating event for people over forty."

Parker let out a combination gasp and guffaw. "Mom, seriously? Speed dating? Those things are for losers. Just because that Remy guy dumped you. That doesn't mean you have to stoop so low."

"He didn't dump me," I said, knowing full well that he had, essentially. "And I'm not going there to get a date. I'm going out there in search of the woman who had been stalking our late neighbor. The woman in that silver Crown Victoria. Apparently, she frequents these things."

"So you're trying to suss her out."

"Suss?"

"Yes. Check her out. Get the dirt on her."

I leaned back in my chair and folded my arms. "I guess you could say that. And again, you can't come with me."

He heaved a loud sigh. "Well . . . okay. I guess I don't want to be around a bunch of old dudes hitting on my mom anyway. But I want a full report when you get home."

"Maybe."

Though *probably* not.

That's when I decided it was time for me to redirect this conversation. "Instead of thinking about this case, why don't we go to the attic and look for your grandfather's old tux," I suggested.

"Cool, Mom."

"Right after you finish the dishes."

"I'm bringing in a hose, Mom. Looks like that's what it's gonna take in here."

I rolled my eyes. "Nice try. But I don't think so."

He gave me his usual goofy grin and proceeded to clean up the kitchen at supersonic speed. When he was done, he led the way upstairs to the ceiling hatch for the attic. Since he was so much taller, he pulled the attic ladder down with ease.

Once we'd climbed the creaky wooden ladder to the upper level of the house, I led him straight to an old chest that held his grandfather's things. Parker helped me lift the lid, and we were instantly assaulted by the wonderful, warm scent of cedar. Not only that, but we had no problem finding the old tuxedo. Along with some more skinny ties. He ducked behind an old bookcase to try on the suit and emerged looking pretty dapper in the tux that was a surprisingly good fit. Except the pants were way, way too short. But thankfully, whoever had sewn them in the first place had left a lot of fabric in the hem. Which meant it would be easy to have them let down to fit my extra-tall son.

"This is so cool, Mom. I'm going to send pictures to Cassidy. So she can figure out what she's going to wear."

"Sounds like a lot of fun to me," I added with a smile as I grabbed a tape measure and checked to see how much the pants needed to be lengthened. "I'll take all this to the dry cleaners and have them cleaned and altered. So they'll be ready for you."

"Thanks, Mom. Hey, what's this stuff over here?" he wanted to know as he dusted off the top of a huge cardboard box.

"I think those are some of your dad's old things. There might even be another suit in there you can have," I told him. "We were already able to get one of his old suits altered to fit you, so we should have no problem doing that again."

He lifted the lid of the box and just stared inside for a few moments. "I remember this suit," he sort of murmured as he lifted it from the box.

I nodded. "It's still in style, from what I can tell."

He touched the fabric, his fingers lingering on the lapel. And I knew just how much he was missing Charlie. Just like we all missed Charlie.

Then without another word, he stepped behind the bookcase again and tried on the suit. The fit was so close to being spot on that it was shocking. Still, the jacket needed to be taken in a few inches and the pants let down a couple of inches. So I took measurements for alterations.

"Mom, can I take this box to my room?" he asked quietly.

"Of course you can," I assured him. "I'll help you take everything downstairs."

But before we could take a single step, his phone buzzed. "Hey, Mom, check out your book sales. Your numbers just shot up."

And he would have known. Not only had my son helped me get set up to independently publish my books, but he also liked to watch my sales numbers go up. The same way people watch the number of hits they get on their videos.

Now he showed me his phone, so I could see for myself. Much to my surprise, my sales had suddenly gone through the roof. Though I had no idea why.

"Well, that's good news," I said with a smile. "I wonder what made them spike."

"I dunno, Mom," Parker responded, sounding much less enthusiastic than I would have expected.

With a grim look on his face, he took off the suit jacket and stashed it back inside the box. Then we descended the attic ladder, taking all Parker's treasures with us.

"I'm gonna take all this stuff to my room, Mom. I'll meet you in the kitchen," he intoned in a voice that was starting to worry me.

I pushed the ladder back up to the ceiling, all the while wondering what was going on. Was he upset about finding the box of his father's things? I know I'd been in Parker's shoes myself a time or two when I'd gone through Charlie's stuff in the attic. Even though Charlie was gone, he was ever present in our hearts. Not to mention, our memories. And in a way, he was still in our lives.

So instead of prying into Parker's state of mind, I decided just to give him a few minutes. To collect his thoughts.

Then I headed for the kitchen and poured myself a glass of my favorite Sauvignon Blanc, ready to get back to work on Blaze's next chapter. The wine wasn't quite as good as the one I'd had at Cissy's condo. But it wasn't bad, either.

I had just savored the first few sips when Parker came racing in, having changed back to his regular clothes. "You're not gonna believe this, Mom. But I figured out why your sales went up. She's done it again." He plopped his laptop onto the counter of the kitchen island.

"Who's done what again?" I repeated dumbly.

"You know . . . her!" He flipped the laptop open and pointed to a video on the screen. "Mindie!"

I suddenly felt a little lightheaded. "Oh, no. Not Mindie again. I thought she would quit after making such a mess of her kitchen the last time."

"Nope, Mom, she didn't. And I think you'd better see this."

Then despite my better judgement, I watched the video. At first, all seemed well as Mindie announced to the viewers that she had decided to make my famous beef stroganoff recipe.

A very simple, straightforward recipe.

"That's easy to make," I commented. "She can't mess that one up. There's no way."

"You wouldn't think so, Mom," Parker cautioned me. "But maybe you'd better keep watching."

And so I kept my eyes glued to the screen. I watched as Mindie set a frying pan atop the gas stove and started the burner. Then she poured some olive oil into the pan to let it heat up. Though evidently, she didn't think she had enough, so she poured in a little more.

And a little more.

Then she beamed for the camera. "While my oil is heating up, I'm going to work on the big piece of beef that I bought. I want my beef stroganoff to be extra soft, so I found this thing online called a meat tenderizer hammer," she informed her audience while she held up the extra-large, heavy-duty square hammer that was made from metal, and judging from the way she was having trouble keeping it upright, it must have weighed a ton.

"See all these little spikes?" she went on. "I'm going to hit the meat with these, so it'll make it really, really . . . umm . . ."

"Tender?" I supplied, as though she could hear me.

"Umm . . ." Mindie said again, before she finished with "not chewy."

"Wait a minute," I said to Parker. "She doesn't need a tenderizer hammer. She just needs to slice the beef into nice little pieces. It's in the recipe."

"I hear ya, Mom. I watched Lyndi make stroganoff a million times. She never used a hammer. This is major."

"'Major' is right," I agreed, suddenly finding it a little hard to breathe. "Where on earth did she even get that thing? I've never seen a tenderizer hammer that big before."

"Looks heavy, too, Mom. She's having a hard time handling it."

"I've got a really bad feeling about this . . ." I barely managed to utter.

All the while, I kept my eyes glued to the screen as I watched Mindie lay a big, old slab of beef on a cutting board. Then she appeared to step onto a single-step stool, since she suddenly looked about eight inches taller. Once she was in position, she struggled to lift her tenderizer hammer high above her head, like she was imitating Thor with his magic hammer.

"She shouldn't be doing that," I said with a gasp. "She's got that hammer way, *way* too high. She won't be able to control it . . ." were my last words before I watched in horror as she brought the hammer straight down toward the slab of beef on the cutting board.

And missed it by a mile.

Instead, she landed the thing smack-dab in the middle of the granite countertop. Shards of stone went flying, and there was now a visible crater-like divot in the granite.

But apparently, one divot wasn't enough, and she repeated the maneuver two more times, making mincemeat of what I guessed was her mom's granite counter.

Every fiber of my being told me to turn away, to quit watching, but for some reason, I couldn't.

Mindie, on the other hand, had no intention of giving up. On her fourth attempt, she actually managed to hit the cutting board.

Or rather, the handle of a chef's knife that was resting on the cutting board. This sent the knife cartwheeling through the air, until the point landed on the handle of the frying pan. The pan immediately tipped on edge, sending the hot oil straight into the flames of the gas burner.

Which also sent flames shooting up into the air.

But Mindie wasn't fazed.

"Not to worry," she said with a wave of her hand. "I'm all ready for a kitchen fire. I'll just throw this towel over the flames, and it'll put them right out. I saw this done on TV once."

"Wait, no!" I managed to squeak out. "You need to use a fire blanket! Not just any old towel!"

But of course, Mindie couldn't hear me, and she tossed a couple of tea towels onto the fire. The towels quickly ignited, sending flames all the way to the ceiling.

Thus setting off the smoke alarm.

"Okay, no worries," Mindie announced to the camera. "I've got this!"

Whereby she pulled a taller step stool up just beneath the screaming alarm. She proceeded to climb up to the top step and started to beat on the smoke alarm with her hammer.

Only, she missed again and put some major dents in the ceiling instead.

Seconds later, I heard another female voice, probably belonging to her mother, shouting, "Mindie! What have you done?"

This was followed by a big, plume of white haze that covered everything, including part of the camera. Since the flames were now doused, I could only assume it was foam from a fire extinguisher.

A siren sounded in the distance.

The last words from Mindie came out in a whine. "It's those recipes, Mom! They're *really* hard. Not only that, but Maddie Montgomery recipes are dangerous!"

And that's when the screen went dark.

Though it didn't stop me from sitting there and just staring at it for another few seconds.

Wishing I could unsee what I'd just seen.

Chapter Nineteen

"You okay, Mom?" Parker asked as he scooted his laptop away, probably so I'd stop staring at it.

I thunked a hand to my chest. At that moment, I may have been many things, but "okay" was most definitely not one of them.

"How . . .?" I started to ask, before I came up with a barely intelligible, "Why . . .?" And then reverted back to, "How . . .?" once more.

"Take it easy, Mom. Don't have an aneurysm or something."

There was that word again. Aneurysm.

"No, Parker," I assured him, trying not to hyperventilate. "I am not having an aneurysm. I'm just utterly amazed that one young woman can do that much damage to a kitchen."

"And she did it so fast, too," my son pointed out.

"She only attempted to cook one very simple meal!" I practically shouted in shock. "To top it off, she didn't even know how to put out the fire. If her mother hadn't been there, she would have burned the whole house down."

"I hear ya, Mom."

Whereby I went back to, "How . . .?" And then, "Why . . .?" again for a few more minutes. Before I finally landed on, "How will that girl ever survive on her own?"

"I dunno, Mom," Parker said as he typed some words into his computer. "She's not the kind of girl I'd ever go for."

Thank God for small favors.

I was about to say more when Parker suddenly let out a loud, "Uh-oh. You'll never believe this . . ."

"Not Mindie again!"

I had to say, the whole situation felt so bizarre to me, considering that Mindie wasn't a colleague or a work associate or someone I'd hired. She wasn't a relative or a friend's daughter or a neighbor. In fact, she was a young woman I'd never even met and didn't even know. And for that matter, she was someone I *really* didn't want to know. Yet through her disastrous videos, she had successfully linked my name to hers.

Forever.

Parker glanced at me. "Ummm . . . Mom. She's already got a fundraising page set up. For money to rebuild her mom's kitchen. Tons of people have donated."

I gasped. "What?"

"Oh, yeah, she's raised five-thousand dollars so far."

I felt my eyes go wide. "How can that be?"

"And you should read the comments, Mom."

Which meant I really shouldn't read them at all. Even so, I couldn't help myself.

"You're a very brave girl," one woman told her, along with a twenty-five-dollar donation.

"Your hair looked great the whole time," another said, after making a ten-dollar donation. "Until your Mom used that fire extinguisher on everything."

"Just let your Mom do the cooking," another small donor suggested. "That's what I do. I'm thirty, and I don't go near a stove."

"You should just eat out," someone else chimed in after donating five dollars.

But from that point on, the comments took a decidedly nasty turn. "Maddie Montgomery is a big phony! She probably never tried out her recipes before she put them in her books!"

Then, of course, there was, "Maddie Montgomery is mean, mean, mean."

Followed with, "Maddie Montgomery recipes don't work. And her books aren't any good. Not that I've ever read one . . ."

And on it went, while Parker continued to scroll through the many, many comments that came pouring in. Along with donations.

Personally, I was back to nearly hyperventilating again. "So . . . not only is Mindie ruining *my* reputation, but she's making money from it? Especially since I'm sure her mother's homeowners' insurance will pay for a new kitchen anyway. So the money she's getting from her fundraising page will just be cash in her pocket."

"You got it, Mom. Your brand takes a hit while she gets rich," Parker said morosely. "But hey, there is some good news. It looks like your book sales keep going up."

"So maybe people don't really believe her claim that my recipes are dangerous."

"Ummm . . . well, I don't think so, Mom. It looks like you made the news."

"The news? Wow, that was fast!"

Light speed fast, as a matter of fact.

Parker raised an eyebrow before he clicked onto another video, this one of a brunette newscaster, Taffy Kakel, who stood grim-faced in front of a video of a random bonfire. In fact, the scene looked nothing like what we'd just witnessed at Mindie's house. Wherever she happened to live.

"We have an important news flash," Taffy said with a steely glint in her blue eyes. "We just caught wind of a serious housefire that happened tonight, as a young woman named Mindie attempted to recreate a recipe from one of the Maddie Montgomery mystery novels. As you can see, the results were horrific," she proclaimed for all her viewers to hear. All the while, a news ticker running across the screen behind her read "Not an actual house fire but a reasonable facsimile of."

"At this time," Taffy went on, "we believe all parties thankfully survived the disaster. And according to Mindie, of the Maddie and Mindie videos, the recipes in the Maddie Montgomery books are obviously dangerous. Now the question arises: Will Maddie Montgomery books be pulled from the shelves? Clearly, the government needs to intervene to protect innocent citizens from these potentially deadly recipes."

By now, it felt like the room was starting to spin.

"This can't be happening," I managed to squeak out.

"I know, Mom, but your book sales are going through the roof right now."

Okay, so maybe that old adage about there being no such thing as bad publicity actually was true?

"Amazing . . ." I muttered. "As soon as people were told that my books might be taken off the market, all of a sudden, everyone wants one."

"Yup, Mom. That, and I think some people are 'hate reading' your books."

"Hate reading?" I repeated.

"Yeah, you know, like hate watching. When people want to look at your stuff because they've heard bad things about you."

I dropped my head into my hands. Hate reading. Maybe not my worst nightmare, but definitely right up there on the list.

Since Parker appeared to be such an expert on the subject, I was about to ask if he had any ideas about how to change things around, when I realized that I already knew the answer. It was time for me to make some videos to counter the insanity of what Mindie was putting out there.

Parker put a hand on my shoulder. "Hang in there, Mom. We'll get this all figured out tomorrow. Right now, I've gotta go get some shut-eye. And at your age, you could probably use some, too." Then after a quick "Chin up, Mom," he yawned, said good night, and was off to bed.

Leaving me alone in the kitchen, reeling from what I'd just seen. Meaning, "shut-eye" was going to be a complete impossibility for me any time soon. Mindie's antics aside, I'd already had a crazy, full day. Including my chat with Cissy, my close call with Remy, Belinda's new stalking target, and Olivia's fake jewels. Naturally, my brain had the entire day's events on an instant replay loop.

There were just so many pieces to the puzzle that didn't seem to fit in. Anywhere. In fact, it was almost like I was working on four different puzzles at once. On top of it all, I'd fallen way behind when it came to writing my new book. One that might be banned before it even got released, if the reporter I'd just seen, Taffy Kakel, had her way. Though such censorship was highly unlikely, considering I could still sell my books out of my own home.

Either way, it was important for me to get this new book finished. And re-entering Blaze's world for a bit might be exactly what I needed right now. So I took my glass of wine and headed up my curved staircase to my home office, with Ellery and Agatha trailing behind. Then I booted up my computer while the kitties made themselves at home on the window seat. They watched and purred as I moved over to glance out the bay window and across my cul-de-sac for a moment. The streetlights had gone on, and while most of the houses were dark, with the usual assortment of porch lights and garden uplights, I couldn't help but notice that Olivia's house seemed to be absolutely ablaze with lights.

I instantly wondered why as I closed my own blinds against the night.

Did she have company? Or was she simply a night owl? Or was she scared of the dark, or of anyone who might be out there lurking in it? Namely, Dex's killer.

Then again, if she was the one who'd killed her husband, she might just be up plotting her next murder.

The thought of it made me shudder, especially with the realization that she lived so close by. Which was probably why I nearly jumped a mile when my phone rang.

Thankfully, it was a different neighbor who was calling. Spencer Poe.

"Good evening, Mrs. Montgomery," came his gravelly voice through the phone. "I hope you'll excuse the late-night intrusion. I saw your lights were still on, so I trust I didn't wake you."

"Not at all, Spencer. I was just sitting down to work on my next chapter."

"Then I won't keep you for long, Mrs. Montgomery. I simply wished to offer my assistance tomorrow as you instruct young Parker on the intricacies of driving the Colonel's car. Since the Colonel is no longer with us, you understand. I would be quite happy to help educate your son when it comes to operating and caring for a vintage automobile."

"That's very thoughtful of you, Spencer. But Parker is an excellent driver already, because Charlie used to take him and his sister out for driving practice years before they got their licenses. He wanted them to be well-prepared and comfortable when it came to driving. So I don't think it'll be much of a lesson tomorrow."

"Certainly, Mrs. Montgomery. The Colonel was a fine father and like many military members, he wanted to ensure that his children were capable and independent. Even so, young Parker will need to adjust to a vehicle with rear-wheel drive, along with a different braking system, and less responsive steering."

"Very true," I agreed.

And while I figured I had Parker's driving lesson well under control, I hated to discourage such a thoughtful gesture from an almost elderly neighbor. Not only that, but I didn't want to tell Spencer that he wasn't needed, when maybe helping out Parker was something that gave him a sense of purpose.

"We would love to have you come with us," I told him. "We can all stop for some lunch when we're finished with the lesson. Parker, of course, already has his mouth watering for Abbott's Big Burgers."

"Oh, Mrs. Montgomery, I would hate to intrude in such a manner, and I do have a meeting scheduled in that part of town later. You will still be going to the Glenwood Cemetery, I assume, as you had mentioned before?"

Which immediately made me wonder exactly what kind of a meeting he was having.

"Yes, we will," I confirmed, hoping he wasn't going to again question the reason why we were headed there for a driving lesson.

Thankfully, he went on with, "I've also noticed that you appear to be the victim of a rather nasty propaganda campaign online, Mrs. Montgomery."

I sighed. "You must be talking about Mindie . . ."

"I'm afraid hers is a rather sinister tactic," he said with great concern in his voice. "Though highly effective. I've seen such a strategy employed many times in the past to topple hostile governments."

"In the past . . . through your work?" I asked without thinking, hoping I might get some real insight into his history.

But as always, he dodged the question, though not so skillfully this time. "Oh, in the usual places where one might observe such a technique," he said nonchalantly. "It's an especially effective tactic to discredit and bring down one's enemies. And now it would appear this 'Mindie' person is trying to sabotage your good name."

"Well, she's doing a good job of it, that's for sure. But I think she's just a young woman who has no clue how incredibly lacking she is when it comes to cooking."

"I would not dismiss the situation quite so quickly, Mrs. Montgomery. A good operative often exudes innocence and ignorance. I am certain she is a competitor of yours, or, if nothing else, making every attempt to piggyback off your success. I trust you've come up with a strategy to counter her attacks?"

Words that left me dumbfounded for a moment. "Well, Spencer, let's just say 'I'm working on it.' I've got a plan, but I haven't quite figured out all the details yet."

"Please let me know if I can assist you in any way," came his response.

"Thank you, Spencer," I said, wondering what such assistance might entail.

Given what I believed to be his history.

"I also trust that your investigation into our neighborhood murder is proceeding well," he went on.

"I'm working on that, too, Spencer. I have to admit, it's a very complicated, convoluted mystery."

"Ah, something that makes you the perfect person to solve it, given your ability to construct complex plotlines in your own books. My confidence in you remains undaunted."

"Thank you, Spencer, I appreciate it. I only wish Remy felt the same way. It would be a lot easier if I could discuss the case with him."

"Unfortunately, sometimes we don't get the collaboration we desire. Regardless, it's important to soldier on, and Detective Reagan hardly needs to be aware of your more . . . *ahem* . . . clandestine investigative activities."

Much like Spencer's "clandestine activities" when he worked for the CIA? Or so I believed.

"Well, so far, I've managed to keep him out of the loop," I added.

Though the words "barely avoid him" were probably a lot more accurate.

"I have no doubt that you'll be able to continue. And should it become necessary, we can scrub your information as a source of any evidence that you might uncover and deem necessary to send him. So he will not be able to trace it back to you. In the meantime, I had better let you get back to your work, Mrs. Montgomery. I will meet you and young Parker tomorrow morning."

After that, we made some quick arrangements and said our goodbyes. Then I got back into the zone with my writing and returned to Blaze's world. By now, Blaze and her beau, Detective Angus Steele were homing in on a large cache of even larger diamonds:

"Blaze flipped her copper-colored hair over her shoulder and used her cooking tweezers to pick the vintage lock of the antique lockbox. A lockbox that belonged to Pennington, the chef who was Chloe's boss and, as Blaze had deduced, the head of the smuggling operation.

Angus' eyebrows shot up his forehead. 'Where on earth did you learn to do that?'

'Oh, you know . . . One acquires talents here and there,' she said with a sly smile, seconds before she felt the click of the lock as it released. Then she pulled the heavy lid of the lockbox open. And there, under a pile of packing paper, she located what she'd been hoping to find—a square of blue velvet, cinched and tied at the top with a golden cord.

At once, her heart started to pound, since she knew that Pennington and his men weren't far away. So she lifted the little makeshift pouch and set it firmly on the desktop.

'Now, let's see what we've got,' she told Angus.

'We'd better hurry,' he stressed as she quickly unfastened the cord and let the edges of the velvet drop away. Revealing an entire pile of bright, brilliant diamonds.

Of course, the sight of all those diamonds made her gasp.

That was, until she held one of the four-carat stones up to the light. Then she squinted her green eyes and stared at the gem. She put it back on the velvet cloth and picked up another one, giving it the same examination. By the time she'd looked at the fourth one, she was shaking her head.

'They're fakes,' she announced to Angus.

His mouth fell open wide. 'Are you positive? How do you know they're not real?'

She pulled the jeweler's loupe from her pocket to confirm what she had suspected. And sure enough, she'd been right.

'Because they're perfect,' came her instant answer. 'Too perfect. Not a single inclusion or imperfection in any of these stones. It's extremely rare

for gems this size to be this perfect, and yet every single one of these is perfect.'

'That doesn't make sense,' he told her as they quickly put the pouch back exactly as they'd found it. They shut the lid of the box, refastened the lock, and then got out of there.

'But why would anyone want to deal in fake gems?' Angus asked after they were safely outside and back in his Ferrari.

'It's got me stumped,' Blaze agreed with a shake of her head. 'It seems like a very risky move, considering they're dealing with other crooks who wouldn't be too happy to find out they've received phony gems. In other words, they wouldn't like being cheated out of the real thing.'

Angus skillfully maneuvered the Ferrari around the corner. 'It's a funny thing about crooks. They'll lie and steal and cheat all day long. But if someone does the same to them, well . . .'

'It can be very, very dangerous,' Blaze added. 'Not to mention, deadly.'"

Words that made me sit back in my desk chair and think. Sure, I was well aware that I'd just written those very words myself. And that I'd just let my real life cross over into my fiction.

Regardless, it brought up a very good question. Maybe Dex had purposely given Olivia fake jewels. Or maybe they started out as the real deal, before he secretly replaced them with phony replicas. No doubt, if Olivia had found out, it could certainly be a motive for murder where she was concerned.

Then again, maybe the gems had started out as fakes. And maybe Dex had figured it out and threatened to expose the jeweler himself, Mr. Gage Flause. So how exactly would a man running a shady operation respond to being threatened?

Not well, I was sure.

Meaning, there might be a lot more going on at that jewelry store than simply the sale of sparkly stones.

Chapter Twenty

Parker was surprisingly chatty the next morning as I drove the Continental to Houston's famous, historic Glenwood Cemetery. Of course, he couldn't stop talking about Mindie's mind-boggling video from the night before.

So I told him about my idea of making videos to counter her Titanic-level kitchen disasters.

"Great plan, Mom. But I think I should be the one in the videos. Making the recipes. Since I'm even younger than Mindie."

An idea that surprised me, considering that Parker had never really shown that much interest in cooking. At least not like his sister had.

"Parker, that sounds wonderful," I said as we turned into the cemetery, entering from Washington Avenue and driving past the brick-pillared gate.

"And maybe I could bring a friend."

To which I laughed, now having a better understanding of why he had a sudden desire to cook. "I think it would be great if Cassidy joined you."

Parker grinned at me. "Cool, Mom. I'll text her right now."

And so he did. Then after a little back-and-forth, she not only said yes, but apparently, she was pretty enthusiastic about the whole idea. Much like Parker seemed to be pretty enthusiastic about her. Not to mention, the prospect of having cookies on hand to eat.

"We should probably have Cassidy come over first so I can give you both some basic instructions," I suggested while I drove a little way into the cemetery and then pulled over to trade places with him.

"No worries, Mom," he told me, as we opened our doors. "Cassidy bakes cookies all the time. She's practically an expert at it. For real. Not like this Mindie person."

"She sounds like a terrific young woman."

"You didn't think I'd go for a girl who couldn't cook, did you?"

I gave him the side-eye before I got out of the car. Okay, this was probably supposed to be one of those teaching moments, whereby I told him that he needed to be independent and learn how to bake his own cookies. But for the life of me, I could hardly fault the guy. After all, he'd grown up with a mom and a big sister who both loved to cook. So I guess it only made sense that he'd want a girlfriend who knew her way around the kitchen, too.

Besides, I couldn't help but be excited about the mere prospect of a daughter-in-law who might join me when it came to making holiday meals. Though, yes, I was well aware that it was way, way, *way* too soon for me to even be thinking such things. Given that Parker and Cassidy hadn't even gone out on one date yet.

But a girl can hope, can't she?

I smiled at my son as he jumped into the driver's seat, just as I spotted Spencer Poe's black and completely nondescript SUV coming from the other direction. Which meant he'd already spent some time at the cemetery this morning. A realization that suddenly made me tense. Was it possible that he'd been looking the place over for personal reasons, namely, to find a spot for his own interment one day? Could it be that he was having some serious health issues, something he wouldn't likely share with us? As far as I knew, Spencer didn't have any relatives nearby. None that he'd ever spoken of anyway. I knew he'd been close to Charlie, like a father to a son, which meant Parker and I were probably the closest thing he had to family. Though who knew for sure.

Spencer parked his own vehicle and then joined us at ours.

"Why don't you take the front seat?" I suggested to him after we'd said our hellos.

At first, surprise registered on his face. "Are you sure, Mrs. Montgomery? While I'm here to assist, I certainly don't want to impose on your plans."

But I quickly reassured him with, "If Charlie were looking down on us right now, I think he would appreciate your helping Parker learn to drive his car."

"As you wish, Mrs. Montgomery," Spencer said with a respectful nod before I eased into the back seat, and he took his place in the front. "The Colonel truly cherished this vehicle," he murmured, glancing around. "I must say, sitting here really takes me back."

"Me, too," I said aloud. "Every time I'm in the car."

"Mom is going to let me take it to prom," Parker informed our neighbor.

Funny, but I still didn't remember *actually* granting him that permission.

"Let's see how you do today," I told him in my best *parental* tone, knowing full well that he would do just fine.

And in reality, I guess we all knew that I'd never deny him the opportunity to drive the Continental on such a special night. Without a doubt, Charlie would have wanted him to take it, and for that matter, Parker already had plenty of experience when it came to driving.

Spencer glanced at the dashboard. "Okay, son, I believe you'll find the steering to be a bit stiffer than what you are accustomed to. So you'll have to use a little more muscle to turn the wheel. And the brakes won't feel like what you're used to, either. So, why don't you put it in gear and give it a try."

"Got it," Parker said with a huge grin, probably since he'd been waiting for this day for a long time.

Then without hesitation, he did as Spencer instructed him, and a few minutes later, he was driving us slowly around the various paved lanes of the Glenwood.

"This does feel different," Parker commented.

"You're doing fine, son," Spencer reassured him. "Just continue on. You're getting the hang of things."

"I like driving Dad's old car." Parker's voice took on a definite lilt. "It feels like I'm *really* driving. Instead of just barely turning the wheel and barely pressing the gas."

"You look a lot like your father did when he was behind the wheel," Spencer told him. "He would be so proud of you, son."

Words that almost made Parker choke up. "Thanks, Mr. Poe."

"Watch your steering, though," Spencer instructed him. "This is a rear-wheel drive vehicle. So it's like the car is being pushed by the rear wheels. Rather than being pulled by the front wheels."

"Got it," Parker said with a nod.

Then he turned onto another of the little lanes and stepped on the accelerator, clearly loving the feel of driving the classic, luxury car. He drove slowly at first and then sped up a little. Up and down the brick-lined lanes we went, all around the huge cemetery. Amazingly, it turned out to be the perfect place for my son to practice driving his dad's old car, since all those curvy, little lanes meant lots of steering. From what I could tell, Parker was becoming more and more comfortable with the Continental by the minute. Not to mention, I was becoming more and more comfortable with him driving it.

And with Spencer Poe giving him sound instructions, I simply leaned back and took in the sights of the beautiful, parklike cemetery. I know those aren't words that people usually use to describe a graveyard, but the Glenwood is called Houston's garden cemetery for a reason. Once upon a time, the cemetery actually did double duty as the town's park, and it was the place to take your horse and buggy for an outing. To see and be seen.

The Glenwood sprawls over eighty-eight acres of woodlands and gardens that are home to over thirty different kinds of trees. Including a gigantic Live Oak named "The Cemetery Tree," whose low branches resemble long arms that reach out past rows and rows of headstones. As though in protection of those who have passed on. On top of that, there were statues and headstones that rival things found in art museums. Plus there was a gazebo with a wrought-iron, domed roof that could only be described as, well . . . romantic-looking.

Yet despite all that, I couldn't help but wonder why Charlie might have indicated the Glenwood Cemetery on his treasure map.

If that was actually what he had indicated. Because I still wondered if Parker had interpreted Charlie's notes accurately. But if he had, then what was Charlie's reason for wanting to come here? Was there something he had hoped to find? And if so, would I be able to spot whatever he might have been looking for?

Since I really had no idea where to start, the best I could do was hope that something might stand out to me. And sure enough, before long, something did. Especially after Parker started to relax behind the wheel and picked up a little more speed. And as we went slightly faster around the cemetery, I began to notice circular medallions that were either attached to headstones or on a little stand next to them. In fact, it seemed that there were several graves with such markers. So what in the world were they?

I leaned forward and caught my son's attention. "Parker, would you mind pulling over for a minute?"

"Sure, Mom. I think I've finally got a feel for these brakes."

And so he slowed down and turned the wheel to maneuver the car to the side of the lane. Perfectly.

"What is it, Mrs. Montgomery?" Spencer Poe asked as he glanced at me. "Are you not feeling well?"

"Oh, no, nothing like that. I just want to take a closer look at something. I'll be right back," I told them as Spencer opened the door and held the seat to let me out from the rear.

Then I walked through the grass, pungent with a fresh-cut smell, and stepped over an inches-tall, stone perimeter fence that had been placed around a cluster of four headstones. I moved carefully to the largest of the stones, one that had been carved to look almost scroll-like. The name on the intricate headstone read "Margaret Houston." A name I recognized. "Maggie," as I'd heard she'd been called during her life. She was the daughter of Sam Houston, the General who had led the Texians at the famous Battle of San Jacinto, or Texas' version of a revolutionary war. He was also the first elected president of the newly formed Republic of Texas.

And now, here was his daughter's grave, adorned with the same metal medallion as other graves. I looked closer and noticed the Texas star shining in the center, with words encircling the piece that read "Daughters of the Republic of Texas."

At once, my interest was piqued. This was the second time in so many days that I'd heard the name of that group. Could this be the clue that Charlie had been looking for, somehow or another? But if that were the case, I had to say, it brought up far more questions than it answered.

I returned to the car to find puzzled glances from both Parker and Spencer Poe.

"Did you find anything interesting, Mrs. Montgomery?" my neighbor asked.

I slipped into the back seat again. "Maggie Houston's grave."

Spencer got back in and shut the door. "Ah, yes. The daughter of Sam Houston who commanded the Texas army at the Battle of San Jacinto, and the man for whom the city of Houston is named."

My seventeen-year-old chauffeur nodded and drove the Continental into the lane again. "I learned all about it in my Texas history class. It happened in eighteen-thirty-six. The battle lasted eighteen minutes and Texas won independence. And it happened not far from here."

"Very good," Spencer Poe said with an approving nod. "Of course, there were a number of battles along the way, before and after Texas signed its own Declaration of Independence. The Battle of the Alamo being chief among them. But their quest for freedom culminated in that final battle, whereby Sam Houston and the underdog Texas army defeated the huge Mexican army led by General Santa Anna. After that, Texas became its own country, the Republic of Texas. And it remained so until eighteen-forty-five, when it was annexed into the United States."

"And then it became the twenty-eighth state," Parker added. "Wow, Mr. Poe, you really know your Texas history."

For once, Spencer smiled. "As do you, young Mr. Montgomery. Which means you are probably familiar with the San Jacinto Monument, commemorating the battlefield."

Parker gave him a knowing nod. "Oh, yeah. My class took field trips there every year."

"An excellent place to take young people," Spencer commented. "Of course, the Daughters of the Republic of Texas were instrumental in seeing that monument built."

"And it's twelve feet taller than the Washington Monument," I said, putting in my two cents.

"Correct," Parker and Spencer Poe both said at the same time, as though I were a student hearing all this for the first time.

I glanced around, feeling suddenly in awe. "You know, this whole cemetery is just loaded with history. Even more than you could find in a museum."

"It most certainly is," my neighbor agreed.

Parker turned onto another lane, one that we'd been on before. "Speaking of history, Mom, I'm starving."

Okay, I'm not exactly sure how those two subjects were even remotely related, except that Parker managed to equate everything and anything with food.

I couldn't help but laugh. "What do you think, Spencer? Is Parker officially 'checked out' when it comes to driving Charlie's old car?"

"I believe he has passed with flying colors," Spencer informed me as we neared his parked SUV. "And if you'll excuse me, I must be on my way as well. Since I do have a meeting to attend."

So Parker pulled over across from Spencer Poe's vehicle.

"Are you sure you won't join us for lunch?" I asked.

"That's very kind of you to invite me, Mrs. Montgomery. Perhaps another time." He stepped out of the car and held the seat forward, so I could get out from the rear.

"Well, thank you for your help, Spencer," I told him as I headed to the driver's side of the car, to take over from my son.

Parker slid out from behind the wheel and stood up. "Yeah, thank you for teaching me how to drive Dad's old car, Mr. Poe," he said with manners that made me proud.

To top it off, he even walked over to Spencer and held out his hand to shake. Something that *really* would have made Charlie proud!

Spencer took his hand and completed the handshake, beaming at Parker. "You're becoming quite a young man," he told my son with a smile.

Then after we said our goodbyes, I got behind the wheel again while Parker slid into the passenger side. I turned the Continental around and headed for the entrance.

"That was cool, Mom. I can see why Dad loved this car so much," Parker said, sounding much more solemn than usual. "But I wish I knew what Dad was looking for out here."

"I'm afraid we didn't get time to investigate."

"And we didn't see any of the 'Notably Deterred'," he said, pulling out his phone.

"Notably Deterred?" I repeated. "Maybe you mean 'Notably *Interred*.' Like Howard Hughes and Gene Tierney."

"Yeah, that's it. I've got a map on my phone. There's a few of those 'Notably Interred' on our way out. Let's stop and look at them. Quick."

"'Quick' is the word," I told him, mentally calculating to make sure we had enough time to eat lunch and then make it to the jewelry store on time for our appointment with Gage Flause.

"I already packed my stuff to look at the jewels at that store," Parker told me. "So we don't have to go back home."

"Good move," I said with a nod. "It'll give us a little more time."

And with that, we stopped and looked over a few gravesites. While they were all works of art in their own way, the one that stood out to me the most was just in front of a beautifully carved stone balustrade that flanked a large center stone on either side. But the simple headstone centered directly below read "Mary Jane Harris Brisco," and showed that she had lived from 1819 to 1903. But this time I saw a different medallion just above the headstone, one with the words "Citizen of the Republic of Texas" encircling it.

"Republic of Texas," I murmured aloud. "*ROT*."

"Yeah, Mom. Like on Dad's map. I think Dad was looking into Texas history," Parker said while he snapped a few photos with his phone.

"It's possible," I replied, feeling oddly spellbound by the surroundings. "I know your dad was a history buff, but he didn't mention that he'd been researching anything specific."

"He didn't say anything to me, either," Parker added with a frown.

Which meant that Charlie had either been keeping things hush-hush, or he hadn't been looking into Texas history at all. Something that would probably always be a mystery to us.

Parker and I strolled quietly back to the Continental. Then, as we drove through the gate and left the Glenwood, Parker rolled down his window and took a quick video of the remaining few yards of the cemetery. After that, he stayed surprisingly quiet the rest of the way back to Abbott Cove, until we entered the drive-through lane of Abbott's Big Burgers about forty minutes later. As usual, he ordered two triple-burgers and two orders of onion rings and a large chocolate shake. I opted for a meal about a fourth that size. And since it was such a beautiful day—and the temperatures hadn't quite reached something that resembled the surface of the sun—we opted to take the food to our favorite park.

I could hear Parker's stomach growling as I turned onto the tree-lined street of the park and found an empty picnic table. I had barely parked the Continental when Parker grabbed the bags of food and bounded out of the car. His fluidity of motion amazed me, as he simultaneously unwrapped his first burger, checked his cellphone and sat down on the cement seat of the picnic table. Without looking up, he pushed the bag holding my food to my side of the table. Then he typed into his phone while he devoured the first half of his first burger. He paused only long enough to take a big slurp of his chocolate shake.

Of course, I'd made it a rule that he couldn't use a cell phone during meals. But something seemed different today. Like he was on a mission and looking up something important.

He finally glanced up at me. "Listen to this, Mom. This is major. Remember that last grave we saw?"

I bit into my own burger. "Mary Harris Briscoe?"

"Yup, Mom. Her husband was one of the signers of the Texas Declaration of Independence. Andrew Briscoe. He also fought at the Battle of San Jacinto." He turned his phone so I could read what he'd pulled up.

I nodded, impressed, and read more. "And apparently Mary was also one of the founders of the Daughters of the Republic of Texas. In fact, the group was started in her own living room. Or probably, the drawing room, as I believe it was called in those days." I handed Parker's phone back to him.

He downed a few more onion rings and pulled up another Texas historical website. "You know, Mom, I'm looking at a list of the soldiers who fought at the Battle of San Jacinto. Not only was that Briscoe guy there, but there were also guys with the last name 'Montgomery.'"

I took a bite of my burger and grabbed a couple of fries. "That's interesting. I wonder if any of them are related to your dad's side of the family. Which would make them your ancestors, too."

Parker sat up straight. "Cool . . . so I might be related to someone who founded Texas."

I smiled and took a sip of my iced tea. "Yup, that would be cool, all right."

"I wonder if that's what Dad was trying to find out. At the Glenwood."

"Could be."

If he was actually trying to find something at the cemetery, like a clue that might possibly lead to some treasure. Then again, maybe Charlie was simply trying to track down his own ancestry and see if there was a connection to Texas' battle for independence. But that wouldn't explain the "treasure map" and the gold coins we'd found in the storage unit where he'd kept his vintage car. Even now, I had to wonder why he'd kept me in the dark about it. Though it was possible he'd planned to tell me but didn't get the chance. That, or he might have wanted to keep me in the dark for my own protection, especially if there was a really large, valuable treasure involved. Meaning, the less I knew, the safer I would be. The only problem was, now I didn't know much of anything.

Regardless, it was something I'd have to think about later. Because, at the moment, I had other things to worry about. Like our upcoming visit to Flause Jewelers.

I wiped ketchup from my mouth. "Why don't we talk about a game plan for our trip to the jewelry store. Since we're going in under the guise of you doing a paper for your class."

Parker nodded and finished the last bite of his lunch. "You got it, Mom. I'll be on the lookout for any more fake jewels."

"But remember, that's all I want you to do. Just check out the authenticity of the gems and that's it. Nothing more. No other investigating. Or asking Mr. Gage any questions unless it's about the gems he lets you look at."

Parker grinned. "Mum's the word, Mom. But let's have a signal. So I can let you know if a gem is real or not."

"Sounds like a plan to me."

"Okay, here's the signal," he told me, holding his hand over the table with his fingers bent. Then he moved his hand back and forth while his grin never dipped.

"Huh? Parker, what is that?"

"Don't you get it, Mom? It's a rake."

I crinkled my brow. "A rake?"

"Yeah, it rhymes with 'fake.'"

I shook my head and tried not to laugh. "No, kiddo, that's way too complicated. If a stone is fake, simply touch your right forefinger to your left thumb. Like it's a nervous gesture or something. Then if a stone is real, put your hand to your heart."

"Okay, Mom, that is pretty smart," he said as he practiced both gestures for me to see.

And while I watched, I had a hard time believing what I was about to do. Because here I was, once again, allowing my own son to help me with a murder investigation. An investigation that I wasn't even supposed to be involved in myself. It didn't exactly put me in "Mother of the Year" territory. Especially considering we'd just spent the morning cruising through a cemetery. I envisioned him telling his therapist all about it someday.

On the other hand, I also envisioned him turning out to be a lot like his father. A man full of adventure and life, who took things in stride no matter what was thrown at him. Though I hoped and prayed that nothing horrific would be tossed our way during our time at the jewelry store. The place where Olivia had acquired her vast collection of jewelry, whether the stuff was real or fake before it went out the door. But it was also the place where Deirdre had had her dagger-like scissors set with a wide variety of stones.

Scissors that had been used to stab Dex Degill in the back.

And now, as I drove us to the store and parked the Continental in the second row of the surprisingly large lot, I was acutely aware that Flause Jewelry Store seemed to be a very big, common denominator in this case.

Had that connection somehow gotten Dex Degill killed?

And as I stood before the door of the glass storefront, with Parker bringing up the rear, I steeled myself, ready to walk in, acting so cool that cucumbers would shrivel in comparison. Because I was determined to be so cunning and crafty in my comments and subtle questions that no one would ever know they'd just given me any vital information.

Exactly like my main character Blaze would have done.

Or at least, that was my plan anyway.

But you know what they say about best laid plans . . .

Chapter Twenty-one

The very second I walked into Flause Jewelry Store, I was under a full-blown assault. An assault on my senses, that is. The place was nothing like I ever could've imagined, and I have to admit, it completely caught me off guard. And I suddenly realized that it had been a long, *long* time since I'd been in a jewelry store. Though this place was like nothing I'd ever seen before.

Or *smelled* before, for that matter.

Because the first thing that hit me was the overwhelming scent of roses, so strong that it nearly bowled me over. Probably because there were tons of the long-stemmed beauties everywhere—bunches in vases and one or two individual roses placed casually on each counter. Not only that, but there were clusters of rose petals on the floor in a few specific spots.

Once I got past the overabundance of flowers, I keyed in on the rest of the décor, which could only be described as over-the-top romantic. Maroon, velour wallpaper and white wainscotting. White, molded roses and multifaceted crystals in huge chandeliers. And plenty of artful, black-and-white photos of ecstatic women showing off huge diamond engagement rings. On top of that, the store lights were kept low, like an upscale restaurant, with pinpoint halogen lighting aimed directly onto the display cases themselves, making the gems shine like stars in the night sky. In fact, the whole place seemed to be ablaze with all those dazzling stones.

Then there was the mostly female crowd who, judging by the dreamy looks on their faces, appeared to be completely hypnotized by it all. Most of the salesclerks could have doubled as models, over half of which were men wearing tuxedos. And while those devastatingly handsome, square-jawed men waited on the female customers, plenty of pretty female clerks appeared to be waiting on the few men who had bravely ventured in.

I had barely managed to process it all when I spotted a large bear of a man, waving to me from behind a very long glass display case. His dark hair was slicked back and his beard neatly trimmed. He had an earring dangling from one ear, and he was wearing a quilted, maroon smoking jacket with a shawl collar. In my mind, he was doing an excellent imitation of Blackbeard.

He held out a large, well-manicured hand to shake mine. "You must be Maddie," he oozed. "So nice to meet you, sweetheart. I'm Gage. Gage Flause. So glad Olivia set you up to come over today. Because I've got lots of jewelry for you to see. A beautiful woman like you should be dripping with all kinds of sparkly gems. Let's see if I can't help you out with that."

Parker held out his hand to shake, too. "I'm her son, Parker."

"Glad to know you, kid," Gage replied, hardly even acknowledging him.

"Mrs. Degill set this up for me today. So I can research a paper for school," Parker explained.

"Sure, sure, kid. Whatever you need. Look around while I get your mom set up with something as gorgeous as she is. But first, Maddie, get a load of what's going on over there," he said as he pointed to a scene at another counter.

I turned to see a stunning, blonde woman and an equally stunning, dark-haired man. They were facing each other with arms extended and hands clasped. All the while, they stared deeply into each other's eyes, their faces etched with emotion.

"Just watch, Maddie," Gage whispered. "It's gonna happen, I guarantee it."

And before I knew it, the young man dropped to one knee, still holding one of the young woman's hands. Her other hand went straight to her mouth, as though caught completely by surprise. She flipped her golden hair behind her shoulders, letting the gathering crowd in on the action.

By now, the young man was fighting back tears. "Aurora, my love, you are the most beautiful woman I have ever met. Inside and out. Your beauty only surpasses your charm, your grace, and your intelligence. I've known from the minute I met you that I wanted to marry you. You give my life meaning, and you make me complete. Aurora, will you make me the happiest man in the world? Will you marry me?"

Right at that moment, it seemed that everyone in the store sucked in a deep breath and held it. I swear, I could almost hear the seconds ticking by.

At long last, a teary-eyed Aurora gushed, "Oh, Jeremy, my answer is yes! Yes, I will marry you!"

"Say it again, Aurora. I want to hear those words *again*."

"Yes, Jeremey! I will marry you. And I'm sure you've picked out a ring to seal the deal."

"Oh, I have, my darling. It cost me three months' salary, and I was offered a layaway plan but, of course, I turned that down. Since I've been saving money for this moment for a while now. But price is of no concern, because I'm getting the deal of a lifetime when I get you for a bride. You make me so happy!"

Then Jeremy pulled a red, velvet box from his pocket and very slowly lifted the lid, holding it up so the huge diamond inside shone like a nightlight, especially since one of those pinpoint halogen lights in the ceiling seemed to be aimed directly at it. Jeremy held his position for a good thirty seconds, giving everyone around him a chance to glance at that big, honkin' stone.

With a flourish, he plucked the ring from the box and gently slid it onto Aurora's awaiting ring finger, which was also strategically placed under one of the lights.

Tears flowed freely from Aurora's eyes now, and she appeared to be completely overwhelmed. Jeremy jumped up and grabbed her by her waist, lifting her up and twirling her around and around.

Aurora laughed and cried. "Oh, Jeremy, I love you! I love you so much!"

"I love you, too, my darling," came Jeremy's reply. "Now and forever!"

I glanced at the crowd of women standing around with tears rolling down their cheeks. Most were young, though some were middle-aged, and then there were a few who were even older. Every one of them congratulated the happy couple, and there were hugs all around.

Despite myself, I immediately thought of the night when Charlie had proposed to me. The moon had been full, and it lit the way as we strolled to the end of an ocean pier overlooking the Gulf of America, just the two of us. Then he got down on one knee and presented me with a diamond ring that absolutely shimmered in the moonlight. It was as magical as any proposal could ever be. And now, as the memory flooded my brain, I realized I had a tear or two of my own rolling down my cheeks. I couldn't believe how raw and flustered I felt all of a sudden.

Gage leaned over and whispered in my ear, "I don't see a wedding ring on your finger, Maddie. Do you ever think about getting married? Is there any happier moment than getting engaged?"

"No, not many . . . I *was* married," I managed to murmur while a whole range of emotions seemed to be holding some kind of sporting event inside my head. "I'm a widow . . ."

"Oh, sweetie, you've been through so much, and you deserve to wear a ring of your own. One that celebrates you and your beauty. Inside and out. I've got just the thing. A London Blue topaz, surrounded by diamonds. Here, Maddie, try this ring on for size. See what it feels like to wear something like this."

Then before I could respond, he slowly slipped the huge, teal-blue ring on my finger. A very practiced move, no doubt. But just the sensation of a man slipping a ring on my finger made my stomach flutter. And the sight of that huge ring on my hand made me dizzy.

"Give it a minute," Gage said softly. "Let the idea sink in. You deserve to have something so elegant, right, Maddie?"

As though I were in a trance, I responded with a barely audible, "Right . . ."

From the corner of my eye, I spotted Parker talking to a beautiful salesgirl with long, red hair, and she appeared to be showing him some amethyst rings.

"So does your girlfriend like the color purple?" she asked my son, ever-so-innocently.

"It's her birthstone. She was born in February. Two days before Valentine's Day."

The salesgirl sighed. "How romantic! Sounds like she's a keeper. Have you thought about getting engaged? You don't want to lose her to some other guy."

Parker smiled. "You know, you're right. Maybe I should propose. Like that Jeremy guy just did."

"Then let me show you some engagement rings, too."

"Sounds good," my son said with great enthusiasm. "An amethyst for now and a diamond for later. When I ask her to marry me. I'll need stuff that's nice. And cheap. But not too cheap."

My jaw practically hit the top of the glass counter. Wait a minute . . . Parker? Getting married? If I thought I was dizzy before, well, it didn't even compare to how I felt right at that moment. Parker wasn't even out of high school. And while I was sure Cassidy was a lovely girl, he hadn't even been on a date with her yet. And here he was, already talking marriage?

Through my haze, I watched as he grinned at the salesgirl. "You don't mind if I look at these rings with my stuff here, do you?"

And that's when I noticed the few pieces of equipment he had sitting on the counter, and I knew exactly what he was doing. At least, I *hoped* I knew what he was doing. Because I guessed he was examining a whole bunch of gems under the guise of getting engaged. Though Gage had already told him he could look at whatever he wanted, I suspected he was using his best subterfuge to "investigate," as it were.

Either way, I decided that now might also be a good time for me to intervene. Especially when I heard my son say, "You know, maybe you should show me some nicer rings, too. I'm sure I can get a part-time job to pay for it."

"I think that's a wonderful idea," the salesgirl agreed, absolutely beaming at him. "I've got just the thing."

I started to remove the London Blue topaz from my finger and return it to Gage when he took my hand. "Gorgeous, isn't it?"

"Uh-huh," was the best I could manage as I stared at that blue stone that seemed to have a life of its own under the halogen lighting.

"Thinking about taking it home, sweetie?" came Gage's voice into the haze in my head.

Well, I hadn't been, at least not until that very second. But now that he mentioned it, maybe the ring did need a good home. Still, such a ring couldn't possibly be in my budget.

Gage gazed into my eyes, as though he were reading my mind. "This one is on sale today for a mere three-hundred dollars," he murmured, saying the magic words. "It's a steal, you might say. Keep that on for a minute for me, would'ya sweetie? I've got to take care of something first. I'll be right back. In the meantime, you just stand there and look beautiful with that ring that brings out the blue in your eyes."

And with that, he walked to the back corner of the room where the newly engaged couple stood. The one who had just put on quite a show in the middle of the store.

So, yes, I left the ring on. And I kept on staring at it, completely mesmerized. And discombobulated. Even after Parker waved and pointed to an amethyst ring in front of him after the salesgirl had turned her back. Then he quickly touched his right forefinger to his left thumb, a gesture that no more registered with me than if he'd been using American sign language.

And my comprehension didn't improve one bit even after he waved his arms and repeated the gesture. Mostly because my brain was a little busy at the moment, thank you very much. What with this gigantic ring on my finger, radiating the most exquisite blue light I'd ever seen. And me trying to decide if I had an extra three-hundred dollars in my budget, while the memory of Charlie's proposal played over and over in my mind, and the scent of roses lulled me into a state of pure romantic bliss. Though the effect was diminished a smidge when I noticed the roses were all made from silk, which essentially meant the scent had come from a can.

Parker waved again, rolled his eyes and started to make a clawlike gesture with his hand. After a few seconds of this, the right gears in my brain started to turn and things finally clicked.

Rake! Which rhymed with fake! Meaning, he'd found a fake stone.

"I think I'll take a picture of this one," he said cheerfully when the salesclerk returned her attention to him.

"You've got good taste," she cooed. "I'm sure your girlfriend would love it! I can probably get you a good deal if you'd like to take it with you today."

"I'll think about it," my son said. "But first, I've gotta go see what ring my mom is looking at over there."

He grinned at her before he joined me. "You okay, Mom? You don't look so good."

"Yeah. I'm okay . . ." I managed to say, having trouble uttering more than one syllable at a time.

"Let me look at the ring you've got on," he said, raising an eyebrow.

Whereby I pulled it off and let him do his stuff. Counting the seconds before I could return that stunning ring to the place where it belonged. Namely, on my finger.

And as I watched Parker, I overheard the conversation between Gage and the newly engaged couple. Funny, but I fully expected to hear all the usual niceties between this pair who were about to take a very big step and the man who had sold them her ring.

"Can you be back at three today?" Gage said in a very businesslike tone. "I've got a young couple coming in at three-thirty. So I want you to do your proposal routine again while they're here. And I'd like a repeat of what you did today. It was terrific. Loved the tears, Lydia."

The blonde woman absolutely beamed. "Thanks, I've been practicing."

Lydia? I thought her name was Aurora. À la Sleeping Beauty.

Gage smiled. "Just look at all those people buying rings right now. Every one of my salespeople has their hands full. You two really hooked 'em in."

"Remember, Uncle Gage," said the dark-haired guy. "You owe us an extra two-hundred dollars for every diamond ring you sell after one of our performances."

Once again, things didn't click with me at first. But when I managed to put two and two together, I was pretty floored. So Gage was using shills to put on quite a show, performing highly emotional wedding proposals.

Proposals that were completely fake.

But wow, oh, wow, were they ever good for sales.

And that's when I suddenly broke out of my trance, becoming acutely aware that everything in the store was designed to manipulate a woman's emotions. From the décor to the roses to the lighting. And even the way Gage had slipped that ring on my finger. It was all designed to influence people to part with their hard-earned cash.

Now I just needed to know if the gems in his store were as phony as everything else.

Parker handed the ring back to me and raised an eyebrow.

I slid it back on my finger, where it seemed oddly at home. "I hope you're not going to do the raking thing again," I told my son. "Because I really like this ring."

"Okay, Mom. But let's just say, if you wanted to work in your garden, you would want to wear this."

"Oh, no, not this one, too?" I asked, amazed at how heartbroken I felt.

"Yup, Mom. It's nice. But it's not real."

I sighed, ready to pull the ring off and say goodbye to it once and for all. While three-hundred dollars would have been a major bargain for a real ring, three-hundred dollars for a fake would have been a complete rip-off.

"Sorry, Mom," Parker said, right before he was interrupted by another voice.

"Maddie, what are you doing here?" demanded a decidedly masculine voice.

One that I recognized.

Remy.

Fancy meeting him here. I glanced up and to my left and into eyes that were almost as blue as the ring I was about to pull from my finger. Naturally, I was suspicious that Olivia had set up this setup, so to speak. It was probably just another one of her manipulative stunts.

While I stood there speechless, Parker immediately piped up with, "I'm here getting information for a paper. For my Earth Science class."

"That's nice, Parker," Remy said coolly. "But I believe I'd like your mother to answer the question."

Yet before I could utter a word, Gage immediately joined us, undoubtedly smelling a sale. "And who's this now? The beau? Your girlfriend has her eye on this beautiful ring, and I'm sure you'd make her a very happy woman by buying it for her. Only three-hundred dollars today. Doesn't she look beautiful in that ring?"

"She looks very beautiful," Remy said in a throaty voice.

"Perhaps I might show you something in a diamond engagement ring instead?" Gage suggested, not missing a beat.

Shock flared in Remy's eyes for but a second or two. "Could you give us a moment? Because I need to talk to her."

"There's no need for you to go anywhere," I said directly to Gage. "Because I'm not his girlfriend. Yes, I went out with him, and silly me, I mistook all his cuddling and compliments and our romantic dates to mean there was something between us. But then he just dumped me or ghosted me or whatever the kids are calling it these days. With no explanation and no actual goodbye. While I don't care to ever see him again in my life, I am, however, thinking about buying this ring. Or maybe I should look at one of your big, giant diamond rings instead. Since, who knows, I might be getting engaged one of these days. Just not to this man."

Remy lowered his lids and looked at me through squinted eyes. It didn't help that the gesture made him look ruggedly handsome.

"Okay, Maddie, I deserve that. Can we talk for a minute?"

"Sorry, but as you can see, I am busy, thank you."

Parker gathered up his equipment and nodded to the other side of the store. "I'll be right over there if you need me, Mom." Then he was off to look at more gems.

"And I'll be right over there, sweetie," Gage told me as he pointed to the cash register on a side counter. "Why don't you wear that ring while you make up your mind."

Remy's dark brows dipped across his forehead. "Okay, Maddie, I won't keep you long. You're not really getting engaged, are you? I mean, we haven't talked for a few days, and now you're out ring shopping?"

I squinted at him myself. "It's a free country and I'm a free woman. I can go ring shopping any time I like," I informed him in a staccato beat, barely a step away from spouting off that age-old adage: "You're not the boss of me." Instead I went with, "How did you even know I was at this store?"

"I saw your car out front. And I wondered what you were doing here."

"Oh, really . . ." I seethed. "Maybe you should tell me what *you're* doing here. Are you buying a ring for your new girlfriend, Olivia? According to her, you're quite an item."

But the very minute I let the words come tumbling out, I could hardly believe I'd said them. When had I reverted back to being a teenager again? In fact, even when I was a teenager, I hadn't gone around spouting off such things.

I caught the momentary flinch in his eyes. "I'm working a case."

"In this store, huh?" I said as nonchalantly as I could manage. "How convenient."

"Funny, but you don't seem all that surprised by it. So now it's your turn. If I didn't know better, I'd say you're here for the same reason that I am. You're investigating, aren't you? Maddie, I warned you about that. You're a private citizen. You're not supposed to stick your nose into police business. It's considered 'Obstruction of Justice.'"

That's when I just stared at the man. "I'm not obstructing anything. And my going to a jewelry store is hardly a crime. I am simply here to buy a ring."

"Is that a fact?"

"Yes, it is," I said, chomping on my words.

Then I waved to Gage. "I'll take this big one. Here's my card," I told him as I reached into my purse.

Parker quickly came to join me. "Ummm . . . Mom. Do you think that's a good idea? Shouldn't you think about it first? You know . . ."

"Nope, Parker," I informed my son, speeding forward like a runaway train. "I've decided I really want this."

Gage gave me a warm smile. "Excellent choice, sweetie. I don't think you'll regret it."

Funny, but I already was.

Then with the new ring nestled carefully inside a ring box and placed securely inside my purse, I told Parker I was ready to leave.

Without so much as a "so long" to Remy.

And that's how I came to own a three-hundred-dollar, fake ring that I never intended to buy. Though if nothing else, I decided it would look beautiful with the outfit I planned to wear to tonight's speed dating event.

An event that I hoped wouldn't be as big a mistake as the ring I'd just purchased. Not to mention, my plans to investigate the murder mystery that I probably shouldn't be investigating at all . . .

Chapter Twenty-two

Okay, I don't know which was worse—being the proud owner of an overpriced, fake ring that I didn't intend to buy or knowing that I'd just set a really bad example for my son. Either way, my performance at the jewelry store was not exactly my finest hour. Or something I was terribly proud of.

And judging from the long, assessing look that Parker gave me on the way home, it also appeared to be something he wasn't going to let go of any time soon. "You okay, Mom? You sure got mad at Mr. Reagan. It was pretty major. I thought you were going to have an aneurysm."

There was that word again. Despite myself, I couldn't help but smile. "No, Parker, I didn't have an aneurysm. And yes, I got pretty mad. Though I probably shouldn't have gotten so mad. Honestly, I don't know what came over me."

An understatement, if ever there were one. At a time like this, my romance writer friends would have used a line like, "He was the most exasperating man she'd ever met." Whereby there'd be a big love scene at the end, and the couple would reunite and be together forever.

Thank God I wrote mystery novels.

"It's because you got dumped, Mom," my teenage expert on relationships informed me, matter-of-factly.

I couldn't help but roll my eyes. Though deep down, I had to ask myself—did Parker have a point? Was I a woman scorned, as the expression goes? Yet the more I thought about it, the more I realized my upset didn't actually come from the fact that Remy had ended our blossoming romance. Frankly, if he didn't have feelings for me or an attraction toward me, I certainly didn't want to be in a relationship with him. If I ever had a serious romance again, it would have to be a two-way street.

No, what really upset me the most was the *way* he'd ended things. Leaving me with no real explanation and absolutely no closure. Not to mention, leaving me completely dazed and confused, while I racked my brain trying to understand what had happened.

To top it off, I didn't like the underlying threat when it came to my involvement in solving this neighborhood murder mystery. Okay, technically I knew that civilians weren't supposed to be involved in such cases. But if I hadn't looked into the last neighborhood murder, the killer would still be roaming our streets, since the police had labeled it an accident. But thanks to the urging of my neighbor, Spencer Poe, I soon figured out that it was far from accidental, and I cracked the case. And now, with another murder so close to home, how could I not be involved? Not when Olivia had practically landed on my doorstep, and Belinda had parked in front of my house, and Spencer Poe was urging me on once again. Unbeknownst to Remy, I had uncovered a lot of information and motivations in this case. All things that might be news to him. In fact, it was possible that I'd uncovered information that he, as a police officer, hadn't been able to acquire.

Of course, I would have been more than happy to pass along what I'd learned. But that was pretty tough to do, given his attitude toward me these days.

And that's when it suddenly hit me—did Remy cut me off cold because he considered me to be a suspect in Dex's murder? After all, I lived right across the street, and my empty shrimp platter was sitting there on the counter the night of Dex's death. Then there was that whole "incident" where Dex had latched onto my hand and refused to let go. Was it possible that Olivia, or even Bugsy, had told Remy that Dex and I had a "thing" going on? An affair that had gone awry? Because, let's face it, Dex was known for "getting around."

And around some more.

Still, even if Remy suspected that I had killed Dex, I had the perfect alibi for the murder—I was out to dinner with him.

Yet the more I thought about it, depending on the time of Dex's death, I suppose that, technically, I'd had a window of opportunity to pull off the murder before Remy and I went out. Not to mention, as a mystery writer, I would have had a good idea how to commit such a crime and get away with it. Then there was the fact that I'd gotten my hair done by Deidre that morning, which meant I would have had access to her scissors. Her giving me such a disaster of a hairdo could have been the perfect motivation for me to frame her for the murder.

Plus, my "returning to the scene of the crime" and then appearing to be involved in trying to solve the case probably made me look even more guilty. Especially after Remy had just caught me red-handed, or rather, 'blue-ring' handed, at the very store where Dex used to buy all his jewelry.

Still, Remy hadn't interviewed me. Or investigated me.

That I knew of anyway.

But just because I wasn't aware of him investigating me didn't mean that he hadn't been. For all I knew, he'd been researching me and my movements since day one. Behind my back. And the mere thought of it made me feel like I'd just been dunked in ice-cold water.

Yet it also left me with one very important realization—I now had a new motivation for quietly investigating the killing of Dex Degill. I was no longer trying to solve this case merely to make my neighborhood safe again. No, I was now doing it to prove my own innocence as well.

Even so, I saw no need to tell Parker of my sudden epiphany. He'd already lost his father, and he didn't need to worry about the prospect of losing his mother, too, by watching her go to jail.

So instead, I decided to stick with a safer subject. "Parker, what did you learn from looking at all those gems today?"

"It was a mixed bag, Mom. The diamond engagement rings were real. And the rest of the stuff was fake. But the weird thing is, the fakes weren't just good fakes. I think they were copies of real jewelry. Like your new ring. I just found one exactly like it online."

"Which would make it even more deceptive. Especially if someone could look it up online and think it was real. And then be pretty excited when Gage sold it at a discount."

"Yup, Mom. Mind if I take a look at your ring again?"

"Sure, just grab it out of my purse," I said as I turned onto our street. "And see if there's an appraisal certificate that comes with it."

He quickly found the little, red velvet box and slowly pulled it open. "Yup, Mom, the certificate is there. Folded up at the bottom. It says this ring is a ten-carat London Blue Topaz. With a half-carat worth of diamonds around it. And none of them are real."

"Pretty sneaky."

"Sure is, Mom. And you were really smart to buy that ring. Because now you have evidence."

If I hadn't just been pulling the Continental into the third stall of my garage, I would have given my son a big hug for trying to make me feel better about my gigantic, impulse purchase. Because he was right—I now had evidence that Gage Flause was selling fake jewelry. Even so, that evidence didn't connect Gage to the murder of Dex Degill. Not yet anyway. The most I could prove was that Dex was a good customer, and that was as far as it went.

Yet the concept stayed in my brain long after we went inside, and I got ready for my speed dating event. While yes, I was only going to investigate, I still wanted to look nice for the night. After all, I was sort of "undercover" in a way, and I needed to play the part. So I curled my hair, put on some taupe eyeshadow and black eyeliner. Along with a peach-colored lipstick. Then I donned my favorite cobalt-blue dress, one with a very flattering fit and flare design.

Finally, I slipped into some rhinestone-covered sandals and slid my new ring over my finger. Sure, the ring may not have been the real deal, and I knew I'd paid way too much for it, but I still thought it was pretty. Very pretty, as a matter of fact. And I actually loved having it on my hand.

Then I spritzed on some of my favorite perfume and headed into the kitchen to give Parker a few last-minute instructions before I left.

Parker's eyes went wide. "Wow, Mom. You look pretty good. For someone your age."

I wasn't sure whether to laugh or shake my head. "Thanks, kiddo. I think."

"You know, Mom, they're looking for parents to be prom chaperones. Do you wanna sign up? You've gotta have a date. And you have to dress up."

Well, the dressing up part I had covered. But the part about the date? That one I wasn't so sure about. Regardless, the anticipation on Parker's face was more than I could take. Because, when it came right down to it, I was a Mom, and if my son needed something, I wasn't about to say no.

Even if that meant finding a date for that night.

So I took a deep breath and said, "Sure, Parker. Count me in. I'll be one of the prom chaperones."

Whereby he grinned his usual goofy grin. "Cool, Mom."

"Okay, kiddo, I've gotta run," I told him, glancing at the clock. "Umm . . . do you have your phone with you? And do you have some money? In case of emergency?"

While I laughed and said yes, a big part of me wondered what would have happened if I had said no. Was my son actually going to shell out a couple of twenties?

But that was a discussion for another night.

"How about you?" I asked, turning the tables. "Do you have your pizza ordered?"

"Should be here in ten, Mom. Me and the felines are going to stay in and binge watch *Stargate*."

"Sounds good. Now be sure to keep all the doors locked and . . . well, you know the drill."

Whereby he saluted. "Got it, Mom. Now, go mingle with the middle-agers. And find some clues."

I couldn't help but smile. "Will do, Parker. Call me if you need anything."

"Back at'cha, Mom. Call me if you run into trouble."

Something I would never, ever do. Maybe not so much the part about running into trouble, but definitely the part about calling him if I did.

Regardless, I was out the door and on my way, driving my navy-blue SUV to my very first speed dating event.

I've never been a fan of arriving early to a party, but a few minutes after I turned into the parking lot, I wished I had. Much to my surprise, there were plenty of cars already there. So I quickly found a remaining spot, locked up my car and stepped toward the front entry, feeling surprisingly rushed.

I was greeted by Trevor the second I walked in. "Wow, Maddie, you look hot."

A comment that made me panic for a moment.

Hot? As in sweating? Starting to have hot flashes?

But judging from the way he looked me up and down, I quickly realized that "hot" was a compliment.

"Thank you," I said cautiously.

Then he took my hand and pointed to my new ring. "Let me guess. You got that at Flause Jewelers. It's a beaut, all right. Sorry to break it to you, doll, but it's probably just as fake as most of the stuff he sells."

I felt my eyes go wide. "What . . . you mean, you know?"

He set his chiseled jaw and let go of my hand. "Of course I know. I'm not stupid. And it's pretty much an open secret."

"It is?"

"In certain circles anyway."

I could hardly believe what I was hearing. "So, lots of people know about it?"

He tilted his head from side to side. "I wouldn't say 'lots.' But a few of us know. And speaking of jewelry, you know what you need to go with that dress, doll? A nice necklace."

Then he reached into the drawer of the stand below him and pulled out a red velvet case. He lifted the lid to reveal a stunning, graduated-diamond, tennis necklace with a large, teardrop diamond in the center. Despite the house lights being turned down low, the diamonds of the necklace sparkled up to me.

"Here," he told me. "Wear this one tonight."

I instantly gasped. "Trevor, I can't wear this. It must have cost a fortune." And then the light dawned, so to speak, and I realized what he was saying.

I glanced into his puppy dog eyes. "Please don't tell me this necklace is a fake, too."

"Wish I could, doll. Wish I could. Either way, I own the thing."

"So you were scammed by Flause Jewelers, too?"

"In a way. Actually, this one was given to me by one of my regulars. A guy named Dex Degill."

"Dex Degill? Why did Dex give you a necklace?"

His eyes suddenly turned dark, though his mouth widened in a smile. "Let's just say, he owed me. He was a regular out here at my speed dating events."

"And let me guess, he was married at the time," I murmured as I reached for the necklace and opened the clasp. "Or engaged."

"Yeah, and he didn't exactly want any of his wives or girlfriends to know that he frequented this joint. So he paid me to keep my mouth shut."

"Blackmail."

"Call it what you like. Either way, the guy was a rat. A cheater in every sense of the word. He cheated on his women, and he cheated on me. Cause he paid me in jewels that all turned out to be fake. I figured it out as soon as I tried to pawn the stuff. That's how I learned that Flause Jewelers specializes in mostly fake stones."

"Do you think Dex knew the jewelry was fake?"

This made Trevor laugh. "Yeah, I'm sure he did. How else could he afford to buy all that jewelry for three wives and who knows how many other women? I think he had some kind of deal going with that old pirate, Gage Flause."

"So Gage supplied Dex with good fakes at a cheap price so he could afford to keep all his women dripping in jewels. And made Dex look like a big spender. And in return, Dex kept quiet about the jewelry being phony," I added as I fastened the clasp on the necklace.

"Yup, I think that was the arrangement," Trevor confirmed.

I turned to look at myself in a mirrored section of the wall.

Amazingly, with all those diamonds twinkling like they had a battery pack attached—fake though they may be—I suddenly felt more beautiful and elegant than I had in a long, long time.

"There. You look perfect now, doll," Trevor said with a smile. "Are you ready to go? I'll take you into the main room where the women will be seated. Grab a glass of wine at the bar. On the house for the ladies. Then just sit at any open table. There will be two chairs at each one. Take one chair and leave the other one open. You'll stay put while the men will be rotating around after they're allowed in. They get seven minutes to talk to you before the bell rings, and then they have to move on. You can mingle with whoever you want to at the end. After the rounds are all over."

"Got it," I responded, feeling strangely nervous.

I hadn't exactly been on a lot of dates since I'd become a widow, and the idea of being sized up in seven minutes seemed like a lot of pressure. But I reminded myself that I was simply here to investigate.

Trevor eyed me carefully. "Don't sweat it, doll. You're gonna be great. Just relax and have fun."

So I smiled my brightest smile. "Thanks," I told him as I followed him into the main room, where the lights were even lower than in the entry. This room resembled a hotel ballroom, with a two-tiered floor. Lower in the front and higher in the back. Twelve small, round tables were placed equidistant apart, and I noticed most of them already had a woman seated there. But since it was so dark, I couldn't make out the features of anyone. Despite each table having a battery-operated candle in the center. Thankfully, I did spot an open table clear back in the left corner, so I guessed that would be mine.

But first I headed to the bar for a glass of wine. "Do you have a Sauvignon Blanc?" I asked the young, bowtie wearing bartender.

He stared at me like I'd just sprouted a third eyeball in the middle of my forehead. "Look lady, I'm not the regular bartender. I'm Trevor's nephew. I just work on the nights when they have this dating thing."

"Okay, then . . . I'd like a glass of wine. What have you got?"

"We have white and we have red. That's all I know. Which one do you want?"

"I'll have a glass of white, thank you," I told him.

Without responding, he pulled an already open bottle of some kind of white wine from below the bar. Then I watched in fascination as he tilted a large-bowled wineglass and slowly poured the wine like he was pouring beer and trying to keep the foam down. Once the glass had more than enough liquid in it, he righted it and proceeded to fill it to the brim. Task completed, he slid it over to me, spilling a little on the bar as he went.

And since I didn't want to spill more, I decided to sit and take a few sips before carrying it back to my table. My eyes adjusted to the dim light after a few seconds, and I could see a woman with long, golden-blonde hair stroll over to the bar. Thanks to the modern miracle of spandex, she had managed to squeeze her voluptuous body into a hot pink dress that was probably two sizes too small for her. Something that put her "assets" on full display, so to speak, given the way her neckline had gone way past "plunging" and had reached a whole new low altogether. It also meant her diamond pendant necklace stood out, dangling just above her décolletage.

"Hiya, Ethan," she said to the bartender, sounding like they were old friends.

"Hello again, Ms. Stanke," he said cheerfully. "Need a refill already?"

She giggled. "Yes, fill it all the way to the top. You know me so well," she responded.

In a voice that I recognized.

I turned to get a better look at her, and there, larger than life, was Belinda.

The woman who had stalked Dex Degill.

Chapter Twenty-three

Belinda's hazel eyes went wide when she saw me. "Maddie? What are you doing here? Are you stalking me?"

I took a sip of my wine, being careful not to jiggle the full glass, so I wouldn't spill any. "Cute, Belinda. Coming from you. Besides, you were the one who insinuated the word 'stalker' has such a bad connotation. What was the term you used? Tracker-American?"

She examined her fluorescent pink nail polish. "Make fun of me if you want, Maddie. But it's a lot harder than it looks. You have no idea how time-consuming it is to keep track of someone."

"I would think it would be a lot less time-consuming now. With Dex Degill gone."

"Oh, but I still keep busy," she added with a sly smile.

"By keeping track of the man's first wife? Cissy?"

She visibly flinched. "How did you know about that?"

"It doesn't matter. Though I have to wonder why you'd be interested in her."

"Dex was the love of my life. So now I keep track of Cissy and anyone who had anything to do with him. His wives, his partner, that jewelry store guy, and anybody I ever saw with Dex."

Right away, I wondered if that might include Bugsy, since the second sip of my wine immediately brought his bug spray to mind. Even so, I needed to down enough of the liquid so I could safely transport the wineglass to my table.

"If it's so time-consuming, then why do it?" I asked Belinda.

"Because I'm sure one of them killed Dex. Which means they ruined the chance for me to be with him, and they ruined my chance to be happy. So if I track them a little and make them miserable, well, they have it coming, as far as I'm concerned."

"All of them?" I clarified.

To which she merely responded with a shrug.

"Have you seen anything that might lead you to believe one of those people murdered Dex?"

She flashed a bright smile at the bartender as he slid an overflowing glass of wine toward her. "Well, no. At least I don't think so. Not yet anyway. But if you ask me, I think it was wife number three who did him in. Because she knew I was going to be wife number four, and she would rather see him dead and buried than happy with me. I'm just sure of it."

"But I haven't seen you keeping track of her. Or parked across from their house lately," I mentioned.

Or rather, in front of *my* house.

"Are you kidding? I can't these days. Not with all the cops who've been around your neighborhood since . . ." And that's when she faltered.

"Since the night when Dex was killed?" I supplied. "Were you in our neighborhood that night?"

Of course, I stopped short of asking her if she'd been the one to kill Dex Degill. Though it took about seven major muscle groups for me to hold my tongue.

She took a big gulp of her red wine. "I was on my usual tracking run that night, about to check on Dex. And I was about to turn onto your street when I spotted all those police cars at the end of the cul-de-sac. So I hit the brakes, turned around, and got out of there in a hurry. Really scary stuff, if you ask me."

"Yup, a murder in the neighborhood is pretty unnerving," I agreed.

"Oh, no, I don't mean that! I mean, a gal like me could end up in the clink for getting caught in such close proximity to Dex's house. With so many cops around."

"What with that pesky restraining order and all," I added, trying not to roll my eyes.

"And well, a few other . . . minor . . . infractions."

"Really, like what?" I asked, using my best Southern Belle charm.

I took another sip of my wine, something that was not becoming an acquired taste. Much as I hated to be a wine snob, I couldn't help but compare it to the perfect vintage that I'd had at Cissy's condo. For which there *was* no comparison, except when it came to the price tag. In the meantime, I tried to calculate just how much more of this swill I needed to drink before I could successfully carry the glass across the main floor and up a step to my table. Without spilling it.

Belinda shrugged. "Oh, you know . . . I may have slashed a few tires here and there. And put a few scratches on a few paint jobs. You know, stuff that comes with the territory. Mostly from before I moved here."

Right then and there, I reminded myself to never, *ever* make Belinda angry. That, and to keep my cars locked up in my garage at night.

"Is that why you moved to Texas?" I asked her, noticing she didn't seem to have any issue with her wine at all.

"Well, like they say . . . If you can't stand the heat . . ."

"Then get out of the kitchen," I said, finishing the expression. Right before I suffered through another sip of my wine and wondered if I would look out of place if I switched to water. "So what happens with that restraining order now? I suppose that, with Dex among the dearly departed, that restraining order is more or less . . . defunct. After all, you can't stalk a dead man."

She, in turn, took another huge gulp of her own wine. "Tell me about it. Especially since the police haven't released his body yet. And I'm betting that Olivia will have him cremated. Knowing her."

"So there might not even be a funeral for you to go to?"

"Lousy, right?" She shook from head to toe, causing her large hoop earrings to swing and her diamond necklace to shimmer in one of the few overhead lights of the bar.

I glanced at the diamond. "Belinda, did Dex give you that necklace?"

A dreamy look flashed across her face. "Yes, as a token of his love and affection."

Which actually made it an appropriate token, given that his "love" was probably just as fake as the diamond she was wearing.

Then she turned to size me up. "Wait a minute . . . what about *your* necklace? I think I saw Dex with it once. Did he give you that? Here you are, getting on my case about Dex when it looks like you were special to him, too. And you didn't have to go anywhere to keep track of him, either. You could have done it right from your own living room."

That's when my breath caught in my throat. Earlier, I'd wondered if Remy thought I had something going on with Dex, and now Belinda practically accused me of having just such an affair, which included Dex's giving me (what appeared to be) high-dollar jewelry. Where in the world did people get such ideas? How could anyone ever think I'd date a philanderer like Dex? Regardless, this was a train of thought that had jumped the tracks and needed to be stopped right away.

Before Belinda started to stalk me, too.

"No," I told her in no uncertain terms. "You've got it all wrong. This is just a necklace that Trevor loaned me for the night. And for the record, I did not have a relationship with Dex. Frankly, I wasn't attracted to the guy."

"Uh-huh . . ." she muttered, before adding, "You didn't kill him, did you?"

Words that shocked me to the core, that she would even think I was capable of something like murder.

"No, Belinda. I wasn't involved with the guy. I'd barely even met him."

She gave me a wan smile. "Sometimes, that's all it takes."

Well, she had that right. Meeting Dex once was enough for me to want to stay away from him. *Far* away.

But before I could say another word, Trevor suddenly appeared beside us. "Are you ladies ready? We're about to start."

"Ready," I said with a nod.

"Me, too," Belinda told him, playing with her necklace.

Trevor glanced at it. "Let me guess. I'll bet Dex gave you that."

She smiled. "Yes, as a matter of fact, he did. Isn't it beautiful?"

"For a fake," Trevor said with a snort, verbalizing what I already believed to be true. "Just like all the other jewelry that Dex gave away."

His words seemed to shake Belinda to the core, and for a moment, I thought she was going to throw her glass of wine in his face. Though considering the amount of wine in the large glass, it probably would've taken more than one toss.

"Dex never would've given me fake jewelry," she said with a huff.

Trevor laughed. "Sure he would. That's all he ever gave anyone. Fake, phony, faux. Looks like the real stuff but it's not."

I saw Belinda flex her claws, and I thought there might be a fight before the speed dating even got started.

But then Trevor left us, stepped to the center of the room and rang a little bell. "All right, ladies, take your seats, please. We're about to let the men in so they can see what they've been missing."

Belinda took a few more quick gulps of her wine and got to her feet, wobbling on her stiletto heels. "Good luck tonight, Maddie. Hope you land a big fish."

And with that, she was off. While she carried her huge glass of wine to a table nearby, I started the trek to my table with my still nearly full glass of wine. Thankfully, I made it to my spot without swishing out a single drop. And I had barely gotten myself situated when the doors flung open wide and in walked the men, making a beeline for the individual tables.

A man with flyaway, white hair and vivid blue eyes, probably in his early sixties, sat across from me.

I started in with, "Hi, I'm Maddie . . ." right before the man cut me off by fanning out a deck of cards and practically sticking it all in my face. "Pick a card. Any card."

I felt my brows go up. "Huh?"

He shoved the cards closer. "Haven't you ever seen a card trick before? Pick one and let's get on with it."

"All right," I said, suddenly realizing how incredibly long seven minutes could be.

So I picked a card, glanced at it and saw it was the seven of diamonds.

"Now put it back . . ." he started to say as I shoved it back into the center of the pack, having done this same trick for hours on end with Parker when he was in grade school and going through his "magic trick" phase.

"Wait," my temporary date whined. "That's not how you're supposed to do it . . . You're supposed to put it back on top . . ."

I faked a smile. "Okay, find my card. Better hurry, we've only got a few minutes. Have you done this before?"

"Card tricks?"

"No, speed dating."

My date began to sift through the cards. "Sure. Been at it for a while now. I find a few card tricks always help to break the ice. A guy's gotta have a schtick, you know."

Silly me, here I thought being nice and starting a conversation would be plenty.

"What's your name?" I asked.

"It's Stan. Stan the Magic Man. I like to make magic with the ladies, if you know what I mean," he added with a wink. "You've gotta have a catchy moniker, you know, so women will remember you."

Which wasn't going to be a problem, as far as I was concerned, since I pretty much guessed I was going to have a hard time forgetting this guy. Try as I might.

"Nice to meet you, Stan. If you've been coming here for a while, you probably knew another man who used to attend these events. A guy named Dex? Dex Degill?"

"The guy who got murdered?" he asked, as he continued to look through his deck for my card.

"Yup. Did you know him very well?"

"Oh, please. I knew who he was, but he didn't bother hanging with the men. He was all about the ladies, believe me. They loved him. All of them. He was big competition for the rest of us guys out here," Stan said with a sigh as he continued to sift through the cards. When he reached the queen of hearts, he held it out before me. "Is this your card?" he asked hopefully.

I shook my head. "Nope."

So he sifted a little more and pulled out the ten of clubs. "How about this one?"

"Sorry."

And on it went, until I was finally saved by the bell. Literally. Without ever finding my card, Stan the Magic Man took his deck and headed for the next table. I took a sip of my wine as the next man slipped into the chair across from me. This second guy was probably a little older than me, and he had a pronounced bald spot while the rest of his long, gray hair was pulled back into a very messy ponytail.

"I only have six months to live," he immediately announced, clearly not wasting any of that time with small talk or minor, little things like getting each other's names. "And I want to spend that time with a beautiful woman by my side. Could that woman be you?"

That's when my jaw practically dropped to the top of the table. "I'm so sorry to hear about your prognosis. But no thanks. I've been widowed once, and I don't care to do that again. Not for a long, long time."

"But I need someone to take care of me."

"You could hire a nurse."

"And pay for that?"

"Well, you can't take your money with you, you know."

"I suppose that's true. But wow, those healthcare people are expensive. Plus I'd have to find someone to cook and clean and mow the grass. Sure you don't want to do it?" he asked, looking up at me with pleading eyes.

Kind of reminding me of Agatha and Ellery when they were begging for food.

"Yes, I'm sure," I informed him. "Very sure. And by the way, did you ever meet a man named Dex Degill? I guess he used to attend these speed dating events."

"Dex? Sorry lady, if you're not interested in a man with six months to live, you're really not gonna like Dex. Because he's already a goner. Dead. Deceased. Kaput."

"Did you know him well?"

"Me? No. You'll have to ask the women. They were all after him. Even though it was rumored that he was married."

"Any idea why they wanted him so badly?"

"Oh, I don't know," he said sarcastically. "Probably for his money. He had lots of it. And he liked to spend it on women. He showered them with jewelry. But I'm not here to talk about Dex. And if this date isn't going anywhere, I don't have time for it. I'm gonna go take my pills and get ready for the next date."

And without so much as a "so long," he left me alone, feeling oddly thankful to be by myself. I took another sip of my bottomless pit of a wineglass and waited for the bell to ring again. While I sat there, I did my best to get a glimpse of all the other attendees, but it was too dark to really make anyone out.

Then the bell rang and a new round started. This time, the man who sat before me was decidedly handsome with his wheat-colored, curly hair and his deep brown eyes. For the first time since I'd arrived, I wondered if I might actually meet someone special tonight.

He held out a warm hand and took mine. "Hi, I'm Daniel. And you're . . ."

"Maddie," I said in response.

"Very nice to meet you. And I must say, I'm surprised to see such a beautiful woman like you here. You really take my breath away. I mean, I am really, really taken with you."

"Well, that's very thoughtful of you to say. This is the first time I've ever done something like this, and I really didn't know what to expect. Not to mention, my teenage son pretty much made fun of me before I came out here . . ."

Zzzzzt!

I glanced at my date, who now appeared to be sound asleep and snoring. Had I bored him? And so quickly? Or was the poor man just exhausted?

I shook his hand to wake him. "Are you all right, Daniel?"

"Oh, sorry? Did I fall asleep?"

"Up past your bedtime?"

"Oh, no, nothing like that. As you were saying?" he asked, staring dreamily into my eyes like it was love at first sight.

"Well, let's see . . ." I began.

Zzzzzt!

My mouth fell open, and I gaped at the napping man before me. Wow, was I really so dull that a guy couldn't even stay awake while I spoke?

I shook his hand again.

"Oh, sorry," he informed me. "I was nervous about coming here tonight. So I took a couple of tranquilizers to calm me down."

Words that left me speechless.

Not that I would have had a chance to respond anyway, since a raven-haired woman suddenly appeared next to the table. "Daniel!" she screamed. "What are you doing here? Looking for a woman to date? How could you? I've given you twenty years of my life . . ."

I gasped. "You're his . . . wife?"

"Yes, I'm his wife, you hussy! Where do you get off, trying to steal my man?" she went on, her laser-beam eyes practically burning a hole in my head.

Thankfully, she quickly turned her attention back to her husband. "Daniel, why are you here? What are you doing?"

"I'm bored with you, Lindsey!" Daniel shot back. "After all these years, I wanted to live a little!"

"How could you possibly be bored?" she screamed.

Zzzzzt!

"Maybe you should take him home," I suggested.

"Gladly," she hollered at me.

And the next thing I knew, Trevor materialized and helped Daniel to his feet, whereby he woke up again and let his wife lead him away.

"Are you all right, doll?" Trevor asked. "We never had a wife show up before."

I shook my head. "I'll be fine, thanks. I guess that guy forgot to mention that he was married when he signed up."

"They never do," Trevor responded with a wink. "But we always find out, and it can be a real moneymaker, you know."

Unfortunately, I knew full well what he meant by his remark. I'd already learned that Trevor had been blackmailing Dex. How many other married men had Trevor lured in for speed dating, only to turn around and blackmail them later?

But if that was the case, what, if anything, did it have to do with Dex's murder? Unless Dex had threatened to expose Trevor's setup. Yet somehow, I doubted it, since that meant Dex would be exposing his own illicit activities as well.

"Thanks for being here tonight, doll," Trevor said with a smile before he returned to the front of the room and rang the bell again.

Seconds later, another man slid into the chair across from me. But this time I recognized the man.

Hayes. Dex Degill's old business partner. With his classically handsome features that were picture perfect, except for his hair that refused to lay down properly. Though I had to say, his hair looked a little better tonight than it had the last time I'd seen him.

He flashed me a dazzling smile. "Well, Maddie. This is a nice surprise. I never imagined I would see you at one of these events."

I laughed in return. "That makes two of us. Tell me, Hayes, you're not married, are you?"

He let out a little laugh. "No, not me. I almost got married once. I thought she was the love of my life. But it didn't work out. I got dumped, if you want to know the truth. Unceremoniously dumped. And then I just never found the right person. I guess I've been married to my work since then. How about you?"

I sighed. "I'm afraid I'm no stranger to being dumped, either. But I was married for a long time, and I've been a widow for a few years."

"I hope you won't hold my performance at Olivia's house against me. I know Dex left provision for her to live comfortably for the rest of her life. But, of course, Olivia is demanding more. She wants money, as much as she can get her grubby, little hands on. She's like a black hole when it comes to money. But Olivia is not entitled to a dime from the business. I made sure of that."

"So you and Dex were friends for a long time?"

"Oh, yeah. Since college. He was always the babe magnet, and I was the wingman. I guess you could say that I lived in his shadow."

"I find that hard to believe," I said, without adding, "since you're so amazingly handsome."

He shook his head. "Dex had a way with women. It's almost like he could read them or something. And he was always showering them with things. Jewelry, flowers, and compliments. He told them what they wanted to hear. To be honest, I don't think he ever really loved any of them. For him, I think it was the thrill of the chase. Like big game hunting."

"Wow," I said, shaking my head. "Almost like chasing women was his favorite hobby."

"And a very expensive hobby at that," Hayes said, leaning back in his chair and taking a swig of his beer. "Which meant our business had to make a lot of money, because he wasn't shy about spending it. I had to bring in a consultant to train us in our overseas mergers and acquisitions and . . ."

And on and on and on he went. Once he got onto the subject of his business, the world around him ceased to exist, including me, and suddenly I wondered if I might end up like my date before him—sound asleep.

At long last, he glanced at his watch and said, "We should go out sometime, Maddie."

But I simply demurred and said, "Let me think about it. I'm on a pretty tight deadline with my next book."

He shrugged. "Okay. But I think we'd get along great. So here's my card. You can let me know when you decide."

Though the truth was, I already had. Sure, Hayes was magazine-model handsome, and he was basically a nice enough guy, and clearly very hardworking. Even so, I found it hard to connect with him. Partly because he didn't seem interested in me at all, except for my talents as a good listener.

Which meant I was pretty much striking out when it came to this speed dating event.

That was, until the next man sat down at my table.

A man who was tall, tanned and muscular, with a true Texas drawl. He gazed at me with dancing blue eyes that went nicely with his curly, blondish-brown hair. Though he was very different from Hayes, in that he was not classically handsome, but he was still completely attractive, given the way he carried himself.

He greeted me with a firm (but not too firm) handshake and said, "Howdy, ma'am. May I have the pleasure of learning your name?"

And just like that, this charming stranger before me had already figured out my Kryptonite—manners. Good manners.

So I told him my name and asked his in return.

"The name's Guy, ma'am. Guy Goodwin."

"Guy?" I repeated, trying not to let out a little laugh.

He flashed me a smile. "That's right, ma'am. My momma and daddy named me Guy and my twin sister, Gal."

Right about then, I'm sure my eyes went wide. "Really?"

He laughed. "No, just kidding. People never know how to take a guy named 'Guy,' so that's my standard joke."

I couldn't help but smile. "Please tell me, Guy, that you're not married or dying."

He laughed again. "Now, that's the first time I've heard that question tonight. Mostly the women want to know what I do for a living and what my financial prospects are. But no, I'm not dying. Not that I know of anyway. And no, I'm not married. I've been divorced for about three years. Not on bad terms, mind you. She got her dream job in Indonesia and left. She wanted me to go with her, but I couldn't afford to leave the company I'd built up for years. Plus, the kids were in school here, so I stayed put. It wasn't long before we grew apart, and she asked for a divorce. Not how I planned for our lives to go, but there you have it. How about you?"

"I'm a widow, and like you, it wasn't the way I planned for things to go, either. I've got a fantastic, genius son who'll be leaving for college in the fall and will probably go into engineering."

"Sounds like a great kid, making a smart choice for a profession. That's how I got my start. As an engineer. My oldest daughter is already working on her engineering degree, and my youngest will start nursing school in the fall. She's the one who set me up with this speed dating thing here tonight. She insisted that I 'get out there' again. Mostly because my girls are worried about me being alone once they're both at school."

"Sounds like my son, Parker. He worries about me constantly. I don't think he understands that he's the child and I'm the parent."

"I've got the same thing going on at my house. Celia signed me up for this and practically pushed me out the door. And I've gotta say that, until I landed at your table, I was starting to regret my decision to come."

Oh, didn't the man just say the sweetest things?

And so the conversation went. Easy, comfortable and fun. I loved Guy's relaxed confidence, and the way he laughed and found humor in things. Not to mention, the give and take of our conversation. He asked about my books, and I asked about his company. He wanted to know about my life, and I wanted to hear about his.

For the first time the entire night, the seven-minute date went by much too fast.

When the bell rang, he looked straight into my eyes. "Maddie, if you'd be agreeable, I'd love to continue this conversation later. Over dinner, preferably. Would you like to go on a date with me?"

"I'd love to," I practically gushed.

Then we exchanged phone numbers and information, with a promise to be in touch, after we checked our calendars at home.

"It was such a pleasure to meet you," he said, taking my hand and raising it to his lips. He gave me a smile and a wave, and then he was off to the next table.

Mesmerized, I sat there, practically purring, remembering the warmth of my hand in his as I watched him walk away.

I sighed blissfully and hardly even noticed when my next date took the chair across from me.

But my bubble of joy was shattered the instant I saw the man who was now seated at my table.

Remy.

Chapter Twenty-four

For a moment or two, I could hardly believe my eyes. Because there, looking as handsome as ever, was the man I once thought I might have a future with. And until the moment when he abruptly ended our relationship, with next to no explanation, I truly believed the growing bond between us might develop into something serious. Now here he was, wearing the same blue, button-down shirt and the same subtle cologne that he'd worn on our last date. Only this time, he wasn't here for me.

He was looking for love elsewhere.

So many emotions passed through my brain, and probably across my face, that I didn't even know which one to start with.

"Fancy meeting you here," I said through clenched teeth.

"Maddie . . ." he started to say, sounding conflicted himself.

"So . . . this is why we needed to 'cool it,' because you simply wanted to see other people? Why didn't you just come out and say so? And why act so romantic only hours before you decided it wasn't what you wanted. Or more importantly, that I wasn't *who* you wanted. It's not like we were engaged or something."

"It's not what you think . . ."

"Wow, that's funny," I seethed. "Because I'm pretty sure it *is* what I think. You dumped me without any kind of explanation, and now you're at a speed dating event. It all looks pretty clear to me."

"Maddie . . . I'm working."

I shot daggers at him with my eyes. "Oh, how convenient! You think you can do whatever you want and just call it 'work' and that makes it all okay?"

He leaned forward and put his elbows on the table. "Seriously, I'm here to investigate."

That's when I shook my head. "Not buying it, Remy. You know, if you didn't have feelings for me and didn't want to go out anymore, that's fine. I can accept that. But you set some kind of land-speed record going from hot to cold. Sweet and loving one minute and then titanic-sized-iceberg chilly the next. All without any kind of explanation or real goodbye. It was a rotten thing to do. And cowardly, I might add."

"Maddie, I didn't really want to end things . . ."

I rolled my eyes. "Oh, sure, you say that now because you're being confronted with your lousy behavior. I'll bet you just got scared because we were getting close. So you turned tail and ran."

That's when he hesitated for a moment. "Okay, fine. There may be some truth to that. Yes, I did get scared because I was developing feelings for you. Way faster than I expected. As for being called out on my behavior, okay, fair enough, I probably have it coming. But as long as we're putting our cards on the table, why don't you come clean, too. You came out here tonight to investigate, didn't you?"

Funny, but I didn't remember agreeing to putting any "cards on the table." And how was it possible that I suddenly felt like a suspect who was being interrogated?

Maybe because I was, in his mind anyway.

"What I'm doing here is none of your business," I shot back, feeling my inner adolescent rear her defiant head. "I'm a free agent, and I can go wherever I want, do whatever I want, and date whomever I want."

Once again, I stopped short of saying, "You're not the boss of me."

Remy leveled his gaze at me. "Maddie, I want you to stay out of this."

"Out of what?"

"You know exactly what I'm talking about. This world. These people. This case. Do I have to spell it out for you? I know what you've been up to."

I furrowed my brow. "I'll just bet you do. It took me a while, but I finally figured out that you included *my* name on your list of suspects. Didn't you?"

With those words, he looked away. "All right, you've got me. That's why I had no choice but to cut things off with you like I did. I can't be personally involved with a suspect in one of my cases. And I can't let my personal feelings impact my judgement as a law enforcement officer."

"How handy. Here you were, needing a good excuse to ghost a woman you'd been dating, because you didn't have the intestinal fortitude to tell her that you weren't interested. And instead of being a man about it, you conveniently fell back on the whole 'work' thing."

His eyebrows went up. "Ghost?"

"I'm sure you know what it means. But how could you possibly see me as a suspect?"

He sighed. "Let's start with this. When I interviewed Olivia Degill, she told me about how you came over to her house and then stood there holding hands with her husband. Intimately. Right in front of her. Like the two of you had something going on."

Gee, funny how Olivia had failed to mention *that* little aspect of her conversation with Remy when she landed on my doorstep and did her best to manipulate me into investigating Dex's ex-wife.

Manipulation that worked, I might add.

I gaped at Remy. "You've got to be kidding me. I didn't want that man's hand clamped onto mine. In fact, I was struggling to get away from him. I thought I'd have to resort to some kind of self-defense tactic to get him off of me."

For some reason, this made Remy smile. He did his best to hide it, by looking down and taking a sip of his drink, but I still spotted it, even in the dim light.

"And of course Olivia would say something like that," I went on. "She wants to divert suspicion away from herself. Besides, she says lots of things. Did you know she also claims the two of you have something going on?"

He swallowed hard and just stared at me.

I gasped. "It isn't true, is it? *Do* you have something going on with her?"

Again, he simply kept up his unblinking gaze.

His lack of denial shocked me to the core. "Oh, my goodness, you're just waiting to clear her name before you make a move on her, aren't you? Her being a rich widow and all."

At long last, he looked away. "No, Maddie, it's not like that. And I can't talk about an ongoing investigation. But this isn't about me. Olivia seems to think you were having an affair with her husband. Since, well . . . you're a very beautiful woman and, apparently, he couldn't resist beautiful women."

To which I responded with a loud, "*Eeeewwww!*" I shuddered as I recalled the sensation of Dex's hand latched onto mine. "You can't be serious. The man practically oozed slime."

"Plus you had time to kill him before I picked you up that night. It would have been in the time of death window. And let's face it, dating the man who would be investigating the crime would lesson your odds of ever being arrested."

"So you think I dropped over to their place, murdered Dex, ran back home and popped into the shower to wash off any blood splatter? And then put on a nice dress and greeted you?"

He shrugged. "Technically, it could have been done."

"What possible motivation could I have had for murdering the man?"

"Well, according to Olivia, her husband chose her over you. And you were 'a woman scorned.'"

"There was no 'choosing.' And there was no 'scorning.' I wanted nothing to do with Dex. Parker and I simply took food over to the Degills to welcome them to the neighborhood. Period. That's it and that's all."

He quirked an eyebrow at me. "Then there's the fact that you're a mystery writer. Murder is your business. You plot out crimes for a living."

I shook my head, completely stunned by what he was saying. "Only on paper, Remy. Only on paper. And I can't believe that *you* think I could kill someone."

Though in all honesty, I *was* considering such a move right at that moment. But I wasn't sure who I would start with first—Olivia or Remy.

He frowned. "All right, Maddie, the truth is, I've pretty much ruled you out as a suspect."

"Oh, how terribly kind of you," I said in a voice that was so dripping with sarcasm that I had the urge to wipe off the table. "But you forgot about one important, little detail when it comes to any possibility that I could have raced right over and murdered my neighbor before you picked me up. And that's my doorbell camera."

"Something you could have easily altered. Which is why I never asked to look at it in the first place. You could've erased any part that showed you running across the street. And the Degills didn't have their doorbell camera working yet. The rest of your nearby neighbors don't seem to have one."

Which meant he clearly hadn't spoken with Spencer Poe.

I glared at him. "So . . . in my great expertise of altering my doorbell camera video, do you also think I created the image of the dark sedan that was briefly at the Degills' house while we were out to dinner?"

"Dark sedan? You should have told me about that."

"Oh? When, exactly, was I supposed to tell you? Before or after you cut me off or refused to talk to me?"

He closed his eyes for a moment, as though fighting hard to be patient. "Was there a license plate visible?"

"No. And there wasn't a valid license plate on the silver Crown Victoria that kept parking in front of my house, either. Naturally, the driver had to park there, so she wouldn't be in violation of her restraining order."

His eyebrows shot up. "Restraining order? Wait a minute . . . are you talking about that same Crown Vic that you told me about the day before we went out?"

I crossed my arms. "That's the one. Driven by Dex's stalker."

"His *stalker*?"

"Yes, Belinda Stanke. A woman who has quite a long history."

"How did you find out about her?"

I rolled my eyes. "Well, she's here tonight, for one thing. If you haven't met her yet, I'm sure you will. Otherwise, you can find her stalking pretty much anyone who was associated with Dex Degill."

"Okay . . ."

"Also, thanks to your nasty, hot-and-cold, cut-me-out-of-your-life decision, I didn't have a chance to tell you that Olivia's decorating style could only be described as 'Modern Cissy.' Meaning,

Olivia seems to be obsessed with Dex's first wife. But who wouldn't be, considering Cissy stands to make a fortune now that she's inherited a big chunk of Dex's business, which she's about to sell to Dex's partner, Hayes. Probably to help pay for her very, very expensive tastes. Of course, Olivia has been demanding but not getting money from Dex's partner, since she seems to think that money should be hers, too. And speaking of Olivia, did you know that all her gems—with the exception of her diamond engagement ring—are fake? Compliments of Flause Jewelry Store?"

"Some of the jewelry is fake and some of it is real?" Remy repeated in a mocking tone. "Maddie, that doesn't add up."

I rolled my eyes. "To the contrary, I think it explains how the man has managed to stay in business. Because most women have their wedding rings appraised and probably insured. And maybe not at the same place where the rings were purchased."

The light seemed to be dawning in Remy's eyes. "So he makes sure those rings are the real deal."

"But other jewelry, especially a gift? Women hardly ever take such things somewhere else for a full-blown appraisal. And Gage already provides a phony appraisal certificate with every purchase. Something that would work just fine for insurance purposes. So it sounds to me like he's got his racket pretty well figured out."

"You've picked up a lot of information," Remy murmured.

"Yes, I have. And you're welcome, by the way."

"Maddie, you've got to listen to me. I don't want you mixed up in this," he said in a low voice. "This is dangerous. Dex Degill led a sordid life, and whoever killed him wouldn't hesitate to get rid of you like they got rid of him. I want you to stop any investigating. This isn't a game. This isn't one of your books. I'll have you arrested for Obstruction of Justice if that's what it takes."

"You couldn't arrest me as a suspect, so now you might try to arrest me because I found out information that will help you in your case? Information that you'll end up taking credit for, I might add. Just like you got credit for solving the last murder in my neighborhood, though we both know I was the one who solved that case, and you just showed up in time to receive all the evidence and haul away the murderer. Practically all wrapped up in a neat little bow. So from what I can see, you just want to threaten me with arrest, one way or another. I think it's time you left my table."

"Maddie, please don't overreact. Yes, you did a great job solving that last case, and I do appreciate it. But I don't want anything to happen to you, that's all. In fact, after this case is solved, I was kind of hoping we might put all this behind us. Maybe start again?"

"In what universe would that ever work?" By this time, I was so furious I thought steam might shoot out of my ears, like a cartoon character.

"I can think of a few. And for what it's worth, I'm sorry, Maddie."

I sat back with my arms crossed. Staring. And seething. And wondering why it was taking so long for that bell to ring.

His gaze met mine. "Maddie, please go home and stay away from all this."

"Sorry, Remy, but I came out here to meet a nice guy. Someone who doesn't run hot and cold at the flip of a switch. Not that it's any of your business."

"I don't believe you."

Just then Hayes strolled over. "Maddie, are you okay over here? You sound a little riled up. Is this guy giving you trouble?"

He glanced at Remy, and the two men squared off and squinted at each other for a few moments, Clint Eastwood style.

I turned to my rescuer. "I'm so glad you came back, Hayes. Because my answer is yes. I've decided that I would like to go out with you after all. How's Tuesday night sound?"

Remy touched my hand. "Maddie . . ."

I yanked it away.

Hayes' eyes went wide. "Well, sure, Maddie. Let's do it. Tuesday night. I'll pick you up at six?"

And that was how I ended up accepting a date with a man that I didn't really want to go out with.

Even after Remy made a second mention of "starting over" and "trying this again."

But I wasn't in the mood for it. In fact, I returned Trevor's necklace to him and left shortly after the speed dating ended, not wanting to hang out in the same room as Remy. Parker was in bed by the time I got home, and it wasn't until after church the next day that he tried to pry the details of the speed dating event out of me.

"Mom, you've been cranky all day. Really cranky. Mind spilling it?" he demanded. "I've got Cassidy coming over today to make one of those cooking videos. And I don't want her to think I've got a mean mom. Because I want her to like me."

"Sorry, kiddo. I'm just not myself today."

"You can say that again. So what happened last night? I guess nobody asked you out, huh? Don't sweat it, Mom. It's okay if you didn't get a date. Like I said, those things are for losers anyway."

I sighed, wondering how much I should tell Parker.

He gave me his usual goofy grin. "But did you pick up any clues for the case?"

"A few," I simply said. "And don't worry, I will change my attitude. Right this minute," I added, just as the doorbell rang. "Is that Cassidy already?"

Parker's eyes went wide. "I don't think so. She's not supposed to be here for a few hours."

"Got it. And I need to get things set up for the first video," I added as I opened the front door.

And there stood a bald man, who was probably a foot shorter than me. Though I had a hard time seeing him clearly since his face was blocked by the box he was holding before him. Or rather, it was blocked by the big bunch of flowers inside that box. Had I made another date last night that I didn't remember?

"Delivery for Maddie Montgomery," the man announced.

"Oh, my goodness, I wonder who sent me flowers?" I practically gasped.

"You'll find out soon enough," came his reply as he handed me a lovely little bowl filled with carnations and daisies. "Let's start with the cheapskate."

"Cheapskate?" I repeated. "I think the flowers are very pretty. And cheerful."

"Uh-huh, whatever you say, lady. Now let's get to the good stuff." He then handed me a tall, thin crystal vase that held three long-stemmed red roses and some decorative leaves and baby's breath.

"These are beautiful," I gushed, holding both bouquets.

"Not a good as this one," the deliveryman told me as he picked up the last bouquet from the box.

A very large bouquet in a nice crystal vase that was filled with multi-colored roses. A stunning display that took my breath away.

I handed the two smaller bouquets to a very wide-eyed Parker, so I could hold the heavy crystal vase loaded with long-stem roses.

The deliveryman looked me over. "I don't know who you are, lady, but you seem to be pretty popular. I'm thinking of asking you out myself. But if I were you, I'd stick with bachelor number three." He smiled at me and kept on smiling even after I'd signed for the flowers, and he took off down my front walkway.

That's when I noticed that Parker seemed to be frozen to the spot, with his mouth gaping wide open. He still had a deer-in-headlights look even after I closed the door, and he followed me into the dining room.

"I wonder who sent these?" I murmured as I managed to ease the largest bouquet onto the dining room table. Parker slid the other two beside it.

I picked up the card from the carnations-and-daisy bouquet and read it aloud. "Looking forward to Tuesday night. Hayes."

I glanced at Parker, who was clearly still dumbfounded.

"Well, that was sweet," I commented, before I picked up the card from the set of three roses and read it out loud, too. "Great to see you again. Hope we can patch things up. Love, Remy."

"Remy?" Parker repeated. "He's back?" His eyebrows dipped into a deep *V* across his forehead.

But I really didn't want to talk about Remy right now, since I was dying to see who had sent the huge vase full of roses. So I took a deep breath and slowly pulled the card from the envelope, savoring the moment. "Looking forward to getting to know you better. Yours, Guy," I finally read aloud.

"Wow . . ." was all I could say, as I suddenly felt a little lightheaded and dizzy from the sight of all those flowers sitting on my dining room table. Was I about to swoon?

Ellery and Agatha jumped up onto the table to take a sniff and a nibble of some of the roses. And just so you know, no, I do not allow my kitties on the table. But right then, I was feeling much too mushy to tell them to get off.

Not to mention, I couldn't stop smiling. I turned to see a definitely "unsmiling" Parker who had crossed his arms and was just short of tapping his foot in annoyance.

"Well, Mom, it appears you had a really good night last night after all. Tell me, exactly how many men *are* you dating? And how do you plan to juggle them all?"

A good question, if ever there were one. And one I didn't have an answer for. Especially since I only planned to go out to dinner with Hayes once. As for Remy, I didn't plan to see him at all. But then there was Guy . . . a guy with real possibilities.

Though I didn't actually feel the need to explain all that to my son. Not at the moment anyway.

"My own mother," Parker said sternly. "A philanthropist."

I glanced at the ceiling for a second. "Ummm . . . I think you might mean 'philanderer'?"

"Yes, that, too."

Oddly enough, it was the same word I'd used to describe Dex Degill, not long before he was murdered. The thought of it made the little hairs on the back of my neck stand on end. And I instantly wondered if my actions might end up putting me in the line of fire, too.

Because let's face it, Dex's cheating was probably what got him killed. And though I technically wasn't "cheating" on anyone, I did, apparently, seem to have more than one man on the line.

But by "sort of" following in Dex's footsteps, was I essentially setting myself up to suffer the same fate that had befallen him?

I suddenly felt a cold chill, making me think of an old adage. The one about someone walking over my grave.

Chapter Twenty-five

Thankfully, I was able to shake off my sense of impending doom. And I was also able to postpone an explanation to my son about why I had received three different bouquets from three different men with a simple, "I'll explain it all later."

Not that I needed to explain a single thing to him. Still, I knew full well that any dating on my part could certainly have an impact on Parker, and I wanted to be up front and honest with him.

At another time, that is.

After I had solved the mystery of the murder of Dex Degill.

"Right now, we'd better get set up for your video with Cassidy," I told him.

He looked at me through squinted eyes. "Okay, Mom. But if I'm going to have a new dad, I want to meet the guy first."

Something that made me laugh as I arranged my three beautiful bouquets on my dining room table. "No worries, Parker. I am not even close to that."

"Good to know, Mom," he said as we headed to the kitchen.

Then I immediately started to grab things from the pantry so Parker and Cassidy could make my chocolate chip cookie recipe.

My son pulled up the recipe on his tablet. "Don't forget, Mom. We've gotta start from scratch, just like Mindie did. And we've gotta do all the measuring and melting and mixing by ourselves."

"Meaning, without any help from your mother," I said with a smile.

"You got it, Mom. We don't want this to look like a science project that our parents did for us."

"Sounds good to me," I told him while I checked the battery level on his camera and set it on a tripod.

Then I scooted it over to the usual spot, next to a floor-to-ceiling column, which concealed it nicely. Parker had recently added a remote control to the whole setup, so now the camera could be started and stopped with the press of a button. A handy feature that we tested out a few times before the doorbell rang.

"It's her," Parker proclaimed with a full-blown smile, before he raced for the door.

I barely got there in time to see him let Cassidy inside. She immediately smiled up at him, and for a moment, the two of them just stood there, gazing at each other. Lovestruck, from what I could see. Today, she had her strawberry blonde hair pulled back in a ponytail, making her big eyes stand out even more. She wore a purple t-shirt and jeans, along with a heart-shaped locket.

When the two finally managed to break away, she turned her bright smile up to me.

I smiled right back. "You must be Cassidy. It's lovely to meet you. I'm Parker's mom."

"It's really nice to meet you, too, Mrs. Montgomery," she said sweetly. "My mom has all your books. She loves them."

"That's so thoughtful of you to say. And thank you so much for agreeing to do this video," I told her.

"Are you kidding? I am *soooo* honored. Anything to help out Parker's mom. Besides, I love to make cookies. My mom and I make them all the time."

Then she turned back to my son, who now had a googly-eyed look on his face. Though I couldn't be sure if he was reacting to her or the thought of having cookies in the house. Or the fact that he'd found a girl who loved to bake cookies. Or all of the above.

Even the kitties got in on the action as they came racing in to greet her. While Agatha rubbed around her legs, Ellery reached up to her waist, and she immediately picked him up.

"Oh, I love cats," she cooed before she dropped a kiss on the top of Ellery's fuzzy, orange head.

And clearly, we all loved Cassidy as she followed me into the kitchen, carrying Ellery and continuing to spread sunshine as she went. A still grinning Parker brought up the rear of our little procession.

Soon, I had the kids all set up for filming. With matching aprons, they were naturals in the kitchen and on camera. Parker started by reading the recipe aloud while Cassidy pointed to the ingredients they would be using. Then they went about measuring and mixing and commenting, all while baking the same chocolate chip cookie recipe that Mindie had attempted to make.

But the difference between this duo and the disastrous Mindie was night and day. And Cassidy and Parker made the recipe look as easy as it really was.

Yet while I stood back and watched them work, I couldn't help but notice the way my son lit up around this young woman. And I loved the way the two interacted. Not only did the pair seem absolutely smitten with each other, but they made a fantastic team in general. Something that was even more apparent on camera.

So was it fair to hope this young woman who was going to be my son's prom date might also become my daughter-in-law one day? Yes, I knew they were both so young. But honestly, I couldn't imagine a nicer girl for Parker. And I knew in my heart that Charlie would have approved.

"This recipe was super easy," Cassidy said once the cookies were done and piled up on one of my antique china platters.

Parker tilted the platter up for a better camera angle. "Anyone could make these cookies."

"Just remember to follow the directions exactly like they're written," Cassidy said with emphasis.

"And you'll get some great cookies," Parker finished with a gigantic grin.

Then he slid his arm around Cassidy's shoulders, and she leaned into him. They each picked up a cookie and took a bite.

"*Mmmm* . . . so delicious!" they said together, before I hit the off button on the camera remote.

"Wonderful, you two! You did such a great job," I gushed when they had finished. "Cassidy, you are welcome to come over and bake cookies anytime you like."

"Yeah, Cass, anytime," said a grinning Parker.

She laughed, and then they just gazed into each other's eyes again.

I smiled and decided to leave them alone together in the kitchen with their cookies. And as I headed for my office, I heard the unmistakable sound of the kitchen being cleaned up and dishes being done. Somehow, I figured Cassidy had taken the lead there, and that was probably her routine. Which made me want to add her to the family even more than ever.

She left shortly before it was time for me to cook dinner. Of course, I headed back downstairs to say goodbye and insisted that Cassidy take half of the remaining cookies home to her family. I was especially pleased that Parker had practiced some manners, in that he didn't simply devour every single cookie there.

I was also happy that my dreamy-eyed son seemed to forget all about my speed dating night, and he didn't demand an explanation when it came to my three bouquets.

But he did want to know what I thought of his "friend."

"And please don't make a big deal about it," he insisted, before he proceeded to down half a lasagna and half a side salad.

So I reigned in my excitement and simply said, "I think she's terrific, Parker."

"Yeah," he said with a sigh. "She really is."

"What's she going to do after graduation?"

"She's going to A & M, just like me. She wants to be a scientist and do genetic research or something."

"That's sounds nice," I said with a restraint that bordered on being heroic. Though on the inside, I was cheering and doing a happy dance.

A major happy dance.

I let him off from kitchen duty that night, so he could go to his room and edit the cooking video. And yes, I knew better, but I already had visions of their wedding flashing before my eyes. I loved what she brought out in Parker, and the two were so complementary.

Something that was incredibly evident in the well-done and well-edited video that Parker showed me on his computer a few hours later. "It'll go live tonight, Mom. I've even posted the link on several websites so we can counter Mindie's video."

"You did such a great job, kiddo. Thanks for doing this."

"Is it worth letting me take Dad's car to prom? For sure?"

I laughed. "Yes, Parker. You can take the car to prom. But there will be a few rules attached. After all, it is a very expensive and very rare vintage car."

"Understood," he said seriously, before the realization seemed to fully hit him. Then he suddenly grinned. "Thanks, oh, mom of mine. You're the greatest." And with that, he was off to bed, with Ellery and Agatha following behind.

He was still grinning the next day when he left for school.

And frankly, it made me happy to see him so happy. It had been a few years since his father had died, and God knows, he'd certainly had more than his fair share of tough times and adjustments. Though I was going to miss him terribly when he went to college, I was still pleased to see him getting on with his life.

I was even smiling myself when my phone rang. It was Hayes. Right away, I wondered if he was going to cancel our date. Not that I would have been too terribly disappointed, given that I'd only agreed to go out with him as a childish reaction to Remy.

"Thank you for the flowers," I told him. "They're lovely."

"Glad you like them. I don't send a lot of flowers, so you might consider it a compliment. So are we still on for tomorrow night?"

"Yes, as far as I'm concerned."

"Oh, good. Because I've got a request that might sound a little bold, considering I don't know you all that well. I was wondering if we could go back to your place for dessert. After dinner. I hear you're amazing in the kitchen."

And that's when my breath caught in my throat. It had been a long time since I'd had a man mention "dessert," and say that I was amazing in the kitchen. Or any other room for that matter. And frankly, the only other man who'd spoken such words to me was one I'd been married to. So yes, call me old-fashioned, but I was a little stunned to hear this coming from a man I barely even knew. A man who was moving way too fast for me.

"Hayes," I began, feeling flustered. "You're very attractive and the thought of being with you is, well, 'breathtaking.' But I don't think I'm ready for what you have in mind."

"Seriously, how long would it take someone with your skills to 'get ready'?"

"Excuse me?"

"I mean, what goes into a dessert? Sugar? Maybe flour? Butter?"

Words that made me roll my eyes. "Oh, you mean actual 'dessert' dessert."

"Well, yeah . . . What did you think I meant?"

"Never mind. But yes, I can make a dessert for us."

In fact, I quickly realized it would be a good chance to make my Cherries Jubilee recipe again. To do a trial run before I made a video of it, or asked Parker and Cassidy to make a video of it.

After I got off the phone with Hayes, I felt a sudden pang of guilt. For some reason, I just wasn't as into him as he probably deserved. Despite the cowlicks and the occasional uncontrollable spikes of his hair, he was as devastatingly handsome as a man could be. Not to mention, a pretty nice guy, especially with the way he came over to check on me when Remy had upset me during the speed dating.

But the problem was, he wasn't exactly what I would call "interesting." And no matter how I looked at it, I couldn't see much of a future with him. So this one date would be it. I wasn't going to lead him on. Though on the plus side, having dinner with Hayes would give me a chance to question him about Dex and his "activities." Which included information about Dex's exes. In fact, I might even end up with that one specific clue that I needed to finally solve the mystery of the murder across the street.

In the meantime, I decided it was time for me to go back to the beginning and chat with Deidre again. So I called her to make an appointment. After all, having a date was the perfect excuse for me to need another hair appointment so soon.

"The only time I have open is two o'clock tomorrow afternoon," she said, sighing.

"That would be great," I responded with a cheerfulness that was as fake as the ring I'd bought from Gage Flause. "I've got a date tomorrow night."

"Oh, how lovely, Maddie. I'll make you look beautiful. I promise."

A promise that I was pretty sure would go unfulfilled.

And yes, I knew it was risky, getting my hair done only hours before I was supposed to go out with Hayes. But it was a risk I was willing to take. Because I truly needed to question Deirdre, since the scissors that were found shoved into Dex's back belonged to her. And for all I knew, Deirdre was the one who had put them there.

Truth be told, I should have questioned Deirdre days ago.

The memory of Dex lying dead on his kitchen floor made me shudder. But I tried not to dwell on it as I grabbed a cup of coffee, all ready to head upstairs to work on the next chapter of Blaze's book. But I had barely started up my front staircase when the sound of my Peter Gunn ringtone filled the front entry.

Much to my irritation, it was Remy.

I sighed, wondering if I should answer it or not. But I figured it was better to talk to him on the phone rather than have him just show up at my house.

"Hello, Remy," I said as evenly as I could. "Thank you for the flowers. They are very pretty."

"Glad you liked them."

At that point, I wasn't sure what to say. Mostly because what I *wanted* to say was completely immature and irrational. Not to mention, purely adolescent. What was it about this man that brought out that side of me? A side of myself that I didn't particularly like.

Now I fought hard to wrestle with my emotions and get them under control. "Remy, I don't think we should see each other anymore. I don't believe we're good for each other."

"More specifically, I'm not good for you."

"Something like that."

"Well, I'm calling to let you know that I met the woman who'd been stalking Dex Degill. Belinda Stanke. I met her at the speed dating event. And yes, you were right. There had been an open restraining order on the woman, and she has a pretty long rap sheet. Though I'm guessing she probably didn't know I was a cop when she was hitting on me."

I rolled my eyes. "Well, I'm glad you got to meet her. I wouldn't have thought she was your type, but hey, whatever works for you. Maybe you're into that whole 'bad girl' persona. And that restraining order won't make much difference now that Dex is dead."

"Probably not, Maddie," he said, chomping on his words. "Especially now that she's dead, too."

That's when my heart skipped a beat. "Belinda? Dead? I can't believe it. I just saw her at speed dating. How can that be?"

"We fished her Crown Vic out of Abbott Cove early this morning. It was mostly submerged, and her body was inside."

I gasped. "So she drowned?"

"No, no fluid found in her lungs. It looks like she was stabbed first. So she probably died before someone rigged her car to drive it into the water."

"She was murdered . . ." I breathed, hardly believing my ears. "Did any camera catch her car? And was anyone riding with her?"

"There was only one camera in all of Abbott Cove Park. And we can barely make out a second person in the car with her when she drove in, around one in the morning. It looks like the other person was wearing a hoodie, or a scarf or something. And they kept their head down. Plus, the picture is too grainy to tell who it is for sure."

I slid onto the first step of my staircase, feeling a little dizzy. "So it could have been a man or a woman."

"That's exactly right," he said matter-of-factly. "We figured the person stabbed her after the car was parked and then sent her and her car into the water. To cover up fingerprints and DNA and everything else. The killer probably hiked out of the park to avoid being seen. And her car was spotted by an early morning jogger."

"What about the knife that she was stabbed with?" I asked as I glanced out the window and noticed Bugsy's van was parked in Olivia's driveway.

"It was left in her body. It appears to be a plain old kitchen knife. And they stabbed her in the back."

Just like Dex had been stabbed in the back.

"Could it have been a robbery? Or an assault?" I wondered out loud.

"No signs of a struggle and no signs of an assault. And her purse with credit cards and money were all there."

"Remy, why are you telling me this? You were so adamant that I stay out of this investigation. You even threatened me with Obstruction of Justice."

He took in a deep breath. "I know, Maddie. But with the information you gave me on Saturday, I think you've proved that you're a top-notch investigator. And I'd like to hear what you think about this. Do you know anyone who might have wanted her dead?"

"Maybe," I told him. "Since she seemed to be stalking anyone who had been close to Dex, it's very possible that she accidentally saw or heard something she shouldn't have."

"Meaning, someone might have murdered her to shut her up."

I took a sip of my coffee which was now starting to become lukewarm. "Uh-huh. Plus, I know she was pretty upset with Trevor the other night. When he told her the diamond necklace that Dex had given her was a fake. I think it was the one and only thing she had to hang on to, when it came to Dex. The man she considered to be the love of her life."

"Hmmm . . . maybe she went after Trevor. Or threatened him with something she knew about him."

"And it's very possible that she *did* know something. Since she frequented those speed dating events."

"Anything else?"

"Not off the top of my head. But I'll let you know if I think of anything."

"I'd appreciate it," he said, sounding sincere. "In the meantime, I want you and Parker to stay home and keep your doors locked. Don't let anyone in until we get this case solved."

I laughed. "Remy, that's just not possible. Parker has school and we both have plans and appointments. We have lives."

"All right, Maddie. I get it. But please be careful. There's a killer running around and the murders seem to be centered around your neighborhood. I'd be pretty upset if something ever happened to you."

And with that, we said our goodbyes, without making any plans to get together again. Which suited me just fine.

I was still at the bottom of my staircase when I ended the call. For a moment or two, I just sat there, taking in the news. Sure, I didn't like Belinda's stalking activities, and to be honest, I wasn't really a fan of hers. Regardless, I still hated to think that someone had murdered her.

But I didn't get time to dwell on it. Because my doorbell rang, making me nearly jump a mile. On my feet, I glanced out the peephole of my front door and at the person standing on my front stoop.

A person I had hoped I wouldn't see again for a long, long time.

If ever at all.

Olivia.

Chapter Twenty-six

I blinked a couple of times and kept on staring out the peephole of my front door. Just the sight of Olivia on my doorstep sent shock waves running through my body. As far as I was concerned, she had a lot of nerve showing up at my house after telling a police detective that I was having an affair with her husband. Not only had Olivia's lie landed my name on Remy's list of "People Who Might Have Murdered Dex Degill," but it had essentially ruined my relationship with him, too. Funny thing, but it was kind of hard to be romantically involved with a man who considered me to be a suspect in a homicide investigation. Especially when his profession required him to shut me out with no explanation, since he couldn't have a personal relationship with someone he was investigating.

So why had Olivia done something so underhanded? Frankly, I could only think of a couple of reasons—either she was a nasty, self-serving woman, or she wanted to draw suspicion away from herself.

Or both.

A whole range of emotions suddenly raced through my brain, starting with anger. And when that fizzled out, terror took over. Mostly because Olivia had landed high atop my *own* list of "People Who Might Have Murdered Dex Degill." And now Belinda Stanke. Maybe Belinda had seen something incriminating, something that could send Olivia to the big house once and for all. So Olivia had silenced her.

She rang the bell again. "I heard you in there, Maddie. Open up. I need to talk to you."

That's when my fear and anger gave away to another feeling—determination. If Olivia had killed her husband, I wanted to see her behind bars. Meaning, I was more determined than ever to make sure the crime from across the cul-de-sac was solved. By me. Or by Remy. It didn't really matter to me who actually figured it out. I only cared that the killer was caught, so our neighborhood could go back to being safe again.

So—good, bad, or otherwise—I opened the door. "What do you want, Olivia?"

She practically pushed her way into my house. "I have something I want to tell you about Dex's second wife. Deirdre. I think you need to check her out."

"Why do you say that?" I asked, careful not to invite her to sit down.

Because I'd lost all patience with Olivia and the way she'd been trying (and usually succeeding) to manipulate me. I'd allowed it before, but I wasn't going to allow it again.

Olivia's gaze moved up my curved staircase to the Juliet balcony on the second-floor landing. "Deirdre claims that Dex ruined her life. She says he lured her away from the man she really loved."

"And you lured Dex away from Deirdre. So, technically that would make *you* the one who ruined Deirdre's life."

Her head swung around so fast that I thought she might get whiplash. Her green eyes practically shot out laser beams, about to burn a hole in my skull. Apparently, no one had ever spoken to Olivia like that before.

I wondered how she would handle it. But to my surprise, she managed to keep her cool. Or so it seemed, as she squinted her eyes and continued to glance around my house. That's when I got the strangest sensation, that she was looking around to make sure I was alone.

Something that made me realize I needed to get her out of there. And quick.

"If you'll excuse me, Olivia. I'm expecting a phone call," I lied. "From my editor."

"Sure you are, Maddie," she said in such an icy tone that I feared I might get frostbite. "I heard you had a busy night on Saturday. At the speed dating. Looks like you made a big impression. I was told that Dex used to frequent those things. Before and after we were married."

She spotted the bouquets that I had on my dining room table and moved over to look at the flowers that Hayes had sent. She glanced at the card and then gave me the side-eye. Without asking if I minded, she grabbed the card from Remy's bouquet and read the note. Then she immediately glared at me, anger flashing across her face.

She turned to Guy's bouquet next, but I raced over and snatched up the crystal vase with the roses before she could read the card.

"You never mentioned how you learned that I was at the speed dating event," I said quietly, feeling my skin crawl.

"No, I didn't," she said in a low sneer.

"And by the way, Olivia, do you happen to be missing a kitchen knife?" I inquired, unable to stop my runaway mouth from annoying the person who might possibly have stabbed two people.

And possibly wanted to add me to her list of victims.

She stared at me, and her eyes seemed to darken a few shades. But instead of answering, she simply spun on her stiletto heels and stomped out of my house. She was halfway down my walkway when she stopped and looked back at me.

Naturally, I didn't wait another second to close the door and lock it up. Tight. Then I turned toward my staircase and leaned against the door, breathing hard. Olivia hadn't said much, but somehow, I felt like she'd threatened me all the same.

I wrapped my arms around myself, trying to stop the shaking that had practically taken over my body. I was barely under control when my phone rang. Was it Olivia calling? Though I didn't remember ever giving her my number.

Thankfully, it was Guy who was phoning instead. "Maddie? Is everything all right? You sound a little rattled."

"Just for a moment," I told him, instantly calmed by his strong, steady voice. "But I'm better now. And I was about to call you. Thank you for the beautiful bouquet. The roses are lovely."

"Glad you liked them. I was afraid they might be a little over-the-top. But my mama told me long ago to treat a lady right."

"I like her already," I said with a laugh.

"I did, too. Up until we lost her a few years back. She was beauty-queen beautiful on the outside and tough as nails on the inside. A great lady. Anyway, I wondered if you'd like to go out on Saturday night."

"I'd love to, but just so you know, I've signed up to be one of the chaperones for my son's high school prom on Saturday night. Would you be interested in being my date?"

"Why, Miss Maddie, are you asking me to prom?"

I laughed. "Why, yes. Yes, I am."

"Well, in that case, I would be happy to escort you to your son's prom. Do I need to get you a corsage?"

"No, I think the flowers you sent already are plenty."

"Should I wear a tux? I've got a couple. Seems I always have some black-tie event or another that I have to go to."

"I think a tux would be nice. My son is going to wear a vintage tux to go along with my car that I told him he could drive that night."

"Please tell me it's a classic car . . ." he practically pleaded.

Words that made me laugh. "It's a black, fifty-six Continental Mark Two."

He let out a low whistle. "*Whooaaa* . . . wait a minute, you didn't tell me you owned a fifty-six Mark Two. That's a gem of a car. One of the best ever made. Would you be offended if I date you just for your car?" he joked.

Or at least, I hoped he was joking.

I laughed again. "I'll even take you for a ride in it."

"Okay, now my life is complete. I probably didn't tell you, but I'm a car guy."

And from there, the conversation flowed naturally. And we talked for a few more minutes before he had to run to another meeting. I was smiling by the time we ended the call, and more than a little excited about Saturday night.

I was walking on air as I returned to my kitchen to reheat my coffee in the microwave. Then I headed back to my staircase again, about to go up to my office and get back to work on Blaze's current mystery.

But I had only gone up a couple of steps when the doorbell rang again. Between phone calls and people at my front door, it seemed like my house had suddenly turned into Grand Central Station. And at the rate I was going, I was never going to finish writing this new book.

More than likely, I figured it was Olivia at the door again. Though I had no intention of letting her in.

I stepped to the bottom of the stairs and moved next to the front door. "Olivia, I have nothing to say to you. Now go back home."

That's when a masculine voice replied, "It's not Olivia, ma'am. It's Bugsy. Olivia is really upset. She said you were terribly ugly to her. Ma'am, I need to speak to you. Now."

I glanced out my dining room window and saw Bugsy looming on my stoop, with Olivia standing in her driveway. Her arms were folded in front of her. Apparently, since she couldn't get me to do her bidding, she had sent Bugsy over. But to do what, exactly?

That's when I finally and fully understood what a world-class expert Olivia was when it came to manipulating people. In fact, she was clearly at a Ph.D. level, and if there were such a degree, she undoubtedly would have graduated at the top of her class. Worst of all, she always manipulated others for her benefit and at someone else's expense. She had certainly managed to manipulate me on more than one occasion. And I'd seen firsthand how she'd manipulated her own husband. Now it appeared she'd done the same to Bugsy.

But the question was, since Bugsy seemed so complaisant and pliable, exactly how far would he go for her? What exactly would he do at her behest?

Though at the moment, I mostly wondered if I was in any kind of danger. After all, Bugsy knew every square inch of my house and yard, having checked it for bugs just days ago. So he could probably figure out how to get in, even if I didn't open the door for him. And Olivia had probably told him I was home alone.

He banged on my door again, just as I was saved by the buzz, so to speak. Or more specifically, the buzz of my neighbor's drone. The cute, firefly-like craft that I referred to as "Evinrude." Because I suddenly heard it outside, and I knew what would be next. The inevitable phone call from Spencer Poe.

I even had my phone in my hand when it rang. "Mrs. Montgomery, I have detected hostile activity in your quadrant this morning, and I am on my way over," he informed me succinctly and then immediately hung up, something he'd never done before.

In the meantime, I decided to try talking it out with the big, angry man on my stoop. "What's going on, Bugsy?"

I could hear him stomp his big boots on the other side of the door. "Something you said really upset Olivia. I don't like to see her upset. I don't like it when people are mean to her."

"Bugsy, you've met me. You've killed insects at my house. You know I was married to a Colonel. Do I seem like the kind of person who would be mean to someone?"

"Well . . . no, ma'am. I guess not."

"And I've always been nice to you, right?"

"Yes, ma'am. Hey, did you see this drone out here?" he asked, suddenly distracted. "This thing is awesome."

"It's Mr. Poe's drone, Bugsy."

"That guy is so cool. And he's got a cool gadget."

"Well, I believe he thinks you're cool, too, Bugsy," I told him, having the odd sensation that some kind of volatile situation had just been diffused.

I unlocked the door and stepped outside, my fear and concern evaporating now that he seemed to be calmed down. Oddly enough, he reminded me of a big guard dog—all sweet and friendly and gangly until he perceived some kind of threat against whomever he happened to be guarding. Which in this case happened to be my neighbor across the street. Though I noticed Olivia had now disappeared. No doubt going back into her own house and leaving Bugsy to fight her battles on his own.

By this time, Spencer had joined us. And Bugsy immediately stood at attention and gave him a snappy salute and an even snappier, "Sir, yes, sir!"

"At ease, soldier," Spencer told him. "It appeared you were loaded for bear when you came over here to Mrs. Montgomery's house. I'd say you were pretty angry, and acting in a hostile manner. Is that correct, son?"

Bugsy let out a long sigh. "I don't know what came over me, sir. One minute I was out *kee-eell-ing* fire ants in Olivia's yard, and then Olivia came outside, and she was crying and all upset. She leaned her head on my shoulder, and I put my arms around her, and I asked her what'd happened to make her so upset. She pointed to Maddie's house and said Maddie had been really ugly to her. And that's when something just clicked inside of me and took over. The next thing I knew, I was at Maddie's door."

Spencer nodded. "Like a knight in shining armor. Off to avenge the honor of a fair maiden."

"Yes, sir, I guess so," said a very deflated Bugsy. "I just lost my head."

Spencer put his hand on Bugsy's shoulder. "Son, you're a good man. And it's entirely noble for a man to want to protect a woman in danger. But gathering intel on any situation first is of vital importance. And a good soldier must always assess a situation before taking action."

Bugsy's blonde eyebrows shot up. "I thought I did, but it's so confusing, sir. Olivia's had a rough life. She's such a beautiful woman, and her husband didn't treat her very well. And he didn't appreciate her one bit. So you'd think she'd be happy now that he's gone. But she's not, and I don't know what to do about it."

"But you feel like you need to do *something*?" I clarified.

He stood up soldier straight. "Yes, ma'am. Olivia needs a man around the house. Someone who appreciates her and will take care of her. And she seems to like me. So I'm thinking of stepping up to the plate and being the man she needs."

That's when I sighed. "Bugsy, have you looked at your shoulder? I notice it isn't actually wet from all those tears she was supposed to be crying," I said gently.

He touched his shirt. "But I saw her. She was crying. Hard."

"Some women are very good at using tears to manipulate men," I told him. "They're even good at faking their tears, if it gets them what they want."

"Olivia would never do that," Bugsy said as though he were trying to convince himself. "She would never take advantage of me."

Spencer was already shaking his head. "Are you sure, son? She succeeded in getting you to come over to confront Mrs.

Montgomery. Even though you like Mrs. Montgomery and knew she wouldn't harm a fly."

Now Bugsy leaned back and pulled his shirt out, so he could get a better look at it. "Well . . . I'll be the son of a centipede. I could have sworn she was crying. For real," he said, almost like he was coming out of a trance. "But why would she do that to me?"

"She must have had something to gain from it," I said carefully. "Has she ever tried to manipulate you before? She can be very good at pushing people's buttons."

He turned and stared at Olivia's house. "I'm not sure . . . But maybe . . ."

Spencer nodded to him. "I would listen to Mrs. Montgomery, son. I believe she knows what she is talking about."

"Understood, sir. Ma'am. Now if you'll excuse me, I've got a job to finish."

Then he made a beeline back to Olivia's house, forgetting to salute for the first time.

"Thank you for coming to *my* rescue," I said to Spencer, once Bugsy was safely across the street. "Bugsy seemed like he was practically hypnotized when he came over here. Olivia really did a number on him."

"I can see that to be the case. The lad has the heart of a soldier, and it is a shame that he was never accepted to serve," Spencer agreed. "And today, his first instinct was to save a woman whom he believed to be a damsel in distress. Unfortunately, he was misinformed and reacted without learning the truth."

"Yes, he did."

My neighbor nodded to me. "Yet another piece of the puzzle, I suspect, Mrs. Montgomery."

"I believe so, Spencer. And I have to say, there are a lot of pieces to this puzzle. It's been a very tangled web that I've been unraveling."

"I have no doubt that you are very close to solving this case, Mrs. Montgomery. As a matter of fact, I suspect you may be closer than you realize."

Words that surprised me. Yet at the same time, they didn't. Because, deep down, I also had a hunch that I was close to unmasking the murderer of Dex Degill. And now, Belinda Stanke. And there was something at the back of my brain, something just out of reach of my consciousness that seemed to be niggling at me. Something someone had said. But it was also something that I couldn't quite bring to the forefront.

Though I put my thoughts aside after Spencer left, flying Evinrude along with him, and I finally stepped into my office and got back to work on Blaze's latest adventure. I took a break only long enough to put braised short ribs in the oven to slow cook.

But there was no more working after a very excited Parker came home from school.

"The video was a big hit, Mom. We got all kinds of likes and hits and comments," he told me as he showed me his computer screen.

I read a young woman's comment out loud. "I'm loving the 'Passidy.' Passidy?" I repeated.

Parker grinned. "Yup, Mom. Parker and Cassidy. Our names combined."

"Oh, how nice," I said, feeling my heart flutter.

"Plus, I linked your book with the chocolate chip cookie recipe to our video. And your sales went way up."

"Okay, *really* nice," I stressed.

Right before Parker changed the subject.

And wanted to finally know the scoop on the bouquets sitting on our dining room table. So I gave him the lowdown, you might say. And yes, I talked to him honestly, though I wasn't completely forthcoming with all the details, since I still wasn't sure he was comfortable with me dating. Considering how much he loved and still missed his father. But in the end, I let him know that I was on the outs with Remy, and Hayes was simply a one-time-only dinner date, whereby I could gather more information on Olivia and Dex's exes. But Guy, on the other hand, was someone I was truly interested in.

"Cool, Mom. So we're both dating. And we've both got dates for tomorrow night. Now what's for dinner?"

So much for my big moment of coming clean with the kid.

I rolled my eyes while I started to make a double portion of sour cream mashed potatoes to go with the short ribs that I pulled out of the oven. Which by now, were so tender they practically fell off the bone.

Later that evening, I got all the ingredients measured and set out to make my Cherries Jubilee recipe the following night. Then I headed straight for my closet to find something suitable to wear to Parker's prom. With the kitties sitting tall next to my shoes and scrutinizing my every move, I decided on a black, halter-style gown with a few sequins around the neckline. The perfect dress for a mom in the role of prom chaperone.

But the dress needed to be dry-cleaned. Along with the tux that Parker planned to wear.

So I ran upstairs and grabbed the old tux and Charlie's old suit from Parker, before I put the whole bunch on the front seat of my SUV, ready to take in the next day.

Which was exactly what I did, before my appointment with Deirdre. Keeping an eye on the clock, I practically stumbled inside the cleaners and dropped all the clothes on the counter. After giving instructions to the attendant to lengthen the pants so they'd fit Parker, I quickly checked all the suit pockets to make sure nothing had accidentally been left inside.

I started with the tux, and like I suspected, all the pockets were empty. Then I checked out the pants pockets and the front pockets of Charlie's old suit and came up empty again. With one pocket left, I reached into the breast pocket of the suit jacket. And that's when my fingers touched a small, round, metallic object. One with a chain attached.

I pulled it out, and much to my amazement, I found I was holding a gold locket. A very, very old locket. With gold filigree and set with seed pearls and what appeared to be tiny rubies and emeralds. Gems that I guessed were probably the real deal, unlike the ones I'd seen at Olivia's house.

Right away, I wondered if Charlie had bought this for me and died before he'd had a chance to give it to me. Tears welled up in my eyes as I realized the moments we never had because of his early death.

But then I turned the locket over. And saw a name engraved on the back.

Theodosia.

That's when my stomach sank to my knees. Who in the world was Theodosia? Had Charlie gotten this stunning antique locket for another woman? Was it possible that the love of my life, the man I'd spent years mourning, hadn't been as faithful as I'd believed? And maybe even had a woman on the side?

The mere thought of it sent a pang of pain stabbing through my heart.

How could this be happening?

Chapter Twenty-seven

Needless to say, I was pretty shaken up as I left the dry cleaners and headed to the salon for my appointment with Deirdre. Finding an antique locket in the pocket of my late husband's suit had knocked me for a loop and sent my mind whirling. If the locket hadn't been engraved, I would've had no doubt that it was a gift that Charlie had planned to give me. Or to our daughter, Lyndi. But this locket had a name on it, and that name wasn't mine or my daughter's.

Instead, it read "Theodosia."

I had to say, it was a name I'd never heard before, and frankly, I thought it sounded like a very, very old name. I even wondered if it might have been the name of one of Charlie's late relatives. Was it possible he'd had a great-great-great-aunt named Theodosia that I'd never heard about? Honestly, neither one of us could have known *all* the names of each other's ancestors from generations back.

Then again, maybe he'd had a woman on the side, a Greek beauty by the name of Theodosia.

Either way, my imagination had taken off at warp speed, leaving reality far behind. Even though I knew there were plenty of reasons why Charlie might have had the locket. It was possible he'd simply found it lying on the ground somewhere. Or maybe he'd gotten it at an antique store, intending to have the name rubbed out and have my name engraved in its place.

All of which could have been true. But the real problem was, I'd probably never learn the truth about the locket. Since he was gone, it was likely the story of that necklace had died with him.

Unfortunately, that very realization left me completely frazzled as I entered the beauty shop and Deirdre led me to her chair.

"Maddie, you don't seem like yourself today. Is anything wrong?"

"No . . . no," I lied, reminding myself that I was here to question Deirdre and hopefully learn something to help me figure out who had murdered Dex Degill. And Belinda Stanke.

She gasped. "Don't tell me your date cancelled on you. Men can be such pigs! You can't count on them for anything."

A sentiment that made me gulp. Was she right? And had I been wrong all these years, believing that Charlie was a loving and loyal husband? To think, I'd spent so much time aching for him while he was deployed, and now I wondered if he'd been unfaithful to me. Was it possible he'd met some woman named Theodosia during his last deployment?

I took a deep breath and tried to focus. "No, I still have my date tonight," I managed to murmur to Deirdre.

"Okay, honey, in that case, I promise to make you look gorgeous. I see that conditioner I put in your hair last time did wonders. Do you want more of it this time?"

To which I simply said, "No thanks. A little of that stuff goes a long way."

And I do mean a *long*, long way . . .

"I'll just have a wash and a blowout," I confirmed as she led me to the shampoo station.

Deirdre sighed shortly after she started to shampoo my hair. "I wish I had a date, Maddie. It's been such a long time. And I really didn't think I'd still be working in a hair salon. I figured I'd have another rich husband by now so I wouldn't have to do this stupid job. I hate it so much."

Which wasn't exactly what a girl wanted to hear while she was getting her hair done. For a moment, I even considered running out the door. But for the sake of solving this case, I decided to hang in there.

"Well, maybe you'll meet someone soon," I said, hoping to sound reassuring. "You know, there are those speed dating events at the Lytely Char and Grill Restaurant. Maybe you should give it a try."

She wrapped a towel around my head and started to dry me off. "I've heard of those. One of my clients goes out to them all the time. And yeah, it might be the place to find a new husband. But first I'm hoping to get together with my ex."

"You don't mean . . . Dex?"

"Oh, no, of course not. He's, umm . . . you know."

She led me back to her station. "Yes, I heard. I'm afraid I also heard . . . well, about your scissors. I'm so sorry, Deirdre. I know how much you loved those scissors. And they were specially made."

"My scissors," she repeated, her eyes turning dark as she started to comb out my hair.

Very forcefully, I might add.

"I can't believe they disappeared on me," she went on. "I saw them that morning, and then, when I came back from lunch, I couldn't find them anywhere."

"That must have been pretty upsetting," I said softly.

"Oh, yeah," she said, combing my hair a little faster. "The police officer questioned me for hours. That guy named Detective Reagan. He wouldn't let me go, and he wouldn't give my scissors back, either. Men are scum, aren't they, Maddie?"

"Well, you never know . . ." I started to say, remembering my own emotional roller coaster with Remy. Not to mention, my recent revelation about Charlie's possible infidelity.

But Deirdre interrupted me with, "If only I had a rich husband. None of this would have happened."

For a moment, I was speechless, amazed at her ability to go from "men are scum" to wanting to marry one in under a minute.

Tears now formed in her eyes as she slapped mousse onto my head. "I don't know how my scissors got into Dex's back. I wish whoever took them had returned them to me. With all those gemstones in there, those scissors were valuable!"

Of course, I knew better than to tell her they might not be as valuable as she thought. Considering she'd traded in her diamond engagement ring (most likely a real one, at that) for the stones that were set into her scissors. And since those stones had all come from Flause Jewelers, it was likely they were a bunch of fakes.

"I'm sure Dex would have preferred that someone hadn't pushed those scissors into his back, too," I replied.

That's when a couple of big, gloppy tears rolled down Deirdre's cheeks. "Oh, poor, poor Dex! How I loved that man. I could've forgiven him for cheating on me with that little tramp, Olivia. Because it's her fault that my marriage ended. Otherwise, I'd still be rich, and I wouldn't have this crappy job."

With that, she turned on her hair dryer and blasted my head with hot air. I watched as she rolled sections of my hair into a large, round brush, smoothing it as she went. At that moment, I had to say, she was actually doing a pretty nice job. I was even sort of relaxed by the time she had finished and returned the blow-dryer to its stand.

Then she pulled out a small, teasing comb. "I'm just going to rat this out a little, Maddie, and make your hair a little fuller."

Suddenly my heart started to pound. "Okay, but not too full, Deirdre."

"No worries, Maddie. I'm a professional, and I know what I'm doing. By the way, you never told me who you're going out with tonight. Is it anyone I know?"

"Probably. I'm going out with Dex's old business partner. Hayes Hawthorne."

She gasped and her eyes went wide. "Hayes? That old cheapskate? Ha! You'll probably have to buy your own dinner. You'll be lucky if he doesn't charge you for the gas in his car to get to the restaurant," she practically hollered as more tears rolled down her cheeks and her teasing comb suddenly took on a life of its own.

"Deirdre . . . I think that's enough . . ."

But my words fell on deaf ears. And now I wondered if Deidre had tried to get money out of Hayes, just as Olivia had, since she believed she should get part of the business.

And since I clearly didn't know when to stop—much like Deirdre wasn't *going* to stop—I immediately asked, "Deirdre, did you inherit any money from Dex's share of his company?"

That's when the teasing suddenly picked up speed, even though I didn't think it was possible for her to go any faster. Yet I watched in horror as she pouffed out my hair like a baker whipping egg whites into a méringue.

As she did, more tears rolled down her cheeks. "Oh, Maddie, Dex didn't bother to put me in his will at all. I didn't get a dime of his money."

By now, her comb was moving so fast that it was practically a blur. "Men, Maddie, men! They'll betray you every time. They'll cheat on you, and they'll break your heart. Did your late husband ever cheat on you?"

Her words hit me to the core, after finding the locket in Charlie's old suit. It only added to the shell shock I was already feeling, considering the dizzying height that Deirdre had managed to rat out my hair. At this point, I could've easily doubled for a 1960s politician's wife. And while Deirdre sprayed the whole thing with an added layer of hairspray—or something resembling the polyurethane on my antique furniture—I wondered how my hair and I were going to fit into my car. Especially now that I was a good five inches taller, and the finish on my hair had dried to a solid form.

And while I should have been the one in tears, amazingly, Deirdre was completely sobbing by the time she added insult to injury, by attaching a little pink bow to the top of my new hairdo. Making me look like the poodle from down the street after it had been to the groomers.

"There you go, Maddie," she said, sputtering through her tears. "You're all ready for your date tonight. I hope you have a wonderful time. Just remember that men are basically pond scum. You can pay the receptionist at the front."

Though I'm not entirely sure how, I managed to hoist myself from her chair. Then I hung onto the armrests for a second or two, fearing I might tip over since my center of gravity was now entirely skewed. Especially since my head seemed to weigh at least eight pounds more than it had when I walked in.

Taking careful steps, I wobbled to the front, paid my bill, and staggered out to my car. I got plenty of stares along the way, and even a few nasty glares, but frankly, I was still too mortified by what she'd done to my hair to even react to anyone else's reaction. I slid my sunglasses on, hoping it might provide me with a bit of a disguise as I drove home on autopilot. All the while, I wondered how I would ever get all this stuff washed out of my hair, so I could return it to normal. Though I wasn't terribly hopeful, considering my hair felt as solid as a football helmet every time I touched it.

But more than anything, I prayed I wouldn't see anyone along the way. I thought I was home free as I turned onto my street. That was, until I spotted Spencer Poe returning from the mailbox. He flagged me down, and I slowed to a stop and rolled down the window, expecting the inevitable reaction.

What I got instead was a surprise.

"My goodness, Mrs. Montgomery, I haven't seen that hairstyle since I was young. I am quite happy to see it make a return. No doubt, the Colonel would have appreciated it very much."

For some reason, his words stabbed through my heart like Deirdre's scissors through Dex Degill's back.

I fought off the tears that pricked my eyes. "About 'the Colonel,' Spencer. I know you two were friends, and I wondered if you could tell me something about an item I found in the pocket of one of his old suits today." With that, I pulled the antique locket from my purse and handed it to my neighbor.

"My heavens," came his immediate response. "If I am not mistaken, I would say this piece is a few centuries old. It appears he was about to give you a rather lovely gift."

I shook my head. "I don't think so, Spencer. Look at the back."

He turned it over and read the inscription aloud and, for a moment, looked surprisingly startled. "Theodosia?"

"Yup. So I have a very delicate question to ask you, Spencer. I always believed that my husband was true to me. But is it possible that he'd been having an affair? And did he know anyone named Theodosia?"

Spencer's response was immediate. "Fear not, Mrs. Montgomery, for there is one thing that I do not doubt. Your husband was completely committed to you and your children. He believed in fidelity and never would have made the egregious error of committing adultery. So, in answer to your question, the Colonel never, ever would have strayed from his marriage vows."

I smiled for the first time all afternoon. "Thank you, Spencer. I guess I always believed that in my heart, but seeing this set me back a bit. Even so, do you know of anyone named Theodosia? And why Charlie would've had this locket?"

"While I wasn't aware that the Colonel possessed such an item, I do know of one woman named Theodosia."

"Oh? Anyone I might have heard of?"

"Perhaps you have heard of an old and little-known Texas legend. One that involves pirate treasure."

My ears suddenly perked up.

He handed the locket back to me. "It starts with Theodosia Burr, the beloved daughter of Aaron Burr."

"One of our founding fathers?"

"That is correct, Mrs. Montgomery. He, of course, was Vice President of the United States, and his daughter, Theodosia, was married to the governor of South Carolina. In December of eighteen-twelve, she boarded a ship that was sailing to New York to visit her ailing father. But she and the vessel went missing, never to be seen again."

"Wow . . . And you think this might be her locket?"

"It was rumored that she had been taken hostage by pirates, who sailed the Atlantic Coast, but also frequented the Gulf Coast of Texas. And, as legend has it, one ship in particular was stranded up a swollen Texas river, thanks to a hurricane in eighteen-fourteen. A woman of some refinement was said to be found captive on the ship, after the rest of the pirates perished in the severe storm. The frail woman was rescued by an Indian chief, and she gave him her locket shortly before she passed away."

"And let me guess . . . the name on the locket was Theodosia."

"Correct again, Mrs. Montgomery. Did your husband ever mention this to you?"

I shook my head. "No, this is the first I've ever heard of it. But I assure you, I'll be doing some research on it now."

"Be careful, Mrs. Montgomery. Tell no one what you've found. Because, if it is what I believe it to be, your husband may have found the key to a very old and famous shipwreck. One with a true pirate's treasure chest that people have been hunting for centuries."

His words left me stunned as I drove the rest of the way home. It was all pretty overwhelming, and I wondered how Spencer Poe seemed to know all that right off the top of his head. Not only that, but now I was dying to know more about this Theodosia Burr, or whatever her married name happened to be. Unfortunately, it was something that would have to go on the back burner. Because right now, I needed to figure out how to resurrect my hair and get ready for my date with Hayes.

That is, if my hair could possibly be saved.

Parker's face said it all when I walked in.

First his eyes went wide and then he slapped his hands to his cheeks. "Seriously, Mom? Again?"

"Yes, again," I sighed. "I guess it's the price of being an amateur detective."

He touched the top of my head. "Wow, I wonder what the chemical composition of this stuff is. It's amazing. Your hair doesn't even move. I hate to say it, Mom, but your hair is sort of an engineering marvel."

Not exactly what I'd hoped to hear. "I'm sure it is, Parker. But the real question is, can you fix this?"

He stared at my head for a few more seconds. "I dunno, Mom. I may be smart . . . but this could be *way* out of my league . . ."

My heart began to race. If I couldn't return my hair back to normal, then I couldn't go on my date with Hayes. And if I couldn't go on my date with Hayes, I wouldn't have the chance to question him and find out what he might know about Dex's murder and all the suspects on my list. And after my beauty salon experience with Deirdre—and hearing her talk about Hayes—I had a feeling Hayes might just have a different perspective on things.

Not to mention, he might have some of the answers I was looking for. Answers that could help me solve this case.

Once and for all.

But it all depended on whether my genius son had some answers for me first. Meaning, my fate and the safety of the neighborhood depended upon the scientific ability of a seventeen-year-old.

Chapter Twenty-eight

I tried to run my fingers through my helmet-like hair, but I could barely get a few fingernails into the hardened mass. To be honest, I wasn't sure if water would even penetrate the outer shell, and I was pretty sure shampoo would roll right off.

Meaning, Parker was my only hope. Because I needed to be ready for my date in less than an hour and a half. Yet so far, Parker hadn't exactly given me any reassurance. Probably because he hadn't gotten over his utter amazement at the sight of my unintended hairdo.

At long last, he raised a brow. "Gee, Mom, I kind of hate to deconstruct that masterpiece."

"Yes, Parker, I get it. On one level, it is a work of art. But can you . . .?"

"Way ahead of you, Mom. I think I've got the stuff to break down that chemical composition. So you can wash out all those synthetic polymers."

I breathed a sigh of relief, well aware that this was another one of those moments when it paid to have a supersmart son. And while I ran upstairs to take care of a few things in my office, Parker went off to concoct something to save my hair.

If not my reputation.

Minutes later, he brought me a vial of some gooey, blue liquid.

I could hardly believe my eyes. "Parker, is this . . .?"

"You got it, Mom. Dishwashing soap. Same stuff you used last time. I sure hope you don't plan to make this a habit. Because I'm leaving for college in the fall. And I'm not going to be here to rescue your hair all the time."

"Hopefully my days of hair emergencies will be behind me," I told him, suddenly thinking of Cissy and her "nail emergency."

"We can only hope, Mom. Now I've got to go get ready myself. You're not the only one with a date."

"Duly noted."

I emerged from my room almost an hour later, with my hair restored to its original state, though it did look a little shinier than usual. I'd donned a simple navy halter dress and added some bold, gold jewelry and my new fake ring. Compared to the way I'd looked an hour ago, I was practically a beauty queen now. And I don't mean a 1960s-style beauty queen.

But much to my amazement, Hayes was already there, a half an hour early. Thankfully, Parker had finished getting ready and had let my date in.

"Oh, I see you two have met," I said with a smile as I fastened my second earring onto my lobe.

Parker gave me a knowing look. "Glad you could make it, Mom. I told Mr. Hawthorne here that you thought the bouquet he sent was really nice. And I showed him the bouquet that I got to take to Cassidy tonight."

I almost laughed at his antics as he held up the vase with the three roses that Remy had sent me. Minus the card of course.

"I'm sure Cassidy will love it," I said with a smile.

"I'll probably be home a little late, Mom. So don't wait up."

"Okay, Parker, have a wonderful time. Make sure you use your manners and eat slowly. And say hi to Cassidy for me."

"Got it, Mom. Oh, and by the way, I put the other stuff from the dining room table into the pantry."

Meaning, my bouquet from Guy.

"Thank you," I told him, right before he grabbed his keys, waved, and headed out the door.

Then I turned to Hayes, and the man practically took my breath away. He was so incredibly handsome that I even found it hard to focus for a moment or two. Tonight, he was wearing a blue, button-down shirt and a navy sports coat. And for once, his hair had laid down perfectly, and the sparkle in his eyes and his perfect white teeth only offset his perfect jawline.

"Hope you don't mind my being a little early, Maddie," he said in his melodic baritone. "But we get fifteen percent off if we show up at the restaurant before six-thirty."

"Sure, no problem," I replied, still mesmerized by this spectacle of masculinity before me.

Though when we got to the restaurant, I noticed the maître d' was clearly not as dazzled as I was, and he gave Hayes a dark look and a half-hearted smile. "Welcome, Mr. Hawthorne. So nice to see you again."

"You'll remember to give me my fifteen percent off tonight, right, Raúl?" Hayes confirmed.

"As always, Mr. Hawthorne. You've beat the clock again." The man grabbed a couple of menus and led us to a table in the back.

"Good," Hayes said with a smug smile.

"Can I get you both a glass of wine?" the maître d' asked with a sigh.

"No, we'll just have water," Hayes informed him, without asking me what I'd like to drink.

"I'll have an iced tea with lemon," I said, jumping in.

Hayes didn't waste any time looking at the menu the very second we were seated. And he accomplished that task in world-record time, whereby he snapped his menu shut and laid it down on the table with a loud *thump*!

Before I even had a chance to finish looking it over.

I immediately thought of Parker, and I wondered how his dinner was going. And more importantly, whether he was using his manners or not. Thankfully, it sounded like the family was simply going out for pizza, so my son's "ordering from the menu etiquette" would not be put to the test.

I finished my own perusal of the food selections. "It looks like you've eaten here before, Hayes. What do you recommend?"

"The shrimp," he said without hesitation. "I always get the shrimp. They cook it three different ways. Grilled, breaded and butterflied. It's my favorite thing to eat."

And it also happened to be the cheapest thing on the menu.

Nonetheless, it sounded good to me, so I ordered it along with Hayes when a waitress came to our table.

"I'm looking forward to that dessert you're making," he said with a smile as he sipped his ice water.

I added sweetener to my tea and took a sip. "It's a fun recipe," I admitted. "As well as being delicious."

"I can hardly wait. So . . . was that your first speed dating event?" he asked me.

"It was. I guess some of the people who go there are regulars."

"Oh, yeah. They're all hoping for new blood, so they can meet that right person."

"Do they ever have any luck?"

"I'd say so. After all, I'm here with you tonight," he said, flashing me his million-kilowatt smile.

Something that immediately made my heart start to thump, and I couldn't help but smile back, despite his "new blood" comment. "That's very sweet of you to say."

He stared into my eyes. "And I guess it depends on what you'd consider to be luck. Dex ended up with tons of dates from those events."

"Even when he was already married?" I asked with all the innocence I could muster, knowing full well that Dex hadn't let a pesky little thing like marriage interfere with his dating life.

Hayes rolled his eyes. "*Especially* while he was married."

"I'm amazed that all those women put up with that," I said as the waitress brought our entrees, considering the "Early Bird Specials" did not come with soup or salad.

"Dex had a way with women, and he knew how to flash the cash, if you know what I mean."

I took a bite of my shrimp, which, as it turned out, was delicious. "Sounds like he was spending a lot of money on those women."

Hayes laughed and tucked into his own shrimp. "Dex sure knew how to make it look like he was a big spender anyway. But the truth was, he wasn't as rich as he appeared to be. In fact, he was spending money he didn't have. But he managed to keep up appearances, thanks to some 'arrangements' he had with some of the local businesses."

I took a sip of my iced tea. "Like Flause Jewelry Store?"

"Yes, exactly like them," he said with a nod to my ring. "Did Dex give you that?"

I choked on my food. "Oh, heaven's no! I bought this myself. I don't know why everyone seems to think that Dex and I had something going. I'd barely even met the man. And he was definitely not my type."

"Oh? Why's that, Maddie? Women everywhere seemed to fall all over Dex."

I shook my head. "Sorry, but I'm not into men who cheat on their wives or run around. I'm more of a one-man woman, and I would rather have a one-woman man."

I'd barely gotten the words out when I realized just how corny they sounded. That, and they were a bit of a lie, considering I was going out with Hayes tonight and Guy on Saturday.

But Hayes seemed completely pleased with what I'd just said. He went on to ask me more about my work, showing total interest in how I'd built up my own business, before he went on to tell me a lot about his business. It seemed like the more we talked, the more I warmed up to him.

That was, until the check came, whereby he pulled out his phone and double-checked the addition of the bill. Making sure his fifteen percent had been deducted. And as I watched this incredibly handsome man while he calculated the precise amount of the bill—down to the very last penny—I was amazed that someone who was so picture-perfect on the outside had not been married long ago, with a houseful of picture-perfect kids.

Though I tried not to stare at him when he flagged the waitress down again, since apparently, he'd found a two-dollar flaw in her math, and he insisted she redo the check.

Then he turned to me with a smug smile on his face, obviously pleased with himself. "I'll be deducting that from her tip. In fact, I probably shouldn't even leave her a tip at all."

"Why don't you let me take care of the tip," I suggested.

"Fine by me," he said.

And as I grabbed some bills from my purse and slid them next to my plate, that's when it hit me. All at once. Like the pins in a tumbler lock being turned when the key is inserted, the pieces of this case finally fell into place for me.

The fake jewels. The cheating. Olivia, Cissy, and Deirdre. As well as Belinda, and any other women who believed they loved Dex so desperately. While here was his partner, a man who was far more handsome than Dex ever was, and who, by all rights, should have had women falling all over him.

But he didn't.

Because, as much as this case looked like it was about love, it wasn't. It was about money.

And I suddenly realized who had killed Dex Degill. And Belinda Stanke.

My pulse began to pound as the realization started to sink in.

Now I just needed to get rid of Hayes—politely, of course—and call Remy to tell him what I'd figured out.

Chapter Twenty-nine

Amazingly, getting rid of Hayes turned out to be a lot more difficult than I had imagined. No matter what excuses and hints I gave him—headache, fatigue, book deadline or whatever—he was bent on getting the dessert I'd promised to make for him at my house.

And I soon realized that he didn't want me to make dessert simply because I was a famous culinary author and he thought the dish would be so exquisite. No, he wanted me to make dessert tonight because, in essence, it would be free.

For him anyway.

Thankfully, I already had everything set up to make my Cherries Jubilee. So I figured I'd have him in, make the dessert and serve it, and then shoo Hayes out the door. While I had Remy waiting in the wings.

So when we arrived at my house, I told Hayes to make himself at home in my living room while I got to work in the kitchen. But before I started, I sent Remy a quick text, telling him that I wanted to talk to him later. Then I hit the remote control button for Parker's camera that was still set up from the last video. If nothing else, I figured I could record some segments of me making my Cherries Jubilee recipe and splice them into the video I planned to make as a counter to Mindie's disastrous demonstration. That was, unless the "Passidy" wanted to do that video, too.

The thought of it made me smile as I quickly went to work,

explaining the ingredients for my Cherries Jubilee recipe to the camera. Then I started mixing the ingredients in a hot pan on the burner. It wasn't long before I reached the stage where I added the cherries and brought the mixture back to a boil.

I was just turning it to simmer when Hayes walked in. "Wow, that smells good, Maddie. I can hardly wait to try this."

"It won't be long now," I assured him while I added the cherry extract.

Just as my phone dinged.

Needless to say, I was completely astonished when Hayes picked it up and glanced at it. "*Nooo* . . . Maddie, are you kidding me? You're chatting with another man? While we're on our date?"

And that's when I realized that Remy must have texted me back.

"Hayes, it's absolutely none of your business who I chat with. I communicate with lots of people throughout the day. Now please put my phone down."

But instead of complying, he just read on. "Wow, it looks like you've actually got another date with another man tonight. What happened to being a one-man woman?" His eyebrows shot up to the top of his forehead.

"Well, I definitely do not have a *date* later," I told him. "Believe me. It's more of a business thing. And by the way, I don't appreciate you looking at my phone. Now, set it down."

"Wait a minute . . . I know this guy. He's the guy who was bothering you on Saturday night. And he's a police detective."

"So you've actually met Remy?" I asked as I poured the brandy into the Cherries Jubilee mixture.

Hayes sneered. "You could say that. That man is a real jerk. He questioned me for hours after Dex got killed. Then he showed up at the speed dating event. Probably to check me out."

Along with a lot of other people there, no doubt.

"Well, nothing to worry about," I said to appease him. "And for the last time, please put my phone down."

But he was like a dog with a bone. "It looks like you texted this guy right after we got to your house. And you said you'd figured out who had killed Dex. Is that what this date was about tonight, Maddie? You wanted to question me, too? That's unbelievable. I trusted you."

But before I could answer, my phone rang.

"It's him," Hayes said in such an icy tone that it made me shiver. "And you're not going to answer it."

And that was about the time when Blaze's catch phrase rang through my head.

Every good kitchen is loaded with lethal weapons.

Because, by now, I decided that having a self-defense implement on hand was probably a good idea. So while I opened a drawer and pulled out a box of kitchen matches, I turned my back to Hayes and slid my own tenderizer hammer from a drawer into the wide, front pocket of my apron. No, it probably wasn't as heavy as the one that Mindie had used in her video. But it was a good start.

Especially considering the way that Hayes was now staring at me with such fury in his eyes. "I notice you didn't name names, Maddie. When you texted the detective."

"No, I didn't. And for that matter, I think it's time you left, Hayes."

"But I came here for my dessert," he said coldly. "Your son's not going to be home for a while, is he?"

And that's when I knew.

That *he* knew what *I* knew. My thoughts immediately went to Parker, and I was thankful he was out. In the meantime, aside from any self-defense measures or simply trying to escape my house, I decided to run out the clock. Because I had a hunch that Remy would show up if he didn't hear back from me. Especially since I hadn't taken his call so shortly after I had texted him.

"I suppose you trusted Deirdre, too, didn't you?" I said directly to Hayes. "When you were engaged to her?"

"Big mistake on my part, since she left me for Dex. Silly me, but I thought since he was already married to Cissy, he wouldn't try to steal my fiancée. But she couldn't resist what Dex had to offer. Tons of jewelry, and a rich lifestyle."

I carefully turned off the burner. "So she traded a man she loved for a man she thought would give her the world. That must have hurt."

"How did you know that Deirdre and I were engaged? Did she tell you?"

"No, but I put two and two together. She told me she'd been engaged and regretted leaving her fiancé for Dex who later left her. And you talked about being betrayed by a woman. And judging from what she did to my hair after I told her I was going out with you tonight, it all added up," I said while I poured more brandy into the cherries mixture.

"You're pretty clever, Maddie. But in a way, you're not so clever at all. If you've figured things out, well, that means I can't let you talk to that detective."

"Don't you want your dessert? It's almost ready," I told him before I poured in another good slug of brandy and stirred. "It's going to be delicious over the ice cream I've got in the freezer."

"That's good. Because you owe me that after leading me on like you did. You look like you're such a good cook, Maddie. Or you were, I guess people will say."

"Just like Dex was good at cooking the books," I went on, trying to keep him talking as I pretended to be taking longer than usual to finish this Cherries Jubilee.

And so I could give the mixture another big slug of brandy.

"Oh, yeah. You don't know the half of it," he went on. "He hid it all from me, that he was basically stealing from the company, which put us in more and more debt. And the bad part was, I couldn't simply dissolve the company and walk away. Since I was the co-owner and he had me in debt, too."

"Then he was using that money he took from the company to chase all those women."

"And don't forget, he even married some of them. Which led to some high-dollar divorces. Including his divorce from Cissy, where he lost a portion of the business to her."

"If only *you* could have divorced him."

"If only," he murmured as he moved behind me.

"And since you saw no end in sight, you decided to murder the man."

"What else could I do? Especially when he and Olivia bought their new high-dollar house out here in the suburbs. That just meant he was going to be stealing and spending more money." Out of the corner of my eye, I saw him quietly and smoothly grab my huge chef's knife from my knife rack.

"Which is why you're so tight with every dollar."

"How did you figure it all out, Maddie?"

"There were two things that gave it away," I explained, as I noticed his reflection in my microwave. "The first was your love of shrimp. Because you were the one who ate all the bacon-wrapped shrimp with honey-garlic sauce that I'd taken over to Dex and Olivia's house. Because Olivia claims that she and Dex hardly ate any. Yet on the night of the crime, my platter was empty."

"You made those? I guess I should have known. They were delicious. Kind of makes me wish you were going to be around longer, so you could cook for me. So what was the second thing?"

"It was simple, Hayes," I said, keeping an eye on his reflected image as I pretended to stir the Cherries Jubilee. "The first time I met you, I thought you had cowlicks in your hair. And that no matter what you did to your hair, it wouldn't lay down properly. But the last time I saw you, I noticed your hair had improved. And tonight, it looks perfect. No cowlicks in sight. That could only mean one thing." Without turning around, I continued to watch his reflection as he slowly moved toward me, knife now raised and aimed at my back.

"I'm all ears," he said from behind me.

"You'd gotten a bad haircut, Hayes. And you'd gotten it from Deirdre. And when she was done with your hair, you quietly stole her scissors, so you could frame her for the crime you planned to commit a little bit later on. The murder of her ex-husband. Dex Degill," I explained as I added more brandy to my dessert.

"Can you blame me, Maddie? Sure, I wanted Deirdre to look guilty. She was guilty, of course, of leaving me for Dex. But mostly I wanted to punish Dex and stop him from ruining my life, too. Because a guy can cheat on all the women he wants. But cheating on his partner? Well, that's a different matter altogether. A man isn't supposed to cheat on his business partner."

"And Belinda?"

He moved ever closer. "When I met her at the speed dating event on Saturday night, she told me about how she used to 'track' Dex. And right away, I wondered if she'd seen something. Something she shouldn't have seen. It was just a case of 'wrong place at the wrong time.' So she had to go."

"Just like that?" I asked as I managed to pour in what was left in the brandy bottle.

Which meant the concoction on my stove now had about a thousand times more alcohol than it was supposed to have.

"Yes, and speaking of which," he went on. "I know what you're doing, getting me to talk and trying to buy time. Now quit stalling and flambé that thing. So I can eat and do what I have to do and get out of here."

"Okay. As you wish."

It was at that exact moment when I was suddenly thankful for Mindie, the young woman who had pretty much annihilated my recipes online. And oddly enough, I even thought of her when I swiped the kitchen match and held it in my hand, watching the brilliant blue and yellow and orange flame on the tip of the stick. Then much like Parker, who could simultaneously unwrap a burger, read his cellphone and sit on the seat of a picnic table, I held the match up and dropped it into the Cherries Jubilee that was overloaded with alcohol. I hit the deck and covered my head at the exact same time, just as Hayes was about to thrust the huge chef's knife straight into my back.

The explosion that followed was legendary. Not only did it create an enormous *"BOOM!"* but it also resulted in a nice, bright flash. Cherries and syrup went flying across my entire kitchen. Cherries landed in my hair and on my dress, and hot liquid and hot cherries must have blasted directly into Hayes' face and eyes, because he screamed and dropped the knife.

But I wasn't finished with him yet. I grabbed the tenderizer hammer from my pocket and proceeded to tenderize his ankles at lightning speed. He screamed again and bent over, whereby I nailed him in his knees. He fell to the ground, and from there, it was easy. I hit him in the head enough times to knock him out.

I was about to truss him up, ready to be carted off to jail, when Remy and a few officers came bursting in through the side door to my kitchen.

Guns a'blazing, as they say.

"Maddie!! Maddie!! Are you okay?" Remy shouted, mere seconds before he remembered to yell "Freeze!" to a mostly inert Hayes.

But then he and his men were the ones who froze, staring at the war zone that used to be my kitchen. While I wiped cherry goo from my head with my arm, Remy and the other officers glanced from me to Hayes and to my floor and then to my cupboards and finally to my countertops. Then they stared at the ceiling, jumping every time a cherry blob dropped down with a loud *splat!*

"What in the world . . ." Remy uttered.

"I've got your murderer," I told him proudly while I plucked a cherry from my hair.

Right about then, Spencer Poe came racing in. He quickly surveyed the situation, and I could tell he'd put two and two together in a hurry.

Then he gave me a proud, fatherly smile. "Excellent work, Mrs. Montgomery. I had every confidence that you would solve this murder. And it appears that you have. The Colonel would be proud."

And shortly after Hayes had been carted away, Parker strolled in, too, and his mouth nearly dropped to the floor. "Seriously, Mom? I go out for one night, and this is what I come home to? What are you going to do when I go off to college?"

"We can talk about this later," I told my son. "But just so you know, I caught the murderer."

"Was that the guy going out on a gurney? The guy you went out with tonight? Mom, we need to have a long talk about the guys you date," he said, giving Remy a stern look. "By the way, who's going to clean up this mess? You might as well just bring in a hose."

For once, that actually sounded like a good idea.

And from there on, the rest of the night was a blur. I sat on a towel on a chair at my kitchen table and gave Remy my full statement. Then after Parker had made a few copies of the chip that was in his camera, I sent my video with Remy, too, with a promise to talk to him the next day.

After everyone had gone home, I got out a mop and cleaning rags and started in on the long, sticky process of restoring my kitchen back to its original state. Parker sighed and joined in to help, all the while regaling me with the tale of the wonderful night he'd had with Cassidy and her family.

I couldn't have been more pleased.

Chapter Thirty

The next morning, after I sent a very tired but happy Parker off to school—and yes, I allowed him to have a full cup of full-strength coffee before he went—I sat down and enjoyed a cup of coffee myself. With extra cream. I could hardly believe that I'd managed to solve two more murders, with my total up to four. Not a bad record for a mystery writer. Though technically, I only uncovered two separate murderers, since they'd both committed two murders each.

But no need to split hairs.

I had just started on my second cup of coffee when Remy rang my doorbell. "May I come in?" he asked rather sheepishly.

"Sure," I said, thinking it might be official police business.

Which it was. Partly anyway.

"First, I want to let you know, Hayes made a full confession after he was released from the hospital," he said as he joined me at my kitchen table, and I brought him a cup of coffee. "So even though you got it all on tape, this only strengthens the case."

"And you, no doubt, will get credit for this at work," I said slyly, taking a sip of my own coffee.

He let out a long sigh. "Yes, Maddie, I am well aware that you've handed me two killers on a silver platter. Because of that, I've gotten permission from our Chief of Police to bring you into the fold, so to speak. In a consulting position. So we would call on you in some cases to offer your insight and assistance. It won't pay a lot, but I think you've proven you have a knack for crime solving, and this way, you can put your talents to work. Officially. What do you say?"

I smiled at the man. "I say, 'yes.'"

He smiled back. "Good, I'm glad to hear it. And just so you know, it took a lot for me to come around to this. I was pretty worried last night after I got your text and then you didn't take my call. My instincts told me you were in danger."

"Yes, but as you could see, I can handle myself."

He held up his hands. "Okay, I'll concede. But when I saw that 'flash' outside your window last night, I thought it was the muzzle of a gun, at first. And I nearly lost my mind. If anything ever happened to you . . ."

We both just let those words hang in the air.

"Anyway, Maddie, I'd like to tell you I'm sorry for feeling so overprotective. But, well . . . I'm not. But I am sorry for the way things went down with us."

"Yeah, me, too," I told him.

"Do you think there's any chance we could put all this behind us? And start again?"

I glanced out the window for a moment. "It's pretty hard to forget that you actually believed I could commit murder."

"I guess I can understand that."

"But there's something more, Remy. I didn't like who I became as a result of the way you treated me. I didn't like that I turned into a hormonal adolescent whenever I had to deal with you. Because that's not me. And that's not a person I would ever want to be. Not only that, but you brought an awful lot of drama to my life. And as far as I'm concerned, life has enough drama. I don't need someone creating it in a relationship. I'd prefer to have a happy home life first, to make it easier to deal with all the drama of the world."

He stared into his coffee. "Understood. But let's just say, I haven't completely given up hope."

A statement that didn't require any response on my part, as far as I was concerned.

"I should also let you know," he went on, "that we've arrested Gage. Mainly for fraud. But we've got all kinds of charges on the man."

"I suspect his business was about to go downhill anyway, now that Dex is dead. He was probably Gage's best customer."

"Could be," Remy added with a smile.

He left shortly after that. And yes, had my romance writer friends comprised that scene, they would have had it end in a gooey love scene. But I just couldn't go there.

I still wondered if there'd been anything between him and Olivia. Which meant I might have been doing the very same thing that bothered me about Remy—listening to something that Olivia had said. And speaking of my neighbor, a "For Sale" sign appeared in her yard a few days later, and she seemed to disappear altogether, without saying a single goodbye. Then a moving van showed up at her house, packed up her stuff, and took it all to who knew where.

She would not be missed.

Especially not by the person who texted me next—Deirdre. Though to be honest, I wasn't the only one who received a text from her. She sent out a mass communiqué, letting everyone know that she was leaving her job. Yes, Deirdre was getting married. To none other than "Stan the Magic Man," who apparently had stacked the deck by agreeing to support her in the lifestyle to which she had once been accustomed.

I wished them every happiness.

And I was certainly happy myself when Saturday night rolled around, and a very handsome man showed up on my doorstep wearing a well-tailored tuxedo and cowboy boots. A guy named Guy. A guy who hit it off with my nervous and excited son before he took off to pick up his date. In fact, Guy and Parker talked math and engineering and all kinds of things. And Parker left with the promise of Guy taking him out to see a drilling rig in operation, firsthand, and the engineering behind it.

Though Guy had the grace to give me a moment alone with Parker after I finished taking about a thousand photos of him, looking dapper in his grandfather's old tuxedo.

"Are you ready to go?" I asked him, beaming like the proud parent that I was.

"Ready, Mom."

Whereby I handed him a set of keys for the Continental.

He gave me his usual goofy grin. "Dad's car. This is major."

"Yup, kiddo, it is. You're finally getting your wish. To drive your dad's car to prom. He would be proud of you, Parker. And so am I."

"Okay, Mom, don't get all mushy on me."

To which I laughed. "All right. Be careful with the car."

He gave me a salute. "You got it, Mom. See you at the dance."

Then I watched him carefully back the Continental out of the garage, before I returned to my own date.

"You raised a great kid," he told me. "I really like Parker. So are you ready to go, Maddie? Your chariot awaits."

With that, we went out the front door and to his bright red Camaro. "My mother never would've let me go to prom with a boy in a car like this," I said with a laugh as he held the car door for me.

He wriggled his eyebrows at me. "No worries. I drove an old Chevy in high school. But I didn't get to go to my prom. There was some kind of family emergency, as I recall."

"I'm sorry to hear that."

"Better late than never. I'd say that going out with a gorgeous woman in that gorgeous dress tonight more than makes up for it." He took my hand and kissed it and then started the car.

Clearly, Guy was also a guy who said the sweetest things.

That, and he wasn't shy when it came to getting out on the dance floor. He certainly knew how to two-step and waltz and swing dance—all the things a boy learns while growing up in West Texas. Unfortunately, we both seemed a bit stymied when it came to dancing to more modern music. And tonight, of course, there was a steady stream of that, so we sat out during a lot of those songs.

All the while, I kept an eye on Parker. And I was happy that he did his best to take Cassidy out for a spin on the dance floor plenty of times. Though mostly they just hung out with a cluster of friends. He had his arm around her waist, and she had her head leaned on his shoulder.

Ah, young love.

"I have a favor to ask," Guy whispered in my ear. "I'd love to go see your Continental Mark Two."

And so we did.

He practically hyperventilated the second he saw my car. Parker had parked it in the back of the lot where it would be nice and protected, with no other cars next to it.

"That is stunning," Guy sort of breathed. "I've only ever seen one in person, and it wasn't in this nice of condition. Mind if we look inside? Maybe even sit behind the wheel?"

"Sure, why not? Parker isn't going to need it for a while."

And so I pulled out my spare set of keys. I let Guy in the driver's side, and I sat on the passenger side.

"This is . . . wow . . ." he repeated over and over. "This is fantastic. Mind if I turn on the radio? Just for a few minutes. I promise I won't drain all the power from your battery. I could stand to hear something other than 'what the kids listen to these days.' Never thought I'd be saying that."

"Me, either," I said with a laugh as I turned the radio on and tuned it in to an oldies channel. An eighties ballad played while the light of the radio glowed warmly from the dashboard.

"Ah . . . now that's more like it," he said with a crooked grin. "What a night this has been . . . going out with you, having fun dancing, meeting Parker, sitting in this incredible car . . . It's all . . ."

I turned to look into his eyes, remembering the last time I had looked across the front seat of the Continental to a truly handsome man. Charlie Montgomery. Without thinking, I scooted a little bit closer to Guy.

"This has been one of the best nights I've had in a long, *long* time," he murmured.

Then he pretended to yawn and stretch, reaching an arm across the back of the seat, before he slipped that arm around my shoulders. The next thing I knew, I was sliding ever closer while he was pulling me toward him.

"I don't know if it's you or the car," he murmured into my hair. "But I really need to kiss you right now."

And so he did.

Much to my delight.

When we finally pulled away, I rested my head on his shoulder while the radio station now played a fifties tune. I couldn't believe how young and alive I felt. And I was pretty sure I was glowing after we returned to the prom, as Guy held me in his arms, and we moved across the dance floor.

In fact, I think I was practically glowing even days afterward, especially since we already had a second date on the calendar. And we'd even done a little texting back and forth just for the heck of it.

I was about to start dinner one night when Parker came to me with his computer in hand.

I cringed at the sight of it. "Oh, no, what is it? Another Mindie video?"

"No, Mom. Look at this. I was doing research. Trying to figure out if I'm related to any of the Montgomerys who were in the Texas Revolution. And a name popped out."

He turned the screen so I could see, and I read it out loud. "George Washington Poe. Cousin of Edgar Allen Poe. Is this for real?"

"Yup, Mom."

"Poe? As in . . . the same last name as our mysterious neighbor? Spencer Poe? I wonder if they're related?"

"That's what I wondered, Mom. Maybe our ancestor and Mr. Poe's ancestor both fought in the Texas Revolution."

It was new information that sort of stunned me. And I remembered I still had a few things I needed to investigate. Starting with the mysterious letter that I'd gotten in the mail. The one that mentioned the Battle of San Jacinto and the Texas Declaration of Independence. Which, oddly enough, was in keeping with what Parker had just discovered. And then there was the locket I'd found, the one with the name Theodosia on it. Not to mention, the treasure map and the gold coins we'd found in Charlie's stuff. Was there a possibility the whole kit and kaboodle were connected?

Clearly, I still had another mystery on my hands.

And speaking of mysteries, I finished writing my next Blaze McClane book and sent it to the editor I'd hired. So, not only did I have another book coming out soon, but I also had a new beau and a very old mystery to solve. And no, I hadn't found a new hairdresser yet, but even so, I guess you could say that life was good for me, Maddie Montgomery, culinary mystery writer and now crime consultant to the Abbott Cove Police Department.

Who knew what adventures life held for me next?

THE END

About the Author

Cindy Vincent is the award-winning author of the Buckley and Bogey Cat Detective Caper books; the Tracy Truworth, Apprentice P.I., 1940s Homefront Mystery series; the Maddie Montgomery Mysteries; and The Light, A Destiny Moments Novel. She also wrote the daily devotional, Cats Are Part of His Kingdom, Too. She is the creator of the Mysteries by Vincent murder mystery party games and the Daisy Diamond Detective series games for girls. She lives in Houston with her handsome husband and an assortment of fantastic felines.

www.ingramcontent.com/pod-product-compliance
Lightning Source LLC
LaVergne TN
LVHW091031080826
845145LV00002B/451

* 9 7 8 1 9 3 2 1 6 9 9 3 5 *